THE 1-800 SERIES

JOSIE RIVIERA

5 STAR READER REVIEWS

Amazon Review by Amazon Reviewer (1-800-CUPID)
   5.0 out of 5 stars
   "Both Candee and Teddy want to buy the same old, dilapidated Victorian house. While Candee wants to remodel it and use it as a recreational facility for handicapped children, Teddy wants to use it as investment, destroy the residence, and build several small houses on the huge land. Although their goals should oppose them, attraction sizzles between them.

   I enjoyed reading this sweet story, well-written, relaxing, and easy to read and will look forward to the other books in the series."

Amazon Review by Amazon Reviewer (1-800-CHRISTMAS)
   5.0 out of 5 stars"What a delightful story! Keiran is the hero every girl who wants romance in her life would die to meet and keep--especially a heroine like Desiree who had a difficult childhood. This book is a perfect Christmas story that I read in one sitting with a smile on my lips. J. Riviera

digs into the characters and urges them to reveal their emotions, fears and hopes. A well-written romance that I highly recommend."

Amazon Review by D. Zappone (1-800-IRELAND)
5.0 out of 5 stars

"When I looked for other books from Josie Riviera and saw that 1-800 Ireland was coming out I knew right off the bat I needed the book. It's a sweet contemporary romance novella. It is about an independent Irish woman named Kathleen who has always dreamt about opening a tea house in the States. Also about Rob also known as the Muffin Man. What I did like about this book was the main male wasn't this drop dead gorgeous guy. Rob was more like the everyday guy, bald, stocky, and older. Not the typical main character guy I have always read about. Kathleen left Ireland to fulfill her dream of opening the tea shop in a small town."

Amazon Review by S. Wagner
5.0 out of 5 stars

"I loved these stories and really could not put them down. They flowed together nicely with believable characters. You need to read these."

INTRODUCTION

To keep up on newly released ebooks, paperbacks, Large Print Paperbacks, audiobooks, as well as exclusive sales, sign up for Josie's Newsletter today.

As a thank you, I'll send you a Free PDF ... The Beauty Of ...

Josie's Newsletter

Did you know that according to a Yale University study, people who read books live longer?

PRAISE AND AWARDS

USA TODAY bestselling author

DEAR FRIENDS

Dear Friends,

A heartwarming story is the hallmark of every romance. Savor the magic with three fun, sweet contemporary romances in

The 1-800 Series.

3 Books in 1 collection!

Cozy up with your favorite beverage and lose yourself in these fun, joyful home-flipping romances.

1-800-CUPID

A house flipper looking for a quick profit. A survivor with a dream. Can two broken hearts find a place to call home?

1-800-CHRISTMAS

Taking the high road is a whole lot easier with someone to love...

1-800-IRELAND

A strong minded Irishwoman pursuing her dream. A disillusioned businessman ready to retire. Can two determined people separated by years find true love at the end of a rainbow?

USA TODAY BESTSELLING AUTHOR

JOSIE RIVIERA

1·800· CUPID

A SWEET CONTEMPORARY NOVELLA

This book is dedicated to all my wonderful readers who have supported me every inch of the way.
THANK YOU!

PRAISE AND AWARDS

USA TODAY bestselling author

Top 4 Amazon Bestseller Holiday Fiction

Top 6 Single Authors Short Stories

Top 3 Contemporary Short Stories

CHAPTER 1

*T*wenty thousand dollars.

Click.

Candee Contando licked her dry lips. She'd done it. She'd placed an online bid on a home-auction website for the Victorian mansion on Thompson Lane. Her dream home, her dollhouse. Her dilapidated project.

Two years of savings. Gone.

No matter. Under her guidance, she'd transform the mansion to its former majestic state, painted a mustard-yellow offset by ornamental burnt-sienna "gingerbread" trim. The sounds of children's giggling and music and barking beagles—yes, beagles—would echo across all five acres of the property.

She surveyed her offer and beamed, savoring the moment.

Now if she only could ensure that no one else bid on the property and drove up the price.

She studied the ticking clock on the website. Stay optimistic, she told herself. Deteriorated by age and wear, the Victorian would scare off any prospective buyer.

She pushed away from her desk and surveyed her real estate office. Although only one room, she prided herself on the cheery décor. One wall featured photos of North Carolina—the majestic peaks of the Blue Ridge parkway and scenic waterfalls. Below the photos hung a map of the area with local real estate listings highlighted by pushpins.

She peered out the window into the street below. Since noon, a bright sun had been at odds with January's wind—a wind crazy in its intent to blow the streetlights off their wires.

For the umpteenth time, she checked her nonringing cell phone for messages. Surely the real estate market in Roses, North Carolina, would improve. Didn't prospective home buyers begin looking in January? And wouldn't these buyers call her rather than her competitors? Candee prided herself on her professionalism and up-to-date listings.

Then why hadn't she made a single sale since August?

On the heel of that depressing assessment came a cheerful one. In two hours, she and her older sister, Desiree, planned to enjoy dinner at Desiree's country club.

Candee stepped back to her desk and switched off the computer.

Two single women in their late twenties, she mused, spending Friday night alone and dateless, four weeks before Valentine's Day.

Her cell phone rang, most likely Desiree firming up dinner plans and reminding Candee not to be late. Regardless of what time Candee met her older sister anywhere, Desiree always arrived before her.

Candee clicked on her phone. "1-800-Cupid," she said with a laugh.

"Contando Realty?" a man asked.

"Yes, yes …" So much for professionalism. Candee felt her cheeks color. She hurried to her desk, dropping into the chair and switching her phone to speaker. "Are you looking to buy a home today, sir?"

"I am." The man hesitated. "Is this the correct number?"

She powered on her computer. "Absolutely."

"I'm new to the area and checked into the Roses Hotel last night," he said.

Envisioning the rundown hotel, Candy raised her eyebrows. Although in all fairness, the hotel was the only lodging open in the winter. Roses, North Carolina, was a summer tourist town known for bubbling hot springs and cool mountain temperatures.

Her fingers poised on the keyboard. "I'm more than happy to assist. Your name?"

"Teddy. Teddy Winchester." He had a deep voice, a slight southern drawl.

"What type of home are you searching for, Mr. Winchester?"

"The worst home in the best neighborhood."

Yup. It figured. No significant sales commission to pay the mortgage this month. Fortunately, her part-time job at the local hardware store was stable, although the pay was meager.

She scrolled through the listings. "For yourself, sir?"

"I'm an investor."

"How many bedrooms and baths?"

"Three bedrooms, two baths. Single family and one level."

"Budget?"

"Anything below $50,000."

She rubbed the back of her neck. *Who did he think she was, a miracle worker?*

"Mr. Winchester, the nicer neighborhoods in Roses are priced well above $100,000."

"Nope. Too high."

Certainly a man of few words.

"Perhaps—"

"I'll take another look on the Internet." He seemed to ignore her completely. "Thanks anyway."

She wouldn't lose a potential sale.

"Wait." She feigned checking a non-existent schedule. "I may have an opening this afternoon. I know the area well and I'll find properties to show you. Will three o'clock work?"

"In a half hour? Fine. I admire a realtor who works fast. Should I meet you at your office? The address is listed on the Internet."

Candee verified the street number and ended the phone call with a cheery, "See you at three."

She clicked off and checked her watch. Thirty minutes wasn't enough time to drive to her apartment and change. Her worn jeans and blue flannel shirt would have to suffice.

Immediately, she phoned Desiree. "I may be late for dinner."

"I'm so glad it's you," Desiree said. "Scott, a new lawyer at the firm, asked me out tonight. Barring the fact the invitation was last minute, I said yes. Desperation, right?" She paused. "Can we plan for dinner together tomorrow night instead?"

"Right, sure. The reason I called is because I have a client who's interested in seeing some properties."

"You have a real live client?" Desiree cut immediately to the question.

Candee envisioned her sister, thick blonde hair piled high, sitting behind a mahogany desk in her law firm. Proper, well-dressed, every inch the high-powered attorney. Desiree had proven that, with the right help, a disadvantaged childhood could lead to a successful adulthood. She worked late hours at her law firm advocating justice for low-income families and their children.

"He's an investor," Candee said.

"Maybe he's tall, dark, and handsome?" Desiree said with deceptive casualness. "And rich?"

"Investors are usually short bald men." Candee adjusted her shirt's wrinkled collar, then checked out the frayed hem of her jeans. She let out a frustrated groan and ran a hand through her unruly auburn waves.

"You'll need a rich man if you plan to go through with your insane idea to purchase that Victorian," Desiree said. "The place will eat up all the money you hope to earn in a lifetime."

"I'll handle most of the work myself. Remember, when we lived in foster care, I learned carpentry from the family who took us in."

"How will you offer a quality after-school environment to disadvantaged kids if you're busy driving nails into crumbling walls?"

"Watch me." Briefly, Candee squeezed her eyes shut. It was her turn to pay it forward.

"Well, don't discount short men. They prefer tall, willowy red-heads with green eyes," Desiree said. "Who knows? He might be struck by Cupid's golden arrow when he meets you. This guy might be the one."

Candee drew in a breath. "The one what, exactly?"

"Your partner, your love, your support system. The one who can help pay off the mountainous amount of debt you'll incur if you actually buy the biggest dilapidated disaster in the state."

"Someone supportive? For me? After what happened?"

Desiree's voice grew quieter. "Not every guy pretends to be something he's not."

A lump lodged in Candee's throat. No man was worth having her heart broken again, although she didn't vocalize her feelings. Desiree was an eternal romantic.

With a promise to meet her sister on Saturday evening,

Candee clicked off and bent to pick up a broken pencil lying on the floor. Not once since the ill-fated night two years ago when her long-time boyfriend had walked out had she broken the vow to herself and wept. Life went on, although a sadness she couldn't shake remained precariously close to the surface.

Some lessons were more difficult than others. Her ex had taught her the hardest—she wasn't interesting enough, pretty enough or vivacious enough.

Tears welled and she brushed them away. Standing, she tossed the pencil into a garbage can by the door. While she confirmed two house showings for Mr. Winchester, she cast a critical assessment of her reflection in the mirror by the office door. She pinched her pale cheeks and added a touch of rose lip balm to her lips. Then she gathered her hair into a ponytail, securing the thick curls with an elastic band. With a final glance in the mirror, she pulled on her cream-colored woolen jacket and wound an emerald-green paisley scarf around her neck.

Her suede purse under her arm, she pushed open the exit doors and stepped outside. The sun had buried itself under a formless cloud, and a swirl of wind blew her paisley scarf across her face. She tucked it securely beneath the collar of her jacket. The day was typical January weather for Roses, undecided if it was warm or cold.

CHAPTER 2

*T*eddy Winchester pondered for the umpteenth time how he'd ended up in Roses, North Carolina. Certainly the town was charming, tucked along a backdrop of the Blue Ridge Mountains. He'd taken a ride around the region before he'd checked into the hotel. The shopping seemed adequate and the town center exuded storybook appeal, retaining a New England quaintness, complete with a bandstand.

Rob, his not-so-silent business partner in Florida, had assured Teddy the North Carolina weather was always cooperative, even pleasant for mid-January. And the area teemed with real estate bargains because Roses, population five thousand, had never fully recovered from the recession.

Rob was wrong on both counts. Relentless gusts battering under the drafty hotel's window had sent a chill through Teddy all morning while he'd sat in his room, and the inventory of low-priced homes on real-estate websites proved nonexistent.

Roses wasn't what he'd hoped for. He needed a quick turnaround investment to help pay for his nephew Joseph's physical therapy. A horrific car accident and the loss of his nephew's father had left Joseph traumatized and weak, and the extensive physical therapy included strength building and stretching.

Teddy took a deep breath, still reeling from his older brother's death. *Christian, we promised to never desert each other. And now you're gone.*

In an effort to keep busy, Teddy perused his email, then texted an abridged list of instructions to his secretary on how to proceed with the sale of his late brother's farm. He assumed Christian retained life insurance, which would help pay for the mountain of medical bills steadily piling up, as well as lawyers' fees. The papers declaring that Teddy was Joseph's legal guardian weren't finalized yet. The courts took their time, although the will guided the court's decision.

With a sigh, he tapped in Rob's business number.

Rob's gruff voice answered on the fifth ring. "Rob's Marvelous Muffins."

"Hi Rob. Is Joseph around?" Teddy asked.

"He's up to his elbows in Valentine muffin ingredients. A four-year-old's favorite activity is making a mess with a cupful of flour, right?" Rob chuckled. "I'll put him on speaker."

"Hi Uncle Teddy!" Joseph's high-pitched voice vibrated through the phone. "Mr. Rob and I are putting a surprise in our muffins and writing something special on each one. Wanna know what's inside?"

Teddy laughed. "Then it wouldn't be a surprise, right?"

The boy hesitated. "Right."

"Is there anything we can do about that?"

"I can save a muffin for you, Uncle Teddy."

"Great idea, buddy. I'll fly to Miami in a couple weeks, and we'll eat muffins together at Mr. Rob's bakery. Okay?"

Joseph giggled. "Okay."

It was the first time he'd heard the boy laugh since his father had died.

"I love you, Joseph," he said softly.

"Love you, too, Uncle Teddy."

Rob got back on the phone. "He's a good kid. You should see how he's mixing the butter and sugar together."

"Maybe he's a born baker like you, Rob."

"Or a farmer like you."

"I was never good at farming." Which was true. It wasn't until he'd met Rob and gone into real estate that he'd discovered his forte.

"Maybe you haven't discovered the right crop. Try tomatoes. Those plants grow regardless of—Hang on a sec." Rob turned away from the phone, but Teddy could still hear him directing one of his employees to be careful attaching the food grinder to the heavy-duty electric mixer he'd recently purchased. His voice returned to normal strength as he inquired how the house hunting was going.

"I'm meeting a local realtor this afternoon."

"Shouldn't take long. It's a buyer's market." He barked another order to one of his employees, then goaded, "You miss slaving over a hot oven?"

Teddy could easily visualize the twinkle in Rob's crystal-blue eyes. "I haven't baked so much as a boxed cake in years," he said, chuckling.

He and Rob had met years earlier at a cooking class for men. Teddy had soon discovered his speciality would never include burning another muffin, but Rob had gone on to build a successful chain of bakeries in the greater Miami area. Teddy could practically inhale the delectable, sugary aromas coming from Rob's spotless commercial kitchen.

"And I'll take Joseph to his equestrian session this weekend," Rob was saying. "The kid has really formed a connection with horses."

"Exactly the reason his therapist advised it," Teddy replied. "She said horseback riding would reduce Joseph's anxiety after the trauma of the accident."

"She's right," Rob said. "And she's such a pretty thing, isn't she?"

"Rob, she's Joseph's therapist."

"Yeah, yeah, I know. And she's a few years younger than me, anyway." Rob gave an exaggerated whistle. "Remember to keep me in the real estate loop."

"Do I have a choice?" Teddy grinned. He was impatient with lawyers and their endless legal jargon and talk of probate court. However, with the man and mentor he owed his real-estate start-up business to, Teddy's patience was limitless.

"Hey, thanks for watching Joseph for me," he added.

"What are oddball friends for? Your job is to snag the best buy in Roses." The usually brash Rob tempered his tone. "And Joseph's no bother, you know. When someone's down and out they need help, right?"

"These past few months … Thank you. For everything." Teddy clicked off and stared at the phone. Sometimes, he didn't know what he would've done if Rob hadn't been there to pick up the pieces after Christian's death.

He checked his watch, then pulled on a gray T-shirt. He was still half-wet from his shower and the T-shirt stuck to his body. He shook his damp hair, threw on a Florida State baseball cap, stuck his wallet in his jeans pocket, and zipped up an olive-green vest. Out in the parking lot, he fired up the engine of his red truck, and at exactly three o'clock arrived at Candee Contando Realty. He needed someone experienced to help him get just the right property, and from the Internet reviews he'd read, Mrs. Contando had been in business over thirty years.

He walked to the entrance of an older brick building

housing various offices and stopped midstep, admiring the beautiful young woman waiting in the doorway. The collar of a cream-colored jacket framed her oval face, along with an absurdly colorful green scarf. A pair of tiny gold cross earrings dangled from her ears. Her features were all high cheekbones and generous lips.

He tipped his baseball hat. "Hello. I'm supposed to meet Mrs. Contando here."

"I'm *Miss* Contando, although please call me Candee." Her smile enhanced her fascinating emerald eyes.

His heartbeat slowed and he had to prompt himself to swallow. "This is *your* realty?"

"Actually, it was said to be my mother's company for a while." She pushed back a stray wisp of auburn hair, handed him a business card, and then extended her hand. "Are you Mr. Winchester?"

"Teddy." Tight jeans emphasized her shapely legs and rounded hips. This woman's stunning good looks could stop traffic.

"I expected someone older," he managed to say.

She let go of his hand, swept her gaze up his six-foot frame, and grinned. "I expected someone shorter."

He met her grin, debating where he should look next.

Her lovely face enhanced by a sprinkle of freckles? Nope, not at all professional to stare. Instead, he gazed at the weathered door behind her and cleared his throat. "Did you find any listings?"

Her mouth curved into a polite smile. "Yes. Ready to see your future house?"

Unexpectedly, he felt drawn to her. She wasn't at all what he'd expected, although his good sense warned him away. He was completely satisfied with being single, having made peace with that reality ever since his one serious relationship with a woman had ended badly. He'd lost his self-reliance once, and once was enough.

He gestured toward his truck. "Should we use my vehicle or yours?"

"Mine." She pointed to a rusted Honda Civic. "I'll drive. I know these roads well."

He opened the car door for her, then came around and settled in the passenger seat.

She buckled her seatbelt. He buckled his, then took in a quick breath. A faint whiff of her scent lingered in the air. Roses. He grinned. Why not?

"So, Candee, have you lived in Roses all your life?"

She glanced at him. "I've lived here and there."

She returned her attention to the road, and an overlong moment passed in silence.

He waited for her to continue. When she didn't elaborate, he asked if he could turn on the radio. The station was set to Classic Rock and "Unchained Melody" by the Righteous Brothers came on, the heartfelt lyrics about "Oh, my love, my darling," filling the little car.

Teddy was about to suggest they try for more upbeat music when she gushed, "I love this song."

Okay, he thought. She must be a romantic.

"How many showings did you schedule?" he asked.

"Two, both in Glenhaven." Flicking on her signal, she turned onto another road. "You want three bedrooms and two baths, correct?"

"The perfect flip house."

"You don't intend to live in the property?"

"Nope. I want an easy fixer-upper that won't take longer than six weeks to renovate. I'm working with another investor, and we intend to make a quick and substantial profit."

"Don't we all," she murmured.

Their gazes met and they shared a grin.

Soon, they were driving past neatly manicured lawns and one-story homes.

She stopped in front of a beige bungalow, parking on the street. "The previous owners relocated, and this house has been on the market over sixty days." They got out and walked toward the house. As you can see—" she gestured to the tidy neighborhood and matching mailboxes—"Glenhaven is lovely."

"The neighborhood is too cookie cutter." He stood on the front porch and studied mismatched shingle patches nailed to the roof. "Needs some work."

"Inside, the home is beautifully decorated."

"The bigger the mess, the bigger the profit." Automatically, he provided the investor's mantra. "What's the asking price?"

"One hundred thousand dollars, although the owners are willing to negotiate."

He shook his head. "Too expensive." *Why did realtors try to sell homes over the buyer's stated limit?*

Noting Candee's downcast expression, he lightened his tone. "Are there any other homes in this town under fifty thousand?"

"There is … one." She paused and pressed a finger to her lips, seeming to search for a reason not to answer.

He overlooked her lack of enthusiasm. "Price?"

"That particular house is listed on an internet auction site and meets none of your criteria." She paused. "It's a rambling Victorian and—"

"Where is this house?"

"On Thompson Lane at the edge of town. It's unoccupied."

"How much land comes with the property?"

"Five acres."

"Can the land be sold off in parcels? Is it zoned commercial or residential?"

"You can get on the website and download the report." She slid into the driver's seat and shut the door.

Had he heard a grunt of disapproval?

"Sorry I can't help you, Teddy," she continued, when he got into the passenger seat. "I'll drive you back to my office to get your truck, and I'll phone if anything in your price range becomes available."

Now he had to beg her to view a property? She might be gorgeous, but she was certainly the world's worst realtor.

"Do you have the lockbox code to this Victorian, Candee?"

She raised her delicate brows. "Yes, but—"

"I assume an appointment isn't necessary if no one lives there."

She inserted the key into the ignition. "My pleasure."

He didn't know why, although he'd bet she was being sarcastic.

A few minutes later she turned onto Thompson Lane. As they passed an elderly man with gray hair and glasses perched on his nose, she waved, explaining he was Mr. Dunworthy, a widower who owned a Queen-Anne-style home two doors away. He'd lived in the neighborhood forever and refused to give up his large home, although it was becoming more and more difficult for him to maintain.

She drove to the end of the road, sped up a circular driveway and parked in front of an imposing three-story house. An octagonal tower soared from the steep multigabled roof. Century-old trees flanked both sides of the property. On one corner of the overgrown front lawn, an oak tree boasted a tire swing. Teddy imagined himself pushing Joseph on that swing. Joseph needed to play more, needed fresh air. He'd been so pale since his father's death.

No, Teddy told himself. Quick and easy sale.

Of course, he could purchase the property for the land and build five new homes, more than tripling his profit. Or build low-income housing. Rob would agree with that decision.

He rounded the car to open the door for her, but she'd already gotten out. They stood side by side and stared at the house. For the first time in many years, he drank in the stillness of a cool winter afternoon, admiring a home he'd only imagined in his dreams—and was well aware of the insane impulse to hold Candee's hand as they walked to the front door.

He extended his hand to her.

She stared at him in surprise, but then she took his hand.

"The home is beautiful, isn't it?" she said as they walked to the front porch together.

It was, although the Victorian sat beneath layers of peeling yellow paint that marred its exterior and several of the windows were boarded up. A covered front porch curved around to the side, and there was also a side entrance. Teddy imagined white wooden rocking chairs, a row of lush Boston ferns, and ceiling fans spinning lazily on a warm summer afternoon.

The land, the land, he reminded himself.

Candee dropped her hand and tapped in the code for the lockbox. She tipped her head toward the purple front door. "In its former glory days, this home reflected the wealth of the owners—the Langrone family. They owned a prosperous knitting mill in Roses."

"And then?"

"And then the mill went out of business. Too much foreign competition. The Langrones declared bankruptcy and moved out shortly afterward. All the owners since then moved in with high expectations until they discovered they weren't able to maintain the upkeep."

What a waste of a beautiful home.

As if she'd read his thoughts she lingered on the porch, a wistfulness in her gaze. "This Victorian was built in 1889 and definitely requires TLC."

An absolute understatement, Teddy decided, when they walked in. The outside needed extensive work, and the hardwood floor of the grand foyer was badly gouged and scratched.

Candee flicked on a light switch. Nothing happened, and she offered an apologetic shrug. With lights not working, they were left in semidarkness. And although the odor in the entrance hall stopped him cold, she didn't miss a beat and continued walking.

"This is the kitchen," she was saying. "The cabinets are an olive color ..."

"What's left of them." He eyed the traditional arched raised panel doors and a lone cabinet left on the floor. So much beauty amidst so much neglect.

He stepped onto rusty linoleum. Luxury vinyl it was not because the floor felt soft and spongy beneath his work boots. Water damage, and hopefully not too extensive and requiring a floor joist.

Candee caught the focus of his gaze. "Avocado was a popular color in the 70's when the owners updated the kitchen."

"Avocado is back in style," he replied.

Hadn't Rob uttered the same words when he'd designed his showy corporate office in Miami?

Teddy opened and closed a cabinet door and examined the hinges. "With lots of elbow grease and white paint, these cabinets might work. Better than tossing them in a landfill."

Candee shook her head. "Nothing in this kitchen is

salvageable." She opened the oven door. With a shriek, she slammed it shut.

He inspected the grease-encrusted stove burners. "I'd install stainless steel appliances. The stove can stay. Six burners are a good selling feature, and the microwave can be mounted above the stove. Granite countertops, travertine flooring, a dishwasher, disposal ..." He swung around. "If I open this wall, there'd be an expansive view of the yard, which would be great for kids."

He didn't miss her speculative glance at his ring finger when he mentioned children.

"I'm not married," he said. "It's just me and my four-year-old nephew, Joseph."

She hesitated. "Where is he?"

"He's in Miami spending the next few weeks with my business partner, Rob. Rob's the one who got me started in real estate."

He'd said too much. How could he put into words the way his gut split every time he pondered Christian's death, or the pain Joseph had endured because of his numerous operations, or how Teddy had recently debated selling everything and starting over—somewhere quiet and peaceful—away from the high-pressure lifestyle of fast-paced Miami?

"Every home I take on, I treat as my own," he whispered.

Although this home wouldn't be here, because every bone in his practical body insisted it should be demolished.

He ran the faucet, and rusty water spewed into the chipped porcelain sink.

"City water and sewers," Candee said.

"Good. No septic issues or a dry well save money. What's this house going for?"

"No one knows the final price with an auction."

"Square footage?"

"Over 5500 square feet."

"This house is bigger than I thought." He pressed his lips together. "What's the current bid?"

She paused for a long while. "Twenty thousand dollars. You know you'll pour money into a house this size in order to get it back into shape."

"Did you know you're the exact opposite of a sales-woman, Candee?" With a grin, he stepped forward into what he presumed was the formal living room, appreciatively remarking on the marble fireplace with its updated gas fire-place and the twelve-foot ceilings.

"No use in traipsing through a ramshackle house—" Candee began.

"I noticed there's a dining room and parlor," he interrupted.

"Yes. And an adjacent library. And a music room."

That same wistfulness in her voice again.

He struggled to find the right words, debating whether to ask if she was upset about something. Hesitating, he changed direction. "Is the music room next?"

"You're the buyer." Had she silently inserted the adjective *foolish*?

He assessed the lengthening shadows signaling early nightfall. With no electricity, the house was growing darker by the minute.

As they headed into the music room, the toe of his boot caught on a torn piece of shag carpeting. He heard Candee call out a warning as he lost his footing and fell through the floor.

CHAPTER 3

*C*andee peered through the hole in the floor into the shadowy basement. Although she heard Teddy's footsteps, she couldn't see him.

"Are you all right?" she called.

"Sure. I wanted to examine the basement, anyway. It appears to be a walk-out."

She leaned over, her eyes adjusting to the darkness. "What's it like down there?"

"I'll let you know in a minute." He switched on his cell phone's flashlight and peeked up at her, waggling his dark eyebrows. "Care to join me?"

He couldn't possibly be flirting.

"Uh no. I'll wait here, thanks."

Teddy pulled himself back up into the music room. "Maybe next time?"

With one hand in his worn jeans pocket, the other wielding a tape measure, he was rugged and impossibly good-looking, his muscled arms straining against a thin gray T shirt. He brushed dirt from his vest and yanked off his baseball cap. His wealth of black hair was mussed, and the late afternoon sun gilded thin strips of golden highlights to the tips. Perhaps he'd stepped right off the cover of the latest men's home improvement magazine without telling her.

Although she'd walked through this house many times, she hadn't ventured into the basement. Desiree often called Candee the opposite of a realist, although what would the world be like, Candee rationalized, without dreamers?

Teddy carried the broken kitchen cabinet from the kitchen and placed it over the hole in the floor.

As they continued through the house, he snapped photos with his cell phone.

"After I see the upstairs, I'll send these pictures to my partner Rob," he said.

She gestured to the sweeping spindle staircase. "This home has five bedrooms, five baths, and five fireplaces. It's the opposite of a perfect flip house."

"Nevertheless, lead the way. There're two more floors to check out."

After he'd inspected the upstairs bathrooms and admired the worn brass hardware on the master suite's mahogany double doors, they made their way downstairs.

When they reached the foyer, he glanced up from his cell phone and said, "I want to make an offer."

She shuffled back two steps. "You're joking … right?" Her gaze shifted to the entrance. She'd made a serious mistake in mentioning this house to him.

"I never joke about real estate."

"This home"—she swept out her hands—"is a money pit."

"Which is why Rob and I will buy the property for the land."

Candee's heart stopped beating.

"We'll demolish the house," he added.

Her house, she wanted to shout. *Her* land for disadvantaged children. She'd envisioned beagle puppies cavorting across the lawn, perhaps an acre set aside for a working farm. Children needed to connect with nature. It was time to get them away from technology and back to values that really mattered.

And music. The music room off the kitchen would reverberate with glorious sounds again.

Teddy faced her. "Anything the matter?"

There was kindness in his gaze, interest on his handsome features. Should she share her ideas with a man she'd known for less than two hours—a man who was bent on destroying those very same ideas? A man who'd held her hand in his strong grip and gazed at the Victorian with the same wonder and appreciation as she had?

Struggling to hold onto her composure, she reminded herself she was a professional. Besides, this house was nothing like what he was looking for.

She lifted her chin. "Not a thing."

Lightly, he touched her cheek, his gesture completely unexpected. "I understand how you feel about a house like this. It's very beautiful, but beyond repair."

Turning away, she quickly dabbed at her eyes. She settled into the tune she'd known the past two years: no matter how sincere, how charming, men couldn't be trusted. Better to hold him at a polite distance and keep her plans to herself. He'd soon be gone back to Miami.

"Are you sure you're okay?" he asked.

She feigned her brightest smile. "Of course."

He waited a beat, then silently followed her, standing on the porch while she locked the front door.

"Any idea what the current bid is? You mentioned under fifty thousand."

Candee rubbed her temples. A quick search on the Internet would spew all the information he'd need to place a bid.

"Twenty thousand dollars," she finally said. "And bidding ends in three weeks."

So many mistakes today, beginning by answering the phone. 1-800-CUPID. Hah!

"Then I'll offer thirty thousand dollars," he said.

An uneasy quiet descended. A cold breeze brushed across her cheeks.

"The auction accepts bids in twenty-thousand dollar-increments," she said.

"Then I'll bid forty thousand, which is still under my fifty-thousand-dollar budget."

"The bank may not accept a lowball offer." Her remark was nonsensical, since she was hoping the bank would accept her offer, because twenty thousand dollars was all she had. She glanced at Teddy's determined stance. Surely there was a way to convince him not to bid. However, thirty years of proper Southern behavior stopped her from saying more.

"I can offer all cash," he said. "Plus, my partner and I can close immediately. On a foreclosure, the bank will take everything into consideration."

"Don't you want to walk the property? If you're interested in the land, there are building requirements and permits—"

He reached into his pocket and handed her a business card. "I do this for a living, Candee. I know all about due diligence." He gave a lazy grin. "And there's another clause, which can either make or break the deal."

She fisted one hand on her hip. "The bank should just hand over the house to you?"

"A definite bonus." He laughed, rich and full. "I'm hoping my lovely realtor will grant me the pleasure of her company at dinner."

"I can't." Her refusal was quick, a knee-jerk reaction. She hadn't dated in two years and wouldn't start now, especially with a tycoon investor who assumed that by flaunting the cash in his pocket, he could take her castle in the air away from her.

"Not even for a slice of pizza? I don't know my way around Roses yet."

She retreated a step. "Tony's Pizza on Main Street is always open. You can spot the red and green awning a mile away."

"Are you saying no, Candee?"

"Is my refusal a deal breaker, Teddy?"

"Not if I can get this property for under fifty thousand dollars."

"If you decide to bid, you'll have to wait three weeks to find out if you've won."

His gaze lingered on her face. "Some things are worth waiting for."

CHAPTER 4

*T*eddy's cell phone buzzed on the nightstand in his hotel room. Awake anyway, he answered it and heard a recognizable woman's voice.

"Teddy?"

"Yvonne?" He peered at the clock on the nightstand. "You realize it's three a.m.?"

"Are you awake?"

He pushed a hand through his hair. "Should I be?"

"It's nine in the morning here in Madrid."

"I'm not in Spain," he countered.

"Such a shame you aren't with me." A long feminine sigh. "I'll never get used to the time difference. Look, my network in the States wants me in Madrid another few weeks to cover the recent drought. Water levels in the reservoirs are abnormally low, and they're aiming for a human-interest story to boost ratings and land a prime-time slot."

Teddy had met Yvonne—an attractive woman with honeyed skin, her thinly arched black brows offset by a pixie cut of platinum-blonde hair—when he'd been offered a weekly television segment featuring tidbits on flipping homes. His fifteen minutes of fame had lasted, well, fifteen minutes. His relationship with Yvonne was going on five months, although he hardly ever saw her. Her job involved a great deal of travel, and he wasn't diligent about keeping in touch with her. He wasn't adaptable to the ever-changing elasticity of dating a woman he saw only twice a month.

He extended the expected congratulatory remarks. Compliments were a prerequisite when dating Yvonne Evette. She was a career woman bent on reaching the top, although what 'the top' was had yet to be determined. Currently, it meant an anchor position on a major American network.

After good-byes, he clicked off his phone and shifted restlessly on his narrow bed. The previous morning when he'd arrived at the Roses Hotel and realized the four-star rating wasn't accurate, he'd debated about sitting on the bed, much less lying on it. Still, he'd pulled back the bedspread, flopped down, and peered at a stain on the ceiling, trying not to ponder how it got there, for it certainly wasn't a water stain.

Now, in the darkened room, he punched a pillow and rolled onto his side.

Night after night since his brother's death, sleep had been elusive.

That's what happened when two brothers grew up together facing the shared futility of scarcity and endless beatings from their drug-addled father. Nothing was left of the Winchester heritage except the old Florida farm, the rundown homestead sitting on two acres of land at the end of a county road. And no matter how wealthy Teddy became, his roots were fixed in poverty.

Fortunately, his brother Christian had held onto the farm after Christian's wife died a year earlier, refurbishing the place and attempting to grow citrus fruit. The crops hadn't produced one grapefruit, as far as Teddy knew. Neither he nor Christian had the knack for farming, and Christian had always struggled when it came to financial success.

Lately, Teddy found himself talking to his late brother: *Christian, should I do this, should I do that? I'm a bachelor. Am I the best choice as Joseph's legal guardian?*

Christian had been an exemplary father. How was Teddy expected to fill those impressive shoes? Perhaps he should marry, he pondered, providing a stable home for Joseph as his brother had done.

Turning onto his back and linking his hands behind his head he thought about Yvonne—her suggestive words, her open invitations, her sultry voice. However, he didn't want Yvonne. His mind traveled instead to *Miss* Candee Contando, the beautiful realtor with the creamy complexion, a mass of red hair framing her face and long legs that went on forever.

Her realty skills were non-existent. When he'd pressed her for details about any property under fifty thousand, she'd hesitated for a lengthy spell before answering. When they'd stood together and stared at the Victorian, he'd had to fight down the impulse to kiss her while holding her hand. She was gorgeous and witty, with a cool no-nonsense façade. And somehow, he knew she'd require a sizable amount of convincing to date him.

He didn't know the reason for his next decision. He only knew he wanted to see her again.

He'd visit her office first thing Monday morning with some excuse, and then invite her to lunch. Perhaps he'd bid on the property with her assistance.

Envisioning Candee's beautiful face, he drifted off to sleep.

* * *

"Pizza?" Desiree repeated. "The guy's taking you out for pizza?"

Candee smoothed the collar of her royal-blue silk blouse. She wore an outfit appropriate for dinner at the fancy country club her sister belonged to—the silk blouse and a black pencil skirt, and black stilettos.

"If you recall," she said, "I'm not going."

"Was he bald?"

Candee sipped her water. "No. His hair is dark and wavy."

"Short?"

"Wrong again. He's at least six feet tall. If anything, he's exceptionally handsome." Her heart gave a peculiar little pitch as she remembered his outrageous smile when he'd asked if she wanted to join him in the basement.

"Married?"

"No, although he talked about his nephew."

Desiree reached for her crystal wineglass filled with a local red wine. "Rich?"

"I checked his business listing on the Internet. R and T Realty in Miami is legit."

A teasing smile tilted Desiree's lips. "Then why would you refuse his offer to go out for pizza?"

Because all her energies were focused on the Victorian house, Candee wanted to say. Because she wasn't ready for a relationship.

"Because he's placing a bid on the Langrone mansion so he can tear it down," she responded aloud.

Desiree beckoned to a waiter who immediately splashed more water into the women's glasses. "Has he lost his mind like you have?"

Candee assessed her perfectly coiffed sister. Desiree was her usual stunning self, her blonde hair caught at the crown of her head with a glittering rhinestone fastener.

Forking a piece of lettuce, she replied, "Perhaps that's how these high-roller investor types go about flips."

"Once the house is torn down, what's he going to do with a vacant five-acre lot?"

"He didn't explain." Candee pushed her half-eaten meal of salad, grilled salmon and roasted red potatoes aside. "Who spends thousands of dollars to tear down a beautiful piece of property which should be preserved, not destroyed?"

Desiree finished her wine and set her glass to the side. "His reasons might be good ones."

"Well, he won't have the opportunity to tell me. I won't be seeing him again."

"Give him a chance. He sounds utterly gorgeous. Call him."

Candee leaned back and crossed her arms. "I've never called a guy in my life."

"Your life, your decision." Desiree's gaze traveled through the expansive dining room. "Did I mention the club is having a Valentine's Day silent auction and dinner dance? I remember how beautifully you helped me decorate the dining room two years ago. We filled champagne glasses with candy hearts—and the chocolate fondue was fabulous!"

Candee faked a glibness she didn't feel. "You're referring to the night my ex walked out on me for another woman."

"You'll be happier if you don't dwell on the past," Desiree said. "Besides, you'd discussed ending your relationship with George two months before the actual breakup. Focus on what's ahead and let the past stay where it belongs."

Before Candee could answer, Desiree trilled a giggle and waved. "Scott's here, the man who took me out last night."

Candee peered over her shoulder. "The guy with the blond crewcut sitting alone at a table near the bar?"

"Yes. I mentioned we were eating here tonight, and he said he might join us for dessert, and then we discussed he might bring a friend … umm … for you. The friend's name is Allen Allen."

"You planned to set me up on a blind date?" Candee half-stood. "Thanks, but no thanks."

"What's wrong with meeting a man for coffee and dessert? Maybe we can double date for the Valentine dance."

"The dance I'm not attending," Candee reminded.

Desiree peered in Scott's direction. "I don't see anyone with him." She frowned, then pulled her vibrating cell phone from her handbag. She flashed Scott a smile and read his text aloud. "Allen heard the weather might take a turn for the worse, so he decided not to come."

"The guy's name really is Allen Allen?"

"He practices law in a neighboring town. He and Scott went to school together."

Candee was no longer listening. She was peering out the nearest window, assessing the weather. The earlier light drizzle was turning to sleet, and she thought it prudent to leave sooner rather than later. Within a few minutes she was pulling on her jacket, a faux fur capelet, and Desiree was sharing Scott's table with him.

As Candee prepared to exit, she walked straight into a tall attractive man wearing navy pants, a striped polo shirt, and a gray sport coat.

"Candee? What are you doing here?" Teddy's gaze slid slowly up her, from her stilettos and slim-fitting skirt to her silk blouse, finally stopping at her face.

She fingered her gold cross earrings. "May I ask you the same question?"

"My partner has a reciprocal agreement with private clubs around the country. Since you refused my pizza offer last night …" He gave an appreciative male smile. "You know, you're a knockout when you're all dressed up."

Heat flushed her cheeks. "Thanks for the … compliment?"

"I mean, you're a beautiful woman whether you're wearing jeans or—"

Now the flush warmed her ears. "Well, thanks again. I was just leaving."

"Me too. I ordered takeout food and forgot forks." He flourished a bag with the country club's logo as proof, then glanced out the window by the front door. "Roses certainly has unpredictable weather."

"It's not usually like this." She attempted to brush past him. "Whereas Florida's weather is predictably hot and sunny."

"Especially Miami." He grinned. "Where are you parked?"

"I came with my sister, Desiree, who's ditched me. She prefers to drink coffee with her latest conquest, a new lawyer at her firm." Candee glanced over her shoulder at the bar area. Desiree was watching her, and she grinned and offered a thumbs-up.

Candee didn't respond, turning back to Teddy. "She and her newest conquest had planned a blind date for me, although Allen Allen, another lawyer, decided I wasn't worth the effort of driving in bad weather."

Teddy's dark eyebrows quirked. "This guy's first and last name are the same?"

"Yes." She surprised herself by adding, "It would have been my first date in two years, although I would've refused."

"His loss is my gain. I'll take you home."

Absolutely not.

"No, no." Candee shook her head while securing her capelet. "I planned to call a taxi."

Teddy gestured toward his pickup truck. "I'm parked at the curb. And your vocabulary might improve if you substituted yes for no once in a while."

"I can't. Really—"

"Say yes."

No use in arguing with him. His references had checked out and he wasn't a total stranger. She smiled. "All right. I don't live far from here."

"Much better."

With his hand on her elbow, he guided her outside to his truck, opening the passenger door and helping her up and in. Her tight skirt didn't allow for much climbing, and she shifted into the seat, hoping her skirt wouldn't ride up her thighs.

It did, and judging from his appreciative smile, he noticed.

"My address is 121 Juniper Street," she said, after she'd adjusted her skirt to a more proper length.

"I'll plug it into my cell phone."

She glanced at his profile as he slid into the driver's seat. Way too attractive, she thought, in a roguish way.

"What about your silverware for the takeout?" she asked.

He flashed a boyish grin, displaying even white teeth. "The club's signature hamburger can be eaten with human fingers, and there's a supply of paper napkins in my truck's glove compartment."

"You're well-equipped."

For a fleeting second, his gaze turned somber. "I try, although sometimes life throws some unexpected curves."

At close range, she noted a scar below his right eye. It certainly didn't affect his good looks, but she wondered if it indicated some of those unexpected curves life had thrown at him.

CHAPTER 5

The sleet came faster, making visibility difficult. Still, Teddy seemed to recognize where they were as they neared the turn-off for Thompson Lane.

"You know the code for the lockbox, right?" Teddy asked.

"Yes, I have it memorized," she said.

"Mind if we stop there first? I'd meant to check the water heater yesterday. In the excitement of falling through the floor, I forgot."

She caught her lower lip with her teeth to stop from blurting out. He wanted to see *her* Victorian again?

"The weather—" She gestured theatrically to the icy roads.

"I have 4-wheel drive."

"Did you offer me a ride tonight in order to get into the house again?"

He slowed the truck, studying her for a couple heartbeats, and she attributed his silence to his interest in the Victorian. "I had no idea you were dining at the country club this evening," he said.

There was enough truth in his statement to make her cheeks burn. Still, she persisted. "But when you did, you seized the opportunity."

He offered a disarming chuckle. "Perhaps that was my second thought."

She couldn't help a reciprocal grin. Truly, the guy was impossible. "And what was your first thought?"

He glanced at her, and for a moment, she was caught in the spell of his irresistible dark eyes. "How lucky I was to see you twice in two days," he said softly.

A faint smile touched her mouth. She stared out the windshield at the falling sleet, trying to decide if he was harmlessly flirting with her or telling the truth.

"There's no electricity at the house, Teddy. It will be freezing and dark."

"There's a gas fireplace in the living room. I called the gas company this morning. The meter is running as the gas was never switched off." The truck slid on the slick road. He reduced his speed again, gripping the steering wheel and focusing on the taillights ahead of them. "And I keep extra flashlights and candles in my truck."

"Are you always prepared, regardless of the circumstances?"

His lips twitched. "I try to think of everything."

When they reached the circular driveway, he inched his truck along it and slid to a stop. At night, the Victorian loomed majestic and mammoth, set against the stormy winter sky. She imagined smoke curling from all five chimneys, the welcoming fireplaces blazing in the enormous hearths.

"This house is a proverbial jewel in the rough," she murmured.

"Yes, it is." Teddy's expression softened. He got out of the truck, hoisted a knapsack over his shoulders, and then opened the passenger door for her.

"I could get used to this," she said.

He assisted her out of the truck and took her hand. "Used to what?"

"Being treated like a lady."

He blinked. "Is there any other way to treat a woman?"

Unfortunately, yes, there were plenty of other ways.

She drew in a sharp breath, remembering the verbal abuse she'd suffered with George. How he'd yell to silence her when she didn't agree with him; his chiding, "Come on, can't you take a joke, Candee?" after he'd made fun of her cooking, or her clothes, or her mannerisms. Their relationship had sent her into a tailspin of self-doubt and self-preservation.

Teddy interrupted her musings. "Shall I carry you up the stairs and over the threshold?"

"I can walk perfectly fine on my own."

She took one step and skated forward.

He slipped an arm around her shoulders. "Just in case, I'll keep you steady."

"Stilettos weren't made for walking," she joked, accepting his embrace and leaning into his solid chest as her heels crunched along the crusty ice.

He chuckled. "I'm not complaining."

They walked to the house under an onslaught of bone-chilling, wind-blown sleet.

Teddy was proving to be a gentleman, she mused, holding her securely and concerned about her welfare, in a fast-paced era where common courtesies were oftentimes forgotten. Gratefully, she smiled up at him.

When they reached the porch, she punched the code into the lockbox, extracted the key and unlocked the door.

He flicked on his phone flashlight and steered them to the living room. "I'll get the gas fireplace running and then we'll have dinner." He pulled a blanket from his knapsack and set it on the floor, gesturing her to sit. Then he placed his gray sport coat beside her.

"You can't light the fireplace and you shouldn't eat in here. The bank owns the house—we don't." She removed her capelet and installed herself on the blanket with her legs straight out, her tight black skirt tucked securely around them. "There are laws, Teddy ..."

"If anyone asks, you're my realtor and I'm the man buying the house."

"And as your realtor, may I remind you that you're making a mistake by even thinking about purchasing a home in such poor shape? This isn't a wise investment for a house-flipper."

"I'm tearing it down, remember?" He walked to the fireplace and held the pilot button down for a couple minutes. A flame flickered, and the fire soon glowed, warming the room.

She sighed. "What else is in your knapsack?"

"Soy candles." He brought out a tidy boxed candle set along with a book of matches. He lit the candles and placed them on the fireplace mantel. "The box described these candles as part of the 'jasmine and cedar wood atmosphere collection.'"

"Well then, they're perfect," she said, amused.

He sat beside her, opened his takeout box and held up a massive hamburger. "Ah, dinner by candlelight."

"No dessert? I love caramels coated in chocolate."

"I'll bring caramels next time. Dark or milk chocolate?"

"Dark." She chortled. "Bring those, and how could I refuse?"

"Hopefully, you can't refuse anything I offer." His teasing

laugh was potent, and his affectionate appraisal made her heart rate rise. Along with the aroma of the cedar candles, she inhaled Teddy's clean scent, all male, and the air around them heated.

They fell into companionable silence, as he shared his crispy fries and had a bite of his hamburger. On top of the dinner she'd already eaten, she was consuming more calories than she normally ate in two days.

When they were finished, Teddy picked up the napkins strewn beside them. "What do you do when you're not selling real estate?" he asked.

"I volunteer at the Roses no-kill animal shelter every Sunday." She wiped her fingers on a napkin. "And I work part-time at the hardware store in town, since I like making things out of wood. My foster family's business was working with wood."

His hands stilled. "Your foster family?"

"When we were teenagers, my sister and I were removed from our home and placed into the state welfare system as foster children."

Once she blurted out the words, Candee chided herself. What had compelled her to divulge so much information? If she'd blinked, she would have missed the kind interest clouding Teddy's face before he replaced his expression with a teasing grin.

"And what do you make out of wood? Should I book you a spot on the home improvement channel?" he asked.

"I'd wait about fifty years if I were you. I'm not ready for my own television show." She fixed her stare on the burning gas logs in the fireplace. "I made a detailed dollhouse once with my foster father, complete with a rocking chair measuring three inches." She paused as tears threatened. "I still have that chair."

He kept his gaze on her face. "Care to tell me about your foster family?"

"Which one?"

"There was more than one?"

"We were shuffled to five different families." Her throat tightened as the memories washed over her. "The agency urged each foster family to keep us, and then the family would decide not to adopt."

Two teenage girls with no parents hadn't been worthy of love or a stable home.

Teddy was watching her closely. "Go on," he said quietly.

She swallowed. "The last family Desiree and I were placed with ended up being our 'forever' family." Candee commended herself on her steady tone. "We attended church together, and in the evening we often sang hymns around their old upright piano while I attempted to plunk out the tunes."

"I'm impressed." He considered her with open admiration. "You make dollhouses and play the piano and volunteer at a no-kill animal shelter. That is, when you're not selling real estate."

He'd turned the conversation away from her past, and she was appreciative. Most days, she secured her childhood memories in a protected compartment in her mind. Sitting with Teddy, who seemed so attuned to her, she felt comfortable and safe.

She half smiled. "I don't do any of those things remarkably well, except volunteering at the animal shelter. Animals love you no matter who you are or your background."

He shook his head. "I've never had time for animals."

"Doesn't your four-year-old nephew live with you?"

"Yes, although it's only been for the past few months, and we're still getting used to each other. Rob's watching him now while I'm away. Joseph rides horses on weekends at an equestrian center near Miami, and now he wants a horse."

"He'll probably beg for a dog at some point, too."

Teddy chuckled. "He already has asked."

Get him a rescue dog, preferably a beagle, she wanted to encourage. Although, seeing the closed expression on Teddy's face, she didn't pursue the subject.

"Do you read music?" she asked.

"I'm no Beethoven, although I can keep a steady beat on a timpani drum." He stood and gathered their trash in the carryout bag. "I'd like to go with you to the animal shelter—if I'm properly invited. You volunteer every Sunday?"

"Immediately after church."

He paused, then winked. "I'm waiting for an invite."

She couldn't help laughing. "The shelter needs all the help it can get, although volunteers must first attend an orientation, give references and then commit to a certain length of time."

"Can you vouch for me? I'll be living in Roses for the next few weeks."

"All right."

"Flexible hours?" he asked with amusement.

She grinned. "Absolutely."

"Then I'll assist in any way I can." He pulled a battery-operated transistor radio out of his knapsack. Turning it on, he fiddled with the dial until he found a crackly station playing 80's music. "Would you like to dance, Candee?"

"You want to dance—now?"

"You're still shivering a little." He offered a playful smile. "It's better to move around when you're cold."

"I'm not shivering," she informed him. "And I haven't danced with a man in forever."

Any further protest died on her lips as he pulled her to her feet.

"I can't remember the last time I danced with a woman, either." He placed his arm around her back. "Although I remember I liked it."

Candee silenced another protest. *Why not dance? The entire evening had a one-of-a-kind, storybook quality to it.*

"Unchained Melody" came on.

"I love the Righteous Brothers," she announced.

Teddy smoothed his fingers across her shoulders and pulled her closer. "I noticed when we were riding in your car yesterday."

They swayed in step to the enchanting words of the ballad about lonely rivers flowing and sighing.

The glow of the fireplace, dancing slowly with this strikingly handsome man, made her forget the previous two years of heartache and aloneness and dateless evenings.

"This music is in twelve eight time," she said.

He kept his fingers joined with hers. "It's beautiful."

With a quiet sigh, she submerged herself in the melody of the timeless song. The minutes passed and she lost track of the following medley of classic songs. She simply relaxed against Teddy's chest and allowed herself to experience the reassuring presence of his solid body against hers. His heart thudded in a steady meter and her own heart felt strange, beating oh-so-fast.

"Candee?" He lifted her chin. "If I was that guy with the same first and last names, I'd have rented a snowplow to meet you at the country club tonight."

His deep brown eyes darkened. Her body warmed with anticipation as his hands drifted down her shoulders, pressing her nearer.

It was there, an invisible thread drawing them together.

Her mind warned: It couldn't be, not after knowing him for a day.

But it was.

She knew he was going to kiss her, and she met his insistent lips with an eagerness she'd never known. He kissed her slowly, thoroughly. The strength of his powerful body molded intimately to hers, bringing her to life. The longer the kiss went on, the more she responded, straining to be nearer him.

The doorbell rang.

Teddy broke the kiss. "Are you expecting dinner guests?" He tipped up her chin. Affection and desire smoldered in his gaze as his thumbs stroked her heated cheeks.

Her hands flattened against his polo shirt and she rested her head on his chest. "Not unless they brought chocolate."

He laughed. "It must be the wind."

The odd chime of the doorbell ringing a second time prompted her to pull from his arms.

A moment afterward, the front door opened sending a blast of cold air into the living room.

"Anyone home?" a gruff voice called out.

A pair of heavy footsteps tromped down the hallway, and an elderly man with gray hair appeared in the living room doorway. With one hand, he pushed up a pair of thick glasses. With the other, he raised a sizable wooden baseball bat.

"Who are you two?" he demanded.

Candee retreated a step. "Mr. Dunworthy?"

"Candee Contando? What are you doing here?" The aging man hobbled into the room, using the baseball bat as a cane. "I saw candles flickering and smoke coming from a chimney. I figured it was teenagers up to mischief and decided to walk down here to see for myself."

"Mr. Dunworthy." Teddy came forward. "Candee was showing me the house."

"At this hour?" Up close, the dark age spots on the man's

face showed prominently. He squinted and stared at Teddy. "You live around here?"

"No. I'm from Florida, actually. My name is Teddy Winchester. I live in Miami and I'm an investor." Teddy extended his hand.

Mr. Dunworthy placed the baseball bat on the floor and the men shook hands. "I'm Charles Dunworthy. I live two doors down and I'm your basic nosy neighbor.

CHAPTER 6

The following day, Candee attended church services. Upon returning to her apartment for a quick lunch, she checked her cell phone. Teddy had texted her.

Happy Sunday, his text read. *Planning to volunteer at the animal shelter this afternoon?*

She glanced at her watch—half past noon. *Yes*, she texted back. *On my way now.*

Can I join u?

Teddy was persistent and apparently interested in her. He was so good-looking and not at all arrogant. His manner was compelling, gentle, yet with an aura of control. She so regretted that Mr. Dunworthy had interrupted their one kiss.

She suppressed a grin and texted back. *All hands are welcome.*

She sent him the address and then changed into a plaid flannel shirt, old faded jeans, black leather boots, and a light navy jacket. After pulling her hair into a casual pony tail, she tied the green paisley scarf around her neck. Despite the freezing weather the previous evening, the sky was a brilliant

Carolina blue, the sun efficiently melting any sleet left on the ground.

Candee recognized Teddy's pickup as soon as she drove into the shelter's parking lot. Lounging against his truck, he displayed an easy charm, looking exceedingly handsome wearing dark jeans, his olive-green vest zipped over a black T-shirt. He was ruggedly fit, his arm muscles taut and hard.

He strode to her car, his boots crunching on the graveled parking lot, and had her door open before she'd taken her key out of the ignition.

"Did you attend services this morning?" His slow, lazy smile made her shamelessly wonder how it would feel to kiss him again.

As she got out of the car, she drew a long breath to steady her fluttering pulse and focused on the simple wood-sided entrance door. "Yes, and the sermon was amazing. The pastor spoke about how grace is the way to heaven and faith is the route we choose to take. Do you attend a church?"

His nodded. "A contemporary church in Florida. They stream their services online and I watched on my computer early this morning before I called my nephew."

"How is he?"

"He sounded happy. I'll fly to Miami next weekend to see him. He's having a good time with Rob." He peered past her at the modern concrete and brick building. "How long is our shift?"

"Four hours. And an application is required."

"Done," he said. "I attended the orientation already and used your name as a reference. Was that okay?"

"Of course." She paused. "When you texted me, were you already at the shelter?"

He shifted. "I guess I was."

"You guess? You blithely did nothing while I texted directions?"

49

He raised a hand. "Guilty as charged. Last night you invited me to join you, remember?" Grinning, he took her hand. "Shall we go inside?"

She liked his easy-going sense of humor. In the spirt of friendly bantering, she teased, "Do you want to clean the crates, walk the dogs or stuff envelopes?"

"I have a choice?"

She chuckled. "It depends on whether you want to sit or stand. I prefer walking the dogs and love being outside."

He gazed down at her and squeezed her hand. "I'll go wherever you go." His words hung significantly in the crisp January breeze.

The next four hours passed amidst amiable sparring and chatter, with Candee teasing Teddy that he was supposed to be walking the dogs—the dogs weren't supposed to be walking him.

Dusk had fallen by the time Teddy was placing the last dog back in its enclosure as Candee explained the shelter's protocol and safety procedures to help limit the transfer of disease. For the next fifteen minutes, they assisted last-minute customers with animal visitations.

As they got ready to leave, Candee called out a jovial good-bye to Agnes, another volunteer.

"Will you and your boyfriend be back here next week?" Agnes asked.

Candee blinked.

She was coming to value Teddy's friendship … but *boyfriend*? No, no, no. She wasn't ready to open her heart to another relationship—because Teddy would leave, like her parents, like the foster families, like George. Absolutely, she wanted to build a social life for herself again, but not at the expense of another heartbreak.

She took a steadying breath, resolve firmly in control. "Teddy and I met three days ago, Agnes. I'm his … realtor."

"Oh." The woman studied them. "You two just look like you're together. I assumed you were a couple."

From the corner of her eye, Candee noted Teddy's quirked eyebrow, although he said nothing. She glanced at her hand in the crook of his arm. It felt natural, although she didn't remember placing her hand there.

As they walked away, Teddy whispered in her ear. "Well, that opens up a landslide of potential for us, doesn't it? Now will you join me for dinner?" Leaning over, he opened her car door.

"I'm at my realty office by eight o' clock on Monday morning." She bit her lip, debating his invitation. "In the afternoon, I work at the hardware store."

"I promise to get you home early." His grin was wide, his gaze glinted with merriment. "Say yes, because we're a couple now. Just ask Agnes."

"I never said—"

Lightly, he kissed her forehead. "We've been on our feet for hours. Don't you need nourishment? Eating a few slices of pizza won't take long."

Her hand hovered uncertainly above her car keys before she agreed. "I'm starved, actually."

The sun was descending as they arrived at Tony's pizzeria on Main Street. They parked their cars near the entrance, and Teddy came around to open her car door.

She smiled as he complimented her, citing how magnificent she was with animals and how much he prized her nurturing manner.

He gestured to the entrance of the pizzeria. "I made reservations. I didn't want us to sit around waiting for a pager to go off. Especially since you go to work early in the morning."

The soft tenderness in his deep voice took her breath away.

Was it wrong for her to enjoy being well-treated? she

questioned herself. Teddy made her feel special—listening attentively while she spoke, sensitive to her moods and attuned to her emotions. He obviously cared, showing initiative and planning ahead so she'd have a decent night's rest.

He took her hand as they walked into the pizzeria.

Mouth-watering scents of freshly cooked pasta, pizza, garlic, and oregano drifted through the darkly-lit restaurant. A portly woman, looking just like an Italian grandmother, escorted them to a table near a cheery fireplace. The woman was dressed in pressed black slacks and a turtleneck sweater, with "Tony's" stitched in red on the collar. A spiked-haired pizza maker stood in front of an open brick oven tossing pizza dough in the air and then covering the circle of dough with tomato sauce, pepperoni, and cheese.

Candee took in a deep breath. "Italian is my favorite food in all the world."

"MINE, TOO," Teddy agreed. As he pulled out a chair for Candee, he took in Tony's traditional decor—red and white checkered tablecloths, Italian statues and grapevines, the muted atmospheric lighting enhanced by votive candles at each table.

He took a seat, and they accepted menus from the waitress, a sandy-haired teen who seemed far more interested in the pizza tosser than in her customers.

Teddy perused the menu. "I love anything with the word pizza."

"Tossed salad is a nutritious alternative," she said.

After they were both served, Candee tucked into her salad while Teddy loaded up his plate with three slices of Margherita pizza.

"Do you have a favorite dog?"

He stopped in midchew to consider her unexpected question. "I came across many breeds today and it's hard to say. You?"

She smiled, but there was a hint of sadness to it. "I love beagles."

He was about to ask why when the waitress appeared. "More water? Coffee?"

"Black coffee for me," Candee said.

"Two cups, please," Teddy said.

A few minutes later the waitress set steaming cups of coffee on the table, cleared their empty plates, and encouraged them to order dessert.

"You haven't eaten any pizza yet," Teddy said. "There are two slices left."

"Box up what's left," Candee said to the waitress. "Teddy, you can have the leftovers for a midnight snack."

He laughed. "Since I professed my love for pizza earlier, I therefore have a good excuse for eating most of it." He gazed at Candee, who was twirling the ends of her thick red hair. He knew he was monopolizing her weekend, but she had been utterly enchanting while she'd handled the animals, treating every dog with respect and compassion, sensitive to the different breeds. She'd walked the dogs alongside him, hips swaying, her tall willowy figure provocative, laughing out loud at his knock-knock jokes.

Finally, he'd met someone who appreciated his sense of humor.

He loathed giving her up quite yet, and he planned to ask for a coffee refill when the waitress came back.

As the waitress went around the corner to box up the pizza and flirt with the pizza tosser, Teddy leaned forward. "Why do you love beagles, Candee?"

She broke eye contact and shrugged. "Long story."

"I'm a good listener." He scuffed his chair closer to the

table. "Last night you mentioned your 'forever' family. I'm assuming the two stories go together. Care to elaborate?"

She cupped her hands around her coffee cup as the waitress set the boxed pizza by Teddy. He waited while Candee sipped coffee and fixed her gaze on the crackling fire in the fireplace. Setting the cup down, she said, "The Johnsons encouraged Desiree and me to attend college."

"They sound like good people. Are you still in touch with them?"

"Six years ago, they moved to Chicago. I haven't seen them since I graduated from college. We still email, and I hope to visit them someday."

"What about your other foster families?" he asked gently. "You mentioned there were five families altogether."

She waved a hand dismissively. "Why would you be interested in hearing the sad story of my childhood?"

"Because I'm interested in you and everything about you."

She blushed and slowly exhaled. "Desiree and I encouraged each other every time we moved, assuring each other everything was fine, but it wasn't, you know? Between the ages of twelve and seventeen, we'd lived in four foster homes. New parents were complete strangers to us, and every house had its own set of rules—where to sleep, how to dress, what to eat, chores that had to be done."

Reaching out, he traced his finger along the curve of her cheek. "Those must have been very hard and scary years for two teenage girls."

The smile she offered quickly faded. "I always felt like a misfit. We didn't do anything normal teenagers did. No sleepovers, no driver's licenses—only a continuous series of knowing we were outsiders wherever we went."

She paused and stared down at her coffee. She'd hardly drunk any.

He took her silence as consent that she'd continue, and waited.

She gazed out the window at a cluster of clouds sitting low in the sky, then shifted her gaze to his. "Looking back, the hardest part was the beginning. I can still visualize my sister and me packing all our belongings into green trash bags the day we were taken from our home. I was twelve at the time. Desiree was fourteen."

"May I ask why you were put in foster care?"

She stared past him. "Our parents were declared unfit, and the state deemed it necessary for my sister and me to live in a safer place." She fidgeted with her gold earrings. "Although I didn't understand at the time, in hindsight I see there was no other choice. Our parents died soon after we were removed, and the doctors blamed their deaths on substance abuse."

"I'm sorry." He took her cold, fidgeting hands in his. "And now you've grown into a beautiful young woman. From my brief glimpse of your sister, she seems to be doing well. She's a lawyer?"

"And a good one, advocating for children's rights," Candee responded brightly. "I'm committed to making a difference in children's lives too. I have a plan that includes a rambling property with five acres, where children can safely go after school and learn music and play with dogs and finish their homework and eat healthy snacks ..." Her voice trailed off.

"I applaud you." He grinned approvingly and glided his thumbs over her hands. "What's your plan?"

It was just like her to want to help others, he thought. He imagined her as a kind and caring mother—a perfect mother for Joseph.

Perfect for Joseph and perfect for him. He scowled at himself, surprised the idea had drifted into his mind of its own accord. With a long sigh, he acknowledged the truth. Candee was an extraordinary woman, compassionate and warm-hearted. At thirty-two years old, he'd never felt such an instant attraction to a woman. After knowing her for only a few days, he was already half in love with her.

Perhaps fate had brought them together.

"You might as well know all the facts, Teddy," she was saying.

His thumbs froze on her hands in midstroke. He made himself resume, collecting his thoughts before asking, "What facts?"

She pulled her hands from his. "I should have addressed the situation and told you everything on Friday." Her voice was so low, he strained to hear her.

"Tell me what?" He leaned in closer, promising himself that whatever these facts were, it didn't matter.

For a fleeting moment, she closed her eyes, but then she pushed her shoulders back and squarely met his gaze. "The twenty-thousand dollar bid on the Victorian? It's my bid. I'm planning to live there and renovate the downstairs space, making it an after-school day care for disadvantaged children." Her voice caught. She paused before her words rushed out. "Therefore, I'd appreciate if you took your money elsewhere, preferably Miami, because the Victorian is taken."

CHAPTER 7

*T*aken? The Victorian was taken?

Teddy jerked off his vest and threw it on the worn oak chair in his hotel room. He approached the window and gazed out at a thick black sky. In the distance, the twinkling lights of shops in the town square beckoned. Somewhere near, a church bell tolled the hour.

He tapped his hands together and spoke softly to his brother. "Really, Christian? Candee bid on the irreparable property in Roses that I'm interested in?"

With a heavy sigh, Teddy shoved his hands into his jean pockets. There were few moments in his life when he recalled being at a loss for words, but he definitely hadn't known what to say when Candee announced her plans. He'd mumbled something about having no idea she'd wanted the property, paid the restaurant bill while acknowledging her 'thank you,' then matched her swift steps as he walked her to her car.

At first, he'd been angry. Why hadn't she simply told him? True, he'd been insistent about seeing the property. However, if the Victorian meant that much to her—which it apparently did—she should have never taken him to see it.

His anger had evaporated on his drive back to the hotel. In retrospect, her intentions explained her hesitancy, her efforts to talk him out of buying it himself. And if he hadn't been so intent on purchasing a bargain, he would have spotted what was clear in hindsight—she loved the house. He'd clearly seen her wistful gaze when she'd held his hand and stared at the property with him.

He shook his head, berating himself. Here he thought she was the world's worst realtor. Instead, she was trying to protect her investment, and perhaps her heart. Her life had been filled with trauma and transience, yet in what he recognized already as true Candee style, her aspiration was to transform the house into a safe environment for disadvantaged children.

His head-strong, courageous Candee.

He recalled the night before, the candlelight living room and her amused, "You want to dance—now?" After the music started, she'd snuggled close, her soft curves pressed against him. She'd felt warm and responsive, and the mere touch of her hands on his shoulders had heated his pulse. Just thinking about the tumultuous highs of the past three days made the short time they'd spent together all the more significant.

He sensed she was beginning to care for him too. Nonetheless, common sense warned that love had no place in his life. He owned a thriving real estate business in Florida and had a nephew who needed him there.

There was no reason he couldn't continue seeing her, though, his heart encouraged. All that stood between them was the house and a distance of over seven hundred miles. Both easily remedied, he assured himself, between phone calls and Skype, although his conscience nagged about how he didn't do well in long-distance relationships.

With a low exhale, he turned away from the window.

Before they'd departed, he'd pressed a kiss to her forehead and informed her he intended to talk further in the morning. She hadn't agreed, although she hadn't disagreed either. Nonetheless, he'd seen the resistance in her green eyes. It had taken the last grain of his self-control not to bring her to his chest and placate that resistance with soft assurances and numerous kisses.

First thing in the morning, he'd arrive at her realty office and check off the first part of what was keeping them apart. He had decided to visit her office on Monday anyway, although now his reasons were different.

He glanced at the clock, dreading the lengthy night awaiting him. At least there were leftovers, he mused.

He uttered a soft curse as he looked around his room. In their quick departure, he'd forgotten the leftover pizza at the restaurant.

More importantly, he'd forgotten to ask Candee why she loved beagles.

Tomorrow. There was always tomorrow. For her sake and for his, he intended to straighten out everything. Tomorrow.

* * *

AFTER CALLING his nephew and speaking briefly to Rob, Teddy arrived at Candee's realty office at nine a.m. His arms were laden with four boxes of chocolate-covered caramels he'd bought at a local supermarket and a carryout bag from the trendy coffee house in town: two espressos topped with steamed milk, a dusting of cinnamon, and dark chocolate curls. A peace offering.

He rapped on Candee's realty door and walked in, smiling his approval at the tastefully decorated sun-lit office.

Candee sat behind an uncluttered desk with her laptop open, clicking rapidly on the keys. It appeared she'd taken extra care with her appearance, wearing a light-pink blouse and tailored black slacks. Her luxurious red hair was pulled back from her face and fastened with a floral-colored barrette, the rest of it falling to curl naturally around her shoulders.

His heart stopped. She was so beautiful.

She didn't seem quite as enraptured to see him. Her greeting consisted of a curt nod.

He held the candy toward her. "These are for you. I realize it's a little early in the morning for chocolate."

"It's never too early for chocolate." A slow smile came across her face as she stood. She accepted the candy and placed the boxes beside her laptop. "Thank you, although I can't eat all this candy."

"I can help you." Encouraged by his success, he pulled up a chair and set the coffees on her desk. "I assume you expected me, and I have four reasons for coming."

She sat back down in her chair. "Teddy, I … The Victorian …If you knew how much the home means to me."

"That's the main reason I'm here." An odd lump formed in his throat at her vulnerable yet unwavering expression. "I have no intention of bidding on the property anymore."

She pressed a palm to her heart. "You don't?"

"Absolutely not. Prompted by the right incentive, of course." He paused. When she didn't respond, he continued, "Besides, I certainly wouldn't want to go against you in a bidding war."

A determined glint shone in her gaze. "Considering you know I'd do anything to win?"

"Considering that fact and everything else, I won't even

try. When you're bent on a course of action, I believe nothing can stop you."

"You've come to know me well in four days." She leaned back in her chair and grinned. "Besides, my twenty-thousand-dollar bid is all the money to my name, and I wouldn't have the funds to bid against you." Without warning, her grin turned into a sob.

He went around her desk and knelt, sliding his arms around her. Turning into his embrace she cried harder, murmuring between sobs about how relieved she was, and how she knew the house could be salvaged with hard work and diligence, and she planned to use the acreage for a small working farm.

When her tears waned, she stayed where she was, her head resting against his chest.

He offered a napkin from the coffee bag. "Everything better?"

Self-consciously, she dabbed at her eyes and composed her features. "I haven't allowed myself to cry in years."

"I haven't cried in a long time either," he admitted. Rising, he skimmed a kiss across her temple.

She offered a rueful grin. "What are the other reasons you're here?'

"Well, the first was to bring you coffee and chocolates, and the second was to inform you I won't be bidding on the Victorian."

"But you mentioned a 'right' incentive. What might that be?"

"I'd like a thank-you kiss in return for preferring to be your ally, not your adversary."

She smiled.

He lifted her from her chair and pulled her into his arms. Gently, he brushed his lips over hers. Her tongue swept across his lips, and he welcomed her, his body shamelessly hungry in its response. His fingers tightened possessively to draw her closer, and an eternity passed before he lifted his mouth.

"The reason you came to Roses was to find a property and now you're giving it up," she murmured. "You would do this for me?"

He gazed into her glistening eyes, brimming with happiness.

"I would do anything for you," he answered thickly, surprised he'd spoken his thoughts aloud. "Although I truly believe the Victorian is beyond renovation."

She pulled out of his arms. "I'm a fairly good carpenter."

His gaze narrowed, although he didn't want to spoil the moment by informing her the house needed at least a dozen carpenters working around the clock—not to mention plumbers, electricians and roofers.

The silence lengthened. His heart gave a lurch at the resolve in her gaze.

"And do you know what I've learned from being a carpenter?" she asked. "Good old-fashioned perseverance and staying power. Even my simple three-inch rocking chair demanded endless hours and a lot of care."

"Making a rocking chair for a dollhouse is a lot different from tackling a five thousand square foot house that's been abandoned for years," he said.

"I'm not impatient. I'll focus on the process and—"

"I'll support you." His quiet tone stopped her from continuing. "However, from my knowledge as a contractor, sometimes you need to move on. Bringing the house up to par with city and code requirements will take a lot of capital."

Adamantly, she shook her head. "I'll never give up my dream."

He noted the guarded hope in her voice and carefully chose his words. "I have an offer for you. Your plan for after-school care is a good one, and I'd like to invest in it. Make me part of your equation." He lifted the coffees from the bag and handed her a cup. "Will you consent to viewing other properties in Roses that might also suit your dream?"

She opened her mouth, presumably to argue.

"Keep an open mind," he reminded.

"I can't accept any money from you, Teddy."

"Consider it a loan, then. I'll even throw in my free expert advice."

She managed a wan smile before sinking into her chair and thoughtfully savoring her coffee.

He glanced around the room. "Your mother owned this business?" He congratulated himself on changing their conversation's direction.

"Those were the days when my mother wasn't drinking. By the time I graduated from college, this office had been boarded up, so I earned my real estate license and opened using her name."

"Which is the reason I called you and not your competitors," he said. "I assumed you'd been in business for many years and knew the area well." Fate again, he thought.

"I wanted to continue my mother's legacy in some way. She wasn't a terrible parent, just terribly misguided." Candee absently touched her gold earrings. "And of course, the drinking and the drugs ..."

"I've noticed you wear those earrings every day. Are they from your mother?"

Sadness flickered across her beautiful face. "It's all I have left as a remembrance. She bought them at a consignment shop for my twelfth birthday. It wasn't long afterward that Desiree and I were moved to our first foster home." A hint of a smile wavered. "Now you've given me three reasons."

He grinned. She didn't miss a thing.

"I'm flying to Miami in a couple weeks to consult with

Rob and see Joseph," he explained. "Joseph's a wonderful kid. I think I mentioned that on weekends, he goes to a horse training therapy facility."

"Do you have custody of your nephew?"

"Hopefully soon." Teddy exhaled a deep breath. "My brother was killed in an automobile accident a few months ago, and I should be granted guardianship of Joseph fairly soon. It's so hard for him right now … For us …" Teddy glanced out the window and knuckled an unexpected tear. She waited in silence while he cleared his throat before turning back to her. "I'd like you to fly down to Florida with me to meet Rob and Joseph. You alluded to a working farm for disadvantaged children and you might want to expand the concept and include animals as therapy."

"It sounds like a wonderful idea, although I can't go. I have too many commitments in Roses."

"We'll be gone from Friday afternoon until Sunday evening and you'd have almost two weeks to prepare for the trip."

"What about my real estate business?"

"Your one client is sitting across from you."

She hesitated. "I've never seen Miami."

"Bring shorts and flip-flops. You can stay at one of Rob's places. He owns apartments above several of his businesses, and one is a five-minute walk from my condo."

"I'd never impose."

"Believe me, Rob owns more properties than he knows what to do with. And didn't you advise me last evening to fly back to Miami? Well, I'm following your advice, except that I want you to join me."

CHAPTER 8

The next two weeks flew by in a pleasant flurry for Candee, as she and Teddy viewed prospective houses and stopped daily at the Victorian home. He'd offered advice on cost-effective strategies to modernize, while staying true to the house's character. Though they'd viewed numerous modest properties more in sync with her nonexistent budget, none came close to matching the Victorian's architectural design, aesthetics, or sheer grandeur.

Together, she and Teddy researched adding a horse farm to the property; and she'd discovered that horses, with their unique nature, were considered mirrors of a person and an excellent choice for therapy. Furthermore, being around horses bolstered a person's self-confidence, as horses were believed to relieve stress.

"You have the acreage," Teddy had encouraged her after they'd exhausted her property search.

On the last afternoon before their departure to Miami, they volunteered at the shelter. When they were about to leave, a pregnant whimpering beagle was brought in. After the veterinarian examination, it was determined the dog was approximately fifty days pregnant and due to give birth to six puppies within the week.

"Where was the dog found?" Teddy asked.

"This poor beagle was left on the side of the road." Candee gazed at the hound-dog look the beagle gave her, and her heart melted. "I may not be able to travel to Miami with you, Teddy, considering how large the beagle's stomach is. I want to be here with her when she gives birth."

He'd assured her they'd technically be gone for one day—traveling to Miami on Friday and returning to Roses on Sunday.

As he knelt beside her, she whispered, "After the beagle has her puppies, I want to keep her."

He raised his eyebrows. "Do you mean her or the puppies?"

"Both. A dog with puppies is costly for a shelter." Lightly, she caressed the dog's black and tan coat, and the dog didn't try to bite. "I'll be a foster mom until the pups can be adopted. All they need is a warm home."

"And food and nursing and a loving caregiver," he murmured, recovering admirably from his shock.

He carefully carried the compact hound dog to her own enclosure with food and water, and Candee placed a worn blanket beneath the dog.

"Try to eat, girl." She offered the beagle a piece of fruit. The dog sniffed and slowly inched toward Candee's outstretched hand.

"Beagles are known to be loving, gentle, and extremely sociable," Candee told Teddy.

Seeing his expression as he brushed a sprinkling of dog hair, which resembled black pepper, from his vest, she assured, "And beagles don't shed, except in the spring when they're ridding themselves of their winter coats."

"You know a lot about these dogs." At the sound of

Teddy's deep voice, the dog keenly watched him and wagged her tail. "Why do you love beagles so much?"

"We owned a dog once, a sweet beagle, and Desiree and I were forced to leave her behind." She hesitated, not trusting her voice to continue. "We called her 'Kisses.'"

The pregnant dog stared up at them with wide-set pleading hazel eyes.

"'Kisses.' Your dog's name was Kisses." Apparently weighing his words, Teddy carefully replied, "You're taking on a tremendous amount of work with a monstrous house filled with rubble and weeds and all these dogs."

"I cannot abandon her. And in eight weeks her pups will be adoptable. And yes, I'm naming the beagle Kisses."

She'd been ready to puff up with indignation if he'd tried to discourage her. He didn't. Instead, he smiled and offered his assistance, agreeing that Kisses was a perfect name for a beagle. Stating he wanted to "seal the Kisses decision," he pulled her close, his arms cradling her body as his lips passionately explored hers.

Hours later, Desiree joined them for a festive dinner at a new farm-to-table restaurant in downtown Roses. Although their table had ample room to accommodate the threesome comfortably, his muscled leg had touched Candee's throughout the meal. It seemed like he always made a point to keep her close to him.

Teddy had laughingly concurred with Desiree as she waved a forkful of miniature crab cake and declared, "No one in their right mind places a bid on a property that looks like a tumbledown haunted house. And now my sister is stepping up to take on a pregnant beagle about to give birth to a bunch of puppies?"

"'Kisses needs a home," Candee said staunchly. "And the children at the daycare can teach her and the puppies how to sit and stay and fetch."

"And you'll need to hire a full-time staff," Teddy said while aiming a subtle nod at Desiree. "Although knowing you, Candee, you'll attempt to juggle everything yourself."

"You've offered to help, right?"

He studied her face and replied, "Yes, and I never go back on my word."

She stared up at him, his smiling features, the firm line of his jaw, enveloped by his commanding presence. His gaze locked with hers. Both of them completely disregarded her sister's presence as he lowered his head, his lips hovering close before he kissed her lightly. Her breath caught as his bracing outdoor scent tingled her senses.

When she returned to her apartment that night, she fell into bed, pleasantly exhausted. As she did every night before retiring, she checked the bidding on the Victorian, relieved her twenty-thousand-dollar offer remained the highest.

She courted sleep, although it didn't come. She was too excited, her thoughts humming with elated expectation. Soon she would own her dream house, and she'd be building that dream with Teddy. Yes, he lived in Miami and she lived in Roses, but with Internet and phone calls and airplane travel, their relationship could continue to grow.

Her mood had lightened with each hour she'd spent with him, and life was definitely taking a turn she'd never expected. Perhaps Desiree was right and Cupid's arrow had been aimed directly at Candee and Teddy.

Sighing contentedly, she rolled onto her stomach and drifted to sleep.

CHAPTER 9

*T*he following afternoon, Candee made sure every employee at the shelter knew to call her if Kisses went into labor. Then she and Teddy boarded the plane from Asheville, North Carolina, to Miami, Florida. The trip to the airport took less than an hour, and Teddy did the driving. Their flight was under three hours, and sudden air pockets and strong winds prompted gasps from the passengers in the cabin.

Candee was still recovering from the rough flight when an impish boy, echoing Teddy's good looks, raced to greet her and Teddy while they were retrieving their luggage at baggage claim.

"Uncle Teddy!" the boy called.

"Hey, Joseph!" Teddy squatted, fiercely hugging the boy. As he stood, he hoisted his nephew onto his shoulders.

Pivoting, he motioned to Candee. "Joseph, meet my new friend, Miss Candee Contando."

She extended her hand. "I've heard a lot about you, Joseph."

"Hi." The boy leaned over Teddy's head. "Mr. Rob said Uncle Teddy mentions you every time he calls."

"And I'm Mr. Rob." A short, heavy-set, balding man bent at the waist in an exaggerated bow. Along with a good-natured smile, his blue-eyed gaze was welcoming. He stole Candee's luggage from her and thoughtfully cocked his head. "You're too ravishing to be anyone else. Welcome to Miami, Candee."

Teddy swung Joseph back down to the floor as he offered introductions. He kept one hand possessively around her waist, and as she glanced up at him, he was staring down at her with heartfelt pride.

"No wonder she was one of your main topics when we spoke," Rob said, clapping Teddy on the back. "Everything's certainly coming up Roses, eh?"

The group dissolved into good-natured chuckling.

As they stepped out of the airport, the air of the Miami evening was balmy and inviting. Candee pulled off her paisley scarf and tucked it into her carry-on bag. Teddy walked between her and Joseph, holding their hands. As they walked to Rob's car, they passed an outdoor kiosk brimming with Valentine candy.

"No candy for me," Rob said. "I'm on a diet."

"Again?" Teddy teased.

"I haven't cheated in twenty-four hours. I'm on a roll." He kept his gaze fixed on the sidewalk and whistled an out-of-tune melody.

"We're not dieting." Teddy turned to Candee. "Carmel dark chocolate sound good?"

"I can't. My stomach is reeling from the turbulent airplane ride."

"Dark chocolate helps." He picked up two decorative gold boxes filled with candy, along with a red-foil rose and a jumbo heart swirl lollipop for Joseph.

"Chocolate and more chocolate?" she joked as he handed her the rose and boxed candy.

"Sugar and chocolate is the cure for most maladies."

"Yeah," Rob interjected. "That's been my bakery mantra for years."

She chuckled and eyed the lollipop. "You realize, Teddy, that your nephew will be on a sugar high tonight and you'll only have yourself to blame?"

"Guilty as charged." Teddy held up a hand, then swept a kiss on her lips. "I'll pick you up at Rob's apartment tomorrow at eleven."

He was so wonderfully generous, and when he kissed her, she heartily kissed him back. At least until Rob's raucous throat-clearing broke her and Teddy apart.

* * *

FOLLOWING a leisurely shower in Rob's high-end penthouse Saturday morning, Candee checked her appearance in the bedroom's full-length mirror. The weather was a comfortable seventy degrees, and she was pleased she'd brought a soft royal-blue crepe dress accented by gathered cropped sleeves. She rubbed a drop of her favorite rose fragrance to her wrists, and pulled on black leather ballet flats for walking ease.

She had just knotted the gold tie belt around her waist when she heard a light rap on the penthouse door. Teddy had arrived exactly at eleven a.m.

She smiled as she opened the door. Yes, he was devastatingly handsome, standing in the doorway wearing cotton khaki pants and a slim-fitting gray polo shirt that accented his strong physique. However, it was the little things that drew her to him—his kind actions, how he was true to his word, and the way his eyes lit with boyish enthusiasm whenever he described the Victorian's renovations.

"Good morning." He took her hands in his and gazed at her with bold dark eyes. "Your beauty lights up this place."

Self-consciously, she laughed. "You must be focusing on the view behind me. You know, the sixteen-foot floor-to-ceiling windows looking out onto Miami beach and 'millionaire's row.'"

He drew her to him. "No, it's you," he whispered. "Only you." His mouth came down on hers for a long passionate kiss, and her heart thumped hard in her chest.

She placed her cell phone in her handbag and slung the bag over her shoulder. Down in the lobby, they encountered a pacing Rob and an exuberant Joseph demonstrating a cartwheel across the marbled floor.

"About time, you two." Rob pointedly stared at his watch. "What normally takes me five minutes took you ten."

"We were detained," Teddy said, reclaiming Candee's hand. "Shall we all walk to your bakery?"

"Absolutely." Rob patted his round stomach. "Some of us can use the exercise."

In the glittering daylight of the promising morning, Candee tucked her fingers in the crook of Teddy's strong arm. A welcoming breeze lifted her loose hair from her shoulders like a whirlpool.

As the foursome approached Sixty-Fifth Street, Rob's body language punctuated his proud tone. "What's not to like about America's favorite vacation city?" He gestured to the glass skyscrapers on both sides of the street. "Miami boasts a trendy nightlife, boat shows, auto racing, golf, tennis, cruises and deep-sea fishing."

"And we've never done any of those activities," Teddy said dryly.

"We had a lively time on the two-night party cruise a few years back, remember?"

"Lively time?" A knowing grin crossed Teddy's face. "You were seasick the entire forty-eight hours."

They crossed an intersection, and the enticing scent from Rob's bakery beckoned them into the store like a warm embrace. Glazed donuts, masterfully iced rainbow-colored cupcakes, and towering, three-tiered layer cakes frosted with buttercream sat proudly in a row of glass cases.

"I saved your Valentine cupcake for you, Uncle Teddy," Joseph said. And I made one for Miss Candee too. We froze them, and Mr. Rob took them out of the freezer yesterday." Joseph tugged on Teddy's hand. "They're in the kitchen. Come on, I'll show you."

"Save us a table," Teddy said to Candee. "We'll be back shortly."

When half of their group had disbanded, Rob examined a display case for fingerprints while a white-aproned employee boxed an order of cinnamon buns.

Candee hung back, standing behind a parade of customers.

When Rob returned carrying two mugs of coffee and a bag of donuts, he guided her to an inviting seating area adjoining the bakery.

"Freshly baked donuts!" He exclaimed. "Twenty-four hours on a diet is long enough." He set a white bakery bag emblazoned with his Rob's Marvelous Muffins logo and the two mugs on the small round table. "Black coffee, right?"

"Thank you." She inhaled the mouth-watering scent of chocolate iced donuts rolled in sprinkles and the aroma of rich dark coffee. "Your hospitality is generous, and both your places—the penthouse and this bakery—are amazing."

"I don't have any complaints about flattery." He took a large swallow of his coffee. "Keep it coming."

"I'd gain ten pounds in a week if I worked here." She grinned. "A bakery like yours in my hometown would be well-received."

He flashed a smile. "I own a half dozen bakeries in Miami. I haven't considered opening out-of-state, although you never know."

Rob went on to describe the process of running a bakery, embroidering his account of the time he'd changed a hit recipe and used confectioners' sugar instead of granulated, which had resulted in a string of complaints.

Her turquoise and silver bracelets cheerfully clinked against her coffee mug as she drank and listened. He was such a genial man and so talkative, she could imagine him having a conversation without her, chatting non-stop to an empty chair.

"Enough about me." His telescope gaze gave her a measured look. "Let's talk about your grand plans for the Victorian, Candee."

"Hasn't Teddy told you?"

He nodded confirmation. "Now I want to hear it from you."

She blew out an audible breath. "To begin with, every bathroom requires a complete gut job, and the carpeting in each room needs to be pulled up." She paused. "The wood floors are trashed, and Teddy recommended restoring them using four-inch red-oak planks."

"Do you have funds to pay for all these renovations?" Rob flatly asked.

His tone didn't intimidate her in the least. "No. I'll take out loans."

"And how do you intend to pay back these loans? All these restorations will take endless capital."

She let the reality of his words hang in the air between them. She'd learned to stay quiet when she wasn't certain how to answer, and she needed to think before replying. Her foster background, dealing with different people's expectations, had taught her that.

"I'll work extra hours at the hardware store," she said. "And I can wield tools and ladders. There's nothing like carpentry to test a person's patience."

Mentally, she thanked her "forever" foster father for permitting her to work with him in his woodshop.

She met Rob's piercing blue gaze and waved a dismissive hand at herself. "Who knows? Maybe I'll even sell a house or two in the meantime."

"Teddy said your perseverance and goals are admirable."

"I'm going to be the type of caregiver who attends every child's basketball game, every concert ..." She forced herself to keep her tone calm and unemotional. "These disadvantaged kids need support."

"I've invested in Teddy's ventures for years, and he's never let me down. He approves of your project and he oversees numerous home-improvement crews."

"We'll give it our best shot."

"The hallmark of a successful baker is self-discipline, and the same goes for real estate." Rob gave a big throaty laugh. "At first, Teddy wanted to raze the house and build low-income housing on the five-acre lot. Our business ethos is to give to those less fortunate."

In the space of seconds, Teddy's ideas collided with hers, and she could see the merit in his plans for the property.

"He never told me," she softly replied.

"You're the best thing that's happened to him in a long time. Has he mentioned his childhood to you?"

She swallowed a deep drink of the exquisitely brewed coffee. "Hardly anything."

"I encouraged him to show you his old homestead," Rob said. "He said he's too embarrassed."

"It can't be any worse than my childhood homes."

Instantly, she was ambushed by scenes from her adolescence. Whenever her birthday had come around, she had waited, hoping for a birthday cake. The cake never came. Neither did the candles, or the balloons, or the birthday gifts.

"Teddy came from nothing," Rob said, "and he and his brother were constantly beaten by his drunken father. When life gets punched out of you, only the outstanding persevere. Unfortunately, after a hard childhood, a person's trust no longer comes easy."

She confirmed his words with a sad smile. Despite his outward bravado, Rob had an astute understanding of people.

"And what about your foster families?" he asked.

She shrugged. "Nothing to say."

He propped his elbows on the table, the gleam in his eyes matching his shiny round face. "Up until now, Teddy's been a confirmed bachelor like me. I'm the furthest a person can get from being a wedding expert, but he genuinely cares about you. He can't stop looking at you whenever you're together."

She stifled a denial as a giggling four-year-old boy raced to the table with Teddy close behind.

"We're back, Miss Candee," Joseph announced. "And we brought your Valentine surprise cupcake." He held up a basket, revealing a red muffin set on a red doily. Piped white icing gel on the muffin read, "Life is butter with you."

Her lips twitched with a grin. Impulsively, she hugged the adorable boy. "Thank you." She turned to Rob. "Clever sentiment, Rob."

Rob laughed. "They're all different. Took me weeks to come up with appropriate Valentine adages that wouldn't offend any customers."

"Taste the muffin and tell me what the surprise is, Miss

Candee," Joseph said. "I'll give you a hint. It has something do with kisses."

"Joseph, you're not supposed to give any hints to Candee, remember?" Teddy hooked his hands in his front pockets. His slow, devastating smile eclipsed all the busyness of the bustling bakery. "It's a taste test and she's supposed to discover the surprise by herself."

Candee bit into the muffin and briefly closed her eyes. The combination of strawberries and butter was delicious. She washed down the muffin with coffee, then took another bite. "There's chocolate inside. Wait ..." she continued around a mouthful of cupcake. "A candy kiss is in the middle?"

"You guessed the surprise!" Joseph jumped up and down. "Like it?"

She laughed. "I love it."

"Me too." Teddy kissed her forehead, then pulled up a wing chair and sat facing her.

"Where's *your* Valentine muffin?" she teased.

"Gone in three bites."

"What was on yours?"

"The Browning quote." He kept his gaze on hers. "'Grow old along with me. The best is yet to be.'"

Positively emanating good cheer, Rob said, "And they all lived long and happily ever after. Long because it was for forty years, and happy for ... two months."

Teddy grinned, glanced at his watch, then back at Candee. "Later today I want to take you to Joseph's horse ranch so you can see him ride his pony."

"I'm looking forward to it."

The cell phone in her purse rang. She pulled out her phone and checked the caller ID. "Please excuse me." She held up an index finger and answered the call.

When she clicked off, she took several quick breaths. Her

gaze flitted to the threesome staring at her before settling on Teddy. "It was one of the volunteers at the shelter. My beagle has gone into labor."

"Kisses?" Teddy's eyebrows drew together. "Don't labors take a long time?"

"For a beagle, anywhere from six to eighteen hours." She matched his stare with a firm one of her own. "I'm sorry. I have to leave this afternoon."

Teddy pressed his lips together and offered a weak smile. "I know how much this beagle means to you." He took his phone from his pocket and began checking the Internet. "There's a direct fight to Asheville leaving at four o'clock and one seat is available."

"Will you book it for me? I'll text Desiree and ask her if she can pick me up at the airport."

After the reservation was made, Teddy set his phone on the table. "Done. I'll keep my return flight to Roses on Sunday night so I can spend more time with Joseph."

"Yes, of course." Looking at the boy, she said, "I'm sorry I can't see you ride your pony."

"That's okay, Miss Candee," Joseph replied. "I ride him every weekend. I love horses! I love every animal in the world!"

She laughed. "Animals and children are very special."

Teddy stroked the auburn curls falling about her shoulders. "You're not even gone yet, and I miss you."

"Okay you two flames, save it for later." Rob cut his gaze to Teddy. Giving him a meaningful look, he lowered his tone. "Your lawyer called this morning. He couldn't reach you and left a message with me. It's about a court date to finalize your guardianship." Rob raised his tone, apparently for Joseph's benefit, who'd been intently watching them. "Hey Teddy, can I talk to you in the back?"

"Sure." Teddy quickly stood. "I wanted to behold the new commercial mixer you purchased for the kitchen, anyway."

"The heavy-duty one? It broke. The grinder lasted a week."

Teddy gave a sharp laugh. "Aren't you glad you came to Miami to meet the special people in my life?" he asked Candee.

She smiled. "Very glad."

He glided his knuckles down her cheek. "Is it all right if I leave Joseph with you for a few minutes?"

"My absolute pleasure."

Teddy grabbed an activity sheet and crayons at the counter and placed them on the table for his nephew. "How about sketching me a horse, buddy?"

"I want to draw the pony I ride at the ranch. His name is Blackjack because he's black."

Candee swallowed a chuckle as the men headed to the kitchen.

"What an excellent name for a pony," she said to Joseph. "I'm sure Blackjack is a beauty." She sat back in her chair, sipping her coffee and watching Joseph color. When Teddy's phone vibrated, she automatically picked it up and scanned the displayed number.

"You can answer it," Joseph said. "Uncle Teddy doesn't mind. I answer his phone all the time."

She debated. The phone number was identified by two initials—YE. A business call, she wondered? Assuming the call might be important, she answered. "Hello?"

"Who's this?" a woman asked.

Candee frowned into the phone. "Candee Contando. And you?"

"Yvonne Evette. Is this Teddy's phone?"

"Yes. May I take a message?"

"Put Teddy on the line," the woman said.

"He's not here."

"Tell him I'll be in Madrid another week and to phone me as soon as he gets this message. That means immediately." The woman hung up.

Candee stared at his phone as she set it on the table. "Who's Yvonne Evette?" she asked aloud, not expecting an answer.

"You mean Miss Yvonne?" Joseph made a face. "She's Uncle Teddy's other girlfriend and she's famous. We watch her on TV."

The shock of Teddy's betrayal knocked the air from Candee's lungs. She swallowed hard.

Unfortunately, Teddy and Rob chose that moment to emerge from the kitchen. They were obviously enjoying themselves, laughing and talking. Rob veered off to speak with an employee. Teddy was still grinning when he approached Candee's table.

He stopped, his probing gaze fixing on her. "What's wrong? You've gone pale."

She pushed back her chair. "Your cell phone rang and I answered it. I shouldn't have—I thought it might be important."

"Who was it?"

"A call from Spain."

Teddy stiffened. "Yvonne?"

"Yes, and she said to call her immediately."

Unnoticed, Rob strolled to the table. "Anything wrong?"

Heartsick from sadness and fury and defeat, Candee shivered and rubbed her arms. "Rob, where's the restroom?"

He pointed to a sign, and she shot past him.

"Candee, wait." Teddy strode purposefully after her. "I can explain."

She inhaled a tortured breath. She'd heard enough explanations from her ex to last a lifetime. And she'd never allow Teddy to see how much his duplicity had hurt her.

"It's not what it seems." He caught her wrist, and she snapped around. "Look," he said, "I've been seeing Yvonne for several months. She travels a lot and I ... I don't do long-distance relationships well."

Tears sprang to Candee's eyes. Firmly, determinedly, she held them back. "You don't do any relationship well."

"Please let me explain."

She deliberately stared down at his hand until he released her.

"I'll walk back to the penthouse and call a taxi to the airport," she said. "Please don't follow me. And tell Rob thank you for everything. Kiss Joseph good-bye for me and tell him I love animals too." She pivoted and entered the restroom. Inside, she splashed cold water on her face and peered at her reflection in the mirror above the sink. Her pallid complexion emphasized her emerald-green eyes, giving her a much-too-vulnerable appearance.

Again she was a fool, and she only had herself to blame. How could she have believed it was possible to fall in love with a man after knowing him a few short weeks?

Love. Love happened to other people, not to her. The sooner she came to grips with reality, the simpler her life would become. No more broken hearts, she vowed. Not ever again.

Two hours later she stood alone in the Miami airport, waiting for the boarding to begin.

To pass the time while waiting in line, she checked the foreclosure website. She gasped, almost dropping her phone when the house came on the screen. Her bid was no longer the highest.

She refreshed her phone. Surely, there must be a mistake.

No. The new bid was $40,000, driving the next bid to $60,000—money she didn't have.

This couldn't be happening. Her stomach felt heavy, her heartbeat raced.

Quickly, she texted Desiree. *I logged online at the airport, and the Victorian is now at 40K. Who bid on MY house?*

Online means the Internet, came Desiree's reply. *So that means anyone on the world-wide web. No use worrying. Whatever happened, we'll sort it when u get home. Have a safe flight and see u in Asheville.*

Candee attempted to pull her mind away from one looming fear. She might lose the house.

Another text floated across her screen, this one from Teddy. *Have u boarded the plane?*

He'd texted numerous times since she'd abruptly left Rob's bakery, and she'd ignored him.

However, he'd made and paid for her plane reservation and she knew she should text him.

Soon, she replied.

Can I call you tomorrow?

She hesitated. Her cold, clammy hands clutched the phone tighter.

Something prompted her to ask, although surely his answer would be no.

Did you place a bid on the Victorian house? she texted.

Air stopped entering her lungs as she waited for his response. Time seemed to be slowing down until a single word appeared on her phone.

Yes.

CHAPTER 10

*A*s usual, Desiree had arrived at the country club before Candee. Candee hung her fur capelet by the door and greeted her sister with a hug.

Desiree looked gorgeous in a red velvet figure-hugging pant suit. She went back to arranging a plate of chocolate-covered strawberries on a silver serving tray. The club was empty, save for black-suited waiters setting glass vases of red tulips and rose peonies on every table.

Candee appraised her own outfit—a sleeveless petal-pink lace dress. Unlined along the hem, the dress allowed a peek-aboo of her long legs. She'd parted her hair on the side and let the thick curls flow down the opposite shoulder.

Satisfied with the strawberry arrangement, Desiree turned to her. "Finally, I was able to talk you into attending the dinner dance. You can leave those puppies alone for a few hours. Valentine's Day is one of the biggest events at the club. Thanks for coming early to help me finish decorating."

"You insisted you needed help, although there's so much to admire." Candee looked around the room. "The lace ribbons and pom-pom wreaths are glittery and sophisticated, and those smooch balloons are gorgeous."

"White balloons with a stamp of my red lipstick." Desiree puckered her glistening red lips.

Candee smiled and fingered an arrow-toting Cupid on the banquet table. "No use in me sitting in my apartment with Kisses and her six puppies, watching television and hoping that Meg Ryan and Tom Hanks will get me through the evening."

"Her puppies are adorable. So firm and plump."

"And active," Candee replied. "Plus, they've doubled their weight in less than two weeks. Kisses is the best mom in the world. I supply high-quality puppy food and a vitamin mineral tablet, and she does the rest."

Desiree popped a chocolate-covered strawberry into her mouth and smiled. "All is well then."

Was it? The lump in Candee's throat threatened to choke her, and tears burned her eyelids. She swallowed and poured herself a glass of water. She wouldn't cry. She was strong and had made a vow to herself.

Desiree was watching her closely. "Have you heard from Teddy?"

"He's texted me every day and apologized numerous times about Yvonne, although it doesn't matter anymore." Candee forced herself to sound calm and detached. "As far as I know, he hasn't returned to Roses. He said something about being tied up in Miami court because of Joseph's guardianship."

"Did you text him back?"

"Only to tell him I landed safely." She missed him intensely, especially on a night like tonight, Valentine's Day. She squeezed her eyes shut, remembering the feel of his strong calloused hand around her waist while they'd danced, his lips capturing hers.

"If I was that guy with the same first and last names," he'd said. *"I'd have rented a snowplow to meet you at the country club tonight."*

How could he have become so important to her in the short time they'd known each other? Each day that passed, she felt more and more empty without him. She'd even been tempted to answer his texts with an invitation to join her for dinner at Tony's. That night they'd gone there, he'd said that, like her, Italian food was his favorite in all the world.

But Teddy lived in Miami with Yvonne, and Candee lived in Roses with Kisses and her puppies.

Once she allowed them in, her tormenting memories took over. She'd loved listening to his remodeling ideas, the quiet decisiveness in his voice when they'd agreed that horse therapy suited her project perfectly. And then there'd been the comforting reassurance of knowing they were venturing into these daunting tasks side by side.

Hah! Had he played her for a fool the entire time, planning to take her house right out from under her? The auction had just closed, and most likely demolition would begin any day. Candee promised herself she'd never drive down Thompson Lane again. Idly, she wondered if Teddy would manage the project himself, or send one of his many home-improvement crews to demolish the house.

Desiree had advised her to set her sights elsewhere. Perhaps a five-hundred-foot Cape Cod made more sense, considering her budget. Smaller dreams were more realistic.

She opened her eyes.

Her sister's gaze clouded with concern and she clasped Candee's hands. "You know, we tried to raise the funds, but neither Scott nor I had an extra $40,000 hidden under our pillowcases."

"Thank you." Not only was Desiree her sister, but she was also a true friend.

After that, Desiree adeptly changed the subject, resulting in a half hour of setting red candles around the room. But Candee's fragile composure began to slip. Other guests would be arriving soon, and she wasn't sure she could make conversation with anyone. She attempted to bolster herself by remembering she'd agreed to attend the event for only two hours. She eyed an ornate grandfather clock on the opposite wall. An hour and a half left.

Desiree jumped to her feet as two men entered the room. "Scott is here, and he brought ... Allen Allen?" she shrieked. Desiree turned so pale, Candee feared the many chocolate-covered strawberries Desiree had eaten had made her ill.

"You're joking, right?" Candee said to her sister. "You invited him?"

Desiree seemed rooted to the floor. "No, actually, I didn't."

Candee threw up her hands. "I'm leaving by seven o'clock," she reminded Desiree.

"Dinner is served at six, leaving you plenty of time." Desiree's gaze narrowed on Scott. Then she grabbed Candee's hand and started toward the two well-dressed men for introductions.

Dusk was streaking pomegranate colors in the darkening sky when Allen seated Candee to his right for dinner. A waiter set glasses of sparkling apple and pear cider at each place setting.

Teddy preferred coffee, she thought, reminding herself that she should be indifferent to his choice of beverage. She frowned. She didn't feel indifferent to anything about him. She missed the bantering they'd shared, the warm strength of his strong muscled body close to hers.

"The first course is a cheese and hazelnut green salad," Desiree declared to the others at the table, rousing Candee from her thoughts of Teddy. "For the entrée, the club is serving chicken in champagne sauce."

"I'm certain the meal will be delicious," Candee replied graciously. She took a long swallow of cider and lapsed into a reflective silence.

* * *

HOLDING HIS NEPHEW'S HAND, Teddy strode into the Roses country club exactly at six o'clock. The flight from Miami to Asheville had been bumpy, and getting his truck from the long-term rental parking lot had taken longer than he'd planned. The Valentine's Day festivities were well underway. A quick assessment of his worn jeans, polo shirt, and vest assured him he was underdressed for the formal occasion.

"Uncle Teddy, where is Miss Candee?" Joseph hopped on one foot. "Look—they have candy hearts in those little glasses by the window. Can I get some?"

Before Teddy could reply, the boy had scurried off. He gazed at him—a bundle of boundless energy and perfection, his dark eyes framed by thick black lashes. His adorable nephew, now his son to raise to the best of his ability.

I can do this, Christian, Teddy thought. Two weeks of endless paperwork had resulted in Teddy being awarded legal guardianship of Joseph.

It had been a difficult two weeks. After Candee had left Miami so abruptly, Teddy had tasted a painful defeat. No matter how much he plunged into his work, or cared for Joseph, or signed papers in the courtroom, he couldn't fully concentrate.

And then he'd made his decision.

His mind told him to stay in Miami. His heart told him otherwise.

"Are you expecting dinner guests?" he'd asked her that night when they'd danced.

Her beautiful green eyes had stared into his. "Not unless they're bringing chocolate," she'd quipped.

She possessed such enthusiasm, such spirit. And he'd hurt her by not being upfront about his relationship with Yvonne. Although in all fairness, he hadn't considered Yvonne a part of his life after he'd met Candee.

"Uncle Teddy! There she is!" Joseph shouted around a mouthful of pink candy hearts.

Teddy's gaze riveted on Candee. She sat at an elegantly decorated table with Desiree and two men. Teddy recognized Scott from the night he'd seen him at the country club. But the other man? He'd better not be that guy with two first names.

He grabbed Joseph's hand and stalked past a group of waiters serving champagne in fluted glasses to the guests.

He stopped Joseph from grabbing a white balloon, and he let a waiter show Joseph where the balloons were stored in an adjoining room.

When he looked at Candee again, she was out of her chair walking toward him.

"Teddy?"

She was exquisite, a glamorous, stunning goddess. Her glossy auburn hair hung to the side, a rosy tint creeping up her flawless cheeks. Her lacy pink dress displayed her alluring figure to full advantage. He was so relieved. Desiree had responded to his texts and told him that she'd finally persuaded Candee to attend this dinner.

He took her hands in his. "You are gorgeous."

She grinned shyly. "Thank you."

His gaze wandered across the crowded dining room, and he was annoyed at their lack of privacy, for all he wanted to do was kiss her inviting lips. Already, the hum of conversation was fading, and several diners were staring at them.

He slipped his arm around her shoulders and guided her into the hallway.

"Why are you here?" she asked.

"Because I missed you."

Her green eyes were soft and tender. "I missed you too."

"Can you leave?" He gestured impatiently around the corner, indicating the threesome at Candee's table.

"Yes, of course. I'll get my capelet."

"Hi, Miss Candee!" Joseph skipped over to them holding three white balloons. "Did you know Uncle Teddy and I flew all the way from Miami today?"

"Joseph, I'm thrilled you're here." Candee affectionately embraced the little boy.

"Uncle Teddy said today is Valentine's Day. I like balloons," Joseph said.

"We've noticed." Chuckling, Teddy put an arm around Candee's waist and held Joseph's hand in the other. He glanced toward the dining room, grinning when he noted Desiree's thumbs-up and conspiratorial smile.

"Where are we going?" Candee asked as they exited the club. Teddy buckled Joseph into the child car seat, then came around and opened the door for her.

"I want to show you the Valentine's gift I bought you." He started the car, and they covered the miles to Thompson Lane in under fifteen minutes.

"I'm still eating the chocolate from two weeks ago," Candee said. She tackled a white balloon that had floated into the front seat and turned to give it back to Joseph. When she turned to face front again, she paled, "Please, Teddy, don't drive down this road."

"How else can you see your Valentine's gift?"

He parked in front of the Victorian, then went around to

unbuckle Joseph. The boy raced to the tire swing, leaving three forgotten white balloons in the car.

Coming swiftly to the passenger side, Teddy opened Candee's door.

In the deepening dusk, she followed his gaze to the large red SOLD sign posted on the front door.

"Congratulations," she said softly.

"The Victorian isn't mine. It's yours."

She flashed him a dubious look, then gazed blindly ahead. "I don't understand."

"Some men buy roses for Valentine's Day, some buy candy. I prefer to buy houses." He paused, continuing in a solemn voice. "And this particular house is for you."

"Me?" She sucked in a breath and her eyes widened. She stared at the house with the same wistfulness he'd seen on her face the first day they'd met.

"Teddy—I … I can't possibly accept such a gift."

"Yes, you can, under one condition."

"And that is?"

"You allow me to help you renovate."

"How? You're in Miami."

He heard the pain in her voice, and his heart squeezed.

"Not anymore. I'm selling my apartment and moving to Roses, although my realty business will require that I fly to Miami a couple of times a month." He framed her lovely face between his hands and gazed into her shining green eyes. "I'm assuming you'll let Joseph and me adopt one of the beagle pups."

"You can adopt all six," she gladly agreed. Leaning back, she stared lovingly at him. "Will you please tell me the reason you bid against me?"

"I'd intended to bid all along, and your sister knew my plan. Somehow along the way, I managed to mess things up. I never meant to hurt you, and I'm sorry."

She glided her fingers through his hair. "You texted your apology a great many times and you're forgiven." She paused, glancing at the tumbledown Victorian and Joseph skipping up and down the porch steps. "Where will you and your nephew live?"

"I didn't want to stop at one house when I could buy two." Chuckling, Teddy gestured to Mr. Dunworthy's home. "He was more than happy to sell, and he'll be moving into a retirement community so he can be closer to his son."

"You're doing all this for me? Why?"

He hugged her close, breathing in her shiny hair, the scent of sweet and spicy roses.

"Because building a new life often begins with tearing down a few walls." He smiled at the stunning woman nestled in his arms. "Candee Contando, I love you."

"I love you too," she whispered.

And then he kissed her, sealing the most important deal of his life.

THE END

RECIPE FOR ROB'S SURPRISE MUFFINS

Makes: 12 muffins

Ingredients:

6 tablespoons butter

3/4 cup sugar

2 eggs

1/2 cup milk

14 strawberries, fresh or defrosted frozen

red food coloring

2 cups all-purpose flour

1/4 teaspoon salt

1 tablespoon baking powder

Hershey's Kisses, Hugs or strawberry jam

Directions: Preheat the oven to 350 degrees Fahrenheit

In a large bowl, cream butter and sugar. Mix eggs one at a time and add milk.

Rinse strawberries and mash. Stir berries into the butter and milk mixture, adding a few drops of red liquid food coloring.

In separate bowl, sift flour, salt and baking powder, and stir. Add flour mixture to the berry mixture and stir with a wooden spoon to stir until the white disappears.

Line muffin tins with paper liners. Drop the batter from a tablespoon to fill the cups halfway. If you are adding the "surprise", place an unwrapped Kiss, Hug or 1/2 teaspoon of jam in the middle of each muffin. Then spoon batter to fill almost to the top.

Bake until muffins begin to brown and a toothpick inserted near the center (but not in the Kiss) comes out clean, approximately 20 to 25 minutes.

Remove muffins from tin. Cool. Serve warm in a basket lined with red doilies.

Enjoy!

A NOTE FROM JOSIE

Dear Friend,

Thank you for reading *1-800-CUPID*, the first book in my contemporary sweet romance series: *Flipping for You*.

If you loved this sweet romance as much as I loved writing it, please help other people find *1-800-CUPID* by posting your review.

House flipping is a subject I've always been fascinated with. In my spare time I enjoy watching home-improvement television shows, and several were an inspiration for my story.

1-800-CUPID is set in the small town of Roses, North Carolina. The second book, 1-800-CHRISTMAS, is the perfect holiday romance.

The series continues with 1-800-IRELAND, the third book, and features Kathleen, from Oh Danny Boy, and Rob, a reader favorite, from the 1-800 Series.

Then, take a beach trip with Belle and Andrew to beautiful Wilmington and read 1-800-SUMMER.

1-800-CUPID is available in ebook, Paperback, Large Print Paperback, Hardcover, and Audiobook.

I'd love to meet you in person someday, but in the meantime, all I can offer is a sincere and grateful thank you. Without your support, my books would not be possible.

As I write my next sweet or inspirational romance, remember this: Have you ever tried something you were afraid to try because it mattered so much to you? I did, when I started writing. Take the chance, and just do something you love.

My Spotify Play List for 1-800-CUPID is here.

With sincere appreciation for your support,

Josie Riviera

Want more sweet Valentine romances?

I Love You More

A Valentine To Cherish

Valentine Hearts: A 3 book Valentine Bundle

ACKNOWLEDGMENTS

An appreciative thank you to my patient husband, Dave, and our three wonderful children.

ABOUT THE AUTHOR

Josie Riviera is a *USA TODAY* bestselling author of contemporary, inspirational, and historical sweet romances that read like Hallmark movies. She lives in the Charlotte, NC, area with her wonderfully supportive husband. They share their home with an adorable shih tzu, who constantly needs grooming, and live in an old house forever needing renovations.

Become a member of my Read and Review VIP Facebook group for exclusive giveaways and ARCs.

To connect with Josie, visit her webpage and subscribe to her newsletter. As a thank-you, she'll send you a free sweet romance novella directly to your inbox.

josieriviera.com

JOSIE RIVIERA

1·800· CHRISTMAS

A SWEET CONTEMPORARY NOVELLA

PRAISE AND AWARDS

USA TODAY bestselling author

CHAPTER 1

*D*esiree Contando had gained weight. Not a lot, although the extra ten pounds on her five-foot-four-inch frame were enough to make her favorite linen skirt fit snugly around her waist. When she was stressed, she ate pumpkin pie. Lately, she'd eaten a lot of pumpkin pie, and she had blamed it on Thanksgiving.

However, it was more than the delicious turkey dinner her sister, Candee, had served. The cause of Desiree's stress was the rundown Queen-Anne style home she'd purchased that morning.

"Your house is beautiful." Candee's voice came from behind her. "Now we both live on Thompson Lane!"

Desiree swallowed hard. "Maybe my house will be beautiful in a thousand years."

She shouldn't have done this. She should have dashed out of the lawyer's office as soon as the closing papers had been handed over for her to sign.

"Mr. Dunworthy, the former owner, never got around to updating the home, and then Teddy didn't have time," Candee said. "Your house won't take long to restore. My dilapidated Victorian is proof that even the most ramshackle house can be renovated."

Teddy and Candee had met in Roses, North Carolina, when Teddy came from Miami searching for a house to flip. They'd married, and together with Teddy's nephew, Joseph, they'd moved into a sprawling Victorian. Teddy had been granted legal guardianship of Joseph a few months earlier.

Desiree pushed out a tight breath. "Your Victorian still needs tons of work."

"Thankfully, it has come a long way." Candee stepped to Desiree's side and flitted her a once-over. She carried a box of pumpkin muffins. "A housewarming token," she'd declared, with a promise of something better coming on Christmas Eve.

"You've accomplished so much this year," Desiree said.

"I'm following your example. Advocating justice for low-income families and children is a daunting task. Fortunately, you're a talented attorney."

"I'm just doing the best job I can."

"You're ensuring the poorest people receive fairness. I respect you." Candee's gaze wandered to the rambling house. "You have more than enough acreage on your property for horses."

"I'll leave horses to your animal expertise. And puppies."

Months earlier, Candee had adopted Kisses, a pregnant beagle, from the local animal shelter. Of the six puppies Kisses had birthed, only one remained, as Candee had sold the rest.

Candee's emerald eyes glowed. "Boomer is adorable—all black and white and tan. And he loves to eat."

"Are you planning to sell him?"

"He'd make a great companion for a special someone."

"I'm sure you'll find a forever home for him."

"I'm sure I will." Candee smirked. "Speaking of animals,

Teddy finished the stable for Joseph's horse therapy. He converted a large shed, and Joseph loves the Haflinger horse. I did my research and the horse is small, with a calm temperament."

"You're wonderful parents. I'm thrilled for all of you." Desiree stared at her house. It seemed to stare back, taunting her. She took a slight step and pressed her lips together. "I don't know if I can do this."

"Of course you can. You're experiencing buyer's remorse." Candee gave Desiree's hand a gentle squeeze. "Everyone panics after buying their first house. Remember, Teddy and I are only two doors away. If you need anything, text me. Better yet, flag me from your driveway."

"Please thank Teddy for selling the house to me at such a bargain price. I'd never have been able to find such a terrific value on my own." Desiree attempted animation, and knew she wavered.

"You have a successful job, and now a home to call your own." Candee kept her hand on Desiree's. "Look how far you've come."

"We," Desiree corrected, keeping her voice light. If she began reminiscing about their miserable childhood, she'd lose it. If she shared her thoughts, they'd both lose it.

The women had been shuffled to five different foster homes in their teens after the state had deemed their parents unfit. Drugs and drink were only part of the issue, as their parents had also struggled with mental health problems. They had died a short time after landing in jail.

Candee broke the somber mood with an encouraging beam. "Just think, you'll pay off the mortgage in thirty years."

"Thirty years." Desiree groaned. "It'll take me forever to find someone with the expertise to fix this house on my limited budget." She paused, willing herself to say her ex-boyfriend's name aloud. "Scott had promised to help."

Not physically, of course, because Scott never got his hands dirty. Nonetheless, he'd agreed to rent the dormer apartment in her attic. In addition, he'd referred his handyman cousin to tackle the house repairs at a reasonable cost.

Some boyfriend. Some *ex*. Desiree had counted on the rental income to help pay her mortgage, and a jack-of-all-trades guy to get the job done. Finally, she had her own house, but no one to share it with. No happily-ever-after.

"Scott is in the past. Forget him," Candee said. "What's worse than a guy who is only around during the good times?"

"I know. It's just . . ."

It was just that it seemed like years had passed since her and Scott's argument, although the breakup had occurred the previous evening when he'd accompanied her to the final walk-through of the house.

"Are you joking? This tumble-down nightmare is your new house?" he'd shouted.

"Well, if you had taken time out of your day before now to see it, you wouldn't be shocked," Desiree had replied. "The owner before Teddy was elderly, and I told you the house needed a facelift."

"A facelift?" Scott had laughed. "Wow, Desiree. The house is a disaster. Is that your smooth-talking attorney jargon kicking into gear?"

"Are you ready to go inside?" Candee asked.

Desiree shifted and checked her shoulder bag for the house key.

Nope. She didn't have it.

"It's better Scott exited before you made a serious commitment to each other." Candee shuffled forward. "Besides, small-town life didn't fit his high-profile aspirations."

"True."

In Roses, life was slower, and people were friendly. A bandstand featured hometown entertainment. Tony's, the local pizzeria, had been there forever. Quaint and charming, the town hadn't given much thought to modernizing.

And now that Thanksgiving was over, the small town was transformed into a magical Christmas wonderland, a virtual postcard. Soon, snow would dust the pine tree branches and outlying mountaintops with a white sheen. Horse-drawn carriages circled the village green every weekend, and scents of gingerbread and cinnamon courtesy of local artisans filled the air. A holiday baking contest was held every year, and Desiree always entered her pistachio cake. She'd never won, although the twenty-five-dollar entry fee was donated to the local animal shelter.

Certainly, the happy Yuletide season and sense of community were reasons Desiree loved Roses and never wanted to leave.

A gust of icy air swept across the house's expansive front lawn, causing the oak tree branches to sway. The chilliness was a firm reminder that winter would soon secure a foothold on their Blue Ridge Mountain town. The wind was like a physical nudge, blowing across Desiree's thin navy suit jacket and bare legs.

She gripped the blue headband holding her thick blond hair in place.

She was out of luck. Her hair had blown into a mass of unmanageable waves.

Willing herself forward, Desiree stared at the various-shaped slate shingles on the roof necessitating repair, and the patterns of varicolored brick laying up the exterior walls. A century ago, the house had been designed to impress. Regardless, did anyone else use green, red, black, blue, and beige on one house?

She shouldered her red tote bag and matched Candee's steps.

This was a moment that Desiree had envisioned sharing with Scott. A life-changing threshold, embarking on their future together. They'd discuss her vision for the house, spend cozy winter evenings thumbing through decorating magazines, and wander paint stores discussing the perfect shade of dove white.

Velvet red ribbons and vibrant green garlands decorating the home's enormous rooms would celebrate Christmas in department-store style, and glittery white lights strung across the expansive front porch would create festive charm.

Now, all these special yet-to-be created memories would be done without Scott, because he was gone.

Her chest tightened, and she told herself to rein in her disappointment. Quietly to herself, she'd even hoped he'd pop the marriage question, bringing their dating arrangement to a happy-ending conclusion. She'd become Mrs. Scott Black, who lived in the beautiful Queen-Anne home on Thompson Lane.

Wow, had she ever been living in a fantasy world.

Between yesterday and today, the dream had disintegrated, and marriage was no longer in the cards. She was reaching thirty years old and every romantic relationship had resulted in a bad breakup. She was beginning to think she would forever be single and relegated to being addressed as Miss Desiree Contando.

Candee was staring at her, apparently wondering about Desiree's peculiar behavior, and why it was taking her so long to enter her new home.

"Desiree?" Candee tucked a strand of auburn hair beneath her faded baseball cap. "I know you're worried about taking on the house repairs, and I understand. When I mentioned to Teddy about your split with Scott, he made inquiries and found a carpenter for you. The guy's relocating here from Atlanta, Georgia. Apparently, Roses is his hometown. He told Teddy he'd like to give back to the community."

"Why would he leave Atlanta with the holidays a few weeks away?" Desiree asked. "Does his family live in the area?"

"Teddy didn't mention anything."

"And this guy's willing to start giving back by renovating my house?" With an overall sweep of her hands, Desiree gestured to the overgrown lawn, the neglected front porch, the weathered slate shingles on the steeply pitched roof.

"Yes. Teddy talked with him, and the guy will be arriving today."

"Does he know how much work my house demands?" Desiree challenged.

"You'll have to ask him yourself. He's reported to be talented and honest."

"Let's hope he's also cheap."

"He'll give you a good price." Candee firmly grasped Desiree's elbow, guiding her up the gravel driveway. "Teddy wanted to make amends for selling you this house when you clearly have reservations. He knows you're in a bind now with Scott gone."

Right. An understatement, to say the least.

Desiree changed her focus from her home's corner tower to Candee. "Who is this carpenter?"

"Keiran O'Malley."

Keiran O'Malley.

His name lodged in her throat. She had to fight down the feelings stirring within her.

"The O'Malleys owned O'Malley's Irish pub, which shut down many years ago," she managed to say.

The image of a tall, green-eyed guy with wavy dark hair came into Desiree's mind. He'd been on the high school football team, his broad chest and strong shoulders emphasized by his well-fitting jersey. He'd been a couple of years ahead of her, and had never given her a passing glance.

She'd glimpsed him at the homecoming game—the only one she and Candee had ever attended. When you lived in as many foster homes as they had, high school socializing was non-existent. Someone had pointed him out as the wealthiest kid in town. From what Desiree had heard, he sometimes helped his parents with their pub, key word being *sometimes*. Usually he was too busy escorting the current prom queen to country club dances, or driving around in his shiny new Ferrari after football practice.

After the game, she'd thought about talking with him, because her heart skipped a beat as she'd watched him. But, he'd been too engrossed in flirting shamelessly with a pretty cheerleader to notice Desiree.

Talk about a guy being off limits. In any event, they had run in completely different social circles. That is, if living in foster care counted as a circle.

"Teddy believes you can benefit from Keiran's carpentry skills," Candee said.

Panic rose inside Desiree. There would be a huge amount of work involved in transforming this house into her dream, and she remembered Keiran as seeming to be the opposite of ambitious.

Was it too late to sell her house back to Teddy and admit she'd made a mistake?

She pressed back her panic and concentrated on the second-story porch—the bracketed columns and neglected ornamental detail.

And the two words the house screamed: money pit.

She grimaced. "How does Teddy know Keiran?" she asked.

"Keiran remodeled a kitchen and bath in Georgia and

someone from Teddy's crew saw his work and recommended him."

Another gust of wind made the women shiver, and Candee jammed one hand into the pocket of her gray hoodie. "Earlier today, Teddy called Keiran and hired him for your project."

Desiree scowled. "Your husband did all this without asking me first?

"The guy's cheap, remember? He's coming back to his hometown and you'll be his—"

Desiree hesitated to finish the sentence. And then she did. "His first client."

"Exactly." Candee cheerfully ignored Desiree's apprehensive glance. "You want to host Christmas Eve dinner in your new house, correct? You can't do that until your kitchen is in working order."

"Regardless, I've never been known for my culinary skills. Except for my pistachio cake."

Candee laughed. "Um, even that's debatable."

The giggles came easier now, and Desiree's mind raced with trying to find a good reason to refuse Keiran's help before he arrived.

"I'd like to see his work. I have a certain design in mind, shabby chic, and I want it to be flawless," she said.

The laughter faded from Candee's face. "Flawlessness isn't the only thing that matters. Sometimes you take what you can get depending on your budget." She extracted Desiree's house key from her purse.

So that was where the key had gone. Desiree had forgotten she'd given it to Candee for safekeeping. Was this a sign she didn't really want the house?

Don't be ridiculous. If it was a sign of anything, it was that she was absentminded.

Candee lifted the key in the air. "Be content."

"Contentment and flawless should always be part of the same sentence."

"Not in our home-flipping world." Candee did a slow whirl, motioning toward the majestic trees, the worn picket fence, the trampled, overgrown bushes. A recent rain had soaked the lawn, and the grass was smeared with clumps of wet clippings. "Every house is a challenge and yours is no exception." She caught Desiree's hand. "C'mon. We've prolonged the inevitable long enough."

Sharing a chuckle, the women stepped onto the porch. Candee inserted the key into the lock, clicked the brass handle, and held the door open. "After you."

They stepped across a straw welcome mat, leaving foot-prints in the layer of dust on the aged parquet floor. Candee switched on the lights and offered a bright smile. "Oh, and there's one more thing about Keiran."

Desiree hesitated. "Only tell me if it's good."

"He planned on renting a place in town until he got on his feet," Candee said. "So Teddy recommended your attic apartment. He assumed you wouldn't mind if Keiran lived there for a while. The rent payment will help you with the mortgage."

A light fixture in the hallway swung precariously from an unsightly wire, and Desiree silently grumbled. "Is Keiran also an electrician?"

"Possibly, but he may not be licensed. I'm sure Teddy will know someone who is, though."

"Will a free room equal free labor?" Desiree waved off her sister's assurances. "And will his results be immediate? I want the house presentable by Christmas."

"C'mon, Desiree, don't be impatient. You're obliged to supply him with a salary and money for materials. Celebrate your good fortune because he dropped directly into your lap." Candee checked her watch. "Joseph's school bus will be coming soon. The school has early release because of a teacher planning seminar. I'll text you later."

With a nod signaling agreement, Desiree accepted the muffins and thanked her sister.

She took two paces into the foyer. A bone-deep weariness made her anxious, whereas Candee's enthusiasm was a source of inspiration.

Desiree drew on that inspiration. Taking a deep breath, she marched through the foyer and headed to the living room. The stained gold carpeting was peeling at the edges, and she bent to fold it back. Beneath the carpet were hardwood floors crying out for refinishing.

A large marble fireplace took up half the wall, its wide mantel solid oak. At Christmas, she imagined the mantel transformed, complete with sprigs of holly, miniature tealights and classic quilted stockings.

An unexpected downpour spilled across the bay window, and Desiree hoped that Candee had beaten the rain and reached her house without getting soaked.

She passed her fingers over the mantel, locating several candles and a box of matches, a reminder that Teddy had used the fireplace. He'd mentioned the HVAC unit wasn't operating, which meant no central heating or air conditioning.

The lights in the foyer blinked, then went out.

Already? Desiree massaged her temples. She hadn't been in her new home ten minutes.

Have faith, and everything will fall into place. Practical matters first. The encouraging words from her "forever family" foster mother came to mind.

Certainly, Desiree thought, she should hold fast to that wisdom.

First, deal with the electrical problem. And then the plumbing, then the . . .

The list went on and on.

Whereas now she had Keiran, the playboy turned carpenter who was on some kind of bizarre mission to help the community.

She went to the kitchen and placed the muffin box on the counter. Quickly, she captured her tote bag carrying overnight necessities, climbed the oak staircase to the master bedroom, and changed into an old pair of jeans and a flannel shirt. Although the light would soon fade, she'd begin the first afternoon in her new house by scrubbing the tiled floor.

Fun way to spend a Monday evening, she thought wryly. Fortunately, the plumbing was functional, and Teddy had kept a pail of cleaning supplies beneath the sink.

Although she had a love/hate relationship with scrubbing floors, she rolled up her sleeves and eased into a pair of rubber gloves to protect her hands. She loved the way the floors gleamed after a thorough cleaning, and the fresh lemony smell, barring the exhausting, manual labor that went with it.

Either way, she'd prayed over her decision to purchase the house, and with prayer came peace of mind. So she could do this. And she'd accept Keiran's help, because the financial savings would be tremendous.

That is, as long as he cut her a good deal, stayed in his attic apartment, and they maintained a working relationship.

And if he wasn't happy about that arrangement, he could book a hotel in town.

CHAPTER 2

*A*fter finishing a nitpicky adjustment to a kitchen remodeling project in Atlanta, Keiran O'Malley thanked the customer and gathered his tools as the other crewmen departed.

Done. Finally.

He drove his red pickup truck back to his apartment to finish packing, intentionally shifting his gaze away from the picturesque historic neighborhood of Iredell Park. Trendy and upscale, it had been reported as an up-and-coming neighborhood for young professionals. Many of the apartment buildings featured rooftop terraces, while several others were within walking distance of restaurants and shopping. He'd decided it would be an ideal area to live and raise a family.

And, he'd intended to set up a stand at the annual holiday display and sell his homemade Irish whiskey cake.

That was then, and this was now.

Still, they were everywhere—his shattered dreams. He shook his head, acknowledging that Atlanta held nothing for him anymore.

He slowed for the last turn to his apartment and went over what had happened that morning.

For once, he'd been able to complete a carpentry job on time and wasn't delayed because of Patricia, his ex-girlfriend. When they'd first met, he'd enjoyed her dark, sultry beauty.

Not any longer.

Usually, her compulsions to run in overdrive and make his life difficult were at the top of her priority list. Today she'd seemed preoccupied, although she'd slammed the office door in his face when he told her he was leaving Georgia for good.

Startled, he'd laughed and stared at the door. Really? As if this was all *his* fault?

He'd lifted his hand to knock. And then he'd pivoted and strode away. She was officially gone from his life. It was over. If only he could make peace with the fact that the two people he'd grown closest to—his girlfriend and his best friend, Kyle —had deceived him. They'd found each other and forgotten about him.

He bounded up the last flight of stairs and greeted Georges, his roommate, as he entered their fourth-floor walk-up apartment. They rented a place above a pawn shop, and Georges worked there part time, negotiating prices on the various items. Georges spent the rest of his time attending college online, majoring in international studies.

With a thump, Georges set a pizza box on the kitchen counter.

"I ordered pizza for my new roommate, Oscar." Georges's deep chuckle brought Keiran to the kitchen.

"Glad you found someone to take my place so quickly," Keiran said.

"Yup." Georges snatched a beer from the refrigerator and took a long swallow. "And we're planning to get blindingly drunk tonight."

"I hardly ever drink."

"Fortunately, Oscar drinks all the time. Take heart, *mon ami*. I'll miss your cooking." Georges headed to the living room and Keiran followed.

"That's my takeaway conversation?" Keiran asked.

"Most of it." Chuckling, Georges sank onto an armchair and drained his beer. "Because you're leaving, I'm putting take-out on speed-dial."

"Sorry, I don't deliver. You can always learn how to put together a casserole, or bake potatoes in a crockpot."

"Me? Every kitchen appliance runs when it sees me coming." Georges crooked a grin at the unlikely possibility of preparing a meal. "And I checked. Oscar doesn't even know how to fry an egg. He just drinks."

"Does he work?"

"He works at a law firm in town."

Impressed, Keiran inquired, "Is he a lawyer?"

"Nope. He works outside and struts around with a billboard advertising their current specials—you know, divorces, insurance claims if you've been in an accident—"

"What kind of a lawyer does that?"

Georges barked a laugh. "The kind you call if you're in a jam. His firm is a one-stop shop kind of place. Oscar said the lawyer is also a locksmith. You've probably seen his advertising on TV. His name is Abraham Realgood and his nickname is Honest Abe."

Unsuccessfully, Keiran tried to keep his face straight. "Well, thanks for an oversupply of information I'll never need."

"You never know when a lawyer is required, especially one who gets things done in a hurry." Georges lurched to his feet and the men shook hands, Georges joking all the while that he was charging his new roomie a higher rent for their "luxurious" studio apartment in the ancient building.

"You're a good guy, Keiran, and much more forgiving of Patricia and Kyle than I'd ever be," Georges said.

A good guy? Keiran thought.

Not particularly.

Forgiving?

Well, he embraced his faith. But if push came to shove, the answer would be *no*. He wasn't very forgiving.

"Always take the high road, son," his mother had often said.

I'm trying, Mom.

Wouldn't a good Christian man forgive an infidelity, as Georges believed Keiran had done?

Wishing his roommate well, Keiran packed his bags, hoisted his guitar case over his shoulder, and placed his father's precious football card in its plastic case. He tucked the deed to his family's pub, O'Malley's, into his wallet.

He loaded his belongings into his truck alongside the rest of the luggage he'd packed the evening before. Thirty minutes later, he headed east on I-85 through Georgia. He estimated it would take him less than four hours to reach Roses, North Carolina.

This was his opportunity to go back to his roots after leaving his family's pub far behind. He loved to cook and bake, and his father had discouraged him.

"I know the restaurant business," his father had lectured. "It's hard work, and I don't want you tied to a stove night and day, like me and your mother have been all these years. Pursue football. Go pro."

Keiran didn't have the desire, the instinct, or the talent to play football. He really liked the restaurant business. Each night, he'd link his hands behind his head and stare at the ceiling.

He couldn't follow his father's football dreams.

So instead, he'd reacted like an impetuous eighteen-year-old and left town. He'd follow his own road. He'd show his father he'd become a success without his family's support.

In Atlanta, he'd met Patricia. Soon afterward, she'd encouraged him to become a carpenter in her father's construction business, dreaming of million-dollar homes in stellar neighborhoods. Together, they'd climb the ladder of success. He'd learn the carpentry trade while she'd manage his appointments, advertise, and grow his business.

Young and trying to find his way, he'd responded with an enthusiastic "sure," and shelved the idea of opening a restaurant.

Now Patricia was gone and the ladder had been pulled out from under him.

In Roses, he'd be surrounded by the community that had given him an idyllic childhood. And maybe he could find his balance again—reopen the old family pub, visit Ireland for recipe inspirations. The more he thought about this new direction, the more he knew he had planned for the better.

He'd driven thirty minutes when Teddy Winchester phoned, introduced himself as a home flipper, and offered Keiran a job.

Keiran put his cellphone on speaker as Teddy explained that Desiree Contando, his sister-in-law, had purchased a Queen-Anne style home in Roses that was in a desperate state.

"Are you interested?" Teddy asked.

Keiran gripped the steering wheel. "How much repair?"

"I'm estimating a few months' worth. Do you have anything else lined up?"

"Not in the short term." Keiran reminded himself that there was more to life than dreams, and a steady income until he found his footing wasn't a bad idea.

"So will you take the job?"

"Without viewing it? What if your sister-in-law doesn't like my work?"

"She'll like it. Truth is, she's in a jam. The guy overseeing the project bailed, she's moving into 321 Thompson Lane today, and the place is a mess." Teddy paused. "Are you familiar with the road?"

"No, but I can find it."

"It's a definite fixer-upper. Despite that, the house has curb appeal and endless possibilities," Teddy continued in a distinct Southern drawl. "I learned from one of my crewmen that your craftmanship is excellent."

"Roses is my hometown and I'm headed back there as we speak," Keiran replied.

"Yes, so I've heard."

How had Teddy heard? Probably because men gossiped at twice the speed of women.

"As a bonus, I'll offer you an apartment—a remodel in the top dormer of her house. I lived there until my recent marriage and it's in good shape."

"What's the catch?" Keiran asked.

"I'm asking this favor because I sold Desiree the property," Teddy said. "Plus, I live two doors away."

"And you still want your wife speaking to you in the morning," Keiran finished with a laugh.

"Something like that."

"Sure, then," Keiran said. "I've been thinking a lot about making a difference in Roses."

Now why had he said that? Teddy was a stranger who offered employment, not his new buddy.

Serendipity. Fate. A coincidence. Keiran chose to believe the hand of God was bringing him back to his birthplace. A sign to leave his broken heart and Atlanta memories far behind.

Once the carpentry job was finished, he'd reopen his parents' pub. In the meantime, as a favor to Teddy for leading him to his first client, he'd give Desiree an excellent price.

"Thanks. I'll tell her to expect you," Teddy said. "Oh, and by the way, she works full time, so she won't be around much."

"What does she do?"

"She's a lawyer."

Smiling, Keiran clicked off his phone. A lawyer? Really? Two lawyer mentions in one day. He just hoped he never needed one.

He switched on the radio, bypassing the Christmas carols —the cheery "Santa Claus is Coming to Town" sung by a current rap star.

He settled on a classic contemporary station, and his fingers tapped a beat on the steering wheel as an 80's rock song belted, *"Don't stop believin.'"* He knew the lyrics to the Journey hit by heart and sang along.

While sorting his collection of football cards, his father would hum the song after the pub closed for the evening. One particular card had been autographed by a well-known player, a guy he'd met while trying out for a first-pick college draft. His father hadn't made the cut. When Keiran had tried out for high school football, his father had given the prized card to him.

Keiran couldn't imagine his father as young and carefree, full of dreams and aspirations. He only remembered a man with a resigned look on his tired, worn face, his mother cooking diligently by his side.

Keiran glanced at his backpack holding the plastic-encased football card. "Thanks for giving me material things, Dad. I'm sorry I didn't live up to your ambitions. I only wish I had visited Ireland sooner to spend time with you."

But he hadn't.

"Don't stop believin.'"

When the song ended, Keiran clicked off the radio, flicked on his left blinker, and exited the highway leading to Roses. He remembered the area, although he relied on his GPS to locate Thompson Lane.

He admired the natural scenery, the backdrop of the Blue Ridge Mountains, the celebratory way the town center was decked out for the holidays—the streetlights trimmed in decorative red bows, and the garlands strung along every shop's window box. He remembered his parents' love of Christmas had radiated throughout their pub, along with savory scents of homemade relishes, roasted turkeys, and exquisite caraway-seed-filled Irish desserts.

Once upon a time, he'd loved everything about Christmas. Now he was an adult, and the enchantment was gone. The constant arguments with Patricia had cured him of childhood expectations.

He parked at the curb in front of a ramshackle Queen-Anne style home at 321 Thompson Lane. The house stood like a freeze frame of a forgotten time.

"This must be the place," he murmured. He got out of his truck and surveyed the property. "A real fixer-upper, all right."

With his keen eye, Keiran assessed the exterior of the house against the fading afternoon light, grateful he'd arrived in Roses before dark. Patches of spongy moss grew along the slate roof. The window frames bubbled with fading beige paint. All these outdoor repairs would take hours of labor and he hadn't even stepped inside.

Despite the neglected appearance, the house brought back memories, and unexpected emotions rocked him. He recalled his childhood home in Roses, bordered by a white picket fence. The house had been located on the other side of town and was one of the largest in his neighborhood. In his mind, he heard his friends' laughter as they played kickball. He'd had no siblings, but had never felt lonely.

Beams of late afternoon sunshine streamed through the Queen Anne's front bay window. A recent rainfall brought a reflective gleam to the wavy glass. Raindrops trembled and shined along the yellow leaves on thick branches. The house was set in, canopied by four gigantic oak trees that appeared to be over a hundred years old.

Curb appeal, Teddy Winchester had said.

And a whole lot of work.

Keiran hesitated. He was a carpenter, not a demolition crew.

Unlimited possibilities.

Well, that one was negotiable, and depended on how much repair the house required. It certainly exuded charm and a salute to a bygone era. He just had to have faith that the bygone era wasn't so long ago that the home offered no modern comforts.

He didn't blink, hardly moving, debating. A slight drizzle from the tree leaves coated his cheeks and two days' worth of dark stubble. There were no lights on inside the home, although the flicker of candlelight illuminated a window.

He scrubbed a hand over his face, then retrieved his backpack, guitar, and toolbox from his truck. He'd get the rest of his luggage later.

Again, he stared at the house.

He was here, had driven all afternoon, and it seemed foolish not to see if Desiree was home. He went to the front door and knocked once.

No answer.

Twice.

No answer.

He debated about clicking the brass handle to check if the

door was locked. But, even if it was, he couldn't exactly stroll inside.

On the third knock, the door abruptly opened, and he came face to face with a beautiful woman with deep-set blue eyes. She held a lighted candle, sheltering the flickering glow with her small, cupped hand. She could have stepped out of a fairy tale—Cinderella came to mind. Her thick blond hair was piled on top of her head, held precariously by a blue headband. Her fair complexion was smudged with dirt.

"Desiree Contando?" he asked. He thought she flinched, but assumed he was mistaken.

"Just Desiree, please." The expression on her oval-shaped face was calm, and her hair shone in the last rays of daylight. Slender, she wore a pair of worn denims and a plaid flannel shirt with the sleeves rolled up.

A spin of warmth between them sparked an attraction he hadn't expected.

She was drop-dead gorgeous, especially if a guy was drawn to fairytale princesses.

He apparently was. Although he'd tried dating a princess and had failed spectacularly. Patricia had never been happy, despite his attempts to shower her with compliments, expensive meals, and flowers whenever he could afford them.

In the end, it was obvious their values and interests didn't match, and she'd discarded him for his wealthy best friend. Aye, she wanted the castle and the crown. She didn't have time to waste on a guy trying to figure out if he wanted to be a carpenter or a cook.

"Hi, Desiree." Spellbound, he just stared. She had the prettiest golden hair, framing a perfect complexion and generous mouth.

She blinked and took a step back. "Mr. O'Malley?"

"Keiran."

"I've been expecting you." Her tone was dispassionate as

she gestured with her small chin to the home's worn interior. "My brother-in-law said you were driving from Atlanta."

A breeze shifted, the wind carrying the promise of chilly winter nights to come. "Yes, all afternoon."

The weariness in her blue eyes deepened. "Do you realize what you're getting into here?"

"Absolutely." He nodded reassuringly. "I'm a carpenter, more or less."

"With any luck, it's more rather than less. This house warrants an excellent carpenter, plus a whole lot more." Her expression tightened. "Are you also a licensed electrician? I've lost power."

"No," he admitted.

The candle wavered in her hand, vulnerable to the late afternoon breeze.

She shrugged. "Then your services aren't required tonight."

"I was told I had a place to stay when I got here," he said.

"Yes, once you begin working. However, there's nothing for you to do yet, and because it's my first night in my new home, I'd prefer to spend it alone. I'll see you in the morning —and bring an electrician with you." She stepped back and closed the door.

"Well, that's perfect." He stared at the wooden front door, then down at the sagging porch. Evidently, this was his day for women opting to slam the door in his face. "I came all this way, but because I'm not the acceptable tradesman for this evening, I'm supposed to sleep in my truck," he muttered. His earlier enthusiasm at arriving in Roses was quickly waning.

You were planning to come, anyway, a small voice in his head reminded him. *You were going to take a ride by your parents' deserted pub, then find a place to stay in town.*

Aye, before Teddy's phone call.

Nevertheless . . .

He was still muttering when the door opened.

"Mr. O'Malley, are you talking to my porch?" Desiree asked.

"Just enjoying my visit with your broken-down floor. That is, when I'm not having a conversation with the rusty propane grill in the corner." He kept his focus downward. "This porch is unsteady. You'd better hope it doesn't cave in, or you'll be clamoring for a carpenter faster than you can say Queen-Anne disaster."

"Are you saying my house might collapse?" She laughed, and that amazed him. It was unexpected. She seemed so serious, with her slim shoulders and strong posture, her huge eyes speaking of sadness. Slight shadows beneath her eyes gave her an unconscious vulnerability, and one, he guessed, she would never admit to.

Her laugh seemed stilted, though. Just like his had been that morning with Patricia. An ironic laugh of disbelief.

"Minor setbacks. Everything can be fixed." He plastered on a reassuring grin that he didn't quite feel. "We'll bring your house back to her former majestic state."

"For now, she's a good distance from her former crown." Desiree smiled, and this time her smile seemed more genuine. "Why are you still standing on my porch, Mr. O'Malley?"

He studied the lit candle in her hand, and then her. She looked absolutely exquisite, her high cheekbones accentuated by pink color, her classic beauty understated. She wore no makeup, and reminded him of a master painting by Raphael—*Woman with a Veil* came to mind. Alluringly beautiful.

Before answering, he questioned himself. Why *was* he still here? Did he truly belong in Roses? Was he good enough to transform a house in shambles into splendor? Was he good enough to open his parents' pub, a legacy he didn't deserve?

A part of him said aye, although it had nothing to do with the house. Or the pub, for that matter. He wanted to learn more about Desiree Contando.

Not a good idea. Wrong reasons. He was here to work. Besides, he was spinning off of a bad relationship. Better to wall himself off from all women, especially attractive women with enchanting eyes and enticing lips.

He was amazed by his next response, which had nothing to do with his thoughts. "This is my hometown and I haven't been back in ten years. Give me a chance."

"I will, in the morning."

"I would've booked a room in town if I'd known." He pulled out his cell phone. "I'll call Morrison's Hotel on Main Street."

"They closed five years ago."

He didn't think twice. There was Broad Acres, a bed and breakfast on the outskirts. He told her as much.

"They shut down last year," came her cool reply.

He clapped a hand to his forehead. "So here I stand, wondering where I'll be sleeping tonight. Teddy mentioned he lived a couple of doors down. Last name is Winchester?"

"Yes, and … no. I mean, don't call him." Desiree's tone stayed no-nonsense. "He and my sister, Candee, are newly-weds. Plus, they're raising a young boy."

"I'll snooze in my truck for the night, then." Keiran picked up his things. "I've slept in worse places."

"Have you?" Desiree assessed him. "From what I recall, only the finest was good enough for a guy like you."

He grimaced at her evaluation. "Do we know each other, Desiree?"

"I know *of* you. I first saw you at a high school football game. Your nickname was Richie Rich."

Wow, was he ever tired of people assessing him on the basis of his well-to-do background. Sure, his parents had been wealthy and he'd never lacked for anything, although they'd toiled long hours for their success. With the same work ethic, he'd driven himself hard in order to prove himself among the other tradesmen in Atlanta.

He held her gaze. "Rich doesn't mean lazy."

"Not always." Those two words, a slight concession, an assessment of a guy she'd labeled without any facts. Frustration mushroomed inside him.

"Did we talk?" he asked.

"Where?"

"At the football game."

"Are you kidding?" She avoided his gaze. "You were too busy with the pretty cheerleader."

"I can't remember her name."

Desiree started to scowl, but chuckled when he did.

"Do you remember mine?" she asked.

He held out his hand. "I don't think we were ever formally introduced. Let's try this again. I'm Keiran, Desiree."

She accepted his handshake. Her hand was fine and delicate. The idea of living in her house was becoming incredibly appealing.

"So you're an authority about me based on a high school football game?" He still held her hand. She made no move to let go. Neither did he.

Silence reigned for a beat.

Quietly, she shifted her stance and pulled her hand from his. "True. Sometimes one chapter doesn't mean you read the whole book."

"Precisely."

Sure, he'd made bad choices. He'd been foolish and reckless for leaving a town he loved in order to prove he could make it on his own, falling into a profession totally removed from the restaurant scene.

She trained her attention on him, her deep-set eyes considering. "Teddy predicts this house will take several months to complete. I'm hoping he's wrong."

Keiran hoped Teddy was right.

"Hard to tell until I see it." He stamped his feet on the dog-eared welcome mat, a not-so-subtle hint. "May I come in? It's cold out here."

"Why not?" She brushed those gorgeous waves from her face. "After you, Mr. O'Malley." With a graceful turn, she ushered him inside.

CHAPTER 3

*D*esiree led the way through the foyer, pausing to peer at a silvery spider web, an excuse to gain two seconds to compose herself. She'd been totally unprepared. She needed time for this new development she hadn't expected.

And that development was Keiran O'Malley. The handsome, dashing Irish football player. She was certain he was accustomed to plush surroundings, and her house was the farthest one could get from that scenario.

Seeing him, she'd done a double-take, surprised that he surpassed her adolescent daydreams. In high school, she'd heard that he lived on the south side of town, the wealthy side, where tall privacy hedges bordered the homes.

A decade had passed and he'd grown even more striking. His teen body had filled out, and tiny crinkles had formed around his Prince Charming green eyes. The navy-blue parka he wore accentuated his athletic shoulders.

His family had reached financial success owning their profitable pub until it abruptly closed. After Keiran departed (she'd inquired), the pub had gone into a downward slide and never recovered from the economic recession.

The way her heart had thudded when she saw him reminded her that her youthful crush was alive and well. Definitely, she should keep her distance. Difficult to accomplish when she couldn't keep her eyes off him.

She realized his gaze was assessing her, from her messy hair to her disheveled jeans and oversized flannel shirt.

Ten years. During that time she'd earned a bachelor's degree, followed by three years of law school and passed the arduous bar exam on her first try.

Every day since then, she'd had a single-minded vision of creating a picture-perfect life. Her own childhood had been just the opposite. However, she'd learned that as an adult, she could control her destiny. Especially with perseverance and God's generosity.

At present, she focused on the monumental task ahead—transforming a rapidly deteriorating house into the holiday fantasy of her dreams.

"This is lovely," Keiran said.

She swallowed as her gaze shifted to his finely chiseled features. "You're being serious?"

"Aye. The house has good bones. And we'll be able to build on that."

"Speedily, I hope," came her patented reply.

He lifted a dark eyebrow. "In six months this place will be as good as new."

"Six months? I'm hosting Christmas Eve dinner and the kitchen needs to be ready by then."

He gave her a skeptical look. "Does your oven function?" he asked.

"Function? Hah! Fortunately, Christmas Eve isn't tomorrow. I've . . . *we've* got a few weeks."

"To perform a miracle?" He motioned to the mismatched wallpaper in the foyer, the floorboards desperate for major repair, and narrowed his gaze. For a split second, she thought he might turn around and leave.

Purposefully, she didn't meet his stare. "Only God performs miracles."

"Glad we agree on something," he replied. "Six months is a generous estimate and the renovation may take much longer depending on any unforeseen problems once we get started." He set his backpack, guitar, and toolbox in the foyer. "Many times, remodeling goes weeks slower than a customer anticipates. Unexpected delays and spiraling costs are part of the process. When was this house built?"

She rolled her eyes. "Many years ago."

"Please let me know when you find out." He crossed his arms. Tall, athletic, and vital, with his male-model good looks and utterly appealing smile, he was definitely out of place in her shabby interior. He should have been strolling across a Dublin runway wearing designer clothes, not standing in her rundown foyer in worn jeans and a navy-blue parka.

"Surely the age of a home doesn't determine the renovation," she snapped at him, and felt churlish for snapping. Having him stand a few inches away sent unexpected tingles through her nerves. Long ago, she'd secured a place in her heart for him and only him. To have the object of her affection so near made her want to confess her infatuation. Blurt it out and get it over with, so he wouldn't think she was bad mannered for gaping and hesitating and staring.

Whoa. Hold that thought. They'd been together ten minutes and she wanted to tell him how much she'd dreamed about him ten years ago.

No, no, no. She was obviously overtired.

He didn't reply. Instead, he headed for the kitchen. "Other

tradesmen will factor in their estimates and might not cut you the same once-in-a-lifetime deal I'm giving you, and there may be surprises in older homes." He swiped a finger across the double-paneled wainscoting in the adjoining pantry.

That was one of the reasons she loved this house, because of the exquisite detailing not found in cookie-cutter newer homes.

"What kind of surprises?" she asked.

"Termite damage and rotting plumbing, to name a couple."

She winced. Unexpected problems would put a definite crimp in her bank account. "What is your once-in-a-lifetime deal, by the way?"

He paused to check a loose floorboard. "You'll need to trust me."

Easy to say, but words were cheap. She frowned and eyed his strong shoulders.

"Should I start on the renovations tonight?" He pulled off his parka, exposing thick arm muscles bulging from a cream-colored T-shirt. "I feel like I should at least fix that loose wire in your foyer because you're letting me bunk here a day early."

"Sure. Great. Thanks." She had to stop gazing at him.

He'd be sleeping in the attic, which was one floor above her bedroom. She'd hear his footsteps padding across the floor, the water running in the small shower when he bathed. Her heart beat quicker in her chest. This was her teenage dream come true, except the dream was several years too late.

Determined to ignore his desirability, she swallowed hard. Her gaze transferred to the kitchen counter. "Have you eaten?"

"Nope." He peered past her. "Any chance the stove or microwave works?"

"Both appliances are in terrible shape and should be ripped out. Plus, there's no power tonight so you're out of luck." She drew a breath. "Do you cook?"

"My parents owned a pub."

She knew that and waited for him to elaborate. When he didn't, she offered, "My sister brought muffins."

"What kind?"

"Pumpkin. Now you're being selective?" She pointed to the refrigerator. "And there's bottled water in the fridge."

"Any idea when the power will be back on?"

"I checked my phone for an update. A storm hit farther north and affected the lines in this area. The power company estimated everything should be fixed by nightfall."

"Excellent."

Excellent. Excellent would be reporting to her law firm tomorrow morning and coming back home in the evening to a fixed, finished house all decorated for Christmas. Excellent would be keeping her personal life private by living in her own space, far from the gaze of her swoon-worthy new roommate.

She ran a hand through her disheveled curls, wishing she'd pulled a comb through her hair before he'd arrived. And why hadn't she changed back into the proper business suit she'd worn earlier?

Keiran washed his hands in the sink. He slanted a glance at her while grabbing a bottle of water. "You want anything?"

She shook her head, her gaze dropping to her waistline. "After the Thanksgiving holiday, I intend to eat light for the next few weeks."

His gaze did likewise, and he smiled broadly. "You look great to me."

Her heart took a leap.

All day, her emotions had roller-coasted from exhilaration to anxiety. Now, as she stared up at the rugged darkhaired man who seemed sincere in his compliment, unexpected tears sprang to her eyes.

"This has been a difficult week," she admitted. "Usually I can juggle a lot of things with ease—"

"Difficult because of Thanksgiving and working full time? Teddy said you're a lawyer."

His question was so unexpected, so gentle, she smiled despite the tears. "No. Thanksgiving was wonderful. My sister Candee, or rather Teddy, cooked a Thanksgiving feast —a turkey with all the trimmings." She didn't tell him that she and Candee had never experienced a normal Thanksgiving growing up, so they savored every festive get-together. They knew what it was like to go without.

"Holidays are good." Lightly, he covered her hand with his fingers. "They're meant to be enjoyed with loved ones."

Awareness of his masculine presence stirred her pulse. "Mr. O'Malley—"

"Keiran."

She opened her mouth to object, then thought better of it. "Keiran, then."

"Now we're equals, Desiree." Although his tone teased, his expression turned serious.

They were hardly equals. He'd been born with the proverbial silver spoon in his mouth. She'd been born into squalor.

"I . . . I assume your Thanksgiving in Atlanta was pleasant," she offered.

He hesitated, then let out a brief sigh. "I cooked a turkey, a sweet potato casserole, and a round Irish cake filled with caraway seeds for me and my roommate."

"Wow. You'll be a welcome addition to any gathering."

So he'd had a roommate. A woman? she wondered, although she didn't ask.

"I never learned how to fix a proper meal, and now my life is hectic." Despite her shrug, she couldn't quite hold the apology from her voice, although she questioned what she was apologizing for. She hadn't had the opportunity to cook in her foster homes. More often than not, she'd been relegated to a spare room and ignored.

"My favorite pastime is spending afternoons in the kitchen trying new recipes," he said.

"I thought you were a carpenter. I imagined you crafting items out of wood."

He met her gaze. "A guy can do more than one thing, Desiree."

"But can he do more than one thing well?"

"Can you?"

"Absolutely."

"Then so can I." Approval and mirth brightened his face. His hand still covered hers. "Also, I make a mean Irish whiskey cake."

"I bake a pistachio cake that is usually edible, as long as I don't forget it's in the oven."

"How can you forget a cake? Don't you set a kitchen timer?"

"Sometimes." Another shrug. "Believe me, a cake in the oven is easy to forget, especially when I'm immersed in a court case and bring the work home with me. When that happens, I get sidetracked."

He laughed. "When your oven is fixed, we'll set a timer so your cake won't burn, and then I'll challenge you to a baking contest."

"Oh really. Who will be the judge?"

His gaze lit with sharpened interest. "Does Roses still hold a holiday cake contest on the village green?"

"Yes." She acknowledged his question with a smirk. "And always the weekend before Christmas."

"I thought so."

"I'm certain your cake will be a success."

"And so will yours."

She chuckled. "I highly doubt it."

He nodded.

Why was she able to fall into such easy conversation with him when they'd only talked for a short time? He seemed genuinely interested.

Not romantically, though.

No. Guys from his wealthy background didn't give the time of day to women like her.

Still, what was she doing? The peaceful intimacy of his large hand on hers caused her to relax a little too much. However attractive, this man was her employee, and their arrangement was strictly business.

She jerked her hand away.

He didn't seem to notice.

With a flash of white teeth, he offered that devastating grin again. "Do you accept my challenge?" he asked.

"To bake?"

"Aye. I'll make it official. I challenge you to the Roses Christmas baking contest."

"That's not fair. Your parents owned a pub."

"A pub isn't the corner bakery."

"You have more experience in a kitchen than me."

He winked. "I'll teach you all I know."

Cozy evenings baking homemade Christmas treats with him? Immediately, her heart agreed. Her common sense, however, reminded her this wasn't a good idea.

At any rate, she couldn't keep from chuckling and

accepting the challenge. His enthusiasm was contagious, and besides, what was the problem with gaining another ten pounds? Hah! She'd simply buy the next size up in clothes or scope out an elastic waistband.

"We'll schedule oven rights while you're here," she said.

"Sounds good."

Warmth bloomed in her cheeks as she gazed at him. Keiran O'Malley was a strong-featured, devastatingly attractive man who liked to cook and bake. Heads would certainly turn when he strode through town, especially if he toted a cartful of his homemade Irish whiskey cakes.

Opening the bakery box on the counter, he offered her a muffin. She declined and he chose one for himself. The table held a smattering of stoneware, along with boxes of utensils. She intended to arrange the glass-paned cupboards with an artful display of dishes and decided to get started while he ate.

Carefully, she corralled a stack of plates and mounted a chair. At her petite height, she stood on her toes to reach the top shelf of the cupboard.

"Get rid of the doors," he said.

She twisted toward him. "I'm sorry?"

"And lime green isn't trending these days."

"Just like that?" His confident attitude annoyed her. "Doesn't my opinion count? I *am* the owner."

"Of course." He waved a hand around. "Though in the latest designs, kitchens are painted white. And for a more open quality, remove the cupboard doors."

Plates in hand, she remained standing on the chair. "I've already decided to paint the walls dove white. I may want to leave the cupboard doors intact, though, so don't go throwing anything into the junk pile without my permission."

He nodded. "At least wait a few days before you decide."

Digesting his information, she agreed as he helped her off the chair. She loved an open floor plan, and took notes while she watched the home improvement TV shows for modern-day ideas.

While he leaned against the sink, she relit several candles. His gaze assessed her, assessed her kitchen, assessed the flickering candlelight.

She ran warm, sudsy water into the sink and placed several dusty dishes to soak. "You still haven't told me how much the renovation will cost."

Slowly, he bit into the muffin, chewed, swallowed, and took a swig of water. "I haven't seen your house yet."

"You're standing in the main room. Surely you have a rough estimate in your head."

A winning smile lit his features. "A million dollars, give or take a hundred thousand."

"That's not funny."

"I'll know better after you show me around." He strode into the foyer for his toolbox. "First, I'll fix that loose wire hanging from your ceiling."

"You're not an electrician."

"I learned a few things while working on construction sites all these years." He pulled a screwdriver from his toolbox.

"Do you know what you're doing?" She hurried after him. "I don't want you electrocuted before you begin working tomorrow."

He stopped dead and directed a grin at her. "If that happens, your repair list might be delayed a few days."

"You're brimming with not-so-funny jokes today."

"How's this?" he asked. "Providing I'm okay, I'll whip you up an omelet. I noticed you have a dozen eggs in your refrigerator."

"The stove isn't working."

"There's a grill on your front porch. If you have a cast-iron frying pan in one of those boxes, we're all set."

She burst out laughing as mixed reactions filled her. Keiran O'Malley embodied the best qualities in a man. And no matter how much she'd questioned his expertise, he was rapidly becoming a true blessing.

CHAPTER 4

A week passed, bringing the first Friday in December to a close. Along with record-breaking cold temperatures, the promise of snow was in the air, and daylight hours were rapidly becoming shorter.

Despite her desire to snuggle indoors and eat platefuls of carbohydrates, Desiree's over-filled schedule demanded she spend her days at her law firm filing last-minute appeals. Hours, days, had gone by in a blur, and she hadn't devoted as much time as she'd initially earmarked for remodeling her new home. As a lawyer fighting for those who couldn't afford it, she knew her service was critical. Many parents were without the financial means to support themselves or their children, and some spouses were victims of domestic violence. On numerous occasions, she'd provided free legal assistance by working pro bono.

At half past seven in the evening, she eased her car into her gravel driveway. During the day, a number of pickup trucks parked there, although all the tradesmen clocked out by three-thirty. Not Keiran, of course. Keiran worked nonstop.

A light drizzle wet the streets, and she yearned for snow —to sit lightly on her eyelashes, to gift wrap the magical season of Christmas.

She stepped onto the front porch, which Keiran had fixed, and admired the pine-scented, evergreen wreath strung with holly berries and pinecones.

"The first sign of Christmas." He greeted her with a lopsided grin as she opened the front door and smacked into him. Through the thin denim of his shirt, his body was warm, his broad chest hard and toned. She gazed up at his thick midnight-black hair, his well-defined features, and took in a sharp breath.

The smile on his face changed from humor to something else. Something deeper. He gazed at her lips, and she instinctively held her breath. His daily presence in her life was a sweet enticement she refused to acknowledge, and it took all her effort to resist his magnetism.

He dusted off his hands, then took her wool coat and set it on a hallway chair.

The renovation had come an incredibly long way in the short time since he'd arrived, and she peered around approvingly. Although she'd immediately wanted to shop for paint swatches, he'd advised focusing on the practical rather than the aesthetic. The roof, windows, and masonry repairs came first. The house required secure sealing, especially with winter approaching.

She'd approved, and in the course of a few days he'd taken on the role as general contractor, quickly becoming fast friends with Teddy. Keiran relied on Teddy's expertise, as well as his contacts. Once the house was watertight, he'd enlisted a crew to sand and sheetrock the kitchen walls.

As she did every evening upon entering the foyer, she peered at the ceiling and muttered, "Eventually, I'm getting rid of that hideous gold fixture."

"I like it." Keiran came to stand beside her. The harsh light of the open bulbs splayed across his face, and she reached up to brush a trace of sawdust from his cheeks.

He caught her hand, squeezing it warmly. "How was your day?"

"Busy. Yours?"

"The same. And I wouldn't have it any other way."

They'd come to an amiable understanding. He'd maintained a professional, friendly distance and, consequently, they'd built a trusting friendship. Somehow, he'd known intuitively that that was the relationship she wanted, and he'd quickly adapted to her unspoken request.

Her gaze swept the foyer, coming to rest on the hardwood floor. "Can the unevenness be fixed?" she asked.

"Any problem can be fixed. The question is, can you live with an imbalanced floor? I checked with a professional and the house's structure is okay, so I'd leave it and save the money." He gestured toward the bay window in the living room. "Same with the wavy glass. These qualities add character to an older home."

"Beautiful imperfections," she mused. "Like people."

"Perfectly imperfect, my chaplain in Atlanta preached at Sunday services," Keiran replied. "People are setting their sights on happiness, but searching in the wrong places. None of us, and nothing we create, is perfect. We expect a lot of others, though."

"And of ourselves," she said. "It may be that perfection isn't always the best way."

"Better to get over ourselves and think more about serving the people in our lives."

She nodded, reflecting, knowing she was forever striving to create a textbook world for herself, the one she'd read about in fables when she was a child.

Nonetheless, attaining the accomplishments her friends

often displayed on social media brought about exhaustion. Consequently, she didn't enjoy the here and now.

"Wise words," she replied.

And Keiran personified those words. He acted knowledgeably and humbly, and performed his work with a consideration that made her admire the person he was—kind, steadfast, and capable.

Each evening, he'd help her unpack endless boxes and order takeout, with a promise to cook her a proper meal once the stove and oven were installed. In the meantime, he'd rearranged her meager furniture and added a touch she would have expected more from a professional decorator than a carpenter with no formal design training.

"My chaplain is an inspiring person," he went on. "If you're ever free on a weekend, I can bring you to a church service in Atlanta. The drive takes a few hours, although it's doable in one day."

She gazed at him, and pretended she didn't. Her first inclination was to immediately decline his invitation, to maintain their cool, professional relationship.

But how could she?

She could hardly feign disinterest in this six-foot-two man with sparkling green eyes and an utterly masculine appeal. She loved talking with him, laughing with him. And she was impressed by his attention to elements and setup. He had an excellent discernment for arrangement, and was resourceful and creative, keeping her strict budget in mind at all times.

A fun conversationalist, he sported a keen knowledge in topics ranging from child advocacy to football, and, of course, cooking and baking. All in all, she considered him a Renaissance man, a term she'd once heard applied to a man blessed with intellect and proficient in a wide range of areas.

Although the term had originated in Italy, with his mesmerizing charm, Keiran was the epitome of the quick-witted Irish male.

"How's the kitchen coming?" she asked as she set down her briefcase.

"I was waiting for you to ask. Quicker than I anticipated, thanks to Teddy's efficient crew. The walls are painted, and your new appliances were delivered and installed this morning." As always, every sentence he uttered was enhanced by a hand gesture. "Do you want to see it?"

"Of course."

"Close your eyes." Obediently, she squeezed her eyes shut as he led her down the hallway.

He gave her hand a light squeeze. "Open."

She stopped at the kitchen entryway and gasped. Surely, this wasn't the same kitchen that had resembled a demolition area only a few days before.

As she and Keiran had discussed, the walls had been painted a dove white, and shiny new countertops were set in marbled granite. The white freestanding farmhouse sink was a surprise, paired with an old-world style pull-down faucet. A glossy tiled backsplash completed the ambience, along with open cupboards. She'd taken his advice and discarded the doors, giving the space a fluid, chic design.

He gestured to an empty corner. "A base cabinet is on backorder. Once it arrives, I'll install it. Hopefully it will be here in time for Christmas."

She sighed dreamily. "Thank you."

Her kitchen was exactly how she'd envisioned it, and a trendsetter's dream. Natural light spilled inside, thanks to sliding glass doors leading to her two-acre plot of land. A consistent thread of sunny yellow complemented the shelving rims, which were the colors they'd agreed upon. An oversized island in a high-gloss finish created a work triangle between the stove and refrigerator and seamlessly accommodated gleaming stainless-steel appliances. Her kitchen table and chairs had been tucked beneath a set of framed picture windows.

Awestruck, she put her fingers to her mouth. "All you've done in a week is more than most contractors could accomplish in a month."

He laughed. "The credit goes to Teddy's large, efficient crew. I'm merely one person supervising the project and helping wherever warranted."

"Truly, you are a genius."

He gazed down at her with tender amusement. "And while I was overseeing the renovations, you were protecting innocent children. If anyone deserves praise, Desiree, it's you."

Her heart skipped a beat.

Retrieving her coat, he strode to the hallway closet while she kicked off her black leather pumps, pulled on her favorite cardigan, and claimed a stool at the counter. She breathed in the aroma of seafood chowder simmering on the stove, and the sweet, enticing scent of a cake rising in the oven.

"And, in addition to the remodeling, you cooked?" she asked.

"Seafood chowder was my parents' signature dish. During my lunch hour, I shopped for the ingredients. For dessert, I baked an Irish whiskey cake."

"The very same cake you're challenging me with for the baking contest on the village green? It's totally not fair if you get a head start."

"I'll make it up to you."

She crossed her arms. "How?"

"We'll shop for a Christmas tree tomorrow, and I'm

buying. Only a ten-foot spruce will complement your living room's high ceilings. Aye?"

"Aye." How could she refuse a hardworking Irishman? In fascinated admiration, she watched him snap up a wooden spoon and adeptly stir the chowder.

"We'll eat dinner together after I shower and change?" he asked.

"Sure. Everything is wonderful."

He chuckled. "Brilliant."

A jumble of sensations made her pause. No man had ever cooked dinner for her before, inquired about her day, or taken a sincere interest. His consideration went way beyond their work relationship.

She stood and took a bottled water from the refrigerator. "Don't you have anywhere else you'd rather be on a Friday night?"

He studied her face, came closer, then pressed a light kiss on her forehead. "The more time I spend with you, the more time I want to spend with you. Does that make sense?"

There was no reason to offer a blasé answer, so she nodded a yes, because it made perfect sense. That pure attraction for him, a feeling she couldn't shake. Enjoy the moment, she told herself.

The thought made her absurdly pleased.

As he made for the stairs, she paused to take in the splendor of her polished, cheery kitchen. Previously, Keiran had drawn a sketch on his computer and gotten her approval, and his ideas had panned out. Ensuring the interior wall wasn't load-bearing, Teddy's crew had torn down the wall between the kitchen and dining room to make the most of her square footage.

A large communal area for family and friends was ideal for entertaining, Keiran had said.

She hadn't purchased a dining room set, and didn't foresee one in her immediate future.

Smiling, she arranged place settings on the kitchen island using her good china dishes and silver flatware. She'd started a hope chest when she graduated from college. It was silly, and most people had never heard of one. Despite her difficult upbringing, she believed in love and marriage, and a future with a special man. Starry-eyed dreams, she contemplated, while she folded white cloth napkins.

Keiran was down the stairs fifteen minutes later in his favorite pair of lived-in jeans and a T-shirt that revealed his fit physique. His thick jet-black hair was still wet from a shower, and he hadn't bothered to shave. His stubbled chin and prominent cheekbones made her pause. And his scent . . .

Oh, my. Now he even smelled like an Irishman—like early morning and whistle clean.

He raised a questioning dark eyebrow over his teasing gaze. "You own a service of fine crystal and china, your dining area is large enough for a twenty-person feast, and there's no place to sit and enjoy a meal?"

"Pull up a stool, like I did." She nodded to the island. "Or I'll pile cushions on the floor and we'll sit cross-legged. Someday, when I win the lottery, I'll buy dining room furniture."

He regarded the brass flush-mount light above the island. "What type of fixture do you want there?"

"I love French country design." She bent to a stack of magazines she kept in a wicker basket in the corner, and thumbed through one. "I saw a distressed frame fixture with candelabra detailing. See?"

He peered over her shoulder. "Excellent taste. I approve of all you've done." His breath was warm and tickled her ear.

That pull again, drawing her to him.

"You mean, all *you've* done," she corrected.

His lips twitched. Reaching up to the cupboard, he brought out two wine glasses. "I also bought a bottle of sparkling cider for our date."

"You're categorizing eating seafood chowder together at home as kind of a date?"

"Not kind of a date. It is a date."

"Is it a proper date?"

He sobered. "No. But it's here and now and let's embrace the moment."

Her heart did a double-turn in her chest. She didn't want this. Someday . . . maybe . . . when her house was finished and her career was established. And that would take years. Slowly, she was working her way up the ranks, though she owed thousands of dollars in student loans.

Besides, Keiran lived here. Did that count as a date?

At any rate, the man in question strode to the stove and stirred buttery seafood chowder with a wooden spoon.

"Want a taste?" he asked. "I baked a loaf of soda bread to mop up the soup. It's sitting on the table in a wicker bread basket I found in your cupboard."

"Okay, now you're showing off," she teased.

A chuckle tugged at the corners of his mouth. "Do you like the appliances?" As he stirred, he gestured to the six-burner stove and double oven. "Exactly what you ordered."

She kept herself from staring at him by concentrating on slicing the bread.

"It's impressive," she said. "And the low price Teddy's warehouse supplier gave for the cabinets was a relief. A huge thank you."

She'd taken out a home equity loan in addition to her mortgage to cover the improvements. Although she was realistic enough to understand she wasn't financially equipped to afford a total house renovation, she presumed the kitchen and bathrooms were most important. To save money, they'd concentrated on what Keiran labeled "mid-range renovations." He'd upgraded the countertops and changed the lighting.

"You're welcome," he said. "My pleasure, Desiree."

"A modern kitchen has always been my fantasy."

His gaze locked with hers. "Do you have other . . . fantasies?"

You, she almost said aloud. Swallowing, she pushed her gaze to his Irish whiskey cake baking in the oven. She whistled lightly and adeptly changed the subject. "Tell me again how you managed to get all this done, plus bake a cake."

"I delegate." He lifted a clean spoon from a drawer and scooped several spoonfuls of the chowder into a bowl, then brought the bowl to her for a taste. "I learned the skill from my father. When you own a pub, you can't do everything yourself."

She savored the hearty taste of cream, corn and potatoes blended with tender clams and sweet red peppers. "Mmm," she murmured. "This is delicious."

"A secret family recipe."

"Really? You won't share your recipe?"

"It's been handed down through several generations." He watched her, and his gaze shifted to her mouth. Gently, without warning, he kissed her. "Although I can assure you that the chowder isn't nearly as delicious as you."

The oven timer dinged. Reluctantly, he about-faced and gripped a mitt by the stove. He pulled out the cake and set it on a trivet.

"I'll glaze it in a few days. I'm testing a new glaze recipe." He gestured to the sugar and butter glaze, blended with whiskey, and grabbed a spoon so she could taste it.

"More deliciousness," she said softly.

He didn't mention the kiss. It had been quick and light. And memorable.

They'd fallen into a pattern of spending their evenings together, and her first home-cooked meal in her new home proved a mouthwatering delight. After slicing his cake, still warm from the oven, for a "taste test," they washed and dried Desiree's fine china and crystal by hand.

Afterward, Keiran led her into the living room, where he pointed out the detailing on the marble fireplace. Pausing, he got to his knees and inspected the chimney.

"I thought we'd light a fire again tonight," he said. "Eventually, you'll need a chimney sweep. Until then, the fireplace is safe to use."

"Teddy lit the fireplace several times when he lived here," she said.

Still on his knees, Keiran glanced up at her. "So is that a yes? Aye?" When she nodded, he gestured to the matches on the mantel and she handed them to him.

"The crew and I checked your central heating system too," he said, as he lit a match and checked the draft.

"Don't tell me, let me guess. The entire unit died."

"Aye, but don't worry." He offered a reassuring nod. "Fortunately, a reasonably priced HVAC guy stopped over. He's one of Teddy's crewmen."

"How much does a new HVAC cost?"

"Depends on the square footage of the house." Keiran lit the fire and waited for the logs to burn before standing. "I'd estimate your house is around three thousand square feet."

"You're right on target."

"Then your unit will cost six thousand dollars." He gave her the box of matches, his rough fingers brushing against hers. An electric current passed between them, and she felt that insistent magnetism. Not the youthful yearnings of an adolescent. On the contrary, hers were the dreams of a grown woman.

Instinctively, she pulled her hand away and wandered to the bay window. Outside, the vibrant colors of a Carolina winter day had faded, and twilight merged to darkness. The pavement gleamed with the slickness of a wet evening.

Across the street, Mr. Juno, a graduate student with a young family, had decorated his porch with an impressively lit display. Gold, red, and green boxes, wrapped in dazzling silver ribbons and bows, glowed with Christmas color and light.

She wiped unexpected tears from the corners of her eyes. What was it about Christmas that always got to her? Was it because she'd never experienced a real celebration because of her alcoholic parents? Because she'd never had a truly loving home? When life was bleakest, she'd searched for the warmth of faith and community. The Yuletide season was a time of celebration, just never for her and her sister. At least, not until this past year when Candee had married Teddy, and Desiree had purchased her first home.

"Desiree, I realize you're overwhelmed because of the renovations, but everything will evolve into the home of your dreams. I promise." Keiran came to stand behind her. His voice was sincere and deep, and a heat of longing pulsed in her veins. She blamed it on the romance of the candlelight, the flames flickering in the fireplace, the patter of raindrops on the bay window.

With its poignant reminders of the approaching holiday, she hoped that this house was the answer to her prayers. Finally, her days would be filled with the elusive elation everyone around her seemed to experience.

"Will it?" She wrapped her hands around her arms and didn't turn. He'd see the tears shining in her eyes and he'd ask questions—about her, about her past—that she wasn't prepared to answer.

"Aye. You can trust an Irishman's word."

She saw his reassuring smile reflected in the glass. The expression in his eyes, though, was a mirror of her own. Intense and probing.

And she knew what it meant.

He was beginning to fall for her, just as she was falling for him.

He turned her around to face him, his hands resting loosely on her shoulders. "I'm here for you, and I won't leave until this renovation is finished."

"Thanks. It's just—" A wave of emotion choked her voice, and she couldn't get out any words. Strange. She never lost control. After she and her sister had been passed from one foster home to another, she'd learned to keep her feelings securely bound. Not a single person was interested in two teenage girls with no money and no skills. No one had wanted them.

Not even their own mother and father had cared—so why would anyone else?

A ripple of sadness caused tears to stream down her cheeks. Swiftly, she caught the wetness with her fingertips and avoided Keiran's gaze.

"You're a nobody." The harsh words of one of her foster mothers came to the forefront of Desiree's mind. In her early teens, arriving at a brand-new foster family's home, Desiree had broken a dish by mistake. She'd tried to be useful, drying the dishes. Her foster mother had been furious, reprimanding Desiree about having no respect for other people's things, and shouting that Desiree was a useless girl.

Desiree had cried herself to sleep that night. She remembered the loneliness, the sadness, the sense of never belonging. Feasibly, that was the reason she felt inept in the kitchen.

Keiran watched her closely. He seemed unsure what to say next.

Lightly, he kneaded her shoulders. "Are you okay?" he asked quietly.

Grateful, she accepted his silent comfort, his reassuring presence.

"Of course," she murmured. She averted her gaze and thrust her fingers through her hair, attempting to right her curls into a semblance of order. She hadn't bothered to run a comb through her tangles since she'd gotten home, and probably looked a mess.

I'm not a nobody, she reminded herself. *Lift your chin and compose your features. 'Unsophisticated' and 'unimportant' do not belong in your vocabulary anymore. You're a poised, professional, educated woman.*

Although sometimes, oftentimes—she attempted to convince herself more than anyone else.

Gradually, she realized that Keiran was still staring at her, still had his hands on her shoulders.

She raised her gaze to meet his. "What's the matter?" she asked.

"Nothing." He cleared his throat, his face so near that his clear green eyes reminded her of Irish shamrocks, vivid and vital. "I was thinking that I debated about coming back to Roses and starting over. When I first arrived in Atlanta ten years ago, I assumed I was going to live there forever. And now I'm glad—"

Her heart responded in a slow, steady beat. "Glad about what?"

"And now I'm glad I came back. If I hadn't, I wouldn't have met you."

"I'm glad you came too." He was so close she could feel his sweet breath on her cheek. "I would have spent the week trying to find firewood to keep this fireplace burning."

Clearly amused, he said, "I assume you found enough wood."

"Yes, I brought in a few logs the other night, remember? You had stacked a cord behind the fence."

He didn't respond at first. His amusement was replaced by a slow, simmering intensity.

"So you found the firewood." He lowered his head, his lips meeting hers. "And I found you."

CHAPTER 5

*A*nother week went by, marking the fourteenth day until Christmas.

On Friday evening, Keiran experimented with a new dish, mushroom stroganoff, which delighted Desiree. It was heartening to have a simple, unpretentious meal waiting for her when she came home after an exhausting workday.

Following the meal and clean-up, he shadowed her into the living room carrying two glasses of sparkling cider, plates of another Irish whiskey cake he'd baked, and napkins. He stacked kindling over crumpled newspaper in the fireplace, lit the newspaper first, then added large logs. Satisfied, he took a seat beside her on her gray-fabric sofa.

She gazed at the ten-foot spruce tree he'd purchased. Placed in a corner of the large room, the forest-green pine made a majestic statement.

After visiting several Christmas tree sites the previous weekend, Keiran had maintained that the largest tree on the lot was the ideal size to complement her living room's grand design. The tree seller had assisted Keiran in securing the tree to the roof of his truck, and Keiran had driven back to her house slowly with the tree swinging precariously on top.

Between making creamy eggnog and cranking up Yuletide music on a holiday radio station, Desiree and Keiran had decided on traditional red and green lights and a dazzling angel tree topper. Desiree had insisted on sparkly silver tinsel and a popcorn garland, and Keiran had enhanced the glittery embellishments with an array of wooden toy soldier ornaments he'd carved. The result was vibrant, festive, and in Keiran's words, "a masterpiece."

"I might pick up another tree," he casually said.

"One isn't enough? Completely decorated, this tree is practically taking up half my living room."

He grinned impishly, highlighting his boyish features. "I'd like to sprinkle Christmas all through the house. A small tree for the dining room would look festive."

"Especially because I don't own a dining room table or chairs." Desiree picked up the two glasses of sparkling cider from the end table beside her, handed one to him, and beckoned to the fireplace. "You know, everyone at my law firm is encouraging me to convert my fireplace to gas."

"It's your house and you've worked hard to acquire it. You should do what you want." His encouragement was gracious, and a surge of happiness flowed through her that had nothing to do with the delicious meal, the enchantment of a heartening fire on a cold winter's night, or the approaching holidays.

It was him. It was Keiran.

Seeing him like this, relaxed, wearing dark-wash jeans and a sea-green sweater that hugged his wide shoulders to perfection, he lounged beside her on her ten-year-old sofa. How could she remain unaffected when he was so breathtakingly handsome?

"Yes, this house is mine, and I still can't believe it," she replied. "And . . ." She hesitated, trying not to get ahead of herself. This was just the beginning. This was just a house. He was just a man she loved spending every waking hour with.

Just a man.

"And what?" He sipped his cider, set it on the coffee table, and moved nearer. His male presence was compelling, and a quiver of attraction went through her.

Quickly, she pushed the thoughts away, attempting a composure she didn't quite feel.

"I love the smell of a woodburning fireplace, so I'm passing on the gas insert," she said. "Call me outdated."

He pressed a soft kiss to her cheek and murmured agreement.

She gave him a questioning glance. "Can I ask you something?"

"Sure."

"Why did you leave Roses? You had the world at your feet."

"Did I? Tell that to an impulsive teenager." He reached for his glass and drained the cider. "I'll give you the short version, and please don't be sympathetic."

"And if I am?"

He hesitated, his features unreadable. "Don't be."

"Is my question too personal?"

He gave her a look that said it wasn't. "My father and I didn't agree about what I wanted to do for a living," Keiran said. "So, being reckless and headstrong, I decided my way was best."

"Which was?"

"Moving to Atlanta. I planned to become tops in my profession."

"Doing what?"

"Opening my own restaurant."

"And what was your father's way?"

"He wanted me to become an NFL football player. Trouble is, I didn't have the drive, or the interest, or the talent. I was the tallest on the team, but certainly not the fastest."

"I remember seeing you in your football uniform at the homecoming game I attended," she said. "It was the first time I ever saw you."

He offered an indifferent shrug. "Did you actually watch the game?"

"A little, I think. I don't remember you on the playing field."

"You have an awesome memory."

"Why?"

He hesitated. Her question sat in the space between them.

"Because I hardly ever played and frankly, I was relieved, although I knew my father was disappointed." Regret shadowed Keiran's gaze. "The football coach put me on the team to please my father because our pub was one of the sponsors. Soon after that game, I quit."

"I caught glimpses of you in the high school halls. Quitting didn't seem to affect your popularity."

A statement, not a question.

"I suppose." He shrugged. "Although popularity is a difficult word to define, especially when it's used to categorize people."

Wistfully, she gazed at the twinkling tree lights, the shades of red and green belonging to a simpler time, offset by the muted tones of the rustic toy soldiers. Could Christmas be celebrated without glossy bulbs and the sophisticated backdrop of her living room?

Of course.

As a child, well, she had certainly longed for Christmas, although it had never been celebrated at her house. Beer cans littered the floor and food was scarce. Christmas was a luxury her parents couldn't afford, and Santa Claus had never visited.

As an adult, she couldn't imagine life without Christmas. She loved the gift-giving and feasting, the religious celebration, the sacredness of the special holiday.

Profoundly moved by a feeling she couldn't explain, she blinked as her vision blurred. "In my childhood, I wanted a real home so badly—the picket fence, a cute puppy sitting by a welcoming fire burning in the grate, surrounded by people who loved me. When my mother was well and not drinking, she said she envisioned herself as a grand lady living on a beautiful estate." Desiree's lungs and throat felt sore, and she swallowed. "Considering our two-room shack, my mother had quite the imagination."

Tears pricked Desiree's eyes and she wiped them away. She scolded herself for dredging up emotional memories, better kept sealed in a safe corner of her mind. Inhaling, she sat erect. "So what you're saying is that at the end of your senior year, you took off because you didn't get the opportunity to play on the high school team?"

"C'mon, Desiree. Do I seem as shallow as all that? I said I quit football."

"Sorry." She paused. "I mean, you lived in one of the most expensive communities in Roses. I would have given the world to grow up in your shoes."

"It's never just about the stunning home and expensive neighborhood," he said softly. "There's more to a person's story than what's on the surface. I went to Atlanta to pursue my dream, got sidetracked, and failed."

* * *

Desiree tipped her face back to view him. He expected to see disapproval on her beautiful features. After all, he'd had everything and given it all up, while she'd had nothing.

"You're young and can achieve anything you want." A positive smile played on her lips. "Also, you're one of the most talented people I've ever met. But look, we can talk about something else if you're uncomfortable."

"I don't mind our discussion, Desiree." He nodded his assent.

He'd been undecided about what to say, about his past, his future, although being with her lightened his concerns. With Desiree, everything would be okay.

He realized she was watching him, apparently waiting for him to continue.

He put his hands on his knees and focused on the wood sparking in the fireplace, the frosted pine cones and garland adorning the wide wooden mantel. The stylish adornments gave the room a celebratory spirit.

"My father discouraged me from what I wanted to do with my life," he said. "I intended to own a restaurant. Therefore, I rebelled."

"And here I thought you wanted to be a carpenter," she teased.

He pushed out a sigh. "I like woodworking, although my passion is the restaurant business. It's how I grew up. I love the hustle and bustle, the busy dinner hours, the scents of shepherd's pie, potato and leek soup, and thyme complementing my parents' famous corned beef recipe."

She gazed at him, openly interested. "I'm surprised."

"Mind if I ask why?"

Her unpretentious warmth set her apart from any woman he'd ever known. Was that what captivated him about her? Besides her vivaciousness, her sensational figure, and her utterly polished appearance when she came home each evening.

That is, until she pulled her hair from her severe bun and let the blond waves fall down her back. Then she looked irresistible.

She studied his face with a concerned frown. "Because most parents would have been thrilled their kid wanted to follow in their footsteps."

"Mine weren't. They insisted that owning an eating establishment was too difficult because of the long hours, which included early mornings, late evenings, and most holidays." He forked a corner of cake on his plate and chewed around the lump in his throat. "Did you know only one third of all restaurants succeed?"

"I've heard it's one in ten."

He paused, forming his words while he stared at the pile of sheetrock marking the next space in her home to be renovated—the small study attached to the living room via French doors.

"Living in Roses, you probably heard talk that my parents lived beyond their means," he said. "At first they did well and their pub was a huge success. Sadly, they didn't plan for the lean years."

"Yes. I heard." Despite her polite nod, he could tell she knew more than she let on. It was no secret his parents had neglected the pub after his departure, eventually forcing it to close. Even their most loyal customers could no longer endure the erratic schedule and so-so meals.

"They moved to Ireland soon afterward. Dublin," he clarified, briefly closing his eyes. "Although they reached out to me, I never flew across the pond to see them except to attend their funerals years later. They died within a day of each other. In the end, discouragement broke their hearts."

"Keiran."

He opened his eyes. Her gaze held his.

"I'm genuinely sorry. You realize none of this is your fault," she said. "My parents died while serving sentences for several robberies. They were alcoholics."

He felt a twist of sadness in his gut. For her. For him.

She was so sweet, so vulnerable, so totally gorgeous, he was torn between kissing her and commiserating on their losses.

He decided on the latter, and enfolded her into his arms.

Would kissing her mess things up? They got along brilliantly, although he often felt off balance. Could they keep their relationship casual, yet professional, living under the same roof, coming to terms with their attraction? His thoughts scattered, although he already knew the answer.

Nope.

With Desiree, his feelings were too deep to be casual.

He gazed at her mouth and cupped her chin in his hands, forcing her to gaze at him.

What would it be like to kiss her again and again?

Nope, his conscience chimed in a second time. She'd made her intentions known without saying a word. This was a business relationship.

Then why did life with her seem spot-on? Was the universe telling him something—bringing him back to Roses after all this time to open a pub, and bringing him to her? He was at the tail end of one profession, embarking on another. And she was the bridge in between. Or was she more? Perhaps she was the missing link . . . the real reason he was here.

She drew a sharp breath. "Keiran, I—"

He lowered his head and brushed his lips against hers. If she rejected him, he'd deal with it.

She didn't.

With a whisper of acquiescence, she twined her hands around his neck and pressed her delicate body closer.

He shivered. "Do you know how many times I've wanted to kiss you these past two weeks?" His hands slid down her back. "I mean, really kiss you?"

"Then what were you waiting for?" came her teasing reply.

He hadn't planned to spend Friday evening kissing her, he told his intrusive conscience. He'd planned on conversing with her, bantering with her, comparing recipes and paint samples.

Or had he? Because devoting every minute of his free time to her felt like the most natural thing in the world.

Slowly, tenderly, he took her lips in a lingering, passionate kiss.

Her cell phone chirped.

She always had it near in case one of her clients experienced a family emergency. For a second, she hesitated, then drew away from him. She picked up her phone and read the screen. "It's Candee," she said. "She and Teddy and Joseph want to stop over. Candee is helping me plan my Christmas Eve dinner menu."

"Tonight? Christmas isn't for a while yet." Keiran couldn't hide his disappointment. He wanted to spend the evening alone with Desiree. "When? If they've started walking, they'll be here in two minutes."

"They're still at their house." Desiree tapped a text on her phone. "I'll tell her tomorrow is better. Besides, I'm electing you as head preparer for Christmas Eve dinner. You're much better suited to the task, so you should be the one to talk with her."

He brought Desiree back into his arms, fingering the lustrous texture of her hair, breathing in the scent of vanilla and a fresh winter breeze.

"If you'd like," he said, "I'll teach you everything I know."

"Didn't you already offer me that once? Umm, no thanks. You know way too much about too many things—carpentry, decorating, football—"

He laughed. "I'm hardly an expert on anything, especially football."

Her gorgeous eyes sparkled. "Keiran, I hear you play your guitar every night when I'm in bed. You're also an excellent musician."

He'd forgotten her bedroom was directly below his attic apartment. "Do I disturb you?"

"On the contrary. You play really well."

He placed his hand along the curve of her velvety cheek. "Shall I serenade you sometime, my stunning Queen Anne?"

"You sound like a chivalrous knight, although I'm no queen." She grinned. "You're confusing *me* with my Queen-Anne style *home*."

"You're not a queen?" In exaggerated surprise, he splayed his fingers across his chest.

She laughed. "The bay window and spindle work in my home are—"

"Exquisite. Just like you."

"Hardly." The color rose in her cheeks. She didn't meet his gaze, instead looking toward the wavy glass windowpanes splattered with rain. "Most people define me as a workaholic."

"There's nothing wrong with being a workaholic. I prefer the term 'overachiever,' which is an admirable trait."

She shifted and pulled her blue cardigan closer around her shoulders. "Oftentimes, my work gets in the way of the important things in my life—family, friends, and good times."

"I've been accused of the same."

She nodded, agreeing. "I've always believed my career

169

came first. I've analyzed myself because I've read that understanding the problem is the best way to heal."

"Overachieving isn't a problem, Desiree."

"In some ways it is." Her smooth forehead knit into a pensive frown. "Candee and I have discussed our childhood. More often than not, we were neglected and now we're trying to compensate."

"By buying dilapidated houses?"

"It seems like that, doesn't it?"

"A little." He tried to think of words to encourage her, because he was picturing her as a young girl with fine blond hair and delicate features, helpless and alone. He realized he hadn't spoken for several moments and reminded himself to keep the conversation going. "And what else did your discussion with your sister uncover?" he asked.

Desiree slumped against the couch. "We were parentless children, raising ourselves the best we knew how."

"You had a mother and father."

"They were absent even when they were around. And the parent-child roles were reversed. Candee and I took care of them."

Gently, he slid his arm around her shoulders. "Candee and I spoke one afternoon, and she mentioned your last set of foster parents became your forever family."

"Yes, they're good people." The pensiveness in Desiree's gaze stirred his heart. "They love Candee and me, and email us regularly since they moved away. I'm grateful they came into our lives and offered love and stability."

But still.

She didn't say it, despite the words hanging in the air. She was trying to make up for the negligence in her childhood by . . . by what? Overachieving?

Something about the desolation on her face made him want to do whatever possible to shape her world for the better. She had a successful career, a lovely home, a caring sister.

And she had his heart.

He paused.

His heart?

Aye—and the realization took a firm place in his gut. He'd been half in love with her since the first day they'd met and she'd slammed the front door in his face, then teased him about talking to her porch.

With great effort, he stopped himself from repeating his thoughts aloud, although the shout-in-his-face awareness of their chemistry made him catch his breath. He liked being with her, conversing and comforting her.

No, it was too soon. He wasn't seeking a romance after his breakup with Patricia.

Better to keep things light. Besides, he didn't plan on staying in Desiree's home much longer. As soon as the holidays were over and her house was in better order, he planned to rent an apartment in town.

Move on.

But now, things were different. Fixing her home, spending memorable evenings beside her, anticipating the joyous holiday, and yes, discussing their childhoods—with all the hurts, all the dreams—was the most natural thing in the world. They were content, and he felt as if he'd known her his entire life. She'd given him a peephole into her past, and he'd done the same.

He cradled her face between his fingers, stroking an errant tear from her cheek.

"I'm grateful you came into my life. Or rather, I'm grateful I came into yours."

The tenderness in her soft eyes and lips tore down his defenses. She sparked a yearning in him he barely recognized, reminding him that there was more to life than successful pubs and impeccable carpentry. And these feelings were new. Not even with Patricia had he felt this utter sense of fulfillment.

His mouth descended on hers. She followed his lead, sliding her hands down his shoulders. Her lips were warm and smooth as velvet, tasting of sweet caramel and Irish whiskey cake.

He told himself to go slowly. His lips said otherwise. Their breaths heated the air around them.

An eternity later, the kiss ended.

As they gazed at each other, longing shown from her intense blue eyes.

Along with another emotion.

Wariness?

"You are beautiful," he whispered. "And that was—" How could he find a phrase to describe it?

"Not a good idea," she said.

"You're kidding!" He jerked his head back. "That's what you were thinking?"

"Keiran, we have a business arrangement. Anything else will only complicate things."

He was still searching for an accurate description of their kiss, while she was headed to the other side of the couch.

As usual, she was spot on. They'd only just met.

"Then will you go on a date with me?" he asked.

"After what I just said?"

"I understand you want to take our relationship slowly and I respect your wishes. Let's start with a real date."

She moistened her lips, just enough to captivate him. "A date where? To the kitchen?"

"I was thinking somewhere a little farther." He laughed. "Lunch or dinner in one of the town's restaurants?" His plan was to get to know her. Sure, he was living in her house and familiar with her daily routine, but it wasn't enough. He wanted to learn more.

She spoke what was on her mind, and she was interesting to be around. She was a brave woman. A Christian possessing a kind spirit. Strong, yet gentle. Courageous, yet yielding. Open, yet unassuming.

And these attributes fascinated him.

"Will you play your guitar for me?" she asked.

He widened his eyes at the unexpected question. "Maybe later," he said.

She granted him an audacious smile. "Please, Keiran?"

He knew he could never deny her anything.

Within minutes, he tromped to the attic and reappeared with his father's acoustic guitar. He tuned the strings and strummed a few chords. "What do you want to hear?"

She sat erect, glancing at him, then his guitar. "Something Christmassy."

He plucked the melody of "Jingle Bells" while she sang the lyrics, her voice light and in tune.

When he finished the final refrain, he broke into the beginning of "Don't Stop Believin'."

"That's the song you play in the attic," she said. "I couldn't place the group."

"Journey," he supplied. "Often, my father played the piece after our pub closed for the evening. My mother used to complain it was the only song he knew."

"I read somewhere the composer of that song was inspired by his father's words of encouragement."

"Aye, and the song held special significance for my father, also," Keiran said. "He came to this town disillusioned after he wasn't picked in the NFL draft, and rose to success when he met my mother and they opened the pub. Sadly, the pub closed when he ran out of funds."

"Why, when the pub was so popular at first?" Waiting, she

surveyed him, giving him the kindhearted expression he was coming to know so well.

"Maybe because all along my father was disheartened. Although he worked hard, his initial dreams of becoming a professional football player didn't pan out," Keiran said. "And then, of course, I left."

He shifted, silent for a beat.

"Did this guitar belong to your father?" Desiree asked, breaking the silence.

"Aye. He bequeathed it to me in his will. This and his abandoned Irish pub in town."

"So you own O'Malley's?"

"There's nothing to own. It's my father's broken legacy. This beat-up guitar, an abandoned pub, and a trading card autographed by a famous football player my father met while he was training."

"Hold on. Is the card worth anything?"

"I checked a few years ago because my former roommate, Georges, works at a pawn shop in Atlanta. The card is a 1976 Topps card, and the player didn't sign many, so the estimated worth is around fifteen thousand dollars."

"Certainly, it's a card to treasure and hold on to."

"And it brings back memories, both good and bad." Keiran released a deep breath and set the guitar to the side. "When I attended my parents' funerals in Dublin, I'm ashamed to tell you I was angry and bitter. My cousin William reassured me that although I wasn't there for them, they were always in my heart."

She squeezed his hand. "I know."

"I didn't walk away from my parents because I didn't care. I walked away because I didn't know if I had it in me to live up to my father's expectations. I knew I couldn't be a pro football player, so I disengaged. I found myself in a state of panic."

Caught in the spell of her captivating blue eyes, he placed his arm around her shoulders.

"Go on," she prompted. "You mentioned your cousin William."

He didn't want to spoil their evening by speaking about sadness. Attempting to recover their former gaiety, he replied with an expressive beam. "William lives in Ireland and has the proverbial Irish philosophy. He connects with people and believes forgiveness is most important. It's called Irish craic."

Desiree shot him a quizzical look. "I'm not following."

"Irish craic is fun and good times. William is humorous and witty and earnestly interested in others. You'll like him."

"I'll like him . . . when? I've never visited Ireland nor do I plan to in the future."

"Someday."

Silence lingered between them.

"With my investment in this house, an overseas trip isn't possible," she quietly replied.

"Never say never," Keiran advised. "My father threatened he wouldn't take me back if I ever appeared in Roses again. And here I am, not certain if I'm moving forward or backward, only knowing I was wrong to leave in the first place."

"Don't feel guilty." She touched his arm. "That's life, isn't it? We make mistakes, we brush ourselves off, and we go on."

"Do we ever forgive ourselves?" His voice came as a whisper.

"It's Christmas, the season of forgiveness," she said. "And the answer is an emphatic yes."

CHAPTER 6

"Tomorrow is the bake-off contest," Keiran reminded Desiree as she entered the foyer.

"It's written in bold on my calendar." Desiree set down her briefcase and joked, "How could I ever forget?"

Finally, it was Friday, the last day of another grueling work week.

"I'm glad to see you, gorgeous." He helped her off with her sunny-yellow raincoat and took her in his arms for a long kiss.

He'd been waiting for her at the foot of the stairs, the sparse lighting glinting over his hair. Thick, wavy, and midnight-black. And he looked oh so incredibly handsome.

He was dressed in a cotton chambray shirt unbuttoned at the neckline, showing a deep vee at his throat. His denims were well fitted. Tall, well-built, and confident, he sent her pulse racing. His physique would stop any woman in her tracks.

She linked her fingers around his nape, thinking all the while that he was the type of man she could easily fall in love with.

Wow. Whoa.

Love was the doorway to sorrow, and she'd had enough disappointment to know better than to risk her heart again.

Still, Keiran might be worth the risk. It was pure bliss having his strong, secure arms around her. Love was a quiet, joyous peace with no barriers. Love was exactly that with this man.

For an instant, she squeezed her eyes closed. *No. No. No.*

As much as she cared for him, they could never be together. Although he was talented and creative, he hadn't decided on a career for himself. Cooking or carpentry?

After her chaotic childhood, she knew stability was her primary goal.

Her feelings warred ferociously, and she considered telling him how much she cared, and what she most feared if they were to go forward in their relationship—that he could easily pick up and leave at any time.

Stability. Stability.

Numbly, she pulled from his arms.

He watched her, his gaze penetrating. He was always in tune with her emotions. "Is everything okay?"

"Of course." She dragged her gaze from his and focused on the authentic tin ceiling tile he'd replaced in the foyer. The edges were trimmed neatly and seamlessly overlapped.

Before she could remark on his excellent workmanship, he brushed a kiss across her temple. "Are you ready for an amazing time tomorrow, gorgeous?"

Gorgeous. No one had ever called her gorgeous. Profoundly touched, she brushed away a tear before his perceptive green-eyed gaze leveled on her. She wasn't used to praises, to his unbending good nature, and didn't know how to react.

"I'm ready to win the cake contest." She gave him her best challenging gaze while she shook lingering droplets from her black pencil skirt. Raindrops had chased each other across her car's windshield all the way home. If only it would snow to complete the holiday season.

"We'll see about that." He hung her raincoat in the foyer closet, then laid a callused hand on her cheek. His touch was reassuring. "So how was your day?"

"Demanding, as usual." Without prompting, she lifted her face for a kiss. "I'm delighted I only have one more work week to go before Christmas. You?"

"Hectic. The study off the living room has been sheetrocked and sanded, and the guys left some of their tools there. All you have to do is choose a paint color."

"My specialty."

"That's my girl." He grinned, drawing her to him. "Desiree, I have a confession."

The way he said her name, low and husky, resembled a loving caress.

Her gaze narrowed on his grin. "What is it?" That feeling, that draw, grew stronger each time they were together. That little flip of exhilaration.

"For the first time in a long time, I'm anticipating an amazing holiday." The sentiment in his voice melted her heart. "And it's all because of you."

"I am too." She was helpless to resist him, moving automatically into his arms. "And I'm glad to be home."

"To see me," he clarified.

"Indeed."

"Did you think about me today?"

"Often," she admitted. *Very often.*

"Good. I thought about you too. See how much we are alike? We both love Christmas and we both love—" He bent his head and kissed her deeply, thoroughly.

Both love what?

Each other?

She'd spent far too long trying to figure out men and relationships, and reveled in his kisses instead. She couldn't pull away from him even if she wanted to.

Excuse me, her conscience kicked in. *You're losing your focus.*

Yes, well, because around him she could hardly think. She wasn't good at this—dating—the entire courting process. Her career had always been most important.

Now she wished for more, wished for him.

He'd never mentioned a girlfriend, dismissing Desiree's inquiry with a wave of his hand. He'd explained that he'd dated in Atlanta, although no one worth mentioning. She'd been relieved he hadn't had a serious affair of the heart, although she'd told him about Scott, her ex. She hadn't said much, but apparently just enough, because Keiran had remarked he was sorry she'd been hurt.

His lips twitched as he drew her closer. "I'm glad you're glad to see me."

"Is that proper English?"

His lips moved within an inch of hers. "It is now."

She felt her cheeks flush as she gazed at his ruggedly handsome face.

"Who is judging our cakes?" she asked.

"Excellent change of subject. What cakes?" Smirking, he took her hand and led her to the kitchen. "First, have a cuppa tea with me. I brewed loose leaf tea using a strainer." He pulled out a stool for her, then poured her a steaming cup. "Sugar? Milk?"

"No thanks." She savored a swallow. Loose leaf tea was definitely more flavorful than tea bags. Again, she asked, "So, who is judging our cakes?"

"Several ladies on the town board, and some guy named Rob who owns a chain of bakeries in Florida," Keiran said.

She gasped and set down her cup. "Rob, as in Rob's Marvelous Muffins?"

"Aye." Keiran claimed the seat across from her. "Is he famous or something?"

"He certainly is famous, at least in Miami." Desiree rested her elbows on the island. "Rob is Teddy's mentor and a good friend. He lent Teddy the money for his start-up real estate business. Rob wants to expand his bakeries to another state and is considering Roses because Teddy and Candee are here."

The subject came up again an hour later, after they'd dined on a savory beef and Guinness stew brimming with carrots, potatoes, onions, and chunks of beef.

"I met him when Teddy and Candee got married." Desiree scraped plates while Keiran loaded the dishwasher. "Rob is great fun. You'll like him. Plus, you're both restauranteurs." She paused. "Is that a word?"

An amused gleam lit Keiran's eyes. "Absolutely, and it means the owner or manager of a restaurant. Although technically, I never owned a restaurant. My parents owned the pub."

"Same difference. And you own the pub now."

"True."

She finished wiping down the kitchen counter. "Who else is participating in the baking contest?"

"It's open to everyone. From what I gather, the town will set up tables for our cakes and an awning is being erected in case of bad weather." A lazy smile graced his face. "By the way, Candee is baking a Christmas cake."

"She's participating? To my knowledge, she's never turned on an oven in her life."

"The cake is a surprise. Or rather, it was a surprise until I spilled the beans." A sheepish grin crossed his lips as he gave an apologetic shrug. "Rob flew in from Miami and is staying with Candee and Teddy. Word is that Rob is baking the cake."

Desiree's competitive spirit jumped into true form. "So I'm competing against Rob, who bakes for a living, and you, the guy who's been basting an Irish whiskey cake for four days?"

He chuckled. "The odds are in your favor, though."

"How?"

"You're the prettiest." He stepped behind her and wrapped his arms around her waist. Nuzzling his lips against her neck, he murmured, "Are you certain you have to work next week?"

"Yes, if you want to get paid."

"I work for next to nothing," he joked. "I want a raise."

She laughed, shook her head, and tugged from his grasp. "Not happening."

That morning, she'd driven with a smile on her face all the way to her law firm in the middle of town. Keiran's parents' pub, O'Malley's, was located a few blocks away. Years earlier, the building had been abandoned and boarded up. A "For Lease" sign had hung on the door for ages.

As she'd walked from her car to her office, she'd tried to stop thinking about Keiran.

The more she'd tried, the more she'd failed. And now, another week had passed and Christmas was closing in. So much had happened since he'd arrived. And it was all good. So, so good.

He was a miracle worker, transforming her home into an enchanting, welcoming place. He spent hours in the kitchen after Teddy's crew knocked off for the day, and often sent Candee his baked goods, which she, Teddy, and Joseph enthusiastically praised.

Each evening, Desiree finished her last client's filing with an eye on the clock, counting the minutes until she could see Keiran.

And tomorrow, a week before Christmas, she and Keiran were participating in a baking contest.

She shook her head and added a grin. Her dashing Irishman, her one-of-a-kind Renaissance man, was as equally at home measuring and marking drywall as he was experimenting with a new recipe, or strumming a melody on his guitar.

She closed her eyes and thanked God. During the most blessed season of the year, when she was worried and despondent, He had brought Keiran into her life.

Certainly, she had much to be thankful for. She was no longer stuck in a bad situation with an ex who didn't care about her.

Have faith, her chaplain had preached numerous times.

But how?

She had wondered—as an orphaned teen, as a grown woman with a broken heart.

God had seemed invisible, but He hadn't been. He'd been working for her good all along.

* * *

THE FOLLOWING morning dawned bright and chilly, and sunlight shone through the wavy glass bay window in the living room.

Keiran and Desiree relished their first cup of coffee for the day. Even when their mornings began before dawn, he brewed a fresh pot of coffee and prepared a hearty cooked breakfast. He loved cooking for her.

"You're staring at me again," Desiree said.

"Am I?" He set down his cup. "I can't help it. You're gorgeous." That figure, dressed in flattering faux-leather leggings, suede ankle boots, and a creamy tweed sweater. And those cornflower-blue eyes, even more fascinating than her legs.

Delight quickened inside him. He'd come to Roses to pick up what he'd abandoned ten years before. A timeworn pub. He'd assumed he'd go it alone, far from Atlanta and Patricia.

Except he wasn't alone anymore.

With Desiree, he instinctively felt a sense of coming home and knew that embarking on this journey without her was unthinkable.

He openly admired her as she picked up their empty cups. Her beauty was stunning.

"I'll finish clearing," he offered, coming to his feet.

She held up a hand. "Keiran, I may not be the world's greatest cook, but I certainly know how to keep things tidy. Please let me do a little something to repay all you've done."

"Okay." His gaze shifted to those figure-hugging leggings before doubling back to her face.

She regarded him with her lovely, shiny eyes and smiled.

He thought about her throughout his day while he multitasked, installing molding, cutting and sawing wood, and picking up debris after the other crews clocked out.

She'd asked him once if he ever slept, and he'd teased that he obviously didn't require as much sleep as she did.

"Ready for the contest?" he asked, following her to the kitchen where their cakes sat on the counter.

"I feel anything but ready." She set her coffee cup in the sink. "Otherwise, yes, sure."

He helped her on with her cobalt-blue coat. She'd worn her blond hair loose, and she ran her fingers through the ends in that graceful, unassuming way of hers.

They placed their finished cakes on cake boards, then packed them in sturdy, clean covered boxes.

Desiree insisted on them both driving their vehicles to

the event, as she had to pick up a bag of groceries at her favorite green grocer when they were finished. He drove behind her car and parked in an empty parking space. As they got out of their vehicles, Desiree remarked that she felt motivated by seeing all the small-town celebrations.

Her pistachio cake, garnished with powdered sugar and maraschino cherries, presented an eye-catching display. Although Keiran's Irish whiskey cake didn't appear as vibrant, his baking process had taken longer. He'd carefully wrapped the cake, refrigerated it for three days and added a glaze on the fourth.

The first prize for the event was an apron, stamped with a red and green *Kiss Me, It's Christmas* motif.

He and Desiree set their cakes on a long table beneath an expansive white canvas awning on the green. The judges provided cake stands that elevated the cakes to a magnificent new level.

"I'll be wearing that apron when I cook the Christmas Eve dinner you volunteered me to prepare," Keiran baited.

He expected a teasing rejoinder, and she didn't disappoint.

She leaned toward him and joked, "You'll be wearing that apron because I let you *borrow* it. And don't forget we eat dinner at six o'clock sharp."

He gave a shout of laughter as they wended through the crowd and perused the food kiosks. Near the judges' stand she halted in midstep. Spotting Candee and Teddy, Desiree took hold of Keiran's hand and rushed over to them.

As planned, Candee and Teddy were manning a booth distributing free hot chocolate and candy canes to the participants and attendees. Nearby, Joseph skipped and played tag in an adjacent play area with a couple of new friends.

Teddy had confided to Keiran that the boy had changed

significantly since moving to Roses. His demeanor was perky, his gaze gleaming with delight.

"Uncle Teddy, watch me!" the boy called. He'd settled down to working with his playmates to build a sandcastle in the sandbox.

"There's Rob." Desiree waved gaily to an older, bald-headed man, then brought Keiran over to meet him.

"Hello, I'm Keiran O'Malley, Desiree's carpenter." Keiran extended his hand as they met. "I've heard a lot about you."

"I'm Rob the baker." The man beamed good-naturedly. "Although you've got me beat because you're the baker *and* the carpenter. Do you also make candles?"

Keiran blinked.

"You know, the butcher, the baker, and the candlestick—" Rob laughed heartily, gripped Keiran's hand, and vigorously shook it. "An old nursery rhyme. Mother Goose and what-not. Never mind. You're too young for rhymes, and I'm too old to be able to recite them correctly."

Keiran nodded. What was Rob getting at? "Sorry, I'm not following."

He glanced at Desiree, who grinned and shrugged. "Rob's not talking about nursery rhymes," she said. "He means—"

"I've heard about your baking and carpentry skills, Keiran," Rob interrupted. "Teddy expounded at length. You're good at one, exceptional at the other."

"That's a fair assessment," Keiran replied. "Should I ask which one is better?"

Rob checked out Keiran's Irish whiskey cake, set on a white platter and topped with spiced chopped pecans. "Your baking won by a landslide. Can you cook too?"

"Lots of down-home food including corned beef and cabbage and shepherd's pie. Although I like experimenting with new recipes, Guinness stew is my specialty."

"I can attest to that," Desiree said with a Mona Lisa smile.

"Excellent. You can experiment on me anytime. I told Teddy I was going on a diet." Rob patted his protruding stomach. "Though I've decided to wait until the New Year. Maybe my local gym will have a special."

Keiran laughed. He liked Rob's responses. He was a good, honest guy. "My parents owned a pub in town. They served authentic Irish food and homemade desserts."

"Oh?" Rob gave the surrounding streets a once-over. "Which one?"

"Walking distance from here. The pub's been empty a long time, although it was once busy with customers lining up outside the door when we opened for the day."

As Keiran pointed in the pub's direction, Desiree and Rob followed his gaze.

"Is the place available for rent?" Rob asked.

Desiree placed a hand on Keiran's arm. "The pub's been boarded up for years, although Keiran inherited it from his parents."

Keiran shifted. She was telling Rob more than he needed to know.

He and Desiree had visited the pub a few days earlier. Peering through grimy windows, he'd been anxious to assess the place when he'd first arrived, although he'd delayed seeing it, wanting to view the property with her, hesitant about coming to grips with the fact that his parents were no longer alive.

With a tight throat, he'd asked Candee, who was a realtor, to install new door locks. The permit had been provided to him, as the owner, when his parents had passed away. Because the pub was historically significant to the town, O'Malley's had been grandfathered in.

As he'd feared, memories had assailed him when he'd stepped inside—the sticky spilled beer beneath his boots, the heady smell of buttery Irish scones, the pennants from the local sports teams hanging on the timbered walls.

The charm and character of a timeless design.

And he was overwhelmed by his emotions—regret, sadness. And aye, excitement.

Fear of failure, fear of not trying. Was he capable of upholding the legacy of his parents' beloved pub?

Although he didn't have enough capital, should he dare hope he could reopen it? The huge project entailed purchasing inventory, cleaning the place, and passing inspections. Since working for Desiree, he'd saved most of his weekly salary. He'd said goodbye to Atlanta with limited funds, anxious to get away from Patricia.

His Atlanta pastor had once said that if you've gone through a storm, then it was a sure sign that God would be coming. Although Keiran's faith was strong, he'd been skeptical. A storm was difficult. How could it make a person stronger?

More important, was he entitled to success after abandoning his parents? In Roses, in Ireland, they had missed him.

He was selfish. He was undeserving.

He looked past Rob and Desiree. "I own nothing," he said.

"You own a piece of Roses' past." Desiree leaned against him. "Someday, you'll make your pub whole again."

Your pub. *Whole.* Like him, with Desiree by his side.

He knew her well enough to know she'd used the terms on purpose, to give him hope, to support his dream.

"Tell the vendors to start showing up again, and get the word out to former customers that you're planning on reopening," Rob put in. "Then roll up your sleeves and get to work."

Keiran glanced from Rob's firm expression to Desiree's unwavering one.

That day, after viewing the pub, they'd held hands on their way back to his truck.

"I want to make a difference in Roses," he'd said softly.

"So I've heard."

"Once the pub is up and running, I'd like to offer a free meal and worship service every Sunday for the homeless in the community."

"I'll help you." A radiant smile brightened her lovely face as she matched his strong steps. "You're the son who wants to set things right again."

"I feel I must do this."

"Good. This is the place, and this is the time."

The quiet tenderness in her tone was all the reassurance he longed for.

Besides, he loved it here in Roses. The slower pace of life, the sound of children's laughter, the colorful display of twinkling lights around each shop's window.

As Keiran conversed with Rob, gaining insights into running an up-and-coming restaurant, Keiran's questions multiplied.

Desiree gave his hand an encouraging squeeze, excusing herself to go chat with Candee at the hot chocolate stand.

"I have a question," Keiran said to Rob. "Can you guide me?"

"Certainly." Rob's cellphone chirped. "Excuse me. One minute." He held up a hand in apology, pulled out his phone from his colorful plaid jacket, and read the text.

He sent a brief reply. "It's always something in the restaurant business." Rob rolled his eyes and swore under his breath as he clicked off the phone and stuffed it back into his pocket. "One of our customers in Miami complained the service at the bakery was too slow. An employee called in sick and we were short-handed."

"How did you handle it?"

"I'm sending the customer a coupon for a free box of muffins, along with a heartfelt apology. In my opinion, the customer is always right"—he chortled—"even when they aren't."

"Will you hire more employees?" Keiran asked.

"Yes, especially with the busy Christmas season heating up. I own a half-dozen bakeries in the Miami area, so when I think about expanding, I'll employ someone reliable who knows the business." Rob motioned toward Teddy, who was talking with Candee and Desiree while refilling the five-gallon hot chocolate container with water. "I hoped to stay in Roses a couple more days. However, between getting married, formally adopting Joseph, plus renovating his new home, Teddy's got enough to do." He glanced in the direction of the judges' stand. "At any rate, I'll head to Miami tomorrow. What's your question, by the way? Do you need start-up money for your pub?" He dug into his chinos pocket and pulled out his wallet.

"Thank you, but no thank you." Keiran motioned to the wad of hundred-dollar bills Rob extracted, and shook his head.

"Well, from what I hear, you have an excellent work ethic. When the times comes, toss your pride aside and phone me."

"Thanks." Keiran hesitated. "If I ever do, I'll consider it a loan. I'll pay every penny back."

"No worries, as long as your pub becomes a Roses sensation. How's the place looking?"

"Like it's crying out for lots of TLC."

"So, what's your question?" Rob glanced at Desiree, his blue eyes shrewd. "If it concerns a gorgeous blond lawyer who bakes pistachio cakes, then I'm no expert. Inquiries about dating women should be posed to men who have successfully dated them."

"Meaning that, from your experience, women split after the first date?"

"Meaning that, from my experience, women are a full-time job."

"Desiree's not like that." Keiran gazed at her while she and Candee served steaming cups of hot chocolate to a group of teenagers. In the midst of conversation with her sister, she combed the green with her gaze, found him, and gave him a secret smile. He glimpsed the fire smoldering in her eyes and drew a wobbly breath. She was an attraction pulling him to her like a magnet.

Realizing Rob's piercing gaze was fixed on him, Keiran carefully composed his features. "She's brainy and successful and we've become good friends."

"And that's not all." Rob stuffed his wallet back into his pocket and directed a meaningful glance toward her.

"Look, we're taking it slow."

"Uh huh." A skeptical smirk crossed Rob's round face. "Do you want my unasked-for advice?"

Keiran shrugged. "Sure. Why not?"

"If she's anything like her sister Candee, don't let her get away." Rob's smirk widened into a grin. "Besides, I can see that she's already got you smitten. Are you up for the challenge of starting a new life and a new career with a new wife? That's a lot of new."

Rob was dead-on. Aye, Keiran was ready. He embraced challenges and he cared about Desiree. More than cared. He was in love with her. He was in love with her snappy humor, intellect, and especially her openness.

"We'll talk further." Rob hung a left when his name was called at the judging stand. Over his shoulder, he said, "I hope I gave you some food for thought. Get it? Food?" He chuckled at his own joke, then added, "Seriously, I hope I answered your question."

Keiran paused, wondering how he'd started to ask Rob one question—whether Irish whiskey cake could be baked in a jar—and ended up receiving guidance about dating and romance. Although the dating advice Rob had offered was far more significant than a whiskey cake.

Don't let her get away.

Desiree gave Keiran a thoughtful glance as she approached him with two cups of hot chocolate. "Well, you two were deep in conversation."

Keiran accepted a steaming, frothy cup topped with miniature marshmallows. "He's extremely knowledgeable and I'm fortunate to have met him."

"He knows the restaurant business and he can give you lots of excellent tips." She sipped her hot chocolate. "He's a blessing to Teddy and Candee, and stepped in many times to help with Joseph after Teddy's brother Christian died."

"I didn't know."

"The pain of losing Christian was almost Teddy's undoing. Candee helped him begin a new chapter of his life here in Roses."

"Teddy's never talked about it." Keiran was beginning to realize that Desiree's sister and brother-in-law were genuinely good people who cared about others above themselves. He'd also noted the camaraderie between Rob and Teddy as Rob paused in his judging duties to joke with Teddy.

Desiree set her cup down on a tray. "Loss is always hard. Nonetheless, the certainty of a blessed future is guaranteed through faith in God."

With a glance at the holiday festival taking place—the face painter and balloon artist for the children, the four-piece brass band playing Christmas carols—Keiran took heart. Truly, God had brought him to Desiree.

He gazed around, entertained by the small town oozing

with big-time charm. Market stalls along the side streets sold ornaments and nutcrackers, and children mailed their letters to Santa at the corner post office. Historic walking tours were scheduled as soon as the judging finished, and the shops were becoming increasingly crowded with holiday customers.

While a pleasurable morning awaited them, he brought his attention back to the main reason they were here. He slung his arm around Desiree's shoulder and guided her to the colorful array of cakes, lovingly made, and the mouthwatering aromas of butter, sugar, and cherries. The contestants had been instructed to stand behind their respective baked goods to answer questions from the judges.

Delight surged through him. This was perfection. His enchanting birthplace, his exquisite Desiree, and the delight of spending Christmas with her family.

By ten o'clock, the event was finished. Although the contest had been close, the judges announced Desiree had won first place, and Keiran had taken second.

Loud cheering erupted and Desiree blushed gorgeously as a judge tied the red and green *Kiss me, It's Christmas* apron around her cobalt-blue coat. Graciously, she thanked the judges and gave a special mention to Keiran for buying her a kitchen timer.

In a last-minute decision, Candee hadn't entered her Christmas cake. Because Rob had baked it and he was one of the judges, it wouldn't have been fair. Consequently, Rob sat at the judges' stand, along with a plate filled with the cake. At last count, Keiran estimated that Rob had eaten at least three slices, along with a thick wedge of fudge from a food kiosk.

Keiran caught up with Desiree in the middle of the congratulatory crowd. In a laughing voice, she said, "All that powdered sugar paid off."

"Well done." Keiran brought her into his arms for a breathless kiss. Truly, the day couldn't have gone any better.

She hesitated. "You're kissing me here, in front of the entire town?"

"I'm just following directions." He glanced at her apron and grinned.

"It's not Christmas yet."

"I've designated the entire month of December for celebrating Christmas."

Chuckling, she said, "I want to catch up with Candee for a minute."

"Hurry back. There's a Christmassy silk scarf in the front window of one of the boutiques, and I immediately thought of you. You mentioned you wanted a scarf for Christmas."

"I did? When?"

"Well, maybe I just thought you did because I plan to buy it for you."

With a laugh, she pulled off the apron, carefully folded it, then scurried off with it securely tucked under her arm.

Out of the corner of his eye, Keiran noticed Rob speaking to a woman near the judges' stand. Although her back was turned, Keiran felt a wave of familiarity.

The crowd began dispersing and he was facing that same woman a minute later.

A woman he'd assumed he'd never see again. His ex-girlfriend, Patricia.

He gaped. His heartbeat raced.

She stared back at him with a cool smile, her dark hair streaked with blond, and her even white teeth. She was dressed in thigh-high boots, a short pink mini skirt, and a coyote-trimmed puffer jacket. He recognized the expensive jacket, as she'd coveted it the previous year. It had taken all the money he'd set aside, five hundred dollars, but she'd been happy. At least for a little while.

"Patricia?" He said her name and heard the shock in his voice.

"Hi, Keiran. Did you get my text this morning?" Deliberately, she perused Desiree, who'd bounced back to snuggle close to him.

"No. I've been busy," he replied.

He wanted to shout that this was his world, not hers. What was she doing here?

Patricia's gaze slid back to his face. "Well, I arrived."

His stomach plummeted. This couldn't be good. "I see that."

"You two know each other?" Desiree inquired.

Keiran nodded. "Aye," was all he could manage.

"We were practically engaged." Patricia directed her response toward Keiran. "You've been missed."

"Our relationship ended in Atlanta, remember?"

"Maybe our personal relationship." She gave him a heavy stare. "Unfortunately, our business relationship has hit a snag."

Heat flushed through his body. "I left you everything."

Before Patricia could reply, Desiree asked, "Were you two in business together?"

Patricia swept her fingers across Keiran's sleeve, a possessive gesture and decidedly intimate. "He worked for my daddy's company."

The way Patricia had always thrown it up to him twisted Keiran's stomach. In the beginning he had worked for her father, until he'd built his own carpentry business.

"I don't punch a clock for your father anymore," Keiran said.

"True," she rejoined with wry exasperation. "I heard you own a pub in Roses. And I want half the proceeds when you sell." She gestured to the street where O'Malley's was located.

"I'm not selling. And besides, the place hasn't been in business for years."

Her response was a derisive sneer. Few people believed Patricia was anything but a sultry, gorgeous female and ultimate charmer. He knew better. She was a woman who always got what she wanted.

And if she didn't?

Then she'd make life exceedingly unpleasant.

"Everything is for sale for a price." She was talking louder, her shrillness drawing the stares of passing shoppers, as she obviously intended. "Earlier, I went by the pub. It's not worth much, though it's worth something."

He sensed the desperation in her tone and looked her straight in the eye. "So you're here for money?"

"Obviously," she said.

"Where's Kyle?"

"He's long gone."

"And your father?"

"He refused to give me any more money." Her voice lowered to a stage whisper. "Now it's time for you to pay up, Keiran. I get half of everything you earn."

He planned to tread carefully before she went into a fresh fit of anger, although he couldn't contain himself. He just couldn't.

"Our verbal agreement ended." He started to pull his hand away.

"What about our written agreement?" Her grip tightened. Sagely, she shook her head. "You never were good at reading the fine print, darling, were you?"

*L*aughter burst from the judges' stand, and Desiree jerked at the sound. Keiran shook from Patricia's grip and grabbed Desiree's elbow. He guided her toward the canvas awning, using the excuse he wanted to admire her cake again.

Under her breath, she asked, "What was that about?"

But it didn't matter, because she already knew. And something was shattering deep inside her. Although she tried, she couldn't tear her thoughts away from the lushly provocative Patricia. The woman had the self-confidence of an exceptionally stunning female who commanded attention.

Keiran heaved a sigh. "Her father owns a construction business in Atlanta, and when I met her she got me a job at his company. I learned the trade and became one of his carpentry men."

Desiree felt her face heat, recalling the conversation between Patricia and Keiran. No doubt, they'd been close. Very close. The thought brought a stab of jealousy, along with recalling how the strikingly gorgeous Patricia had ogled Keiran.

Desiree yanked from his grip. "I think this is about a lot more than carpentry."

Neither of them broke the loaded silence as they advanced toward the cake display.

"She's trouble," Keiran said. "Supposedly, she helped me when I was building my carpentry business."

They'd come to the edge of the awning. Desiree leaned against a makeshift pole and crossed her arms. "Supposedly?"

"Aye. We rented an office together. She answered phone calls from customers, scheduled my jobs, and advertised my business. And, I trusted her with all the bookkeeping duties. Now that I look back, though, there were several times that I suspected money was missing."

"Did you confront her?"

"Are you kidding? Of course, although her answer was always the same. She'd nearly bite my head off and her resultant tantrum would last for days."

Desiree glanced at Teddy and Candee near the judges' stand. Teddy had his arm around Candee, and they chatted amiably with Rob.

Oh, to be able to give her heart to a man she could trust, Desiree thought, a man who loved her unconditionally.

She studied Keiran. "And that was okay with you?"

"Unfortunately, aye. I thought she was a prize—pretty, well-heeled, efficient. And then, she cheated on me with Kyle, a moneyed stockbroker."

The tension in the cold air between them crackled.

"You never told me any of this."

"I should have," he admitted. "Except it's demoralizing for a guy to have his girlfriend cheat on him with his best friend. They became a couple and—"

"And you skipped town to land on my doorstep."

"Patricia and I had a rocky relationship from the start. It's odd. Once the truth hit me, I realized I wanted the happily-ever-after ending. Just not with her."

"And yet, you couldn't bring yourself to tell me these revelations."

"I'm sorry. I should have." For a moment, he closed his eyes and breathed aloud. "Teddy said the same thing."

"You told Teddy, yet you wouldn't confide in me?" The surprise that had seized her when she'd realized who Patricia was to Keiran evaporated, along with the belief he actually cared. In a blinding flare of realization, she tore from his hold. "I'm a good listener, I would have understood. Now . . ."

"Nothing's changed."

The lump in her throat was so thick she could hardly manage any words. "Everything's changed."

"Because you're judgmental?"

"You're blaming me?" To stop from splintering into a million pieces, she shielded herself by opposing him. "You're the one who lied by omission."

"I couldn't admit it, okay? I thought I cared about a woman who was nothing more than a liar and a cheat. And then I realized I never cared at all, but wasn't sure how to make a proper exit."

"So your pride got in the way of your decision-making."

"Look, can I show you the silk scarf I saw earlier?" His jaw set with determination. "I think you'll like it."

"Please tell me you're joking."

"I'm completely serious." He laid his hands over one of hers. "We've got something good, Desiree. Surely you realize it too."

He didn't understand. He never could, considering his silver-spoon background. She'd been hurt and disappointed her entire life.

She winced. The only way to protect herself was to stay

away from precarious situations—the risk of heartache was too great.

"You don't get it," she said. "You weren't there when Candee and I were growing up. You didn't live where we lived."

A look of persistence passed across his features. "True, but I'm not to blame."

Angrily, she swiped at a tear running down her cheek.

"This isn't about me." He kept hold of her hands. "Or Patricia. It's about you growing up in the foster care system. You're afraid to open your heart because you might get hurt again. You can trust me, Desiree. I made a mistake and I'm genuinely sorry." He took her in his arms, lovingly stroking her hair. "Let's discuss this in a quiet place. We can have lunch at the new Chinese restaurant near my pub, and designate the occasion as our first real date."

"A date? *Now* we're dating?" Methodically, she removed his hands as Patricia headed toward them with sheer determination planted on her porcelain features.

"I'm back, Keiran," Patricia said, plunking dainty hands on her nonexistent hips while she perused the village green. "Where do you suggest we eat in this single-traffic-light town before we drive back to Atlanta together?"

"How about Chinese?" Desiree indicated the street where the restaurant was located. "It's across from the pub."

Keiran regarded Desiree levelly. "I'm buying you a silk scarf, and then I'm treating you to lunch to celebrate your cake victory."

"I've lost my appetite for eggrolls." Desiree cut her gaze to Patricia. "Although you'll love the food. Try the fried rice too. I've heard it's the best in Roses."

"I will, as long as he's buying. He's a generous guy." Patricia's thin eyebrows lifted in amused mockery. "Keiran, we can visit our pub too." Possessively, she touched his sleeve and beamed up at him.

"Desiree, please listen to me." He edged away from Patricia. "I can make everything right between us."

"You can't," Desiree shot back.

Her retort reverberated in her mind.

Or could he? They'd grown so close that they'd even begun finishing each other's sentences. One emotion bombarded her—hope—but hope would leave her brokenhearted if it didn't work out.

No. She couldn't take the chance.

"Enjoy your lunch, Keiran." For a second, Desiree forced herself to look at him. So handsome, so striking, so utterly appealing—and she faltered.

And then she reminded herself she wouldn't allow any more disappointment into her life. "We're done here," she said.

He met her look. "Really? You won't hear me out?"

She shook her head.

His green-eyed gaze froze to solid ice.

She twisted, trying not to recall the times in his arms, the pleasurable, passionate thrill of his kisses. Blindly, she made her way to the judges' stand, feeling the keenly inquisitive stares of strangers.

"We're not finished. I'll see you as soon as I get things sorted," he called out to her. "Back at the house. Wait for me there."

Drowning in sadness she couldn't control, she struggled to keep her shoulders straight and her gait sure. All around her, cheerful festivities rang out. The boutiques were filled to capacity. Shoppers spilled into the streets, and light-hearted conversation abounded.

"There you are." Candee raced through the throng and hauled Desiree to the side. "Teddy and I want to invite you and Keiran to our house for lunch. By the way, where is Keiran?" She peered around Desiree, shaded her eyes, and scowled. "Who is that woman he's walking with? I've never seen her before. Does she live in Roses?"

"She's from Atlanta."

"Why is she here?"

Why, indeed.

Desiree didn't answer her sister's question, although she agreed to lunch. The trembling that had started in her arms had spread to her legs, and later, she couldn't remember how she managed to get to her car, bypassing the green grocer as she drove home.

One fact she knew for sure. She wouldn't be waiting when Keiran arrived at her house. She couldn't bear the thought of facing him, yet she didn't have the prerogative to confront him. They weren't engaged or even officially dating, unless one counted nightly home-cooked meals as dates.

Sure, she'd presumed he'd told her the truth about his life in Atlanta, but he'd omitted a key point. He'd been seriously dating Patricia.

What did a lie by omission mean? Her lawyer brain clicked into gear. *Leaving out an important fact, thus fostering a misconception*, she automatically supplied. Yes, that described it.

As soon as she arrived home, she dashed off a note telling him to pack his things and leave, and set the note on her kitchen table. Then she planned to stay at Candee's house until midnight. Or longer, if Desiree saw his truck parked in her driveway.

CHAPTER 8

$\mathcal{D}$esiree needn't have worried, because Keiran came and went while she lunched and spent the afternoon with Candee, Teddy, and Joseph.

Keiran had penned his own note and placed it on the kitchen table next to hers, explaining he was driving back to Atlanta with Patricia.

Not sure when I'll return. Will keep you posted, he'd written in his typical bold script.

She crumpled up his note and tossed it on the floor.

A dire, stabbing ache grew as she climbed the stairs to the attic apartment. Hesitating, she slowly opened the door and stared at the room in silence. His bed was neatly made. His scent pervaded the space—raw wood and the outdoors, a hint of sawdust and pine. All related to his job.

And his belongings had vanished.

She inhaled and leaned weakly against the door. Here it was, a week before Christmas, and he'd abandoned her to be with his former girlfriend. For all Desiree knew, Keiran and Patricia planned to return to Roses and renovate O'Malley's as a team.

Her feverish brain refused to accept that scenario, and she seriously considered moving out of her beloved town if that ever occurred. In comparison to Patricia, Desiree felt like an adolescent girl again—ordinary and inexperienced.

Goodbye Keiran, she thought, coming to terms with the fact that they'd gone in opposite directions.

After arriving in Atlanta, he texted and phoned numerous times.

She replied with a brief text: *Don't contact me. No texts, no calls, okay?*

A date when I return? he immediately countered. *It's Christmas, after all.*

And Christmas brought memories of when she was a little kid, feeling alone and deserted while her parents lay drunk on the living room couch. She knew she must come to grips with her emotions in order to move forward. But, oh, this was so hard. Acceptance and forgetting, these were weaknesses in her life she had a hard time acknowledging, although her favorite pastor had assured in a sermon that weakness led to strength.

When, exactly? Had God brought her a Christmas miracle in Keiran? And if so, was she throwing that miracle away with both hands when she refused to speak with him, allowing pride to dictate her lonely path?

She pressed her cell phone to her heart and asked the empty room, "How can I fight you, Keiran, when I'm warring with myself?"

The sparks between them had flamed with his every touch, his every kiss, and she missed his solid strength, calm reassurances, and good humor.

With a deep sigh, she tried to come to terms with the desolation weighing her down. How could she face another day without him when he made her feel so complete? Finally, she'd had a chance to be happy.

But happiness was a funny thing. The fear of being alone stemmed from her childhood, and she'd proven she could succeed on her own.

She reminded herself of all she'd accomplished, that her colleagues had remarked on her spirited, confident nature. With firm determination, she lifted her chin and pushed her thoughts of Keiran aside.

And then she texted him back. A final, single word: *No.*

By Monday of the following week, she knew he'd departed for good. Still, her heart jumped whenever the doorbell rang. Despite her firm reprimands to herself, she'd hurry to the front door, thinking he'd returned for Christmas after all. A secret fantasy come true, despite her conflicting emotions.

Although the opposite prevailed in her real world, and it turned out to be the postman, or an online store delivery.

Very well, then. The next time the doorbell rang, she would take her time answering it.

By the end of the week, she'd established a pattern. No longer did she live in suspended anticipation that Keiran might stride into her foyer. Nonetheless, neither was she able to anticipate the upcoming holiday with delight. She'd thought she'd find the peace she'd been looking for if she bought her own home.

But she hadn't.

Peace had little to do with the most expensive home, the most beautiful neighborhood, she decided. It was who you shared your home with that mattered most. And now that Keiran was gone, despite her attempts to deny it, the truth hit hard.

At six o'clock on the Friday evening before Christmas Eve, Desiree pulled off her black leather boots, hung her jacket in the hall closet, and pulled her blue cardigan over her silk blouse. She was done working for two weeks, and had won a case involving Julie Wallis, a single mother of two children, who was being jailed and fined for a minor offense. When it was clear the mother couldn't afford to pay, Desiree had argued for another solution. The court had accepted a community service plan, and Julie had cried with relief when she was released.

Cause for celebration, Desiree thought, although the day didn't feel at all celebratory.

It felt empty.

Aimlessly, she wandered the spacious rooms of her home, fingering the prominent wooden staircase, the paneled oak walls, the built-in china cabinets.

She barely glanced at her wristwatch as she stepped across the spacious foyer, although her mouth tightened when she realized the time. Candee was coming over in an hour to finalize their Christmas Eve plans.

As much as Desiree liked talking to Candee, she'd avoided her sister's phone calls because she'd been dreading their imminent discussion. Most likely, the topic would center around Keiran and his notable disappearance.

As Desiree headed for the kitchen, Candee phoned, launching into a lengthy monologue regarding the sweet rolls she was bringing for Christmas Eve dinner. Desiree cut her off, making an excuse that a thorough kitchen organization required her attention, and she'd see Candee at seven o'clock.

She poured herself a glass of sparkling cider, sat on a stool, and rehearsed their upcoming exchange in her mind.

"*What happened?*" Candee would ask, referring to Keiran. Most likely, she'd expected to find Desiree and Keiran acting like an official couple by the time Christmas rolled around.

"What happened?" Desiree would repeat. "Keiran lied to me, knowing I was falling in love with him. And then he went off with Patricia."

An unbearable ache pierced her heart. She set down her glass and perused the kitchen. A box of pots and pans required sorting, and her pantry could be more orderly.

As she arranged a variety of spices closer to the stove, a trio of deliverymen knocked on the kitchen's sliding glass doors. Her base cabinet had arrived, they announced, and her contractor had requested they bring the cabinet through the rear door rather than muddying up the new wood floors.

"Is the cabinet heavy?" She invited the men inside to unbox the cabinet in the earmarked corner near the pantry.

"Just awkward, ma'am," the youngest of the three replied, test-fitting the cabinet by what he clarified was dry-fitting. "Do you have a carpenter to install it?" he asked.

She shook her head.

"We're booked until the first of the year, but you're missing the stainless handle for this cabinet. If it's in stock, I'll make a note for a special delivery before Christmas."

"Thank you, and Merry Christmas," she replied.

As the men cheerfully departed, she bid them good-bye with a quiet smile.

She went into the pantry, intending to declutter the shelves by stacking the flat containers on top of one another. Instead, she found herself rummaging in a drawer to retrieve Keiran's note, which she'd salvaged from the floor.

Not sure when I'll return. Will keep you posted, he'd written.

Rereading the simple sentences, she traced the letters with shaking hands, feeling a pang of longing so intense, her knees weakened. He was so magnificent, so unbearably good-looking, she'd taken unabashed pleasure in spending every spare second with him.

If he phoned her even once more, she might cave and answer his call.

Might? Ruefully, she decided that she would answer.

Of course he hadn't, and her phone had sat silent for two days.

"I thought I had everything worked out," she whispered to the quiet pantry.

Apparently not this time. The storybook life she'd planned out hadn't gone the way she'd expected. And despite reaching her goals—her successful career and a home of her own—happiness remained elusive.

Pivoting, she walked into the living room, taking heart in its remarkable transformation, the Christmas tree illuminated in dazzling splendor. She lit a fire in the fireplace, and the flickering light assured her of comfort through the bitter winter ahead.

All week since Keiran's departure, she hadn't allowed herself to cry, and had accomplished her workdays briskly and efficiently. However, now that she didn't have court cases and clients to occupy her mind, the heavy burden of keeping her feelings bottled up threatened to spill over.

As tears welled, she shuffled back to the kitchen. The wintry December wind whistled through a small opening in the sliding glass doors and burned her eyes. She slid the doors closed as tears streamed freely down her cheeks.

She let them come, weeping until there were no tears left to shed—no more sadness or resentment. The picture in her mind's eye of where she was supposed to live, where the man in her life was supposed to stand, and the children she would be blessed with hadn't happened.

She sank onto a chair, her shoulders drooping with desolation. Why had Keiran refrained from telling her about Patricia? And why hadn't he returned to Roses by now? He'd given up so quickly. Wasn't he interested in knowing how Desiree was faring after their break-up?

Her thoughts went back to the previous weekend, and she

visualized Patricia's seductive eyes as she'd gazed intimately up at Keiran.

We were practically engaged, Patricia had said, her words intended to pierce.

Hurt, confused, and angry, Desiree refused to allow that image to dominate her thoughts. Instead, she recalled how Keiran had held her afterwards, murmuring to her, caressing her hair.

You can trust me, Desiree. I made a mistake and I'm genuinely sorry. His voice had been rough with self-reproach.

And later, the guarded hope in his tone as he'd called out, *I'll see you as soon as I get things sorted. Back at the house. Wait for me there.*

A stinging pain punctured her chest with each memory. He'd sounded sincere, and she remembered the despair that had crossed his handsome features.

She half-rose from her chair as a thought struck her. With surprising clarity, she recognized that the pain she felt was more for Keiran than herself.

Angrily, she swiped her wet cheeks and sprang fully to her feet. Surely this proved she was a besotted fool. How could she feel sorry for him when she was the person who'd been deceived?

Surprisingly, with that realization, her mood began to elevate. In fact, by the time she stood by the table and item-ized her to-do list for Christmas Eve, she felt better than she had all week. Her sadness began turning into fortitude.

She opened the refrigerator and brought out two bags of fresh cranberries she intended to frost with sugar for a festive centerpiece. She'd also purchased a variety of prepared side dishes including creamy mashed potatoes and a green bean casserole topped with pecans. In the morning, she'd tackle the fresh turkey preparation.

So, the meal was set, and she'd slated her pistachio cake for dessert.

Her gaze travelled to the adjoining dining room.

Where would they all sit—Teddy, Candee, Joseph, and Desiree?

She paused, considered the lack of furniture, then recalled her conversation with Keiran.

You own a service of fine crystal and china, your dining area is large enough for a twenty-people feast, and there's no place to sit and enjoy a meal? he'd teased.

I'll pile cushions on the floor and we'll sit cross-legged, she'd replied.

Dashing back into the living room, she dragged her coffee table into the dining area. Then she draped a red tartan tablecloth over it and arranged colorful throw pillows around the table.

With great care, she set the table with four place settings using her finest china and silver, embellishing the tablespace with shiny silver candle holders and a string of sparkling white lights.

Pleased with the result, she went into the kitchen and sat in the middle of the tiled floor, eyeing the base cabinet waiting to be anchored.

The deliveryman had stated she needed a carpenter. Well, Keiran wasn't here.

However, she was.

On her phone, she searched tutorials on how to install a cabinet, and selected a step-by-step video that assured installation was easy with the proper tools, which included a level, a screw gun, screws, clamps, and a hammer and nails.

"Carefully measure and draw the exact location," the woman in the video instructed. "Drive screws into the wall studs to anchor the cabinet."

Quickly, Desiree changed into jeans and a sweatshirt,

chose the necessary tools from the study where the crewmen kept their supplies, and set to work.

An hour later, she was kneeling on the floor, concentrating intensely on the installation, when Candee entered the kitchen.

"Sorry I'm late," Candee declared as Desiree jerked back, startled by her sister's voice. "Boomer was doing his favorite thing—eating—and then I took him for a quick walk. You didn't hear the doorbell, so I let myself in." Candee's mouth trembled with laughter as she admired the cabinet. "And now I see why. You look remarkably determined."

"Base cabinets aren't difficult to install if the area has been measured accurately and you have the correct tools," Desiree said, parroting the singsong tone of the woman in the video. She finished driving the last nail into the toe kick beneath the cabinet, set the tools on the floor, then stood.

"Bravo!" Candee gave her a high-five. "The place looks great."

She smiled. "Thanks."

"Have you eaten dinner?" Candee's gaze skimmed the kitchen.

"No, and I'm starving." Desiree reminded herself that she needed to set aside a half hour a day for exercise in order to shed the extra ten pounds she'd gained. Appreciating Keiran's magnificent cooking, she hadn't had the opportunity or the inclination to diet.

"Teddy and I are so busy with Joseph and his horse therapy that I haven't eaten, either." Candee peered into the refrigerator and extracted cold cuts and bread, motioning for Desiree to join her. "I'll make us both a sandwich and brew a pot of tea."

The women enjoyed a cozy light supper at the kitchen table.

"You seem much better than I imagined," Candee said as she poured tea. "I mean, after last Saturday."

"I feel better."

"Care to fill me in on what happened between you and Keiran?" Candee fixed Desiree a mug of tea without milk, and added milk and sugar to her own. "Teddy mentioned he and Keiran have been in touch, but when I pressed him for details he was extremely close-lipped."

Desiree debated, opening her mouth to defend her position, then closing it. Today, for the first time in a week, she'd begun to feel purposeful again. A delicate newfound serenity had emerged through her tears. Should she take the risk of talking about it?

But Candee seemed so resolute, Desiree knew holding back was futile. Besides, who was better to confide in than her dear sister?

"Ask away," Desiree said.

"Tell me everything."

"Well," Desiree sat back in her chair, "I suppose our relationship began when he first arrived and began talking to my front porch."

"You mean talking *to you* on your front porch."

"No, I mean talking *to* my front porch," Desiree said with an amused smile. She couldn't explain her attraction to Keiran from that first moment. At night her dreams had been of him. During the day, she'd daydreamed about him. His capable hands as he cooked, or his bass voice as he sang an Irish tune, had awakened her desire for a secure, centered life with the man she loved. Often in the past weeks, she'd told herself that the uniqueness, the unqualified novelty, of having a charismatic Renaissance man living in her house would pass.

Instead, her feelings had intensified.

Noting Candee's raised eyebrows, Desiree set aside her

teacup. "When Keiran arrived, I told him I needed an electrician, not a carpenter, and to return in the morning. So I shut the door on him and when I reopened it, he was still there, muttering to the porch. I invited him to move into the attic because he had nowhere else to stay."

Candee laughed softly. "And then the relationship began."

"A practical relationship."

"A romantic one."

"At night after dinner, we'd go into the living room and he'd light a fire." Desiree drew her legs up in the chair, curling her arms around them. "He'd play his guitar and . . ."

When she finished her story, Candee dabbed at her eyes. "Truly, your entire courtship is enchanting."

"We've never even been out on a formal date."

"In all those hours you spent together you probably know him better than anyone. Teddy said that just because Keiran moved into your house didn't mean a relationship would develop, especially in a short period of time." A satisfied smile wreathed Candee's face. "But I felt certain he was wrong. I heard Keiran talk endlessly about you whenever he came to the house to confer with Teddy. And I watched you two at the cake judging contest, and I knew. He's deeply in love with you."

Desiree stood and wiped her palms on the folds of her sweatshirt. "He has an odd way of showing it, running off to Atlanta with Patricia."

"Has he tried contacting you?"

"He's called and texted many times."

"Have you responded?"

Desiree stared impassively at the glossy white backsplash above the farmhouse sink Keiran had installed. "Only to tell him not to contact me again."

"Well, that's a brilliant way to go about things."

Desiree gave a guilty start. Her heartbeat raced with a

surge of annoyance. Or was it culpability?

Candee crossed the room and took Desiree's cold hands in hers. "Do you love him?"

Understatement. Sweet memories hastened to her mind. With a rush of happiness, she recalled his attentiveness, his patience, the pride she'd felt when he complimented her for fighting court battles against injustice. This broad-shouldered, rugged man gazed at her with such heartfelt tenderness, sometimes words would lodge in her throat.

"Did you think about me today?" he'd asked.

"Often."

"Good. I thought about you too. See how much we are alike? We both love Christmas and we both love—" Then he'd drawn her into his arms and kissed her.

Desiree willed herself to say no, she didn't love him. Instead, she heard herself saying, "Yes. I fell in love with him at a high school football game ten years ago."

Candee tightened her grip on Desiree's hands. "I thought I recognized his name when Teddy first brought him up. Then O'Malley's pub was discussed and I recalled you going on and on about him when we were teenagers. So often, in fact, I suspected you had a crush on him."

"You were right," Desiree said. "But now I'm a grown woman."

"Who loves a grown man. And that man loves you very much."

Desiree shook free and peered out the window at the thick dark night, chilly and moonless.

"He's gone," she said quietly.

"He's not gone." Candee went to the sink and ran soapy hot water over a stack of dishes. "He's just waiting for you to give him the opportunity to make amends. You can't repair a relationship if you avoid him."

"He hasn't texted or called in a couple of days."

"He's probably come to accept that you don't want anything to do with him."

"That's not true."

"Then go to him in Atlanta. And tell him face to face."

Desiree's brain frantically groped for a way to refute Candee's argument. Suppose she failed? He was obviously more interested in Patricia.

"I can't. Tomorrow is Christmas Eve. We're attending church service, and I'm cooking. See?" Desiree gestured to the dining room. "The table's all set."

"Then I'll give you a one-day pass because you admitted you love him."

Her love for him was out of reach, but she knew if she admitted her thoughts to Candee, her sister would argue her point a tad too vehemently.

"Yes, I love him," Desiree said. Desperately loved him. And when he gazed at her as if she were the only person in his universe, her pulse surged with excitement.

"Settled. On Christmas Day, you're driving to Atlanta," Candee said. "Teddy knows where Keiran used to live, and you'll start there. Or, you can phone him."

Desiree hesitated. Would Keiran be angry with her, or coolly polite? Or would he be thrilled to see her, because he still cared?

Desiree blew out a breath. "I'll surprise him."

Although, as she closed the door after Candee's departure, she felt a sickening fear of failure straight to her belly.

Suppose she interrupted Keiran while he was with Patricia?

Suppose he didn't want to see her?

With resolve, she pulled her thoughts away from irrational worry and concentrated on their reunion in Atlanta.

Please love me, my affectionate, gentle Renaissance man, she thought, *as much as I love you.*

CHAPTER 9

Keiran didn't return to Roses in two days, which was the time frame he'd originally planned. Neither did he spend his days with Patricia.

He'd passed on lunching with her in Roses, and hadn't taken her inside O'Malley's. He'd left her in town, driven back to Desiree's home, and read her note with surprised alarm. She wouldn't hear him out.

He'd been raised a gentleman, and quickly packed his bags as she requested and loaded up his truck. It didn't matter who was right or wrong. He'd kept the truth from her, although not intentionally. He'd simply removed Patricia from his heart and mind because Desiree had taken over his thoughts. When he was with her, everything else fell away.

After a silent four-hour drive with Patricia back to Atlanta, he'd dropped her at her apartment. He intended to get to the bottom of her demands, settle any financial score once and for all, and return to Roses, his true home.

And his true love, Desiree.

When Desiree hadn't answered his phone calls or texts in

the ensuing first hours of his departure, he'd tasted a bitter defeat. But not for long. They weren't finished by a long shot.

He bunked in his former apartment, where he discussed his situation with Oscar and Georges. Oscar made a hasty phone call and booked a consultation with Abraham Realgood, Honest Abe, the lawyer he worked for. Although the lawyer wasn't accepting new clients, he'd offer his consultation services as a favor to Oscar.

The following afternoon, Mr. Realgood's receptionist showed Keiran into a dark-paneled office where the lawyer greeted Keiran with a friendly tilt of his head.

"What can I do for you?" He gestured for Keiran to take a seat across from him.

"I'll come directly to the point." Keiran sank into the cushioned chair. "My former girlfriend, Patricia, believes she's entitled to half my earnings, including a pub I inherited."

A pair of astute hazel eyes measured Keiran. "I've heard some of your story, thanks to Oscar and Georges."

"Then can you advise me? I want Patricia out of my life."

"She's requesting money."

"Yes, and more money than I have." With Patricia, it had always been about an extravagant lifestyle, and when she had a goal in mind there was no stopping her.

"Is she entitled to your money?" the lawyer asked.

"When we were together, we had a verbal agreement that we would split half my earnings. I did the work, and she maintained the office and books. However, I've reviewed the paperwork I held on to, because she implied there was some fine print," Keiran said. "I couldn't find anything written down."

"How much does she want?"

"Twenty thousand dollars. I wish it was less. She found out I inherited a pub and she wants me to sell it and she'll take half the proceeds. However, I'm not willing to sell, and besides, the building isn't worth much in its present condition."

"Not functioning?"

"It hasn't been open in many years."

"Is there a possibility she'd take you to court?"

That was a worrisome and infuriating thought. Keiran stretched out his long legs and blew out a sigh. "Knowing Patricia? Aye, although she couldn't possibly win. Could she?"

"Probably not, if your agreement was verbal, but this battle could go on for years. It all depends how badly you want her out of your life."

Furious with himself for getting involved with her in the first place, Keiran glanced out the window at the overcast sky. "I'd like our relationship to be finished, once and for all."

"Then there's a solution because money talks." The lawyer examined the paperwork on his desk and idly pushed it to the side. "Georges mentioned you inherited an autographed football card that might be valuable."

With a nod, Keiran pulled the card from its protective case, as Georges had urged him to bring it to the meeting. He felt a deep, almost agonizing sadness about giving up the card that had meant so much to his father. He'd prayed about it, and realized he needed to get over the sadness and guilt if he sold it. If he reopened the pub, his parents would undoubtedly be grateful and proud. As much as his father's dream had been football, the pub in Roses was his legacy.

Keiran shifted his gaze to the lawyer's sparsely furnished, dimly lit office. He'd expected an oily charmer with a law degree, but Abraham Realgood seemed on the up and up.

"We appraised the card at the pawn shop Georges works for," Keiran said. "The estimate from the pawnbroker is fifteen thousand dollars."

Seemingly impervious to Keiran's emotional state, the lawyer grinned. "I advise you to sell the card and pay the ex. If your past agreement was verbal, you're in the clear, but it's more the matter of guaranteeing she won't be able to badger you for any more money. Otherwise, she may turn up again. More time. More money. Do you want that?"

Keiran shook his head. "I'd like her gone from my life."

"Then I'll draw up a contract, a full and final release stating clearly she's not entitled to anything else after this payment."

"Do you think she'll accept less than she's asking?"

Mr. Realgood rubbed his jaw. "From you and your friends' descriptions, I'm positive she'll jump at it. Fifteen thousand dollars is a lot, especially around Christmas."

"Excellent." It was all Keiran could do not to burst into an Irish song. This was going to work. "How soon can the contract be drafted?"

"By tomorrow. I'll handle everything from here." Slowly, the gray-haired lawyer leaned back in his chair and folded his hands behind his head. "Now I'm not judging, mind you, but if I were you I'd avoid any further correspondence with your ex—verbal or otherwise."

The lawyer *was* judging, Keiran reflected, although he was too relieved to do anything other than watch Mr. Realgood write out a bill and hand it to him.

Keiran looked over the number and gaped.

"Admittedly, my services are costly on account of the short notice and holiday season," the lawyer said. "But your problem is solved. And if you ever need your locks changed, I'll cut you a good deal."

"Thank you." With a deep, relieved breath, Keiran shook hands with the lawyer and left.

By noon the next day, Abe Realgood phoned to report

that Patricia had received the email and accepted via her electronic signature.

Another deep breath of relief.

"The thing is," Keiran told a frowning but somewhat amused Georges and Oscar, "I can't stay to cook Christmas Eve dinner because I'm driving back to Roses."

Georges flashed Keiran a mischievous grin. "What will we eat then, *mon ami?*"

"Why don't you call the local pizzeria? They deliver on Christmas Eve, and pizza goes great with beer." Keiran chuckled as he hoisted his belongings over his shoulder, thanked the men for their help, and wished them a Merry Christmas.

He glanced at his watch. He had two stops to make in Roses, and one important phone call. He hoped he wouldn't be late for Christmas Eve dinner. They ate at six o'clock sharp.

* * *

"You burned the turkey?" Candee hovered over Desiree, who'd dashed into the kitchen to extract a charred, smoking turkey from the oven. "How can anyone burn a fourteen-pound turkey?"

"Fortunately, it didn't catch fire. When the smoke detector went off, I was worried," Desiree replied. "I went into the living room for a few minutes to start a fire in the fireplace and plug in the Christmas tree lights. Then, while I was lighting the candles on the mantel, I got sidetracked when the radio started playing 'Silent Night' on repeat."

Desiree wore the red and green *Kiss Me, It's Christmas* apron over a red silk blouse and black velvet pants. Christmas Eve was a special occasion, and she planned to slip on suede ankle boots and her cobalt-blue wool coat for midnight church services. To keep her hair away from her face while cooking, she'd pinned it into a chignon secured with a red jeweled clasp.

"I should've helped you with the dinner preparations. Sorry I lost track of time. I love watching Teddy and Joseph play a game of flag football," Candee said. "It's amazing—we haven't gotten any snow this year so the guys are still wearing sweatshirts and jeans."

"The weather forecast predicts a light dusting by midnight." Desiree glanced out the kitchen window at the energetic twosome. They'd decided on another game and were flipping a coin. Then Teddy placed the football in the middle of her large backyard. Starting with a snap, Joseph passed the ball in one fluid motion to a third player.

"Recognize that handsome guy? He looks like he could be a male model." Candee feigned fanning herself as she came to stand by the window with Desiree.

He certainly seemed familiar, with his broad shoulders and midnight-black hair and . . .

Desiree's knees buckled. No, it couldn't be. The guy must be one of the neighborhood men, perhaps Mr. Juno taking a break from his graduate studies.

"I'll try flipping the turkey," Candee suggested. "If I drop it, then we can remember this Christmas as the year you burned the turkey and it fell to the floor."

Desiree laughed. "As long as it doesn't roll into the dining room and—"

The front doorbell rang. The cabinet door handle delivery man, Desiree surmised, because she wasn't expecting any visitors.

Or was she?

She told herself to take her time answering, but scratched the idea as she hastened to the door and swung it open.

It wasn't the delivery man.

He stood on her front porch, tall and lean, his green eyes reminding her of Irish emeralds glimmering in his handsome face. He wore his navy-blue parka, unzipped, accentuating his toned physique. His denim shirt and jeans were rumpled. He was holding a small gift, wrapped in brown paper and tied with a red satin ribbon.

"Keiran." She stepped back and attempted to breathe. Part of her functioning brain reminded her that she should stay calm and composed.

"Merry Christmas, Desiree." He held out the gift.

She kept her hands at her sides. "Why are you here?" Her voice shook. He still offered her the gift, his hands outstretched.

"To finish our discussion from last week. And to tell you what I've wanted to say since we met. Listen—"

"Keiran, you're a little late." Candee approached and gave him a mildly sardonic smile.

"It started to snow in Atlanta and the limited visibility on I-85 slowed traffic," he said. "Plus I stopped in town to buy Desiree's gift, then ducked into my pub. Rob is coming in the morning."

"Rob?" Desiree regarded them both. "Why?"

"Rob and Keiran are reopening the pub. Rob is loaning him the start-up money, much as he did for Teddy when he began his real estate flipping business," Candee said.

"Rob and I will be serving Christmas dinner tomorrow to the homeless in our community," Keiran explained. "Several of the markets in town, including your green grocer, are donating food. We're using the ovens at the local supermarkets to prepare the meals. I hope you'll join us, Desiree."

Blinking, Desiree gaped at Keiran, and then Candee. "And you knew about all this?"

"Only recently," Candee replied. "Teddy and Keiran arranged everything."

"And about Keiran returning here? Tonight?"

Feigning innocence, Candee gushed apologetically. "You wouldn't answer his texts. Tonight, Teddy told me they've been in touch all week. And now I'm going to see to dinner." Candee rolled up the sleeves of her glittery silver blouse and hurried away.

"Keiran." Desiree touched her throat. "I don't know what to say."

His strong fingers were gentle as he pressed them against her lips. "Take my gift and invite me inside."

"Please come in." She accepted his gift. "You didn't need to buy me anything. Thank you."

He stepped inside. "I confess I used the gift as an excuse."

"What? I don't understand."

"I've been working all week to make things right between us. I understand you're hurt and justifiably angry. I met with a lawyer in Atlanta, and Patricia signed a full and final release contract. She's not entitled to half of what I earn anymore. Our former business agreement was verbal, by the way."

Desiree's heart was pounding so hard, he could surely hear each beat. "What do you mean?"

"She was demanding twenty thousand dollars, the estimated proceeds if I sold the pub." He shook his head. "You don't know her the way I do. She would have made our lives miserable. So, I gave her fifteen thousand, and made certain she's out of our life for good."

Desiree's gaze narrowed. "Where did you get the money? Rob?"

"Rob's been great, but no."

She paused for a beat. "Then where?"

"My father's football card. I didn't want to sell it, and I prayed long and hard before agreeing. The pawn shop assured me they'll hold it for a while, in case I can come up with the money to buy it back. I don't see that happening, but you never know. Our pub might become extremely successful, just like it once was."

"*Our* pub?"

"I'm hoping you'll help me bring it back to its former glory."

Through tears of happiness, she found her voice. "With you at the helm, how can it fail?"

"And you," he said solemnly. "I hope I'm the man you deserve, and I want to make all my mistakes up to you."

The pain in his voice brought a new swell of tears. "Keiran, please, we all make mistakes and—"

"I'm sorry, Desiree. And I love you."

When she realized he was threading his fingers through her hair, then cupping her face so he could kiss her, she whispered the words bursting from her heart. "I love you too."

All week she'd dreamed of kissing him—the tenderness of his mouth on hers, the elation of being reunited. For a long moment, she felt mesmerized, like she was floating. His kiss was light and sweet, and magnificently poignant.

She snuggled against his warm, hard chest, feeling the solid beat of his heart. There was so much she wanted to tell him—that she'd installed a kitchen cabinet by herself, that she'd won a particularly difficult court case.

Not knowing where to begin, she burst out, "I burned the turkey. But I set a lovely table for dinner and I wasn't going to let a little thing like charred meat stop us from enjoying Christmas."

He chuckled. "Let me survey the damage and see if I can help." He removed his parka and Desiree hung it in the front foyer closet, then placed his gift on a side table in the living room. She crossed to the kitchen, where Keiran was deftly removing the burnt skin from the turkey.

"If everyone likes the legs and thighs, we're golden," he said.

Desiree set out her turkey platter, and Candee artfully arranged sliced lemons and sprigs of rosemary around the carved meat Keiran placed on the platter. He asked Desiree to stir the gravy on the stove.

"You're a little bossy."

His eyes crinkled as a grin touched his lips. "I'm delegating."

Teddy and Joseph joined the group, and they settled, cross-legged, on the cushions Desiree had arranged in the dining room around the makeshift table.

Dinner was a feast that did credit to all of Desiree's preparations. She glanced uncertainly at Keiran as he tasted a slice of turkey. He proclaimed the meat expertly roasted, and she couldn't help but notice he gazed at her with profound pride.

She toyed with the mashed potatoes, wishing she hadn't felt so nervous about entertaining. Keiran assumed the role as host with a casual, gracious elegance.

After her pistachio cake was served for dessert, Joseph turned his attention to her. "We have a present for you, Aunt Desiree!" he burst out. "It's a surprise! Uncle Teddy said we could go back to our house and get him as soon as we were finished." He turned to Candee. "May I be excused?"

Him? Get *him?* Before Desiree could ask, Candee opened her mouth with the obvious intention of suggesting they wait until Christmas morning, but Teddy forestalled her by grinning at Joseph in agreement.

"This won't take long," Teddy said, as he and Joseph hurried out the door.

They returned ten minutes later holding Boomer, the brown and tan beagle pup.

"Merry Christmas, Desiree!" Candee, Teddy, and Joseph chimed.

The beagle wriggled out of Joseph's arms and lunged for the coffee table laden with food.

"This dog loves to eat, so he must think he's landed in paradise because he can reach the height of this table," Teddy said.

Desiree dissolved with laughter. Her contentment was so real, she thought her chest might burst. This was heaven—a happy home, sharing God's message of joy with the people she loved.

After the meal was cleared, Keiran escorted Desiree to the living room while Candee and her family excused themselves to go back to their house and get ready for church services.

Boomer, apparently full and exhausted, curled up near the fireplace, tail to nose.

"Desiree? There are a few things we need to discuss." Keiran claimed a seat beside her on the sofa. Although he asked gently, she knew by his inquisitive expression that he wanted an explanation for why she refused to accept his phone calls and texts.

She pulled off her apron and smoothed her red silk blouse. Drawing a long breath, she told him her feelings about trust, knowing he'd been correct in surmising her issues had come from early life experiences.

"Trust can be relearned," he said quietly. "It helps if you talk about it. And I'll be here for you, to listen."

"You're moving back in?"

He brushed a wisp of blond hair from her face. "I hope you'll invite me to sleep in your attic. I can't drive back to Atlanta in a blizzard."

"I wouldn't call a few inches of snow a blizzard." She stared out the wavy glass of the front bay window. The snow was starting to fall, its thick wet flakes covering the side-walks and road in a white blanket.

"You don't want your fiancé to be homeless," he said.

"Fiancé?"

Although his tone was light, she heard the rough tinge in his voice.

Tipping her chin up, he gazed deeply into her eyes. "I love you, Desiree."

She laid a hand on his cheek. "And I love you."

Her Renaissance man. She attempted to smile. "Until now, I felt certain I'd never hear those words from you."

"Desiree, I've loved you since you slammed the door in my face when I first arrived, then berated me for talking to your front porch."

"A bit odd, don't you think? Talking to a porch?"

"Not considering the circumstances." With an arm around her waist, he turned to a side table, picked up his gift and handed it to her.

"I thought about something Christmassy, and it's one of the reasons I stopped in town. Please open it."

She unwrapped the gift and slid a silky scarf between her fingers, admiring the holly design in white and green. "Thank you. It's gorgeous."

"The boutique owner said it's a designer scarf, and the colors will go with everything."

"Ideal for the holidays." She tied the scarf around her throat and smiled. "How does it look?"

"Perfect. Like you." He nodded to the box. "There's something else inside, at the bottom."

"What is it?"

He caught her in a long embrace. "Something special that I hope you'll love."

She unsnapped the lid of a tiny black velvet box and

gasped. An exquisite round-cut diamond ring, styled in yellow gold, reflected sparkling white light across the ceiling.

"I've never seen anything so beautiful," she breathed.

He drew back slightly and regarded her. "Will you marry me?"

From the moment he'd returned, Desiree had known he would ask for an open and honest relationship.

Through tears of bliss, she whispered, "Yes."

His arms closed around her. "Good. Because if you don't mean it, I won't bake any more Irish whiskey cakes."

"Maybe it's better, because I need to lose a few pounds." She laughed through her tears. "Besides, you never shared your secret recipe with me."

He took her hand and led her to the kitchen. "We can start this evening. I promise I'll teach you everything I know."

THE END

RECIPE FOR DESIREE'S PISTACHIO CAKE

Easy, fast, and festive, this recipe is always a treat!

You will need:

1 package of white cake mix- any brand

1 package of pistachio instant pudding – sugar-free may be used instead of regular

½ cup vegetable oil

½ cup water

½ cup milk

5 eggs

Blend cake mix with the package of pudding. Add oil, milk, and water. Add eggs one at a time, beating well with electric mixer after each addition.

Pour into a greased (or sprayed with cooking spray) tube or Bundt pan.

Bake 1 hour at 350 degrees. May be done sooner, as ovens vary.

Cool for 30 minutes, and invert onto favorite cake platter.

For a light and festive topping, sprinkle with sifted confectioners sugar and sliced maraschino cherries.

Optional frosting recipe: (Spread on cooled cake)

½ pint heavy cream

1 package instant pistachio pudding (sugar free may be used)

1 container thawed Cool Whip (fat-free may be used)

Beat heavy cream until thick. Blend in rest of ingredients. Frost as desired.

Enjoy!

A NOTE FROM JOSIE

Thank you for reading *1-800-CHRISTMAS,* the second book in my contemporary sweet romance series: *Flipping for You.*

If you loved this sweet romance as much as I loved writing it, please help other people find *1-800-CHRISTMAS* by posting your review, as well as for the bundle: The 1-800-Series.

1-800-CHRISTMAS continued the series in the same small town of Roses, North Carolina, and follows 1-800-CUPID.

The third book, 1-800-IRELAND, brings in 2 favorite characters from my previous sweet romances.

1-800-CHRISTMAS is available in ebook, paperback, Large Print paperback, Hardcover, and audiobook.

My Spotify Play List for 1-800-CHRISTMAS is here.

JOSIE RIVIERA

1·800· IRELAND

A SWEET CONTEMPORARY NOVELLA

PRAISE AND AWARDS

USA TODAY bestselling author

CHAPTER 1

*W*hy *did I decide to do this? I must've been madder than a box of frogs.*

Kathleen Kelly nodded politely while listening to Candee, her Realtor, although she scarcely paid attention. While she tried to come up with an animated reply, her mind spun. She hoped she hadn't made the biggest mistake of her life.

I'm in America. I've done it.

Meanwhile, Candee gushed on and on about Roses, their picture-perfect North Carolina town. Voted one of the best places to live by a national magazine, Roses frequently persuaded travelers passing through to sell their homes and relocate there.

Kathleen grinned, because she was one of those travelers. However, she hadn't passed through Roses. Her Dublin hometown was 3600 miles away.

The internet was a marvelous thing, connecting people from all around the world. Finally, after months of preparation, her dream of owning a business had become a reality.

Cause for celebration?

In truth, she'd been full of starry-eyed dreams and didn't

know what to expect—this being America with its laid-back style. However, she'd found that professionalism and punctuality were respected here, judging by how efficiently Candee had handled the real estate closing.

She eyed the run-down exterior, the broken-down wooden front door that looked like it had once been painted turquoise. Moss flourished beneath the eaves, and numerous shingles were missing. The brick façade was crumbling in several places.

This wasn't Betty's Diner anymore. From here on in, this was her place: Kathleen's Teahouse.

Critically, she assessed her reflection in the smudged plate-glass front window. She'd swept her red-gold hair up at the crown, and pinned the overly long ends back from her face. Tired lines etched the corners of her dark eyes, and the blush of color she'd applied along her cheekbones had disappeared, leaving her complexion pale. Her lips, which she'd always deemed too full, looked a tad solemn.

Despite the sunny day, she'd dressed in a suede skirt, thick black tights and ankle boots.

Budding leaves on the tulip magnolia trees whispered of spring, and buttery-yellow daffodils had begun to open. So different from Ireland, where hawthorn hedges wouldn't bloom until May.

"So, what do you think of your new business on Pine Cone Lane?" Candee asked.

"Everything is brilliant, absolutely brilliant," Kathleen lied effectively. Sometimes white lies were best to hide her reservations because the place wasn't nearly as brilliant as all that.

In its heyday, the former greasy-spoon diner had served countless meals, the floors and countertops spic and span. However, it had been boarded up in recent months, which was why she'd snagged the place at a steal before the building went into foreclosure.

With a silent groan, she estimated the number of weeks it would take to sand and repaint, outfit the kitchen and hire staff, and the numerous unexpected details that would surface.

She came up with months, not weeks, although she reassured herself there was no point in olagonin'—whining and complaining—because it only made things more difficult.

However, since she'd arrived in America, being anxious had become her forte.

The long weeks of anticipation and tension had taken their toll and kept her awake at night, and she could think of nothing she'd like better than a tub soak with the lavender soap she'd brought from Ireland. Followed by a lengthy, leisurely nap.

Resignedly, she knew a nap would be out of the question for a long time.

Perhaps forever.

She paused to stand back, surveying the building. If she thought objectively rather than with her emotions, she understood that she wouldn't be able to accomplish everything by herself, especially within a five-week timeline.

She'd scheduled her grand opening on St. Patrick's Day, deeming the date fitting and appropriate.

She envisioned painting the shingles a serene shade of soft-green, overstated by a burgundy-striped canvas awning, much like the awning gracing The Ground Café, her former employer's coffee shop in Dublin. And she wanted outdoor seating on the patio, allowing customers to dine at wrought iron tables beneath vintage-style Edison light bulbs.

Curb appeal. That's what the place needed.

She focused on which project she would dive into first—the interior or the exterior.

She was weighing the pros and cons when Candee asked,

"You're not having second thoughts about moving to America, are you? I realize it's a huge undertaking."

"Of course not," Kathleen said. "Ireland was getting a little too small for me."

At thirty-five years old, her mantra had become *pursue my dreams or bust*. Besides, it was too late to check out, things being what they were. Her former coworkers knew she was embarking on a refreshingly different chapter in her life, and it would be disheartening to admit defeat.

Kathleen fidgeted with the gold watch on her wrist, a going-away gift from her employer, Danny Brady. "Also," she continued, "baking and the restaurant trade are second nature to me. I've spent half my life managing a coffee shop."

Candee covered Kathleen's hand. "Sometimes a fresh start is as simple as buying a dilapidated building and getting on an airplane."

"Did I say that?"

"Oh, and much more, because you not only said it, you did it," Candee said. "You've created your dream life."

Kathleen shook her head. "I used to be smart and sensible."

"In the present circumstances, you're even smarter," Candee said. "And you're strong and beautiful. The first time we Skyped, I couldn't get over how put together you were. You'd already composed a business plan."

Kathleen offered a brittle smile. "Don't believe everything on your computer screen."

"Positive thinking, plus action, leads to accomplishment. You're a doer."

"Despite what my so-called friends advised," Kathleen replied.

"Weren't they supportive?"

"Aye, in a polite sort of way. They gave me rock-hard, unsolicited advice." For some reason, her thoughts kept darting back to Ireland, and a sense of isolation rolled through her. "They wanted to protect me from making a mistake."

She longed to tell someone about the successful closing of her new property, the deep-blue sky gracing the warm Carolina days, the way the sweetgum tree branches swayed in the pleasant morning breezes.

But there was no one to tell. Danny and his wife, Clara, were busy with their own lives, with a wee one on the way.

"You'll love Roses, and I predict your teahouse will become a tea emporium," Candee said.

"What in the world is that?"

"An emporium is a retail store selling a variety of goods."

"I plan to serve food—Irish tea and scones, sandwiches and cakes. I'm not a chain of fancy shops."

"Well, you should be. Also sell tea and teapots, because you and Roses are poised for success. I can feel it."

Kathleen smiled. Aye, Roses was enchanting. The once sleepy town was thriving, and the lush green grass packed neatly between the brick sidewalks reminded her a wee bit of Ireland.

Except that it wasn't …

Remembrances of lyrical brogues brought a poignant yearning to Kathleen's chest that stopped her cold. She hadn't realized she'd be so homesick. With her accent, she'd already found that oftentimes her words got misheard and misunderstood, and she'd had a hard time communicating even though everyone spoke the same language—English.

"This area will get a lot of foot traffic, especially on warm spring and summer evenings," Candee said. "Here in the Carolinas we enjoy a temperate climate, so don't rule out winter or fall, either."

"Unlike Ireland." Kathleen chuckled.

"Does it truly rain buckets?"

"Our term is bucketing down," Kathleen said, repeating the standard Irish joke. "Although the rain is at least warm in the summer."

Candee laughed. "Is it windy?"

"Not much." Kathleen lifted her shoulders in a teasing shrug. "Except small children and pets are sometimes blown clear away to England."

"Believe me, you'll enjoy the weather here," Candee concluded with a laugh. Gently, she urged Kathleen to the diner's doorway.

Kathleen blinked at the dazzling noon sunlight and realized her stomach was growling. She hadn't eaten anything except a slice of her homemade Irish brown bread when she'd woken at six a.m.

"What do you think of your upstairs apartment?" Candee asked. "Internet photos don't do a place justice, but housing above your teahouse is a money saver. You won't have to pay rent nor commute."

"Aye. Although truth be told, it's all in a little worse shape than I expected."

"Manageable, though, I trust?" Candee's puzzled frown swung from the door to Kathleen. "I realize it needs curtains."

"It lacks a lot more than updated curtains," Kathleen said with a laugh. "And it will take an army of crewmen to get everything in working order by St. Patrick's Day."

"My husband, Teddy, is a contractor. He'll get the place turned around for you in no time." Candee shook back a strand of red hair that had come loose from her braid, exposing a pair of gold cross earrings, the only jewelry she wore except for her wedding rings. Even without an ounce of makeup, the woman was stunning, her green eyes gleaming whenever she discussed her husband and their adopted son, Joseph.

In addition to being a Realtor, Candee had opened an afterschool daycare facility in her home for disadvantaged children in the community. On several occasions, Kathleen wondered how Candee was able to do it all. She'd been inspired to match her stamina and ambition.

"As long as there's running water, a kitchen and a bathroom in my apartment," Kathleen said, "my needs are met."

"Good. Your reference from Danny Brady was excellent, by the way."

"I never missed a day of work."

"And he said your brown bread flew off the shelves whenever it was featured."

"He granted me the option to take my recipe to America, and I ran with it."

"Free and clear?"

"Danny understood I was drained. After countless years as his head assistant, I wanted a change." Kathleen wished the warmth burning her cheeks didn't give her away. Why couldn't she compartmentalize her second thoughts like she did everything else in her life?

Because she was excited.

And mildly terrified.

"I expect he and his wife will come to America and visit me someday," she finished.

Candee studied her. "So, at present, you're alone."

"Aye." Kathleen considered saying more, to explain she always felt lonely despite her attempts to build relationships.

She kept her lips sealed. Some words were better left unsaid.

In a little over two years, she'd been duped by a man not once, but twice. First, by a moneyed Italian she'd met on the internet who had turned out to be, surprise, surprise, a young boy. And then, Alexander, an American businessman, had played her for a muppet—a fool.

Danny Brady and his bodyguard, Ian, had said Alexander was too talkative. Talkative? Hah! What an understatement! Charmer was more like it, and Alexander was so smooth-talking he could sell ya an eye out of your own head. He'd had her believing he was genuinely interested in her. When she'd fallen for him, his charisma had changed to controlling. He'd quickly become domineering and expected her to be subservient.

As Candee continued to study her, Kathleen offered, "The man I believed I loved was actually two different men. He was fine as long as things went his way and I was passive." She shrugged and tried to act unconcerned. "Although being submissive isn't in my nature. As I advanced in my career, our relationship quickly fell apart."

"You said you wanted a fresh start, and you've created it. Here's to new men and extraordinary opportunities." Candee gestured to the doorway.

"I'll take the opportunities minus the men," Kathleen said. Truly, she was done with con men, eejits—idiots—who expected women to take a back seat to them and their opinions. Men who exuded personality while keeping a close watch on their own agendas. Men who fired off derisive comments for no other reason than to feel superior.

She was a woman who had helped Danny Brady's Ground Café achieve fame. Here and now, with determination and hard work, she'd make her teahouse a noteworthy addition to this quaint little town.

"During our Skype sessions, I mentioned that your teahouse will offset Keiran O'Malley's Irish pub nicely." Candee pointed to a side street. "His building isn't far from here."

"Keiran's cousin, William, first spoke of Roses and recommended you as a Realtor, which is why I messaged you,"

Kathleen said. "Fortunately, I zoomed in on this town fairly quickly."

"William lives in Dublin, right?"

"He also knows Sean, my coworker from The Ground Café. Both men wanted to date me, and I turned Sean down flat."

"And William?"

"He frequented the café a couple times a week. We dated for a short while after my breakup with Alexander until I realized I wasn't ready for a romantic involvement." Kathleen swallowed, giving herself a breather before continuing. "Sean still texts me now and then. He wishes to come to America to help me with my new business."

"Is that a good thing or a bad thing?"

"I'm not certain. Sean is competent, but I can't imagine he'd actually fancy working for me. He and I were on the same level as managers." She exhaled. "At any rate, William had told me that Keiran loves it in Roses."

"He's married to my sister, Desiree. They are extremely happy."

"I've heard."

Happy. Such an elusive term.

"Keiran said that life called him back to Roses. Maybe the town called you here too."

Kathleen reflected on Candee's words. She'd read about life's calling in self-help books and tuned in to endless podcasts on the subject. Sometimes, it seemed like she'd waited her entire life for a voice to explain which bend in the road led to happiness.

Nevertheless, if one's calling was a voice whispering in her ear, she hadn't heard a sound. Perhaps a calling was the Lord tapping her on the shoulder. Either way, she'd known in her gut that Roses was the ideal spot, and everything had clicked into place.

"In any case, here I am," she replied.

Candee opened her arms, firmly clasping them around Kathleen. "And this is the dawn of the grandest adventure of your life."

Tears welled in Kathleen's eyes—a mix of joy, fear, and reservations. She'd chosen her destiny, following in the footprints of the Irish immigrant.

Don't be an eejit, her inner voice chided. *You're launching a teahouse, not fleeing from a potato famine.*

"And I can't wait to introduce you to everyone," Candee said. "Desiree and Keiran, my husband Teddy, and our son, Joseph—"

"Aye. When the time comes." Now she was sounding standoffish.

She drew a see-through container from her leather shoulder bag. "Before I forget, I baked a loaf of my brown bread for you this morning."

Candee stepped back. "You haven't been here two days and you're already baking bread in your apartment?"

"I ran the oven before I even unpacked." She handed the container to Candee. "This is a thank-you gift for taking care of the million incidentals that came with an international real-estate transaction. And, for fixing up my apartment before I arrived."

"My pleasure. Decorating is my thing, and you advised me on your likes and dislikes. In fact, you were quite decisive."

"I don't have much of a knack for it."

"Oh, but you do."

Kathleen envisioned the packing boxes strewn throughout her flat's hallway, the luggage and clothes piled by her bed. She should have put away her belongings a while ago. Instead, she'd drawn on a ruffled apron, let a batch of dough rise, and baked.

"Take a bite," she urged.

Candee obliged, closing her eyes as she nibbled. "This bread is one of the best baked goods I've ever tasted. And that's saying a lot, because my friend in Miami owns ..."

"I plan to sell Irish brown bread every day," Kathleen said, grinning broadly at the compliment. "Although I'll need to sell more than bread."

"What about pizza?" Candee asked.

"I'll leave pizza to the pizzeria in town. Presently, I'll turn my energy into outfitting the bakery with delicious Irish desserts and an array of tea selections. In Ireland, people aren't in such a hurry. We savor every moment, and I intend to create the same experience in my teahouse."

"Unlike America," Candee said.

"Comfy couches and free Wi-Fi," Kathleen went on. "Brewed tea in a variety of flavors—chamomile, mint, and a host of exotic herbal leaves."

Her ideas overflowed. Were they too ambitious?

"Have you set your hours?" Candee stooped down at the doorway, muttering about the weather stripping not being sufficiently tight to prevent air leaks.

"I'll open at eleven, and close by nine at night."

"You realize you're describing ten-hour work days?"

"Aye." Like a shot, Kathleen's brain worked rapidly. "I'm still on the lookout for locally sourced ingredients so I can serve healthy salads, sandwiches, and wraps. For dinner, stone-baked pita bread topped with goat cheese and caramelized onions will be a nightly special."

Candee linked arms with Kathleen and walked to the side of the building, where rickety exterior stairs led to the second floor. "What you're describing is enough work for twenty people. And that pita bread sounds a lot like pizza."

"It's Irish pizza, so no competition with the local pizzeria." Deciding on her menu options, Kathleen hardly realized

Candee had come to a determined stop while saying a man's name twice.

Rob. Rob.

"Who is Rob?" Kathleen asked.

"He's a dear friend and owns a string of popular bakeries." For some reason, Candee's pitch heightened. "His chain is called Rob's Marvelous Muffins and is based in the Miami area where he lives. He's delightful and funny and easy-going—"

"Brilliant, I'm sure." Kathleen went back to the menu choices in her mind. Irish bacon and poached eggs, or a traditional Irish breakfast complete with roasted tomatoes and mushrooms? Perhaps beef burgers and cider glazed salmon for lunch.

No. She reined in her thoughts. This wasn't a full-scale restaurant.

"I'll begin advertising for employees soon and start with a modest staff," she said, "Did I tell you I won't be serving alcohol?"

"Yes, and I applaud your decision."

"Thanks. I've had enough of that in Ireland. People going out on the lash and stumbling home in the wee hours." Kathleen waved a dismissive hand. "I'll leave the drinking to the pubs."

She looked back on the intervention Clara Brady had staged for her alcoholic brother, Seamus. Little good that had done. Once a person was addicted, it was often a long road to wellness.

"What are the requisite number of ovens for a bakery?" Candee asked.

"Certainly a small commercial oven, plus a full-size convection oven is necessary. Also, a deck oven for layer cakes and breads." Kathleen frowned as she considered all the equipment yet to purchase. "Where will I buy a mixer and a—"

"You'll need someone knowledgeable to advise you. Fortunately, Rob has extensive retail bakery experience. He studied at a prestigious culinary school in Florida offering lots of hands-on experience." Candee plucked her cell-phone from her purse. The excitement in her voice matched the glow in her eyes. "He was voted Miami's most successful entrepreneur, and he's just the right person to help you."

Whoever this Rob was, he'd be overwhelmed when he saw what needed to be completed in five weeks.

Unless, of course, he was a miracle worker.

CHAPTER 2

"Rob's Marvelous Muffins." Realizing both hands were a sticky mess from rolling out pastry dough, Rob Taylor answered his cell-phone, then balanced the phone against his shoulder. His gaze landed on the commercial mixer on the counter. He switched it on to prepare twenty batches of cupcakes.

Mondays weren't usually hectic, but with Valentine's Day over and the forthcoming St. Patrick's Day holiday, baking green cupcakes galore became the blueprint of the day.

Pushing out a sharp breath, he wiped his hands on the white apron tied around his protruding waist, trying to remember how many cupcakes he'd tasted that morning. One. Well, no, at least two. Okay, three, although the third had lacked his bakery's signature Irish Cream liqueur glaze.

He eyed that same liqueur set near several pounds of unsalted butter by the commercial mixer, ticking off the items on his to-do list. Next, dozens of cupcakes needed frosting.

A diet was in order, but he'd made peace with that long ago. A man owning a half-dozen bakery shops couldn't resist the smell of mouth-watering chocolate, succulent blueberry, or tart lemon muffins. At least, *he* couldn't. And there was nothing to do except, well, keep tasting.

"Rob, are you there? Hi. It's Candee."

He grinned. "How's my favorite daughter-in-law?"

"Umm, are we all of a sudden related?"

"Your husband is like a son to me." Rob silently motioned one of the bakers to shut off the timer going off on a convection oven. "So if Teddy is my son, then you're my daughter-in-law."

"I've always loved your logic, Rob." Candee chuckled. "How's the muffin business?"

"Busy. Can't complain." He muffled the phone as an employee wearing a company hat and sporting nonslip clogs ran past looking for the espresso. The featured cupcake was a combination of flour, sugar, espresso, and that Irish Cream liqueur.

"How is everyone in Roses?" Rob asked. "Is the weather warm in the Carolinas? The temperature is in the mid-seventies here in Miami."

"We're all well. It's a pleasant, sunny day and quite typical for February. Teddy sends his love." Candee paused. "Can I ask you something?"

"Anything, my lovely daughter-in-law."

"What are your views on helping a damsel in distress?"

"Like in the original silent movies where the villain wearing a top hat ties the woman to the railroad tracks? What was that guy's name again?"

"Snidely Whiplash. And no, I mean a beautiful woman needs your help."

"Wait. Who in Roses ..." Rob stopped in the middle of his sentence. "I assume you're not referring to yourself."

"Correct."

"Okay then. Who? And why me?" He glanced at his wristwatch. The lunch-hour crowd would be flooding into the bakery soon. Mentally, he estimated the hundreds of cupcakes required to refill the soon-to-be-empty display cases.

"Because you're a professional baker," Candee said. "Plus, you're a perfect gentleman."

"I appreciate the compliments, but where are we going with this conversation?"

"Do you remember my telling you about Kathleen, an Irishwoman from Dublin? She managed The Ground Café."

"Actually, I do," Rob said. "That coffee shop chain recently opened in the States."

"At the time, Kathleen was considering relocating to Roses and starting a teahouse. Well, all that talk became a reality."

Vaguely, he recalled the discussion from a few months earlier. "Congratulations. She made it over the pond okay?"

"Yes, and she's enthusiastic and vivacious and—"

"Good. Wish her luck." He paused to bark instructions to David, a new employee plunging a rack of croissants into a roll-in oven. David had been recommended by a friend of a friend, and Rob had hired him on the spot. High employee turnover and a shortage of staff left him no choice. Too bad the kid hardly looked eighteen, his checkered trousers a size too big for his skinny body, a white torque hat overpowering his small head.

According to his application, David was twenty-something.

Either kids were looking younger, Rob mused, or he was getting older.

"Don't take shortcuts," he directed the newbie. "Check the oven temperature again."

"Yes, Mr. Rob," the newbie acknowledged with a slight bow.

"Do I look like the king of England?" Rob held up a hand, palm up. "Check the temperature, or I'll have you clear out the moat around the bakery."

David gave Rob a blank look and scurried away.

Rob eyed the liqueur. He was inclined to grab the bottle and pour himself a large glass.

Clueless. This next generation was absolutely clueless. Surely the kid realized there was no moat.

The clanging of a pan had him cupping the phone to his ear. "Sorry, Candee. I'd like to chitchat, but it's busier than I anticipated today. Can I call you back tonight? Or better yet, in April."

"Things won't be busy in April?"

"I forgot Easter is in April. Maybe May."

"Isn't Mother's Day in May?"

"June. We'll say June." He ran an irritated hand over his bald head and sighed. "June is the month for weddings. Apparently, a baker's job is never done."

"Coincidentally, Rob, she's a baker too."

"Who?"

"Kathleen. The Irishwoman."

"Right. As we've established, so am I. Tell her cheers, or whatever those Irish people say, and to prepare to never sleep."

"She's lovely."

"Bravo."

"She baked me an Irish brown bread," Candee said. "Her special recipe, and it's delicious."

He slanted over the table to snap off the electric mixer before the over-mixed batter resulted in dense, gummy cupcakes.

"How delicious?" He tried to decide whether he should put the phone on speaker so that he could spoon the batter into tins, or grow a third hand.

"How delicious compared to your cupcakes?" Candee asked.

"Yeah."

"Her bread is the best baked good this side of the Atlantic."

Whoa. Compared to his award-winning cupcakes? Rob frowned and held out a hand to stop an employee from rushing over to him.

"Hold on," he said to Candee. He laid his phone on the counter, yanked off his apron, and stalked to a quiet spot by a window. "Okay, I'm back."

"She is overwhelmed," Candee said. "Relocating to a different country, launching a business from scratch … I can't imagine how she'll accomplish everything. Do you recall the broken-down diner on Pine Cone Lane? It's been unoccupied for a while."

"The diner is located not far from Keiran's pub, right?"

At his mention of Keiran, Rob rubbed a hand over his eyes. Perhaps he should tell Candee how guilty he felt that he'd been unable to attend the grand re-opening of O'Malley's, the pub Keiran had inherited from his father. Although Keiran and his wife, Desiree, had assured Rob they understood he couldn't leave Miami during the middle of an extensive baking exhibition, he'd missed being in Roses to support them.

"Good memory, Rob," Candee said. "And Kathleen intends to create an old-world teahouse. The problem is the place is screaming for a total remodel. She's experienced, but—"

"What can I do?" Rob conjured up the image of a cherubic, delicate Irishwoman. Slight and fragile, with flaming-red hair and freckles, staring wide-eyed at an undertaking far too large for her.

"You have the expertise and bakery know-how," Candee said.

"Does she need capital and an investor?" Understanding that all new restaurants were under-capitalized, Rob automatically reached for his wallet. A foolish move, he realized, unless cash flew through the phone lines. And even more foolish because he wouldn't see a return on his investment for three to four years.

"She needs advice and support," Candee said. "She's laser-focused on a St. Patrick's Day opening."

"Does she have a business license and sales permit?"

"All set. Fortunately, the diner was already permitted as a restaurant."

"Health and fire department permits?"

"Done."

"Is she making alterations to the building?"

"Major." For the first time, Candee hesitated. "Why?"

He peered out the window. The wrought-iron tables facing his bakery were filled with customers. Between the palm tree border outlining the seating area, low-flowering crepe myrtle trees added pops of vibrant pink blossoms. The effect created a natural arbor, and shade from the bright Florida sun. If customers were comfortable, they tended to stay longer and buy more baked goods.

"She'll need a building permit and possibly a parking permit," he said.

"Good point. I'll check into it."

"Does her business have a name?"

"Kathleen's Teahouse, and the sign is being designed as we speak. She's keeping true to the logo of the old diner. And she's planning to be open ten hours a day and serve break-fast, light lunches, and dinner, as well as tea and baked goods."

"She should add five hours to the beginning and end of

her shift for preparation and clean-up," he said. "Tell her to hire a lot of help, which is forever challenging. Bakery employees find the labor exhausting—both mentally and physically."

"Because of those hot ovens, and they're on their feet so much," Candee commiserated. "Anyway, it's my long-winded way of asking you to come to Roses and give her a hand."

He delayed his response, preparing to launch into a thousand reasons why he couldn't leave his bakeries at such a chaotic time.

"Rob," Candee said, "I know how busy you are."

"You read my mind."

"And I wouldn't phone you if she wasn't in such a bind. The woman is beyond desperate and the place is bleeding money."

Frowning, he strode to the counter and took a sip of the liqueur directly from the bottle. There were plenty of other bottles in the storage room, he rationalized.

"She can email me. No charge for free advice," he said.

Silence on the other end of the phone. Oops. Maybe he'd sounded a little too harsh. A second glance at his watch revealed half past noon. The bakery would be overflowing with people.

He pondered. He hadn't been able to attend the opening of Keiran's pub. However, if he booked a quick trip to Roses, he could be back in Miami by Tuesday.

His bakeries were all closed on Sunday. He'd made the decision since going back to church. It was a religious choice, and a way to honor God.

"You can stay with me and Teddy," Candee pressed. "It will give you an opportunity to see Joseph, the beagles, and Joseph's horse."

The trip made perfect sense. He'd visit with everyone, plus extend his expertise to the Irishwoman. Furthermore,

Roses was absolutely delightful in its slow-paced, countrified way. It would be good to get out of Miami's rat race for three days. Lately, he'd felt exhausted both emotionally and physically.

"Maybe you're right," he murmured.

"Fabulous," Candee said. "You'll love Kathleen. She's all Irish wit and charm. Trust me, you'll want to listen to her brogue all day."

For some reason, Rob felt a little toss of excitement.

Why?

This trip was about a hurried getaway, not meeting an Irishwoman with milky-white skin who brewed perfect cups of tea. She couldn't possibly deal with all that owning a bakery, teahouse, and full-fledged restaurant entailed, so he'd set her straight.

If she was the determined type, she'd remain in Roses, although it was more likely she'd high-tail it back to Ireland before the end of March.

"So when did you say you were arriving?" Candee asked.

"Can Teddy pick me up at the Asheville airport?"

"Absolutely."

Rob took another swig of liqueur. "I'll fly out early Sunday morning, because Saturday is a high-volume day. I'll attend church services on Saturday evening here in Miami."

"Hurray," Candee said with a joyous laugh. "We'll do the same. See you soon."

He started to say more, then stopped, bidding goodbye and clicking off the phone.

How had he been talked into something so quickly?

Truth be told, he was intrigued. This Irishwoman displayed grit by leaving everything behind and coming to America. He guessed she was probably homesick.

He braced a hand on the window sill and stared at the roll-in oven, where smoke was emerging.

"Mr. Rob, do you think the croissants are finished baking?" David, the newbie, asked.

"Did you set the timer?"

"No." David rummaged through a stack of boxes near the oven. "Where is it?

"Do you smell smoke?"

"A little."

"I'd say the entire batch is burned." Rob handed the newbie two oven mitts and snapped a string of instructions. The young man paled and promptly complied, apologizing because it was all his fault.

Rob agreed.

Mitts at the ready, David opened the oven door to a large quantity of burned croissants. He cursed, then swung around. "Are you going to fire me on my first day, Mr. Rob?"

"For cursing?"

"Because ... because the croissants are burned."

"I'll give you another chance because I like you."

With that, Rob pushed open the adjoining door to his bustling bakery. Fortunately, no one realized that under his gruff exterior, he was really a marshmallow.

CHAPTER 3

$\mathcal{T}$he following Sunday, Rob stepped off the plane at the modern Asheville airport. He and Teddy exchanged greetings with a clap on the back.

Now that he'd arrived, Rob checked his phone for messages. Although his bakeries weren't open, he oversaw a skeleton crew as they prepared products and ingredients for Monday.

Freeze the stock we selected before you punch out, Rob texted his associate manager.

Roger, his manager replied.

Roger? Really? Who said that? Wasn't the term used for radio communication?

Teddy chuckled, eyeing Rob's exasperated sigh. "I don't miss those days."

"Of slaving over a hot oven? I wish I could say neither do I, but I'm still baking after all these years. Sometimes I wonder if I should sell everything and move to Hawaii."

"Or the Carolinas," Teddy suggested.

"You're always trying to convince me to relocate here."

"I'm simply fulfilling my role as your best friend, and

friends like to be near each other. For camaraderie. And support."

The men had been chums for years. A decade earlier, they'd met at a men's cooking class. Rob had discovered he loved baking and pursued a culinary arts degree. Upon graduation, he'd opened a prosperous bakery chain. Teddy decided he didn't want to be in charge of all that dough (he'd quoted the pun from Julia Child), and, with Rob's capital, became a real estate professional and flipped homes.

After Rob retrieved his luggage, he and Teddy settled into Teddy's pickup truck. Morning sun lightened the sky, and the beauty of North Carolina—from the majestic waterfalls to an old-fashioned swimming hole—brought a sense of relaxation.

"Beautiful state, isn't it? Candee and I love it here," Teddy said.

"Yeah. I may rent a car for an afternoon trip tomorrow."

"You won't be able to explore everything in a few hours, so file it under your list of reasons to move here."

"I don't have a list of reasons," Rob said.

"You should." A grin flashed across Teddy's features. "The other day, Candee read a travel brochure advertising outdoor dining by a pool of water in Asheville. She also cited many art galleries tucked away in little towns within an hour's car ride of Roses."

"Sightseeing it is, then."

"I'd go with you, but I'm tied up with renovating the teahouse, plus helping Candee with her daycare facility. And, needless to say, seeing to Joseph. I assume you'll go by yourself?" Teddy asked.

"Who else?" Rob laughed gruffly. "I can't remember when I last toured anywhere with a companion." He drew down the mirrored sun visor for a quick glance at his reflection, keenly studying the lines of fatigue around his mouth. He was closing in on fifty years old, and the strained creases were showing.

"Frankly, you seem like you need an extended vacation, my friend."

"Uh-huh. Thanks for the advice." Rob flipped up the visor, then smoothed the wrinkles on his Rob's Marvelous Muffins T-shirt. He'd worn the shirt under a navy sport jacket paired with khaki pants. A white cotton square handkerchief showed from his breast jacket pocket.

"I thought my age looked good on me, although I don't see as well as I used to." He chuckled. "Get it?"

Teddy grinned. "I can always count on you for the one-liners. I'm glad you're here. I wish you looked more rested."

Dismissing his fatigue with a wave, Rob replied to a sequence of text messages.

Teddy flicked on the blinker and merged onto the road leading to Roses. "Mind if I ask you a question?"

"Not at all," Rob replied, still absorbed in his text messaging. "I'm perfectly willing to listen. I won't guarantee an answer, though."

"When have you ever actually relaxed?"

Not in forever. Rob didn't share that fact with Teddy, as he'd probably encourage Rob to extend his stay. Although he might be tempted, his bakeries could never operate without him.

"It's high time you enjoyed life," Teddy said. "Worrying about every minute decision will only magnify your problems."

Rob paused, reflecting how best to answer. He switched on the radio to the Bee Gees singing "How Deep Is Your Love".

"Since when have you become so philosophical?" Rob asked.

"A wonderful woman changes a man." Lightly, Teddy

261

tapped the beat of the song on the steering wheel. "Makes him stop and think about what's truly important."

A ping on his cell-phone drew Rob's attention. His manager asked whether to close an hour later in order to customize a cake for a last-minute wedding.

If you need extra time to get the job done, then sure, Rob texted.

You'll be paying the staff overtime, the manager reminded.

What else is new? With that, Rob snapped his phone shut and jammed it into his pocket. He felt his blood pressure rising. A visit with his physician had confirmed that blood pressure medication would soon be a part of Rob's future. For the time being, he'd refused the brigade of medicines his doctor was all too willing to prescribe.

"That nice-looking Irishwoman might make the ideal companion on your sightseeing excursion," Teddy said. "She hasn't explored the area yet, either."

"Not interested. You and Keiran married the last two good women on the planet."

"There's more than two good women in the world, Rob. And a third is waiting for you to sweep her off her feet."

"Based on the number of my failed dates, a successful match for me is probably somewhere on a remote island in the Pacific. And because I'm not vacationing in the Pacific islands anytime soon, I'd say my dating days are over."

"I don't believe that for a minute." Teddy's expression puckered into a pensive frown, and Rob was reminded of Teddy's older brother, Christian, who had died in a horrific car accident. Teddy had stepped in and gained legal custody of his young nephew, Joseph.

Like his brother, Teddy was dark-eyed and tall, and Rob knew Teddy mourned the loss of his brother every day. Teddy and Candee were exemplary parents, raising a child who had been left frail and devastated after the accident.

Fortunately, hours of physical therapy and boundless love had enabled the boy to rebound triumphantly.

"No wonder we never got along," Rob teased. "You're an eternal optimist."

They flew across a bridge, and crushed gravel crackled beneath the truck's tires.

"You'll find your special woman when you least expect it," Teddy said.

Really? Who? He was older now, bald, twenty pounds overweight, and set in his ways. Anyway, bachelor life suited him.

He shifted in his seat. All those long nights in his deluxe Florida condo with a sweeping view of Miami beach had passed in solitude. He filled the void with work, because loneliness only crept up when he had time to think.

He dragged his contemplations away from self-absorption, preferring to stare out the window at the picturesque landscape with a magnificent Blue Ridge mountain backdrop. They traveled past an ancient church, fields of wildflowers, and a garden of violet irises beginning to bloom.

"Candee is preparing a special brunch for us," Teddy said. "Or rather, Keiran is cooking. Desiree hasn't purchased a dining room set yet, so everyone is assembling at my house."

Keiran had met Desiree when he'd been hired to fix up Desiree's Victorian home. They'd married a few months afterward and lived a few doors down from Candee and Teddy.

"Sounds perfect," Rob said. "I'm always up for a delicious meal."

"Be prepared for pandemonium. Our beagle, Kisses, is full grown. Plus, Candee gifted Keiran and Desiree a pup, and the dog goes everywhere with them."

"The more commotion, the better." Rob slanted his head

back, viewing a row of shuttered buildings. "What town are we in?"

"We're going through Hollan Farms. It's a few towns over from Roses."

"Interesting little place." Rob noted mediocre shops and an enormous hotel that dominated the main street. "Someone should give it some TLC. Does anyone live here?"

"At last count there were a few inhabitants. A major factory moved out a while ago, leaving a proverbial ghost town. I heard the entire town is for sale, and the asking price is several million dollars."

Not bad for a place with lots of potential, Rob mused. He was, after all, a businessperson.

A businessperson who could barely handle a half-dozen bakeries in Miami, let alone an entire town.

As they passed through, Teddy indicated the rotted wood on a boarded-up ice cream parlor, then focused a conspiratorial smile on Rob. "Don't even speculate about buying this town to renovate. You have enough on your hands, and should be slowing down to enjoy your wealth."

Rob chuckled. His friend was a mind-reader and knew him like the back of his hand.

"I have absolutely no intention of buying anything," Rob defended brusquely. When skeptical amusement crossed Teddy's face, Rob immediately changed the subject. "How is Keiran's pub?"

"The first few weeks were hectic. At present he's settled in and doing what he loves. Desiree took an extended leave from her law firm to hostess at the pub."

As they entered Roses, Teddy stopped at a crossroads and rounded toward Thompson Lane. The street was lined with trees, large older homes, and plenty of acreage. Window boxes overflowed with velvety purple pansies, ferns, and tulip bulbs, staying true to the traditional origins of the town. Teddy pointed out Keiran and Desiree's Victorian as they drove by.

"Ready to meet Kathleen after brunch?" Teddy eased his truck around the circular driveway and parked in front of his three-story house with its octagonal tower and multi-gabled roof. "Candee has immersed herself in Kathleen's business and vows to make it as popular as Keiran's pub. Too bad the place isn't open yet. Imagine when it is."

"All this Irish charm in one pint-size town," Rob mused. "Sure, I planned on meeting her."

"Excellent." Teddy grinned. "Because she's expecting you."

*　*　*

THAT AFTERNOON, Kathleen stood on her front stoop and watched a well-dressed bald man wearing a navy sport jacket and khaki pants emerge from Teddy's truck.

Her heart thudded with nervousness. The past few days, endless work had muddled the hours. Today she'd been awake before dawn, baking, attending church, and revising her business plan. She made a mental note to ask Candee if there were any local social media sites where she could advertise.

She'd heard so many stories about the legendary Rob and his marvelous muffins that anticipating his arrival had become an exercise in self-discipline. She flattened the collar of her checkered blouse, critically reviewing her navy-print slacks and sensible leather flats. The mint-green cardigan over her shoulders warded off the midafternoon chill.

She'd half-expected Rob to wear a chef jacket and black trousers, while brandishing a wooden mixing spoon. However, the man confidently striding toward her was solid and broad-shouldered, a warm smile crinkling his face and accentuating his electric-blue eyes. Instead of a wooden spoon, he carried a reflective silver wine bag.

"So you're the lovely Irish rose." He came to the doorstep, stopped within a foot of her, and beamed.

"And you're the famous Rob, who owns bakeries all over Florida."

"Only a half dozen, and they're all located in the Miami area." He grinned. "It saves me from driving all across the state."

"Well, I'll leave you two to get acquainted," Teddy called from his truck. "Rob, when you want a lift back to my place, text me."

"Thanks. Probably in a couple hours." Rob's wave to Teddy was quick before he veered to her. "However, I confess I'm at an impasse."

"A confession already? We just met."

"And an impasse."

She lifted an eyebrow. "Impasse?"

"Yes, because I may never want to leave." He extended his hand. "I'm Rob."

"I gathered. Why are you staring at me, Rob?"

"Because you're beautiful, and not at all who I expected."

Near the curb, she heard the purring of Teddy's truck engine.

"Who did you expect?" she asked.

"Not someone who makes me flustered because she's so gorgeous. I get tongue-tied around women like you."

"What?"

"Tongue-tied. At a loss for words."

"For a tongue-tied guy, you're speaking quite well, although I appreciate the compliment." She forced herself to stop and think. "*Was* that a compliment?"

"Absolutely. You remind me of Maureen O'Hara from *Miracle on 34th Street*."

"I love that film. Maureen was originally from Dublin and only twenty-seven years old when she played the role," Kathleen said.

She felt Teddy's gaze on them for another moment before the engine roared and he pulled away from the curb.

"I'm Kathleen, by the way." She accepted Rob's hand. Large and firm, he had the hands of a construction worker with calluses along the base of his fingers. From hours using a rolling pin, she surmised, because she had the same.

"The beautiful Kathleen." He gave a smile, and her heart skipped a beat.

She regarded him, trying to gauge if his words were sincere. She might have given a flippant response, the cool disinterest she employed whenever she suspected men were coming on to her. But wait. Was he—

No, certainly not. Aside from the age difference, he was accomplished and well-educated. She was a country girl who'd grown up in County Galway before moving to Dublin.

He let go of her hand, tugged a bottle out of the bag, and offered it to her. "This is for you. Do you drink Irish liqueur?"

"Tea. I drink tea." She examined the label. "Imported from Ireland?"

"Yes, although this bottle is from Miami. Consider it a housewarming gift. It's a little reminder of your country in case you were homesick."

How did he know she was homesick? A ripple of sadness brought a sting of tears to her eyes that she quickly blinked away.

His gaze fastened on her. "I use the liqueur as an ingredient for a cupcake glaze."

"Thanks."

"I like it," he said.

"Liqueur? Oh, I'm sure." She stuck the bottle in the bag

and set it on the stoop. "Most Irish men love a drink or two."
Or three or four.

"On special occasions?" Rob asked.

"On any occasion. Many were on the lash."

"Meaning?"

"Irish slang for going out drinking." Ruefully, she laughed.
"I've learned to stick with tea, though."

"In that case, so will I." That beam again, flashing
charisma, and firing an attraction inside her that took her
utterly by surprise.

"And I'll teach you how to create the best buttery glaze on
the East Coast," he said.

When, exactly? Candee had told Kathleen that Rob was
only in town until Tuesday. He was a wealthy, successful
man, setting aside a few days from his busy calendar. Most
likely he was overconfident, a tad entitled, and considered
his time more valuable than anyone else's.

"Like you, I'm also pressed for any spare hour these days,"
she said.

"Oh. Sure." He kept his beam. "I understand."

The appeal of his handsome face caused her pulse to leap,
and an awkward heartbeat went by. He waited, apparently,
for her to elaborate about the host of things she had yet
to do.

She didn't respond, just stared at him as if she'd never
seen a man before. She should invite him up to her apartment for tea. However, while she was usually neat as a pin,
the living room and bedroom were in dusty disarray and
boxes were everywhere.

"However, we have a dilemma," he continued.

So do I, she thought. Aloud, she asked, "Which is?"

"How will I prove who is the better baker if we don't bake
together?"

There it was. A not-so-silent gauntlet thrown down between two professional chefs.

Or did he propose more than a bake-off contest?

"We're together now," she pointed out.

"We're not baking. I can show you my cupcake recipe, the one crying out for my celebrated buttery glaze. I presume you store flour and sugar in your apartment's pantry?"

"Of course. I raced to the corner grocer as soon as I arrived in Roses."

"Good." He brought levity to the moment with another smile. "I've heard your Irish brown bread is fabulous."

Aye, they could bake, but she preferred to chat. Here, on her front porch, sitting on the two white wicker rocking chairs Candee had restored, enjoying a cheery afternoon.

Debating, she gazed at the park across the way. February in the South was being pushed to an early spring, and the flower bushes near her entryway displayed the first pink buds. Candee had assured Kathleen that a few more warm days and all the trees would be in bloom.

"Actually, I'm shattered," she said.

His thick eyebrows drew together. They were so close, she saw the threads of gray weaving between the dark hair.

"Exhausted," she explained. "More Irish slang. How about we just chat?"

"I'm up for that." He glanced at his watch, a high-priced brand she instantly recognized. "We can exchange classified information."

"This isn't Scotland Yard," she said. "And my commercial ovens haven't been installed yet, so I've been using the oven in my apartment to bake my breads."

"Will you show me around?"

She felt her cheeks heat. Her apartment? The setting was so intimate.

Aye, that was what he'd asked, and what she'd alluded to. The teahouse seemed the better choice, although kitchen equipment wouldn't begin arriving until Monday. And the large dough mixer was on back order. However, the vendor had assured it would arrive in plenty of time for her grand opening.

She shifted. She was fairly good at thinking on her feet and making quick decisions, but since Rob had arrived, the edges of the afternoon had blurred. Perhaps it was because she enjoyed being with him and hoped to impress him. Woefully, her place was the furthest one got from being impressive.

And he thought *he* was tongue-tied?

She rubbed her hands on her slacks, knowing he stared at her.

"Alright, then. Follow me upstairs," she said. "Before you arrived, I pulled loaves of my Irish breads and batches of scones out of the oven. I'd welcome your truthful opinion on the texture."

Rob seemed the kind of fella a woman could talk to. Despite his affluence, he seemed approachable. Who else wore a T-shirt advertising his company beneath a sport jacket?

She noticed there was no wedding band on the fourth finger of his left hand. Candee had offhandedly remarked he had never married. So he was alone in life, reminding Kathleen of herself.

"Lead the way, my beautiful Kathleen." He stepped nearer. "Have you ever sung, 'I'll Take You Home Again, Kathleen'? It's an Irish ballad."

"The song isn't Irish, Rob." She picked up the gift bag and ushered him around the building. "It has German-American origins."

"I memorized all the words. I'll sing it to you if you'd like."

Before she could answer, he belted out the melody in a

smooth tenor voice, slightly out of tune, warbling lyrics about a wild ocean and a bonnie bride.

She laughed out loud, and it felt good to laugh with a friend, with a man.

Somehow, as they ascended the stairs, she knew she'd always remember this afternoon. The soft, promising breeze on her cheeks, the glint of a dipping sun changing her Carolina world to a silky, golden glow.

And the appealing grin on Rob's features that engaged his entire face. Women could be completely charmed by a man whose emotions were so utterly apparent. He literally wore his sentiments on his sleeve, much like the Irish.

They made their way to the top of the stairs, and he took her free hand as if it were the most natural thing in the world. When they reached the landing, he belted out the second verse, *I'll take you to your home again, Kathleen.*

She joined him, and they sang in unison.

CHAPTER 4

*W*hen they reached her apartment, they walked directly into her narrow, cozy kitchen as the screen door banged shut behind them. The floorboards creaked as she hung his jacket on a coat rack in the foyer.

The scent of yeast and sugar flavored the air, and Rob sniffed appreciatively. She invited him to sit at a wooden breakfast nook, consisting of corner unit benches and a table polished in a natural white finish and trimmed in yellow.

"Bread lies at the heart of Irish baking," Kathleen said. Efficiently, she sliced Irish soda bread and went to work on a loaf of brown bread. "Before we eat, let's pray a simple thanks to God." She bowed her head, and he did the same. She whispered a blessing, then offered him a portion of each bread.

The brown bread's crust was thick, the texture dense. The soda bread sprinkled with caraway seed tasted like a biscuit. Although hard on the outside, the inside was moist and delectable.

"Wonderful. I like them both." He helped himself to

another two slices and washed them down with a bottle of water she'd pulled from the fridge.

"The trade secret is cooked raisins." She slid onto the bench across from him. "Save and freeze any leftover raisin water for a later batch. It will produce a sweeter flavor in the bread."

"I like trade secrets." *And he liked her.*

"Brown bread is a well-known Irish staple, so what I'm telling you isn't classified information. This bread is a treasured family recipe from my auntie Peggy."

Rob chewed and bobbed his head, encouraging her to continue.

"Auntie lived twenty days shy of her one hundredth birthday." Kathleen dashed tears from her eyes. "She was slim, walked everywhere all her life, and was witty and fun to be around."

"Do you miss her?" he asked quietly.

"Aye. She used to say that without a slab of brown bread every morning, no Irish kitchen is complete. In fact, you can't go into any pub or bakery without brown bread being on the menu."

"I've never visited Ireland." *Perhaps they could go together.*

"You'd love it." Wistfully, she sighed, although she didn't extend an invitation. "After drinking pints in a pub, this bread has saved my stomach at midnight on many occasions. Topped with a sliver of sharp cheddar cheese and heated in the broiler, it's delicious and not too heavy."

He carved another good-sized portion of bread for himself, slathered it with butter, and savored. Awe-inspiring. There were no other words for this woman's baked goods.

"I don't drink, and I'm old enough to admit I've learned a lot through the years," she said. "Giving up alcohol and nights at the pub were two of them. I've witnessed too much heartache. It's been estimated that at least half of all Irish drinkers are problem drinkers."

"Why such a large number?"

"The usual reasons." She looked away. "Affordability, ready availability, and heavy marketing."

"Are you referring to anyone in particular?" Gently cupping her chin in his hand, he directed her to face him.

"My employer, Danny Brady." She eased from Rob's grip, stood and surveyed a decorative ceramic platter in a glass cupboard before reaching for it. "Although not him, because he doesn't drink. His wife, Clara, has a brother who struggles with alcoholism." Kathleen's smoky eyes were remarkably expressive, filled with compassion. "Seamus was a dish-washer for a brief while at The Ground Café. He's been in and out of treatment programs since."

"How is he these days?"

She shrugged casually, a bit too casually considering her shoulders tightened. "Last I heard, he's back in treatment. Success rates for rehab are misleading and aren't as high as people expect."

"If you ever fancy a talk about Ireland, about anything, really, I'm a good listener," Rob said quietly.

"Fancy?" She reached beneath the end bench to a hidden storage unit and retrieved two sage-green place mats. "Is that an American term?"

"I'm trying out your Irish slang."

"*Fancy* is British English." She set the place mats on the table. "And I'll keep your offer in mind."

"Good." He broke the somber mood by gesturing to the counter overflowing with scones. Soon, he'd sampled her blueberry and plain scones baked to a golden-brown, proclaiming them exquisite. As Kathleen directed, he smeared a generous amount of butter and homemade straw-berry jam on each.

He grinned. He liked taking directions from her.

Lulled by her lyrical Irish brogue, he listened to her jokes about Ireland's rainy weather and ran his hand down the bench's smooth pine finish. She had a discerning eye for design—it showed in her comfy, appealing kitchen. A leafy English ivy plant hung by the window, a cobalt-blue toaster splashed color on the counter, and a hand-woven rug in a creamy blue weave complemented the tile floor with texture.

"I like your sense of style," he said. "You must enjoy interior decorating."

"Hardly. I find decorating one challenge I prefer to leave to professionals." A smile bloomed on her face. "Tea? I'll put the kettle on."

"Sure."

"You're supposed to say *no, thanks*."

"I am? Why?"

"Because that's what is expected in an Irish home. No worries. We'll try again." Squarely, she faced him. "Tea?"

"No, thanks."

"Brilliant." She grinned, waited a beat. "Tea?"

"What's the correct answer? Yes?"

She pressed her lips needle thin.

"Aye?"

"Have you suddenly become Irish?" she asked.

"No?"

"Third time's a charm. Let's try once more." She smiled. "Tea?"

"Yes. That would be lovely." He folded his hands on his lap and watched her uncertainly.

"Very good."

"Whew." Dramatically, he wiped his brow. "I feel like I almost failed an algebra exam. Should I have started with a *cheerio*?"

"*Cheerio* is another British term and means farewell. Are you leaving?"

"I just arrived." His gaze flicked to the platter of brown bread and he grabbed another slice. "I sought the magic word, and the word *cheerio* always comes to mind when I think of you Brits."

With a heavy sigh, she bent to pick a crumb from the floor. "I'm from Dublin, which is part of the Republic of Ireland. We're our own country and not part of the UK. Shall I enlighten you on the differences between Northern Ireland and the Republic of Ireland?"

He steepled his fingers. "Certainly. I'm quite interested."

"That's a refreshing change. In the States, this topic doesn't often come up."

"I told you I'm an excellent listener." *Good. Excellent. Same difference.*

She seemed to digest his words before she spoke. "Let's get back to our tea discussion, shall we? In Ireland, it's customary to answer *no thanks* twice when offered tea. It's impolite to say *yes* until the third ask." She took a breath. "Once more for practice. Ready?"

He gave a thumbs-up, considered including the word *aye*, but didn't.

"Tea?" she asked.

He held up one finger, then two, mouthing the numbers. "I assume I'm safe because this is at least the third try."

"It's actually the first because we were trying again," she said. "I'll let it pass, though."

"Then I'd love a cup of tea, thank you."

"Cuppa."

"Cup of."

She laughed. "Soon you'll get the hang of it. Are you ready for more questions?"

"Sure."

"Do you prefer milk and sugar? Or a squeeze of lemon?"

"My choice is black tea with lots of sugar." His mouth twitched in amusement as she approved. "I see you Irish take your tea quite seriously," he added.

"Aye, which is why I'd like to teach Americans how to serve a proper tea." She put water in a kettle and placed it on the stove. While waiting for the water to boil, she retrieved two china cups, saucers, and a matching creamer and sugar bowl embellished with blue flowers. She poured milk into the creamer, added lumps of sugar to the open jar, and arranged china and linen napkins on the table.

He considered telling her that if she spent that long preparing each customer's cup of tea, she'd never earn a profit. Instead, he wisely opted for keeping silent as she poured the boiling water into the teapot and their two teacups.

"This warms the pot and our cups," she explained. She waited a minute before discarding the water from the pot and cups into the sink. Then she added two tea bags into the teapot and poured in boiling water.

While he encouraged her to talk about her vision for the teahouse, they filled their plates with more bread. She kept an eye on her wristwatch in between nibbles. After three minutes, she removed the tea bags to an extra plate, stirred the tea, and glided onto the bench.

"First draw?" she asked, preparing to pour.

"I prefer a dark tea."

"Me too." Quickly, she added the tea bags back to the pot for another minute. "A favorite Irish expression is, *strong enough to trot a mouse in* for dark tea."

"Clever. I suggest you not use that expression around your customers, though."

"Mice in the kitchen. The idea would definitely keep patrons away." Her face lightened with wry laughter. "Did you realize the Irish aren't the world's biggest consumer of tea?"

"Who is? England?"

She shook her head. "Turkey, then Ireland, then the UK."

For the next few minutes, he considered voicing his views on buying and selling, and keeping an eye on profit margin. Because he was a competent entrepreneur, he assumed his advice would be welcomed with enthusiasm.

Painstakingly, she poured the tea.

"Thank you." He relished the rich, deep flavor and smiled. They sat silently for a few minutes, savoring their tea.

"If I opened a teahouse," he said, "I'd insert those attention-grabbing tidbits you shared about tea preparation on the menu. Items of interest will enhance your customers' experience and provide them with something to talk about beyond your delectable desserts."

"Maybe." She stared straight ahead while he sipped. Finally, she said, "I'm glad you like tea."

He hadn't said if he liked tea. In fact, he preferred coffee, even over this exquisite brew. But tea was apparently the Irish way, and he sat back on the wooden bench and warmed his fingers around the fragile china cup. Inhaling the fragrant steam, he plated another sliver of brown bread. "Candee was dead-on. Your baked goods are outstanding. And your scones—"

"Thanks. Coming from you, I'm flattered."

"My cupcakes and muffins aren't anywhere near as exciting as your Irish brown bread." He downed the rest of his tea. "I'm thinking about selling fancier pastries in my bakeries. Every one of them needs a face-lift, and foods not normally experienced in standard American shops might benefit sales. Currently, my blueberry muffins are customer favorites. Mind if I pick your brain for innovative European recipes?"

"Certainly. I'm delighted to share what I know." She placed her teacup on her saucer with a clink. "However, if you're turning a grand profit, which I assume you are judging from what Candee has said, why change anything? My ideas aren't any better than yours."

His instinct was to volley her comment back to her while reciting the adage *two heads are better than one,* or some such sage proverb.

However, that wasn't entirely true. The truth was, he wanted to spend time with her, because he could hardly tear his gaze away from her striking face, her delicate smile. She looked utterly gorgeous, her porcelain complexion flushed from a veil of steamy tea.

Mentally, he went over his flight details, suddenly loathe to leave Roses on Tuesday morning. Maybe he'd stay a few extra days, go sightseeing with her, dine with her at the farm-to-table restaurant Candee and Teddy raved about.

"Would you like to see Asheville with me tomorrow afternoon?" he blurted.

"I can't spare the time, although I'm sure Asheville is splendid." Kathleen busied herself with pouring another round of tea. "After March seventeenth, well, perhaps then. Although you don't live here so timing might be difficult."

"I come to Roses often."

"Do you?"

He'd come more now, even if it meant leaving his precious bakeries in the hands of his assistant managers. And to his amazement, he was okay with that.

"By plane, Miami to Asheville is less than a three-hour flight," he said.

"Rob—"

He couldn't gauge her expression beyond that one sharp word. Was she not interested? Preoccupied?

"I'm just saying," he said. "We can exchange phone

numbers, alright? In case you need to text me about anything."

"Sure." She gave him her cell-phone number.

He sent her a quick text. *Hi. I'm Rob. 1-800-IRELAND.*

Her smile expanded as she scanned his message. "What does that mean?"

"It means you can call me toll free anytime you need my help and never incur a charge."

She grinned. "I'll remember that. In the meantime—" her voice quieted, seeming to soften her refusal—"I want to stand out with an exceptional product so people will flock to my place. What do you judge to be the best …"?

So she sought his opinion after all, although she'd adeptly sidestepped any personal conversation. When they focused on shop talk, her eyes lit with enthusiasm.

And while they faced each other in her inviting kitchen, he realized something extraordinary. His heart, cold for so long, was thawing. He loved a woman with enthusiasm, and her obvious excitement about her business ignited her smile. He saw the evidence in her dark, gleaming eyes and the way she sat straighter, gesturing with her hands. Her grin widened, displaying white, even teeth. She was already striking. When she elaborated on her innovative concepts, she was altogether alluring.

In turn, she fanned a spark in him he thought had been extinguished long ago.

"… vegan baked goods using organic products," she was saying. "What do you think, Rob?"

What did he think about what? He'd been too preoccupied with gazing at her.

"Rob, were you listening?"

"Of course."

"What did I say?"

"You were mentioning using ground flax meal in your … scones."

"Aye, that was ten minutes ago."

"People are opting for a wider variety of choices, so consider customers' lifestyle choices when figuring out your menu." He searched his mind for topics he'd discussed with his managers through the years, and added, "Currently, I'm serving carbohydrates, fats, sugar, and caffeine in my shops, so obviously my menus are on the fattening side."

"It's all a balancing act, isn't it?" she asked.

"Life?"

"I was referring to food, but aye, I suppose life too." Pensively, she regarded him, then fished through a kitchen drawer and came back with two sheets of paper and pencils. "How about we combine taste with nutrition?"

We.

"Don't forget your bottom line," he said. "Otherwise, you'll be out of business within six months."

She seemed not to have heard him, intent on her list-making, mouthing the words as she penned them. "Crave-ability," she wrote with a flourish, then pursed her lips. "Is that a word?"

"It is now. And it's a good one."

"Are you interested in going over my business plan with me step by step?" she asked.

"Can I ask you a question first?"

"Aye."

"Have you begun interviewing applicants?"

"No. I'm running an ad in the local paper soon. If I get stuck, Sean, a coworker in Ireland, has offered to assist me."

"How generous," Rob said sardonically.

"He's a dependable manager, and versed in the restaurant business."

"So he's willing to quit his job in Ireland to fly here to help you?"

"Aye."

"There's plenty of suitable workers here in the US." Rob lifted his pencil off the paper. "Should I start listing my ideas?"

"Aye. Fill up the whole sheet."

A thought struck him. Actually two thoughts.

Without admitting it, she'd concurred that two brains were, in fact, better than one. And any comparing of recipes wouldn't be done that evening. He'd already established that anything baked in her oven came out superb.

He tapped his pencil while she wrote an extensive list in a scholarly penmanship he hadn't seen in ages. Nowadays, everyone typed on their computers.

Soon, her list crammed both sides of the paper.

She nibbled the end of her pencil. "This is too much," she murmured. "I'll never complete all these tasks."

"Have you considered prioritizing?" He skimmed the tasks and numbered them according to importance. "And let's pare down this list. You can do that, right?"

"Aye." She consented, humming a familiar Irish folk song, "Oh Danny Boy", under her breath, as she crossed out a word and added alternates.

Hours later, when he gazed through her sheer white kitchen curtains, a full, round moon sailed high in the sky. He glanced at his wristwatch in amazement. The hours spent with her had been nothing short of delightful.

She was a stunningly attractive woman. A woman who touched something powerful and unfamiliar inside him.

Lifting his cell-phone from his pocket, he texted Teddy.

Pick me up at ten, Rob typed.

Did your two hours change to six? came Teddy's reply. *Glad U R enjoying your evening. We were wondering what happened.*

Worried about me?

Always.

I'm fine, Rob typed.

More than fine.

Across the table, Kathleen smiled at him, and Rob's heart did a little meltdown.

Because she's remarkable.

Rob finished his message to Teddy and clicked send.

CHAPTER 5

*A*lthough he tried, Rob couldn't convince Kathleen to play hooky and accompany him to Asheville. She refused, and with good reason considering her opening date of March 17. Instead of sightseeing on his own, he shelved the idea until his next visit, assuring her that he was more than happy to assist her.

While she spent Monday morning securing a line of credit and visiting warehouses, Rob followed breakfasting with Candee and Teddy to lunching at O'Malley's pub, where he assumed head waiter relief for a harried Desiree and Keiran. Pleased the pub appeared busy and profitable, Rob walked the short distance to the teahouse.

Although spring hadn't technically arrived on the calendar, pale lavender crocuses burst through the soil in backyard gardens, and a lazy breeze swept across the grass. Rob plunged his hands into the pockets of his gray windbreaker, delighting in the fresh air against his face. Roses' weather made him feel more animated than he'd felt in ages. February and March were transitional months in Miami, heralding a brief spring before the intense summer heat arrived.

Admittedly, the bounce in his step had more to do with a certain Irishwoman than the temperate weather, his comfortable jeans, or tennis shoes.

As he strolled at a brisk pace, Rob mulled Kathleen's comment from the previous evening.

It's all a balancing act, isn't it?

Yes, he thought. You're so wise. For years, he'd sought to appease thousands of patrons—tweaking recipes, solving every complaint, adhering to the adage "the customer is always right". He'd been so focused on developing his business, he'd pushed aside any notion of personal happiness.

Love? Nope, not even a blip on his radar screen.

Armed with painful past experiences, he struggled to recall why love was so important—why poets wrote sonnets, why it made the world go round.

Because love was everything. Because love mattered above all else.

"Ridiculous notion," he whispered. Besides, he was too old for love. And Kathleen ... well, when he calculated their age difference, he came up with fifteen years.

Had it always been so clear, so straightforward, these unspoken rules for dating and romance? Certainly, problematic circumstances occurred, although Candee encouraged his interest in Kathleen. She'd sensed it immediately, sniffed it out like one of her beloved beagles. In fact, he and Candee had discussed Kathleen throughout breakfast while Teddy looked on with amusement.

Before Rob left, Candee suggested that Kathleen join them for an intimate evening get-together at her home.

"Don't forget to tell Kathleen dinner is at six," Candee reminded as Rob ducked out the door and settled into Teddy's pickup for a ride to town. "And, Rob, a May-December romance is just the thing when two people are so attracted to each other."

He'd given a brief nod, neither agreeing nor disagreeing, although he'd googled age-gap couples on the internet. Studies showed these couples were extremely happy despite social disapproval.

Still, he felt as if his searches let him down, as the findings had encouraged dreams he'd catalogued as unattainable. He wasn't about to fall in love with anyone, including the beautiful Kathleen. Anyone who knew him could recite his unsuccessful dating record. Regardless of his wealth and achievements, women left him flat, and it hurt more than he admitted. No woman chose a man with a retreating hairline (he was being kind to himself—the correct term was bald), and a waistline that increased with every passing year. More important, the sting of heartbreak was too steep an expense for a few weeks of happiness.

WHEN HE ROUNDED the last curve to the teahouse, Rob was out of breath from the final rise in the road. Beneath the overhang of the wide front porch, Kathleen paced impatiently, coming to a stop as if she'd sensed his arrival.

"Hi, Rob." She scratched the back of her neck, her shoulders tight. "I'm relieved you're here."

He puffed to a halt. "Anything wrong?"

"I'm waiting for a distributor to ring me about the oven delivery. I admit I'm terribly impatient. And the large dough mixer is still on back order."

"Sometimes things move slower in the South," he said.

"The same holds true for Ireland." She sighed heavily. "I've been known to snap at people if they're late. I don't want a reputation in the States for being rude. Folks in Ireland accused me of bad behavior on more than one occasion, and I was ashamed and apologized."

"You're a person who likes to get things done. I'm the same way."

Her shoulders relaxed. "Thanks for the assurance."

He caught his breath at the sight of her. That smile. Those deep-brown eyes. He knew he'd think about her every minute of his flight back to Florida. Pausing, he remarked favorably on the exterior of the building, the white glossy trim and exposed brick.

"Teddy's crew is painting the interior and exterior," she said. "He provided a generous bid I couldn't refuse. They started this morning and accomplished a lot already."

"What was his bid? Thousands of dollars?"

"He's offering the labor for free. I'm paying for materials."

"Another reason why I always liked him," Rob joked. He chased ideas across his mind. How could he top Teddy's generosity?

"Please, please come in," she said. The screen door groaned on its hinges as she guided him inside. He envisioned how the diner had been situated—the long counter and various booths were still waiting to be removed. The greasy cooktop hadn't been cleaned in years. On the walls were large black square marks where paintings had once hung.

"The place looks … good," he said. He searched for another word and couldn't find it.

She winced. "Surely, you're joking." She meandered, pointing out wet stains on the ceiling, bemoaning the former owner who had left the windows open, subsequently leading to water damage on the ceiling.

They stepped across the linoleum floor, coated in thick layers of dust.

Amidst the constant pounding of hammers, an Irish band played "When Irish Eyes Are Smiling" on a CD player.

Sounding as if the song had been recorded in a pub, the rousing chorus prompted Rob to sing along.

"You recognize this tune?" she asked.

"Doesn't everyone? Irish music is well-known around the world."

She grinned. "I'm proud to be Irish."

"And I'm proud to know you. You're a resourceful entrepreneur."

"You're a grand fella, just like Candee said."

He chuckled.

"Am I turning scarlet this very minute?" she asked. "For complimenting you?"

They stared at each other in comfortable silence. "A little," he admitted.

She burst into laughter. "Well, that's settled then. Crack on."

"Get to work?"

"Aye."

The blue vinyl seating had been torn out and sat in a heap by the back door. Gingerly, they stepped around it.

"I'm baffled about pricing the scones competitively and hope you can brainstorm with me," she said.

"I'll try, but I should warn you. As I grow older, I'm baffled more often than not."

"About scones?"

"About life in general."

She grinned. "Right, well, welcome to my life."

She had twisted her strawberry-blond hair into a semblance of a bun, securing the hairdo with pins and a shiny green ribbon. The pulled-back style accentuated her high cheekbones and dainty chin. Her wide eyes seemed too large for her refined features, and the swingy striped T-shirt and baggy sweatpants reflected her commitment to hard work, not to being a slave to the latest fashion.

Once at an empty booth, Kathleen plunged into ordering kitchen equipment, leaving little time for chitchat save for her sharp questions. He pulled off his windbreaker, rolled up his sleeves, and sat across from her.

"Tea?" she finally asked.

"Oh no. Will it be an all-day process?"

"Only a few minutes, I promise. And I'll take your answer as an *aye*." She climbed the interior steps to her apartment and came back carrying a tray chock full of stoneware—cups, a teapot filled with steaming tea, sugar and creamer, and scones from the previous evening.

Today she wasn't glamorous. Today she was simply breathtaking. Despite her flushed cheeks, her complexion was bone-white, revealing dark shadows under her eyes. Bound by the invisible strands of a strong work ethic, he'd later look back on the afternoon as the best he'd spent in decades.

In between her visiting with suppliers who stopped in and a meeting with a service rep, he inquired about her years as head assistant for Danny Brady. He even pressed for information about her dating past, to be sure no man waited for her in Ireland.

Her responses were vague, although she revealed she'd dated a couple fellas and discovered both were liars. Actually, she used the word *eejit*.

"These days, I'm embarrassed I was a stook for believing them," she said.

"*Stook* is another Irish word for idiot?"

"Aye." She wove her fingers together and glanced at the floor.

By late afternoon one of the ovens had been delivered, and the last of Teddy's crew packed his tools and left. She stepped over to a rusty sink to wash her hands for the umpteenth time, and Rob came beside her.

"I'm leaving tomorrow," he reminded. "I hope you'll join me for dinner tonight at Candee and Teddy's house."

She wrenched the faucet shut. "Is that an invite?"

"A sincere invite."

"I'm sorry." Her expression became pensive. "I wish, but I'm drowning here."

"I'm wishing too." He wished he could stay in Roses. Another day, another two days. She hadn't encouraged him, although he'd dropped several broad hints.

He decided to take matters into his own hands. He couldn't help himself.

Gently, he brought her to face him. Before she could reply, he bent his head and kissed her, a feather-light touch of his lips to hers.

She tasted of tea and sugar, her fragrance the subtle scent of lavender.

At first, she didn't move. When his hand curved around her back and the kiss deepened, she broke free.

"Obviously," she said, "we're not going to start dating."

"Why?"

"Because you live in Miami. And I live in Ire ... I mean, Roses."

"That's why they invented airplanes. And cell-phones."

She moved backward. "You, of all people, should know I'm not interested, given you've heard my dating history."

"So you dated a few guys who were rogues. Not all of us are like that."

"*Rogue* is a harsh word." Her reddish-brown eyebrows lifted. "Is the term American?"

"I've never used the word before. I assumed it was British, and I was trying to impress you."

"Irish. I'm Irish." She gazed at him and her smile came slow, lighting her heart-shaped face. She was delightful—part cherub and part tigress. His heart beat in double-time.

"My dating track record wouldn't win any awards, either," he said quietly.

She studied him.

Fearful she might feel sorry for him, an old guy, a desperate bachelor, he waved a hand indifferently. "I'm only telling you so we can commiserate."

"About love and romance?"

"About commonality. We both target accomplishment above all else."

"From the sounds of it, we're both workaholics."

The quiet lasted several beats, punctuated only by the drip, drip, drip of a tarnished faucet.

"You know, I could use someone like you in my bakeries," he said. "Someone energetic and organized."

"*Your* bakeries?" Her Irish brogue thickened. "In Miami?"

"Yes. You'd like Miami. It's—" He'd been about to say it was hot and humid before stopping himself. He certainly couldn't illustrate a Miami travel brochure if those were the only adjectives coming to mind.

She plunked her fists on her hips. "As you are certainly aware, I have my own business right here in Roses."

"How could I forget?" He tugged on his windbreaker. "We've dreamt up a million ideas about it all afternoon."

"Don't you understand? I need to do this on my own."

"I understand that you won't allow me to help you."

"By giving everything up? Why would you ask me such a question?"

Because he didn't want to leave her. And he couldn't just abandon his businesses. Hers was just starting up. Perhaps she could sell the diner. Or the teahouse. Or whatever she preferred to call it.

Thankfully, he kept his opinions to himself, for when he rotated, he confronted narrowed eyes and a stormy expression.

"You'd learn a lot," he said, "and I'd promote you to a manager in my flagship Miami bakery."

"Surely, you're joking. *Flagship* was my middle name in Dublin. Been there, done that."

"You won't earn a decent salary here for months, maybe even years."

Definitely the wrong thing to say, judging by the anger flashing from her dark eyes.

"Haven't you heard a word in all the hours we've spent together? My answer is no. Absolutely not." She spun and gathered up the stoneware, placing cups and teapot on the tray.

"What about this evening's invite?" he asked. "Candee and Teddy are expecting us."

"Tell them I'll probably see them tomorrow." She picked up the tray. "You may not live in Roses, Rob, but I do."

"I can stick around a few more hours. Really. I'll text Teddy and—"

"No. We're done here." Resolutely, she shook her head. "Enjoy the flight back to Miami and thanks for your help."

CHAPTER 6

The following morning, Kathleen was awakened by persistent hammering coming from the floor below her apartment. The sun poured into her bedroom window and she checked the time, knowing she'd overslept.

After a quick shower, she gulped some tea and hastened downstairs.

The five crewmen who greeted her caused her to stop short. All the scene needed was a foreman. As the word came to mind, Teddy appeared. In a lazy southern drawl, he adeptly guided the men to sheetrock, sand and paint. As he joked with them, she could hardly believe he ran such a large construction firm, because he was so laid-back.

Of course, the same held true for Rob. His winning smile was disarming, and he'd been heralded as Miami's most successful entrepreneur.

His dry humor was comfortable, cheerful, and concise. After he'd abruptly left the day before, her reflections continued to revolve around him. Not her business plan, nor her scones, nor a proper cuppa. Just him.

"Good morning, Kathleen." Candee waved from the

doorway of the back room. "Teddy and I came to see how your place is progressing."

Kathleen sucked in her bottom lip. "Good as gold, thanks to Teddy."

"It's a virtual circus around here, but a good sign because it means things are moving quickly."

"Aye." Kathleen fidgeted with the skirt of the apron she'd thrown over her jeans and charcoal-gray sweatshirt. She knew she looked a sight and slanted a glance toward the workers. By way of an explanation, she said, "I was experimenting with a new recipe for scones last night, and went to bed later than I planned."

"You're worn out."

"Knackered is the Irish word."

"Have you eaten breakfast?"

"Black tea."

Candee waved several brown bags in the air. "You must eat a decent meal or you'll fade away. Teddy and I brought you a typical southern breakfast, but I won't take credit for the cooking. Grits and eggs, buttermilk biscuits and sausage swimming in creamy white gravy, compliments of Keiran."

"Thank you. I haven't had the chance to meet him yet."

"As you're aware, he has family in Dublin so you'll have lots to chat about." Candee flashed a sunny grin. "C'mon. Let's eat."

"I won't be able to fit into any of my clothes," Kathleen warned, while Candee led her through the back room, littered with debris. By the window facing the yard, they assembled at a three-legged table salvaged from the diner. A chest of drawers Kathleen had brought from Ireland held some of her personal belongings.

Candee brought out warm food wrapped in foil containers, complete with silverware and cloth napkins. For herself, she set carry-out coffee and sugar packets on the table.

"I assume you drink tea," Candee said as she poured three packets of sugar into her coffee and stirred.

"I've had my fill for now." Kathleen pulled a bottled water from the cooler.

She perched at the end of the booth, gestured for Candee to sit across from her, and said a blessing. Although she'd baked, she hadn't prepared a proper meal for herself since she'd arrived.

"I'm sorry you weren't able to join us last night," Candee said over the rim of her coffee cup.

Kathleen helped herself to another forkful of eggs. Candee had bragged about Keiran's cooking with obvious good reason.

"I'm hoping for a raincheck," she said. "I'd love to see your home."

"Rob missed you."

Kathleen felt her cheeks color. "We had a slight disagreement."

"He was unusually quiet at dinner."

Thinking over his offer tugged hard on Kathleen's mood, and she took a deep breath. "He assumed I'd prefer to work for him rather than run my own business."

"He said that?"

"He suggested I become a manager at his bakery in Miami. Why on earth would—?" Kathleen broke off.

"Only one reason."

"Which is?" After studying Candee's determined features, Kathleen sensed the answer. "You think this was his way of us being together?"

"Are you … together?"

"We met a few days ago. Surely you don't believe we're falling in love."

With a bemused smile, Candee said, "Why do you think people call it falling in love? Love develops quickly and feels like you're losing control. You know—falling, tripping—"

Kathleen dismissed this with a head shake. "I'm not seeking any type of courtship. Too often, I've failed in the dating department. I'm good at business. Strictly business."

She wasn't an obsessed, clingy woman who needed a man.

Nonchalantly, Candee sipped her coffee. "Every person is different. You'll know when the right man comes along."

Like Rob, for instance?

No. Not happening.

Blankly, Kathleen stared at the paneled wall behind Candee. Admittedly, thoughts of Rob consumed her. He made her feel relaxed and encouraged, telling her she could handle the most difficult situation. And he'd made it clear he was available.

She heaved a breath. At this rate, she was focusing more hours and energy on him than her teahouse. How would she ever create a tea emporium if she couldn't even manage to get menus finalized?

"Why don't men ever listen to women?" she asked.

"Because men and women are wired differently," Candee replied. "Knowing Rob, he was only trying to help. He doesn't understand why you should struggle when he can do so much for you."

"He said that?"

"Yes."

"I know he believes in me," Kathleen said. "Now I want him to stand back so I can face the challenges on my own."

"He's a man who looks at a problem and presents a solution. He's practical. Once you learn more about him, you'll understand."

Oh, but she had learned about him. Beneath their light bantering she'd discovered he'd never married and wasn't currently dating. Beneath his laughter, she felt certain he'd been hurt. On their first night, he'd revealed his home life had been filled with rejection. His parents had never responded favorably to his bids for affection and hadn't approved of his profession.

There was more. She knew there was more, although he hadn't spoken of it. Perhaps someday. At present, she wouldn't push, wouldn't pry. Besides, when would she see him again?

Beneath his commanding exterior she sensed an easily bruised sensitivity. And with that insight, she was more attracted to him. Because he was vulnerable, just like her. Sometimes the most prosperous men were the most insecure. Perhaps it was the reason why he was driven to succeed.

She stared out the window. Sunlight exposed floating dust particles. A fluorescent light bulb buzzed overhead, calling attention to the discolored ceiling.

"The thing is," Kathleen said, "Rob is fun to be around. He's well-educated and freely shares his experience."

"When Teddy needed a friend, Rob was there. He's loyal and generous." At Kathleen's inquisitive expression, Candee added, "The next time he comes to Roses, you might see his generosity in action. He's involved in several charitable organizations, including one with Keiran."

"Rob comes to Roses often?"

Candee grinned. "He will now."

Kathleen's heart swelled. When Rob had smiled at her, kissed her, she'd felt a shiny spin of hope. Perhaps here, in America…

No. She refused to dwell on a future that could never be. If she and Rob dated, she knew the ending. Men left her without a care. Every single time.

She concentrated on the last of her biscuit and white

gravy. Some people were meant to live life alone. She was one of them.

"And do you know why?" Candee asked.

"Know why what?" Kathleen glanced up, noting Candee's mischievous grin. "Why Rob will be back? Do you know something I don't?"

"Me?" Candee feigned an expression so innocent, Kathleen burst out laughing. "He talked about you the entire evening and kept looking at his phone," Candee went on. "I think he was hoping you'd reconsidered our invite."

"I couldn't." Kathleen stood and threw open the window to let in some fresh air. "Look around."

"You sent him back to Miami with your rejection." Accusation colored Candee's voice.

Kathleen bristled. "Wasn't he leaving, anyway? He owns a half-dozen bakeries."

"He wanted to stay longer. In fact, he'd been in touch with his Miami assistant manager."

Kathleen knew her cheeks colored. Aye, her refusal had been blunt, but she'd worked for others her entire life. Wasn't sacrificing all those sweat-filled years enough?

"I didn't mean to hurt his feelings, although I doubt he was affected," she said.

"Did you apologize?"

"What?" Kathleen's eyes widened. "He should apologize to me."

Candee settled her elbows on the table and rested her chin on her fists. "Have you heard from him?"

"He texted me last night." Again, Kathleen stared out the window at the post-card perfect sky and shifted on the ripped vinyl seat.

The previous afternoon, she and Rob had tossed designs around. Their conversation had been easy, and she hadn't laughed so hard in years. She'd been impressed with his quick mind, the ease in which he'd presented practical, timely solutions to her questions, writing extensive lists with his bold left-handed scrawl.

"What did he say in his texts?" Candee asked.

"He said he enjoyed his time with me. I wished him a safe flight," Kathleen said.

"Unfortunately, you're both too polite."

Kathleen took note of Candee's set jaw. "Meaning?"

"You didn't discuss what really matters."

"Dating?" Kathleen clenched her hands together. "When I'm drowning in business loan debt?"

"Love is the only thing that matters."

"Maybe in your world. Certainly not in mine. What matters is that I'm starting a brand-new venture and can't concentrate on anything else."

Candee doctored her coffee with another packet of sugar and took a long swallow. "I admit Rob is a little high-handed at times."

"It's because he's skilled and on the ball. And funny and warm-hearted."

Exactly what the other men in her life had lacked. In the short days they'd known each other, Rob had displayed a tenderness she hadn't noticed at first, developing in the course of their hours together. She'd listened as he'd laughingly remarked about his dismal dating history. Although he'd airily portrayed himself as a man who couldn't care less, his admission seemed more heartbreaking than humorous.

"Wow, Kathleen." Candee set down her cup. "You're quick to come to his defense."

"I—" Kathleen rubbed her palms on her sweatshirt.

"I see you're interested in him. It's written all over your face. Admit it."

Kathleen averted her eyes from Candee's attentive gaze. Despite her exhaustion, she hadn't slept well. If she had more time, she might have talked further about Rob, but the sentences wedged in her throat. Unfortunately, time was something she lacked, and life went on.

She dabbed her lips with her napkin. "What interests me is designing this blank space into a charming teahouse in a few short weeks." As she disposed of the containers, Candee wrapped the silverware and napkins.

Through the doorway, Teddy and his crew set up ladders, arranged tools and prepared joint compound.

Kathleen perused the bare walls. She'd never considered interior decorating her strong suit despite Rob's compliments. In any case, he'd only seen her kitchen.

"How can I best utilize every inch of space?" she asked aloud.

"This is where I come in." Candee popped to her feet.

For the next several hours, Candee shared design tips while drawing up a floor plan, adding extra windows and laying out a well-equipped kitchen complete with sinks, a cooler, and oven placement. When Kathleen peered over Candee's shoulder, Candee said, "No worries. I'm keeping in mind the strict health code."

Meanwhile, Kathleen grabbed scrubbing supplies and tackled the shelving.

When they finished, Candee locked arms with Kathleen and yanked her out the front door. "And now, we're going shopping."

"My pantry is stocked with flour and baking soda."

"Good, because we're canvassing all the paint stores for samples. Fun bright colors will look terrific on the interior walls, and I suggest leaving the exposed brick behind the counter. Build a fireplace on the far wall with a wide pine mantel."

"Let's section the rooms to keep them more intimate," Kathleen said. "The smaller room can seat ten to twelve

people, the larger up to twenty. I want worn leather couches
in the sitting area, a loveseat, and blackboard by the entrance
so I can chalk in the soups of the day." A wave of excitement
coursed through her as more ideas took hold. "Creamy broccoli or parsnips with apple and curry are favorite soups in
Ireland."

"Parsnips?" Candee asked. "What are those?"

"A root vegetable similar to a carrot, only cream-colored."

"When parsnip soup is on your menu, call me," Candee
said. "Now, over and above food, let's get back to decorating.
Stripping the wood on the sideboards will create an antique
feel."

"At some point, I'll need a taste tester for the scones and
bread."

Candee paused. "Is that all you think about—food?"

"I own a teahouse, not a bookstore."

Candee gazed at her with an overly satisfied expression.
"I know the ideal person for the job."

"Who?"

"Rob."

Kathleen's pulse skipped a beat. The subject, the man
she'd avoided talking about all afternoon, brought a smile she
couldn't contain.

"Aye," she agreed.

Did her enthusiasm make her look transparent? The
twinkle in Candee's eyes gave Kathleen her answer.

Aye.

CHAPTER 7

*R*ob stood in the backyard of Candee and Teddy's Victorian mansion, gazing at the enclosed pasture. Teddy had converted a large shed into a stable and purchased a Haflinger horse, sturdy and energetic with a flaxen mane, for Joseph's therapy.

When Joseph got off the school bus, Rob was propped against the fence admiring the home's gingerbread trim, which Candee had painted burnt-sienna. The shade nicely offset the mustard color exterior.

"Mr. Rob!" Joseph squealed in delight as he charged down the driveway. "I'm so happy you're back in Roses!" Out of breath, he dropped his bookbag on the ground and launched into Rob's arms. "How long will you stay?"

Rob managed a jovial smile. "A few days, maybe more."

Maybe less. It all depended on how a certain beautiful Irishwoman responded when he showed up at her teahouse.

After Candee had phoned him, breathless with the news that Kathleen had spoken favorably about him, she'd used her finest singsong voice and urged him to return to Roses.

That took some planning, but he'd assembled his managers and arranged the necessary details.

"I'm only a phone call away," he'd assured, with the unspoken hope no one rang.

So here he was, a week later, back in Roses. This time, he vowed not to talk shop with Kathleen. At least, not *his* shop. He was here merely to lend a hand.

As the opening drew nearer, she might fly into a panic. Consequently, he was ready and able to offer his support.

"Mr. Rob, what do you think of my horse?" Joseph tipped his head toward the small horse being led out of the stable by the therapist.

"I think your horse is awesomely pint-sized," Rob said.

"His name is Blackjack," Joseph said with an impish smile.

Nearing seven years old, the little boy had quickly emerged from a preschooler to a thriving second grader. The freckles on his cheeks were disappearing and baby teeth had begun to fall out, leaving a gap-toothed grin.

"Yes, I know. Even though Blackjack is chestnut colored and not at all black."

"Blackjack doesn't mind." Joseph's face shone with happiness. "He likes his name."

Rob touched the boy's chin. "I'm sure he does."

Teddy and Candee's love and affection had strengthened the boy's self-esteem, and he bore little resemblance to the broken child Rob remembered from a few years earlier.

"Rob?" Teddy called from the back porch. "Are you ready? Kathleen's expecting you." Thumbs hooked in his front jean pockets, he grinned indulgently. Whenever he spoke to Rob about Kathleen, he smirked. Just like Candee did.

"Be right there," Rob said.

"I've gotta go too, Mr. Rob." With a breeze tangling his fine hair and an eager smile on his face, Joseph scampered away.

A few minutes later, Rob arrived at the teahouse. In several days, the exterior had been transformed from drab to grand. The old-world appearance Kathleen strived for conveyed a welcoming invitation to passersby. Her signage, Kathleen's Teahouse, stained in lavender and blues and exaggerated by pink teacups, had been fixed high above the entrance.

His gaze roamed enthusiastically over the renovated building. Afternoon had settled, and the windows were aglow with lit electric candles.

A very welcoming place indeed. He just hoped the owner's heart held the same welcome.

WATCHING THROUGH LOWERED LASHES, Kathleen stood on her front porch as Rob got out of Teddy's pickup and waved a thanks. The work crew had retired for the day and the house was empty. They began at seven in the morning and clocked out at three thirty, so without the constant rat-a-tat-tat of hammering, the hollowness echoing through the rooms was oppressive.

"Cheers," she greeted Rob as he approached. "It's good to see you."

"A greeting from a beautiful woman is the best form of welcome," he said.

She smiled. "The Irish are known for their hospitality." As much as she tried, she couldn't tamp down the flurry in her chest at seeing him again.

Should they embrace like great friends, erasing their silly squabble? He had texted an apology and she'd done the same. Since then, the subject of her moving to Miami hadn't been broached. Thankfully, that had been settled.

She kept her hands at her sides while considering what to do next.

"It's good to see you again too." His blue eyes were steady and genial, startlingly intense. His tan golf shirt fit his frame perfectly, and he carried himself as a self-assured man, not a young guy who'd disguised his identity on the internet. Rob's tastes were sophisticated, and he was cultured and witty, an enticing combination.

No doubt about it. No matter how she resisted, she was drawn to him.

An expression of unconcealed admiration touched his handsome face. "I came back for you."

"Because of me, or for me?"

"Both."

"Did you assume I needed help, or did you want to see me?"

"Both."

"So you're not here to sightsee or visit friends?"

"I'm here exclusively for you." Warmly, he appraised her. "And you look gorgeous."

"Gorgeous? Hardly." Self-consciously, she patted her hair and offered a fatigued smile. Then she tugged at the pinstriped blouse and dark-washed jeans she'd changed into after a quick shower. Rob had texted saying when he'd arrive, but, as usual, she hadn't allowed enough time for herself and had settled for braiding her hair and applying pink lip gloss.

"Kathleen." He stepped closer. "I missed you. And I want you to know how much."

"You've only been gone a short while."

"The days were long for me."

The heat in her cheeks became a full-blown fire. Her gaze dropped to the flowers he held.

"I missed you too," she said quietly.

Attraction was a funny thing. It made you forget about feigning disinterest, a game suited for years thankfully well past.

"These are for you." He offered the flowers. "I asked the florist in town for something Irish."

"They're lovely." Kathleen accepted the bouquet of fresh-cut green and white button mums and carnations, the perfumed fragrance reminding her of the bushy plants growing wild in County Galway.

Her beloved Ireland. Nostalgia rushed through her, clogging her throat with emotion.

"Thank you," she managed.

"Are you homesick?"

"A little, although it's childish." Her eyes turned liquid, and a tear streaked down her cheek. "This is what I wanted—America and my own business. Fortunately, I've kept myself so busy my mind doesn't have time to wander."

Gently, he brushed the tear away. "I'm here and not going anywhere. Teddy and Candee said I can stay at their house as long as I'd like."

"What about your bakeries?"

"My marvelous muffins are so marvelous they practically bake themselves."

Despite herself, she chuckled.

He took the flowers from her, set them on the porch's wide railing, and gathered her into his arms.

She'd dreamt of this moment ever since they'd parted, and she didn't resist. Instead, she pressed her cheek along the smooth cotton of his shirt. The steady beating of his heart reassured her that he was here, truly here. And all was well.

He'd texted and emailed nightly since her talk with Candee. Which, he'd admitted, had prompted his return.

His emails were humorous and engaging, often describing a nonsensical situation occurring at work—a customer demanding a slice of huckleberry pie, although his bakery clearly sold only muffins and cupcakes and croissants, or an experimental batch of seaweed muffins everyone refused to eat.

We try to sell healthy selections once in a while, he'd joked.

What did you do with all those wholesome muffins? she'd asked.

I gave them to my skinny employees. Along with the remaining seaweed.

Oftentimes, his solutions to her work-related questions were exceptional. And when she uploaded photos of the daily progress to share with him, he replied instantly. Nothing was too unsettling that Rob couldn't solve with a clever, sensible remedy.

Each evening, when she was too exhausted to decide on another scone recipe or the installation of a gas versus a wood-burning fireplace, she looked forward to the end of her workday. She could finally climb the stairs to her apartment, open her laptop, and eagerly read his email.

When worries about money kept her awake at night, Rob would message her as soon as she logged onto her computer, as if he'd waited up for her. Sometimes, his messages were flirtatious. The actuality that he was eight hundred miles away made their exchanges feel safe and risk-free, and she enjoyed the playful bantering.

"The place looks better in person than in your photos," Rob said as she plucked up the bouquet and they stepped inside. He beamed his approval, sniffing the cedar-scented air and indicating the blazing logs in the stone-faced fireplace. "You decided on wood instead of gas after all."

"Aye." She went to the sink, retrieved a crystal vase, and arranged the flowers. "It's more work, but wood-burning is more authentic. And Teddy's hard-working crew deserves the credit, along with Candee's decorating expertise."

"I love these photographs." He stepped to a white-washed

wall and surveyed the black and white photos of the old diner.

"I chose to pay homage to the diner's legacy. This place is riddled in history and was originally named Betty's Diner."

She'd set a table in Victorian style, complete with an Irish lace tablecloth, bone china cups, and polished silver. She set the vase of flowers in the center.

"Do you like the ambience?" she asked, following his reaction.

"Very, very much." He lifted back a pale-blue wool Oriental rug. "The wide plank oak floors are gleaming and rustic, which was the effect you were going for, right?"

"Absolutely." She tipped up her chin. "The crystal chandeliers will be hung tomorrow. And the paintings depict Ireland's landscapes. I placed them on the wall opposite the photographs, highlighting the old and the new, and two different cultures." She indicated a particularly poignant watercolor of a stone castle atop a hill, the rugged coastline and sea beyond. "I borrowed this concept from Danny Brady. Irish murals grace the walls in The Ground Café."

Rob came beside her. "Kathleen, you are a treasure." His sincere smile melted her heart. He bent his head and kissed her temple, then brushed a butterfly kiss on her lips. Joy surged through her that had nothing to do with his compliment. She couldn't believe this delightful man was interested in her.

And he was. It showed in his avid gaze, his steady eye contact and how he engaged her in endless chats.

"Would you prefer high tea or afternoon tea?" she asked.

"What's the difference?"

She glanced at her wristwatch. "It's around four, so afternoon tea is better."

"Again, what's the difference?"

"Mostly the seating. Afternoon tea is best experienced on low parlor chairs. If it's a high-backed chair, then it's high tea."

"Easy facts to remember," he said. "So these are low chairs."

"Correct."

"Is there a story behind high and low tea you can place on your menus?"

"I'll give you the abridged edition if you're interested."

"If it concerns you, I'm very interested."

"Well, teatime is a British tradition." She steepled her fingers. "Customarily, tea, scones, cakes and sandwiches were served in the nineteenth century. Teatime filled the gap between lunch and dinner, which was usually eaten around eight o'clock."

"I eat muffins every day at four. Should I call my snacks teatime?"

"If you'd like." She chuckled. "Nowadays, obviously, routines have changed. However, teatime is still observed as a civilized tradition. More important, it brings friends and family together and allows everyone the chance to slow down."

His eyes crinkled into a smile. "I'm more than ready to slow down."

Aye, she reasoned, noting the low crease in his forehead. Despite his smile, he looked as exhausted as she felt.

She whisked a glance at a log dropping in the fireplace. The wood sparked and crackled. Knowing his gaze was on her, she donned her prettiest beam. "So, shall we enjoy afternoon tea?"

"Sure. I think."

She laughed out loud at his wary expression. "You think?"

"Mind briefing me on what afternoon tea entails? I

understand the four o'clock part, but is this another no thank you three times discussion?"

"We've done all that." She gestured for him to sit in a flowered parlor chair at the intimate table set for two.

He didn't.

Instead, he pulled out a chair for her before claiming his own. He was a gentleman in numerous ways, opening doors for her, never sitting if she was standing. Always, he was respectful and polite.

She poured the hot tea, which she'd prepared ahead. Gold flatware glinted by the light of tea candles, and metallic gold linen napkins folded in the shape of a crown sat on bone-china plates, the plates so translucent as to be almost see-through. A tiered platter was set with scones, finger sandwiches, clotted cream, and strawberry preserves.

"Is your tea dark enough?" she inquired.

He made a show of examining the brew in his gold-rimmed cup. "Strong enough to trot a mouse in."

"Here, here." She chuckled. "You're learning the Irish sayings quickly."

They bowed their heads and prayed a blessing. When they finished, she presented turkey sandwiches covered in cranberry jelly from the platter.

"I could get used to this," he laughed, taking a bite of a cucumber finger sandwich spread with herbed cream. "How did you make the cream?" he asked.

"It's not difficult. I'll lend you the recipe."

He settled in, slid his teacup closer, and supported his elbows on the table. Tea sloshed over the rim of his cup. "Kathleen, you've made the entire process look easy. You're going to open without a hitch."

The table wobbled, the legs uneven. And with that, the exquisite settings, hot tea, sandwiches, and flower-filled vase clattered to the floor.

Kathleen caught her teacup between her palms, although the brew spilled across her pinstriped blouse, leaving behind a splotchy wet stain. She dabbed at her shirt, her fingertips catching the droplets.

"Aye," she echoed, perching on the edge of her chair. "I'll be opening without a hitch."

CHAPTER 8

To his customers and everyone in Miami who presumed to know him, Rob's bakeries were the epitome of success. To Rob, his bakeries were fast becoming a weight too heavy to carry on his broad shoulders.

And he was seriously considering selling everything.

More and more, Miami had become a place he sought to escape. He was tired of setting aside his personal life for an ever-elusive joy, no matter the vast amount of wealth and accolades he'd accumulated.

He craved laughter and companionship with people he enjoyed.

With Kathleen.

However, he also wanted to make certain their bond was more than a casual exchange between two businesspeople.

The following afternoon, he sat in the back room of Kathleen's teahouse with his cell-phone on speaker. George, his manager, was working in the Miami office, and he'd asked David, the newbie, to be his messenger and relay the bad news to Rob.

Butter prices had substantially risen and were up by 75 percent.

"Tell George to shop around," Rob told David.

"He has, Mr. Rob," David said. "All the local vendors and bulk supply stores have increased their prices."

"Their timing is perfect for the spring baking season. That is, perfect for them," Rob said sardonically. "I'll recalculate our muffin prices so we can stay within profit margins."

"Not possible, sir, unless you're planning to charge five dollars per muffin," David said. "We're currently selling at two dollars apiece."

"And losing money," Rob pointed out. "Although no customer will buy a five-dollar muffin, no matter how marvelous."

"Correct, sir."

"I'm proud of my products. However, I'm not in business to give them away." Impatience thickened Rob's tone. "Tell him."

"Yes, sir." David muffled the phone, and returned a minute later. "George said he's well aware of that, sir."

Heaving a sigh, Rob tipped his head against the back of the chair.

"Rob?" After a light tap on the door, Kathleen's voice floated through the room. "Oh, sorry." She put a hand to her mouth in apology. "I didn't realize you were still on the phone."

The afternoon sun shone through the window, splashing her cheeks with a hint of color. The past three days, she'd worked nonstop from early morning to late evening. Between Teddy's crew and a constant stream of suppliers, organized commotion heralded each new day. Rob had appeared each morning at daybreak, rolled up his sleeves, and worked alongside her.

He smiled at her, stood, and held up an index finger to let her know he was finishing the call.

"Text me later with a better update," he said to David. "Or we'll be churning our own butter."

"No worries. We'll need a cow, though, sir."

Rob stared at his cell-phone in stunned disbelief.

Apparently waiting for a response, David stacked on more assurances. "Actually … we'll probably need two cows, sir."

Frustration reduced Rob's response to a groan. When he did speak, he kept his tone purposefully calm. "Thanks for the helpful tip, David. Goodbye for now." He clicked his phone shut and tossed it across the table.

Kathleen's lips twitched, a twinkle in her sparkling eyes. "You're in the business of buying cows now, are you? I'll take a half dozen. I heard Candee and Teddy own a pasture."

He laughed heartily. With her, every minute was like being in the middle of a splendid dream. She had an aura of exhilaration, a freshness sparking something inside him. Most important, she let him forget his cares, at least for a while.

Strawberry-blond tendrils had worked loose from her high ponytail, which she'd tied back with a teal satin ribbon. She wore a stretchy-knit yellow dress with a pretty V-neck-line and tan loafers.

He'd dated beautiful women in his lifetime. No one compared to Kathleen. Perhaps it was her porcelain complexion, or the figure-hugging dress showing off her curves, or her shiny hair glinting in the sunlight. Perhaps it was because, besides being downright striking, she was chic and confident.

And yet she had never married. What was going on in Ireland? Were all the men blind?

Grinning, he placed his hand on his heart. "Kathleen, have

I told you you're gorgeous? I liked the jeans you wore yesterday, but the dress—"

"Aye, you have, and often." She laughed. "And I've thanked you for your kindness each and every time."

"You're very welcome." He stepped closer and tucked a silky tendril behind her ear, his fingers brushing across her high cheekbone. "I applaud your conviction to follow your dreams. You're a determined, sharp-witted businessperson."

She rubbed her palm against the door which had been sanded and stained to a satiny oak finish. "Same as you, aye?"

"Yes, and I don't know if that's a good thing or a bad thing."

"What do you mean?"

"When you're focused on victory at all costs, it's easy to forget the important things in life."

A quiet smile, not quite reaching her eyes, lit her fine-boned face.

He was extremely attracted to her and wondered if it was a good idea to work so closely. He was caught up in her. She was caught up in her business.

He knew the feeling. He'd lived that way most of his adult life. And if he continued analyzing their situation, the fifteen-year difference between them would clutter things up even more.

She extended her hands, apparently unaware of his thoughts. "I hope butter hasn't risen significantly in the Carolinas," she said.

He took her small hands in his. "I'll check in the morning." He perused her flawless figure before his gaze slid to her face. "In the meantime, there's something else we can do besides churn butter."

"What?" She didn't seem to notice the telltale huskiness in his tone.

He pulled her near and pressed a kiss on her hair, her temple, her cheeks.

"Rob ..." She gazed up at him and licked her lips. "Maybe we should—"

He swallowed hard. "Kiss?" He framed her face in his hands, stared at her mouth and bent his head.

From the entrance, a crewman's voice called out. The workers were leaving.

Immediately, she stepped back. "I should see them out."

"Why? They can find their way through the front door. They've worked every day since I've been here."

"Aye, but—"

"Kathleen, are you comfortable with us ... with me ..." Wow, did he ever sound desperate. Quickly, he closed his mouth before he revealed something he'd regret.

"Surely you understand I didn't come to America to find a man."

"And surely you understand there's a magnetism drawing us together."

"Your businesses will be calling you back soon enough, so we shouldn't get too attached to each other."

He tried his most charming grin. "Why not?"

"It's like giving biscuits to a bear."

There went her Irish slang, and he had no notion of what she was talking about. "Meaning?"

"Our being together is a waste of time. Look at what I've undertaken. I can't manage anything more."

He got it. He'd take it slow. She had mountains of tasks, and it was too soon for a commitment.

"Will you take a wee peek at the kitchen in my apartment?" she asked, her tone shifting to businesslike. "The crewmen have enough to complete down here, and one of my shelves needs an adjustment."

"I'm not a carpenter."

"It isn't a complicated job." She led him through the rooms, separated by brick archways, and paused by the staircase. "If you fix the shelf, I'll best the deal with a warm bowl of colcannon."

At his puzzled expression, she clarified, "Mashed potatoes mixed with kale, scallions, milk and butter. And I'll fry you a pan of sausages on the side."

"Free labor for free food," he said. "How can I refuse when I'm ravenous?"

He was ravenous all right. He wanted to hold her, glide his fingers through her strawberry-blond hair, spend hours chatting with her. Kissing her.

As he accompanied her up the creaky wooden stairs, she remarked, "My father never owned anything he couldn't fix."

Rob grimaced. Aware he didn't immediately respond, and likewise aware she was waiting, he contemplated telling her the truth. He'd never been handy with tools, and if she evaluated a man by his hammer wielding abilities, he'd fail miserably.

"That's the way with most men, isn't it?" she added.

Real men fix things. He visualized the slogan—resembling a television commercial.

The tension in his shoulders tightened with each ascending step. He hoped she wouldn't judge him for not being able to hang cabinets or install crown molding, because his reply would be *I can't*. His affluent parents had deemed carpentry beneath them, and encouraged Rob to perform well in school and play sports.

So he had, excelling at both.

And his father had continued to beat him. They'd kept it hidden, presenting a fake façade to their community. Despite the proper upbringing in the proper home, there was no love; only disinterest, indifference, and cruelty. However, they'd filled their home with material possessions, and Rob never lacked the latest tech toy.

After his father had broken Rob's nose once, he'd whipped out his checkbook and bought Rob a Camaro for his sixteenth birthday.

"I can fix this," his father had said, as if a new Camaro could fix a broken nose.

It had come as no surprise his parents didn't approve of his baking career. Although he became a prosperous businessperson, they'd dismissed his achievements.

And now they were gone. A few years earlier, they'd died within months of each other, both from lung cancer. Rob was an only child, and had tried to accept the fact he had failed them, but he never did.

Ten minutes later, he found himself crouched beneath a loose corner shelf in Kathleen's kitchen.

"Can you hand me a hammer, Kathleen?" he asked with a nail held between his teeth.

"Aye," she obliged.

He pinched a second nail between his thumb and index finger, lined the nails up and gave them several sharp whacks. Two nails hammered at once seemed more efficient. Thankfully, she seemed blissfully unaware of his many misses as he attempted to drive the nails into the board and kept slamming his thumb instead. He held in his colorful curses and tried again. Finally, on the fifth attempt, he succeeded.

He stood and wiped wood particles from his jeans. "All set."

There it was. The shelf was secure. Now he could swing a hammer like any of the burly men on Teddy's construction crew.

Her gracious smile filled with appreciation. "What would I do without all this help?"

He prayed she'd narrow her selection down to one helpful person: him. She simply couldn't accomplish this project without *him.*

She slipped off her loafers. "I have something special for us!"

"A wee bit of whiskey?" He peered at her bare feet. "Will we be stomping the whiskey like the Italians stomp grapes for wine?"

"I don't drink," she reminded, skipping to a CD player on the counter. "And what I planned is indeed better."

A lively jig sounded through the kitchen, played by the traditional Celtic instruments of a fiddle, flute, and tin whistle.

She held out her hands, positioning him to face her. "Dance with me, Rob."

He was almost as inept a dancer as he was a carpenter, and he primed the argument on his tongue. "Kathleen, I'm a baker."

"You've repeated that a number of times. And so am I, but I also can dance." She dropped her hands to her sides, and he followed her lead.

"You're Irish," he said. "You've probably danced a jig your entire life."

She wasn't listening. "First, assume the stance." She bounced with the beat, shoulders back and head held high.

He tried to imitate her and carry out her instructions—cross your feet, point your right toe, do a hop, hop back, and lead with your left.

"Leave it to you Irish to make your dance as complicated as drinking tea," he groaned.

She laughed. "Execute the reel straightaway." She whirled him around in a circle, sending her knit dress flying up and exposing shapely bare legs.

He pulled a handkerchief from his pocket to wipe the

sweat from his forehead. He was dizzy, he was breathless. And he was laughing with an abandonment he hadn't felt since he was little.

She giggled, her deep dimples showing. As the jig ended, she collapsed against him. Tears of laughter streamed down her flushed cheeks. "Not so difficult, aye? You danced grand."

"And you're amazing." He caught her tears with his knuckles. In his arms, she was soft and light and he tightened his grip. He was charmed and totally besotted, and he couldn't recall ever being as in love with a woman.

Whoa. Hold that thought.

"I'll teach you the Irish jig whenever you'd like," she was saying. "There're more steps."

"Uh-huh, I'm sure there's a whole book full. I'll put jigs on a back burner for now, but you're an admirable instructor," he said. "And your cooking—"

"Oh, that reminds me." She tore away. "I'll warm the colcannon. That's part of our deal."

"How about a tour first? I spend most of my life in a kitchen."

She tapped a hand to her forehead. "I forgot you haven't seen the rest of my apartment." A slow smile came across her face. "Although saying it's crying for a complete overhaul is an understatement. I've been too busy to entertain decorating ideas, and I admit it's not my strength."

Evidenced by her charming kitchen, she was more than capable. She obviously set high standards for herself.

They wandered through the half-empty rooms—bathroom, hallway, and bedroom. The bare walls were devoid of mementos—no pictures, no window treatments save for shades, no framed photographs of loved ones. The carpet was bland and tattered, the white paint peeling from the ceiling. A chipped farmhouse stool stood as a table beside a worn plaid couch, a knitted blue blanket draped over an end chair. In the corner, wind whistled through cracks in the walls.

Where were her personal belongings? He considered asking, but didn't. She'd admitted to missing Ireland. Possibly she was hesitant to set down permanent roots in America.

Suppose she decided to leave? He captured the troublesome thought and kept it in the forefront of his mind.

"Lovely," he crooned politely as they reentered the kitchen.

"You're too kind." She removed the mashed potato mixture from the refrigerator and transferred it to a pan on the stove.

He grabbed plates and silverware and set the table before coming to stand beside her. "And you work too hard."

"Not any harder than you. Besides—"

"Therefore, I declare tomorrow afternoon a sightseeing holiday."

"Rob, I can't possibly take off an afternoon. Anyway, I'll be knackered."

He quirked an eyebrow.

"Tired. I'll be tired," she said.

"You'll be more productive afterward. What's more, this town is the size of a postage stamp."

"We'll stay in town?"

"For the most part."

She frowned, crunching her delicate eyebrows together. "What's that supposed to mean?"

"It means I plan to show you something first. Then we'll eat dinner at a farm-to-table restaurant that's drawing glowing reviews. Aren't you interested in your local competition?"

"I'm running a teahouse."

"They serve food. You'll be serving food. Maybe new recipe ideas will inspire you."

Ever the entrepreneur, her face lit up. "I guess I can quit at four o'clock."

"Make it three. Where we're going will require a few hours of daylight." He glanced down at her smoky eyes, placed a kiss on her lips, and added a wink.

"Ooh. Sounds mysterious. We're not staying in Roses, then?"

He shrugged. "There's a surprise first."

"I don't usually like surprises. Is this a good surprise?"

"It's a fun surprise," he corrected. "And one I'd like your opinion on."

She gave the colcannon a quick stir, then twisted. "Alright, then. Brilliant."

He smiled. The main thing was that they were going to enjoy an afternoon outside of work. And, by doing so, he'd show her why she should settle in Roses for good.

CHAPTER 9

The following afternoon, Kathleen hummed "Molly Malone", a favorite tune, as Rob pulled up in his candy-red rental car. The afternoon was balmy, foreshadowing the pleasant weather to come.

They'd stopped working at two o'clock after the power had unexpectedly shut off, leaving the crewmen and teahouse in darkness. Fortunately, the electric company had responded and quickly restored power, giving her the opportunity for a hot shower.

She'd taken care with her appearance, dressing in a royal-blue cotton dress with a flared skirt. She paired the dress with brown leather ankle boots and dark tights, topping the outfit with a twill jacket in a light pink print. She'd scrubbed, blow dried, and brushed her long hair until it crackled and shone. Leaving it to lie in loose ringlets around her shoulders, she donned a jaunty straw hat and pinned it in place.

She called out a cheerful greeting as Rob got out of the car. He was at her door before she'd taken a step.

"My beautiful Kathleen." He kissed her warmly on the lips. "Good to see you again."

"You just left my place an hour ago."

He smirked. "And I missed you the entire time." He opened the passenger door for her, and she settled into the plush leather seats.

"Where are we going?" she asked, buckling her seat belt.

He slid into the driver's seat and did the same. "It's a surprise, remember?"

"Rob, I've never liked surprises and—"

"I'll give you two hints." His teasing voice stilled her protests. "It's a town not far from here and it rhymes with toast."

"We're driving to the coast? But we're near the mountains."

Smiling, he pulled to the curb and turned to face her. "I'll give you another hint."

"Alright."

"Boo!"

She jumped, patting her heart. "What on earth? You scared me."

"Sorry." He planted a kiss on her temple, then eased the car back onto the road.

"So now it's presumed I know where we're going?"

He shrugged, an impish expression on his face. "I assumed my clues were useful."

She smiled. "A town rhyming with toast? Boo?" Her smile widened. "Those are clues? Even Sherlock Holmes would have given up."

Their gazes locked—his filled with mischief, hers with a hint of apprehension.

"The surprise is we're driving to Hollan Farms," he said.

"I've never heard of it."

"Teddy and I passed through when we drove from Asheville to Roses." Rob flicked on his blinker and followed a narrow two-lane road, the only traffic a bicycle rider and a lone scooter. "Hollan Farms is a ghost town."

Images of American cowboys and deserted gold rush cities came to mind. "Here? In the Southeast?"

"Technically, a few inhabitants still live there. Sit back and enjoy the ride." He switched on the radio, and James Taylor sang about seeing fire and rain.

They arrived a half hour later, and Rob parked in a graveled car park at the edge of town. Before she could open the door and reach for her straw clutch handbag, he came around and assisted her.

She linked her hand through his arm, their pleasant banter and discerning observations progressing with each step.

"There's a general belief that ghost towns are creepy and haunted," he said. "From my research, this town is none of these."

"Except it does looks abandoned." She pointed to a string of empty storefronts. "It doesn't take a genius to realize no one has lived here for a while."

"Yes, there's that."

Her cheeks warmed as he regarded her, his gaze moving to her lips before he took her in his arms and kissed her.

She was with him far too often. He was the picture of who and what she'd intended to avoid—a good-looking man sharing precious, remarkable moments with her.

Risky, risky, risky. If she continued along this path, eventually her heart would be broken.

But this was Rob, and he was different.

Aye. Different all right. He was too appealing, too perceptive, too much of a distraction.

Too much of an *attraction*.

A light breeze caused her straw hat to flap, and she placed one hand on top of her head to steady it. Trees on every street corner blossomed, sending tiny white petals floating through the air.

As they wound through a forsaken alleyway, Rob seemed to take in every element of the buildings—the worn scalloped awning on the supermarket, abandoned café tables outside a bistro, an ornamental stone fountain. She imagined water bursting from the basin, children playing around it, street vendors selling bunches of flowers and delectable coffee and desserts.

"This was a boomtown, a resort boasting a healing hot spring, luxurious spa, and top-rate restaurants," Rob said. "The town went belly up because of the economic downturn a few years ago. Sadly, the anticipated clientele—middle America—could no longer afford spa vacations."

She slowed to peer through a dusty café window. Chairs and tables were arranged in the middle of the floor, menus stacked by the receptionist's booth as if frozen in time.

"And the hot spring?" she inquired.

"What about it?"

"Where is it?"

"It still runs through the center of town."

The sky changed to a dove gray, and the sun disappeared. A minute later, a heavy rain shower caught her sleeves with drops of water.

"Hold on to your hat," Rob joked. He grabbed her hand and led her on a race through the streets.

"This happens in Ireland constantly," she said, winded and laughing. "One minute it's sunny, the next, rain is bucketing down."

They ducked beneath the canopied entrance of a once impressive hotel, the windows reflecting a marbled tile entryway and carpet at least ten years old.

"It storms and rains on many hot afternoons in Miami too," Rob said.

Water dripped from the brim of her hat, a puddle forming at their feet. "Except Ireland's weather is a wee bit cooler than Miami, to be sure."

"You think?"

"I know for certain." Her hand was still clasped in his warm one. This close, with his warm blue eyes framed by thick brows and his ever-present smile, he exuded self-assurance. Not arrogant the way some men she'd dated carried themselves, more interested in their lives than anything she had to say.

As she gazed up at Rob, she noticed his nose had been broken at least once. Tenderly, she ran her finger across the bridge. "What happened?" she asked softly.

"He liked whiskey and bourbon and cigarettes."

"Who?"

"My father." Rob was silent for several beats. "The combination was frightening when he was angry."

"Your father." She mulled the two words in her mind. Rob rarely spoke about his family or his past. "Did he ... break your nose?"

"Yes."

"So, he beat you?"

"Often."

"Oh, Rob." What could she say? She knew from Clara's brother, Seamus, how alcohol twisted a person's life into a roller-coaster, the ups and downs catching loved ones in a virtual whirlwind of emotions. Inevitably, wreckage and despair followed.

"It happened years ago. Decades, literally." Rob spoke so softly she wasn't sure she heard him. She thought he dabbed at his eyes.

She pictured him as a small boy, chubby, sweet-faced, an infectious beam in his deep-set eyes. "It's alright," she finally said.

"What I remember most is the smell of my father's whiskey and cigarette breath, and the sight of him asleep at the oak desk in his study, an empty liquor bottle lying beside him. I tried to please him, I really did."

The neediness in Rob's voice warmed a secret place in her heart. Perhaps that was why he'd tried so hard all these years to succeed—in his effort to satisfy parents who didn't care. He was a pleaser, thinking of everyone except himself.

"I'm sorry." Something inside prompted her to squeeze his hand and offer reassurance. "The future is what matters."

They stood quiet, the steady rain beating down on the hotel's canopy. He stared at her so long a shiver coursed through her. He trusted her enough to share his heart-breaking memories.

Truly, he cared about her.

And she, in turn, cared about him. Trusted him.

More than cared. More than trusted. She was falling in love with him.

No. Not here. Not now.

Then where, exactly? And when? All she need to do was gaze at him. The confirmation stood directly in front of her —with his every intention, and devotion shining from his brilliant blue eyes. Somehow, in the madness of two different worlds, they'd found each other.

Knowing her rain-dampened cheeks were a hot pink, she broke the spell and spun to peer through the hotel's grimy window. She tented her hands and read the scrawled sign posted in the lobby. "We are open to patrons during the summer months."

"Wow," Rob said. "Business is booming."

She laughed and pivoted. "For who, exactly?"

"I don't know. It might be an old sign."

"Didn't you say a handful of people still live in Hollan Farms?"

"Yes, but they wouldn't stay at the hotel."

"So, where are they?"

He shrugged. Gently, he wiped rain droplets off her chin. "They're probably in Asheville for the day."

"The entire population?"

"The entire population of ten."

The rain stopped as suddenly as it had started. He kept hold of her hand as they continued their exploration, answering her speculative questions with speculative answers. Eventually, they crossed a rickety wooden bridge.

The famed babbling hot spring nestled beside budding trees and shrubs, and Kathleen caught her breath at the exquisite sight. With mountain views in the distance, the scene could have been a page removed from a travel brochure advertising tranquility.

"Beautiful," she murmured. "Like a fairy-tale reproduction of what real life should be."

"Zen."

At her raised eyebrows, he explained, "Zen is Japanese slang for serenity."

She gazed upward and sighed. White, wispy clouds floated above, drifting leisurely. No rush for the clouds. Nature was never in a hurry. If only she could harness that same inner peace.

Directly opposite the sun, a muted band of colors formed an arc. "Look, Rob." She pointed. "A rainbow!"

"I'll snap a photo."

"Quick, before it disappears."

He pulled his cell-phone from his pocket, stepped beside her, and snapped a selfie of them framed by the rainbow.

She was too enchanted by this fascinating town to object.

"You're prettier than any rainbow." Rob hung his arm around her shoulders. "But I can delete the photo if—"

"No, of course not." She wanted to relish the growing

attraction between them, to spend every precious minute with him. Everything about him was appealing—each shared glance, the feel of his callused hand around hers, his agreeable, mellow nature.

She peered at the sky. Already, the rainbow was fading. A homesickness she hadn't felt in a while enveloped her.

"Are you okay?" he asked.

"I'm fine." She brushed her fingers across her eyes. "Oftentimes, the rainbows in Ireland are brilliant."

"Rainbows are brilliant in America too, Kathleen. And Roses is your new home."

Here. With me.

The words dangled between them.

"Do you desire a soak, my lady?" he asked when they reached the edge of the hot spring. "You know, all those healing powers …"

"I didn't bring my swimsuit," she joked.

"A pity." He moved behind her and wrapped his hands around her waist, nuzzling her neck. She turned, considering, then stood on her tiptoes and kissed him.

He drew an inward breath and folded her in his arms. She wrapped her hands around his nape.

This was decisive.

She was done worrying about dating, or relationships, or whether this was the right time. Because here was Rob, a man she trusted. She loved the way his lips were firm, yet tender and enticing. He was so good to her, polite, calm, respectful.

When the kiss ended, he whispered, "You have no idea how often I think about you."

Likewise. He was in her thoughts every minute.

He beckoned her to dip her hands into the water with him.

"I read that famous actors and actresses who visited here often immersed themselves in the healing waters," he said.

Kathleen splashed water on her face. "Whether the spring is healing or not, this town is delightful."

"I agree." He looked around, pensive, deliberating. "And it's for sale."

"What is?" She aimed her gaze across the street. "The hotel?"

"The town."

Playfully, she swatted him. "A town can't be for sale."

"Sure it can."

The whole town was for sale.

And Rob had a gleam in his eyes she instantly recognized. Once an entrepreneur, always an entrepreneur.

"How much?" she asked.

"I've done some investigating. Plus, Candee's a real estate agent, which is helpful."

"How much?" she repeated.

"Several million dollars."

He might as well have stated several trillion dollars; the amount was so removed from her stratosphere.

"Rob, surely you're not thinking of buying a ... town."

He chuckled. "Teddy and Candee voiced the same reservation."

"What about your bakeries?"

"I'm putting them up for sale. I'm retiring."

She touched a hand to her parted lips. "You'd sell Rob's Marvelous Muffins?"

"I'll keep the name and unload the buildings, retail spaces and my condo. I'll start the paperwork when I fly to Miami."

"Is this wise? You've established a wonderful reputation. What about your recipes, your customer base—"

His jaw set. "All too much work."

"Compared to renovating a town?" She couldn't find a

coherent sentence to sputter. "Along with the actual price, it'll take several more millions to fix all the buildings."

"True." Lazily, he stroked a stray ringlet falling across her shoulder.

She stepped back. "Isn't that a lot of money?"

"Yes. However, Hollan Farms has one thing Miami lacks."

His words caught, and she looked up at him. The entire afternoon had followed its own course. And in his explanation, she recognized a deep emotion. Commitment.

"Healing spring water?" she half teased.

"Guess again."

"Rob, I ..." She'd forgotten her guesses, anyway. When she was with him, she forgot all her troubles.

She knew he watched her, so she ventured, "The town offers dilapidated cafés just waiting for your marvelous muffins?"

"Nope."

"What could Hollan Farms possibly offer that isn't in Miami?"

"You." He brought her into his arms, bent his head, and thoroughly kissed her. "I'm planning to move to Roses permanently."

WHEN THEIR TOUR of the town ended, the sun hung low in the sky, the beginnings of a sunset casting vivid purple and orange hues that shadowed the derelict buildings. By the time they arrived at the farm-to-table restaurant, stars blanketed a clear night sky.

Rob's admission that he would sell all he'd built in order to be close to her had successfully breached the last of her defenses. Here she'd assumed the wall barricading her heart had been honed to perfection and nothing could penetrate it.

And it had been so, until she'd met this honest, mature gentleman. Until the impossible had occurred.

She'd fallen for him, and there was no turning back.

"Are you hungry?" he inquired.

"I'm starving, actually."

"Next time we go to the hot spring, we'll pack a picnic."

Next time. A promise of shared experiences to come. Celebrations.

Seeing the restaurant's parking lot packed with cars, she remarked, "We may not be eating here tonight."

"I made reservations," he said.

His cell-phone pinged. He darted a glance at the caller ID and scowled. "Sorry, Kathleen, I need to take this. One of my managers—"

She drew in a breath before a sharp retort rolled from her tongue. *Rob,* she wanted to say. *Must your business always come first?*

After a clipped exchange, Rob ended the call.

Scents of smoked bacon and fresh-baked rolls wafted from the doorway as they ascended the restaurant's stairs. Inside, the walls were decorated in cherry-wood paneling. Candlelight and a pianist playing soft background music— well-known Broadway show tunes—completed the under-stated elegance.

As Rob hung her jacket, Kathleen removed her floppy hat and peered at her outfit, grateful she'd worn a dress.

When they were seated, a black-clad waiter brought menus, explaining the food was fresh and locally sourced, while he poured glasses of sparkling water.

She enjoyed an exquisite meal of a seared chicken breast served on a bed of roasted mushrooms and cherry tomatoes, while Rob opted for the grilled beef tenderloin with spinach and spaghetti squash.

For dessert, she ordered black coffee and a cherry fruit

cobbler. She forked a piece of the crust and chewed discerningly.

"How is it?" Rob asked. He'd ordered bread pudding filled with frozen grapes, and raisin rum ice cream on the side.

She placed the fork near her plate and patted her lips with the linen napkin. "Surprisingly mediocre. Yours?"

"The same." He toyed with the pudding, then scooped up a spoonful of ice cream. "Odd, because dinner was delicious. I wonder if they outsource their desserts because I know a certain woman who bakes a heavenly brown bread." A not-so-secret smile appeared on his lips.

Chuckling, she shook her head. "I have enough on my plate baking bread and scones for my patrons-to-be. What about you?"

"I'm retiring, remember?"

Sure, by buying and restoring a ghost town boasting a hot spring, grocery store, hotel, and who knew what else.

As she sipped her coffee, she felt an unexplainable surge of pride for his tenaciousness. Although he'd told her he didn't have a bit of Irish blood in him—his surname, Taylor, being French and Scottish—he was as sharp-witted as any Irishman.

"What's the finest dessert you've ever tasted?" she asked.

In the softness of candlelight, his face appeared younger. He looked rested and happy. "Your brown bread."

She smiled over the rim of her cup. "No, really."

"There's a mom-and-pop restaurant near Asheville. I dined there with Teddy a while back, and the owners specialize in homemade apple cobblers topped with a flaky crust. I'll take you there some time." He leaned in. "What about you?"

"Ah, well, in Ireland, any coffee shop or café will likely serve desserts prepared in-house."

"I'd like to visit Ireland someday," he said quietly.

Don't go there, she thought. A small part of her demanded she stay on track—launching an up-and-coming teahouse in America. That meant no distractions.

But then, she'd already made her decision. With Rob, her world had changed. They could enjoy America and Ireland together, as a team, as a couple, as two people devoted to each other.

She sat back in the tufted chair, moving in time to the pianist's rendition of the upbeat "I Could Have Danced All Night" from *My Fair Lady*.

She tilted back her head, her smile lighthearted. "It would be an honor to show you my country, Rob."

"I can't wait."

She inhaled, treasuring the moment. She'd made the correct choice coming to Roses, and she wanted Rob in her life.

The way he smiled back at her told her everything. It warmed her weary heart, and there was no mistaking the love in his expression.

CHAPTER 10

"I'll depart for Miami tomorrow," Rob told Kathleen a few days after they'd dined at the farm-to-table restaurant. They stood on the front porch of her teahouse on a brisk day in early March. A sharp breeze ruffled the burgundy striped awning that had recently been installed.

She swallowed and avoided his gaze. "Seven days seems like forever."

"I'm merely a few hours away by plane. In the meantime, I have a gift so you won't forget me." He withdrew a silver-foil-wrapped box from his sport jacket and handed it to her.

Solemnly, he watched her open a black velvet box and snap open the lid. Inside was a Victorian heart-shaped skeleton key locket on a cable chain, plated in twenty-four carat gold.

"Thank you," she said. "It's beautiful."

"For a beautiful woman." He secured the chain around her neck. "My Irish queen, you hold the key to my heart. Always remember that."

She laughed. "Fit for a queen, aye?"

"Yes." He nodded. "Open the locket."

She popped the magnetic closure, and all laughter vanished from her face. She studied the miniature photo tucked inside—the one he'd taken of them at Hollan Farms with the stunning rainbow in the background.

"Turn the locket over," he instructed.

On the back was inscribed: 1-800-IRELAND.

Tears welled in her eyes. "Thank you," she said again.

"I hope you will always think of me when you wear it."

"Every day."

"That's what I like to hear." He embraced her in a loving hold. Against her cheek, his chest was warm and comforting, his heartbeat steady and sure. "I'll return well before your grand opening. I promise, and I never go back on my word."

He was considerate and compassionate, intuitive to her feelings.

She acknowledged his promise, although tears burned. "I'll miss you," she said.

"Not as much as I'll miss you."

She declined his pocket handkerchief that he offered, her thoughts scattering.

When he was near, she felt treasured. Now these crucial hours leading up to March 17 would continue without him.

Well, she'd steel her shoulders and deal with it. He had a business to run. So did she. Furthermore, she was a resourceful entrepreneur. Rob had told her so himself.

He pressed a kiss on her lips. "I'll call as soon as I land in Miami." His gaze flicked to the crewmen busily making adjustments to the wood floor in one of the dining rooms. "Teddy, Candee, Keiran, and Desiree are all around, so you won't be alone."

Despite his assurances, a moment of sadness went through her, just long enough to cause her chest to ache. She was truly alone now.

Woodenly, she nodded. "Aye."

And with that, the next day he was gone.

As the week passed, she enlisted Teddy's crew as taste testers while she perfected scones and breads. Happily, they obliged.

Candee designed a high-quality menu, and aprons were ordered to match Kathleen's teahouse logo. At the last minute, the crewmen erected a pergola to the outside seating area, where bottled water, tea, and fruit juices would be sold.

Kathleen stationed a NOW HIRING sign near the entrance of the teahouse, and several applicants immediately responded. Interviewing the bright-faced candidates left her invigorated and hopeful.

However, various decisions still loomed. Would customers prefer high tea or a more casual atmosphere? Parsnips in their soup or a traditional creamy broccoli? Spot-on decisions meant enthusiastic regulars, and she counted on Rob's daily answers to her texts.

As the days flew forward, two catastrophes occurred.

First, the large dough mixer wasn't expected to arrive on time after all.

Forcing herself to sound calm and unemotional, she phoned Rob.

"You have countertop hand mixers, right?" he asked.

"Aye, and a dough proofer and all the bakeware."

"Tell the two assistants you hired to use what's available. They're qualified, correct?"

"Which brings me to my second catastrophe." She could hardly voice the words. "One quit before she started because she said the start-up wage is too low. The other is in university and her work days are limited."

"Keep looking."

"I am. There may be a third applicant. Her name is Nancy, and she's enthusiastic and eager."

"How old is she?"

"Twenty-something. She's willing to work alongside me, doesn't mind long hours, and told me that my teahouse is unique and special."

"She's a keeper. People like that are hard to find, so train her well and take any spare minute to invest in her development. And don't forget to phone Keiran too. He's a block away."

"I did. O'Malley's is busier than ever and he can't spare anyone this close to St. Patrick's Day. Teddy has even bussed a few tables there to help Keiran out."

Rob blew out a sigh. "Unfortunately, being short-staffed is typical in this industry."

"Short-staffed is one thing. No staffed is another."

"Part-time employees aren't dependable. I'd refer a couple of mine, but with my stores for sale, everyone is in an upheaval. Many of my steady workers are seeking employment elsewhere."

"Didn't you assure them that their jobs were secure?"

"I tried, although new owners may bring aboard different people."

She paused. "Rob, can I ask you another question?"

"Certainly."

"Should I urge my customers to place their cell-phones in containers when they walk in? You know, to strengthen community, and encourage family conversations."

Through the phone, she heard a man speaking to Rob.

"Sorry Kathleen, it's David," Rob said.

"The cow guy?"

"Yes, and it's apparently urgent. Hang on." Rob muffled the phone. He addressed David's question, then came back on the line. "This place is like a zoo today. What were you saying?"

"Nothing." Kathleen's grip on her phone tightened. "I'll sort it out myself."

"Sorry," he said softly. "Once this place is sold, we'll be together."

When? Selling a huge commercial operation wouldn't be a matter of a few days. It would take weeks, maybe months. Maybe years.

She'd always found herself cheered after talking with Rob. However, her chin quivered as she felt her safeguards being swept aside. She relied on him, but he had enough on his hands without her constant barrage of questions. In the interim, she needed to trust her own business sense.

She inhaled deeply. "Do you remember Sean, my coworker at The Ground Café?"

"The guy who is supposedly interested in quitting his manager job in Ireland to lend you a hand in America?"

"I wouldn't put it that way, Rob," she corrected. "He isn't *supposedly* interested. He is interested and assured he won't accept a salary from me. Plus, he'd work full-time, so there's no dependability issue."

"You've discussed your last-minute problems with him, plus he'll work for free?" She could almost see Rob's eyes narrowing. "Why?"

"Because he's a friend." She bristled. "He's been nothing but supportive. He rang me again last night."

"And now he's phoning you as well as texting?"

"Only twice since you left. He's as experienced as you are."

"Your brogue is thickening, and you sound defensive, which is never a good sign." There was an inexplicable seriousness in Rob's tone, coupled with frustration. "And what did you tell Mr. Sean?"

"I told him I was handling things well on my own,

although these days I'm thinking I can use his support. He's ringing me tomorrow morning."

"Sounds like you talk with this guy more than you talk with me."

"Don't be ridiculous. You and I chat every day. It's just that you're … preoccupied." She couldn't remember the last time her conversation with Rob hadn't been interrupted at least once. And Sean was 100 percent available—and always sympathizing with her.

"Kathleen." Rob allowed the silence between them to go on for twice as long as she expected. "There's a lot involved here in Miami."

"I know." She squeezed her eyes shut. "And I should be more understanding."

He didn't say yes or no. Instead, he continued, "Several of my managers expressed interest in purchasing the entire business. That's heartening, because they've been with me for years and I trust them to maintain the quality. However, bank loan applications are time-consuming. Not to mention, my bakeries are all still running."

She needed him. Now. Didn't he realize that?

She shook her head. She was being selfish.

"I understand," she said quietly, although she heard the edge in her tone.

"Remember our ghost town. Our life together. Remember us."

Us.

The dovelike caress threading his words caused a delicious shiver up her spine.

"I'll remember." She gave a weary smile into the phone.

Hollan Farms. An empty shell of a town. Despite Rob's assurances, she felt similar to that town. Abandoned.

When her cell-phone rang at dawn, she recognized Sean's

number on the caller ID. And when he asked if she required back-up relief, she answered with one word.

Aye.

He was capable. He was more than eager. And they'd worked closely before.

ON A RAIN-SOAKED afternoon a couple days afterward, Sean appeared in Roses. His flights from Dublin to Asheville were brilliant, he assured. He'd hired an Uber for the final leg to Roses.

"You quit your job at The Ground Café?" Kathleen inquired as he met her under the front awning. Despite the heavy travel he looked well-rested, his olive-camouflage jacket and black pants washed and pressed.

"Aye. Howya." He placed his luggage on the stoop and grasped her in a fierce hug. "I'm tired of working for someone else."

"You'll work for me now."

He didn't answer. A shadow crossed his hard-lined face.

"Well, travel certainly agrees with you." She pondered her statement as she regarded him. "When I flew the transatlantic flight, it took me several days to recover from jet lag."

"Kathleen, I must confess." His gaze darted. "I landed in Boston last week."

"Boston?" With keen effort, she controlled her temper while drawing a slow breath. "I assumed you were in Ireland when you rang me."

"I figured I was off to America, anyway. A few days earlier didn't matter."

"And if I didn't accept your bid to help me?"

"Don't know." He waved his hands airily. His hazel eyes darkened. "I may have stayed in Boston, although I knew you'd come round eventually if I kept badgering."

Typical Sean. He'd always hassled big-hearted Danny Brady at The Ground Café, requesting weekends off or extended paid holidays until Danny agreed.

"You're obviously a pro at badgering," she said.

"I suppose I am."

She couldn't keep from staring at him. His medium-length dark hair had been styled into a kinky perm.

"Any comments?" He finger combed the curls. "A man perm is all the rage."

"It's …" She stopped herself before saying *hysterically funny*, assuming he wouldn't appreciate the humor.

"Foxy?" he questioned.

"Aye, especially combined with your dark beard."

"Go raibh míle maith agat."

Thanks a million. The familiar Irish words brought a rush of tears to her eyes.

"Can you recommend a place in town where I can rent a room?" he asked.

"There's a splendid bed-and-breakfast not far from here."

"And a pub with good craic?" He stepped too close, completely disregarding her personal space. "I'm definitely fond of parties."

She moved backward, remembering the times he'd reported to The Ground Cafe after going out on the lash and drinking. Although she'd often smelled alcohol on his breath, it hadn't seemed to affect his performance.

"If you're in search of lively banter," she pointed down the street, "Keiran O'Malley's pub is walking distance from here. Just don't drink on the days you're working here."

"Wouldn't think of it."

"Do you remember Keiran's cousin William?" she asked.

"I do." His gaze leveled on her. "He won your affection and took you away from me."

"We're all just friends, Sean."

"I'd like us to be more than friends, Kathleen. Surely you must know that."

"Sean. No. Although I'm thankful for your support."

"Gotcha. Loud and clear." He raised his hands in feigned surrender. "As soon as I'm a wee bit settled, I'll visit Keiran's pub on my off days." His small hazel eyes left hers to regard the teahouse's green painted shingles. "Your place looks brilliant. The color reminds me of Ireland."

"Do you think so? Decorating isn't my forte, I just wanted an old European touch. Fortunately, my friend Candee guided me. I couldn't even choose curtains until she carried over several fabric swatches and I finally decided on a jewel-tone floral."

"Candee is your real estate agent?"

"Aye. Her husband, Teddy, is my contractor." Kathleen blew out a breath. "I'm trying hard to resist the impulse to text her every time there's a decorating problem."

"Luckily, here I am to solve everything." He picked up his luggage, and they stepped inside, the front bell tinkling to announce their arrival.

"Thanks for coming. You're an asset, Sean."

"It's because our Irish work ethic is first rate."

She grinned, turning her attention to the shelves teeming with tea. "Today I'm trying to decide how many loose-leaf blends to serve my customers."

"Less is better to keep the quality up."

"Sean, there are over 250 teas to choose from."

"From the looks of it, you've bought them all." He planted his hands on his bony hips. "Stick with a basic selection of twelve."

"I planned a high tea every day at four o'clock. Is that too much?"

"Roses is a little-bitty town," he said. "Compromise and

serve high tea on weekends only. You'll end up failing if you overextend yourself."

"You're right," she said.

His boots clicked across the wood floors, and she glided her hand over a lavish tea service she'd polished until the silver gleamed. "I can't believe you flew such a long way for me."

"My pleasure." Lightly, he brushed a curl coming loose from her pony tail in much the same way when they'd worked double shifts together and were exhausted at the end of the day. "You remember I'm the adventurous sort. Like you."

She also remembered he used to point that out a lot. *Spirited go-getters intent on success,* he'd say. Somehow, the words didn't sound as flattering as they once did.

IN THE ENSUING DAYS, Sean inched his way into becoming an integral part of every decision, from improving providers' terms to mounting a decorative box next to each table for cell-phones.

He was shrewd, often voicing her objectives before she did, or latching on to an idea and expanding it. He repeatedly pointed out that her concepts were comparable to The Ground Café's. Therefore, when she described a problem with the teas or scones, he immediately chimed in with eleventh-hour solutions.

Rob phoned numerous times, and she played phone tag with him. She yearned for his quick grin, the sound of his deep voice, his warm-hearted reassurances. However, immersed in a whirlwind of activity, the hours passed all too quickly.

Another snag, Rob texted the evening after Sean's arrival.

I'm coming, but delayed a few more days. I should be in Roses by Friday.

Understandable, she replied, noting Friday was a week away. *I'll send photos of my new menu.*

Sean watched while she texted Rob and smiled knowingly.

"I'm here for you," was all he said.

The following day, Kathleen went through every nook in her teahouse for elements she might have missed. Lightly, she traced her fingers over the herbal tea baskets, honey dispensers, and a row of clear glass pitchers. Teddy's crew had completed the renovation, and the place was quiet, save for a collection of Irish tunes playing on the CD.

Everything in the teahouse was unique and stylish, a far cry from the greasy, cramped, and gloomy interior she'd first encountered. She knew Rob would be impressed.

Rob.

She'd meant to send him photos of the menu. In the flurry of activity, she'd forgotten, falling into bed at night too weary to think. She'd do it in the morning.

"What will the children drink?" Sean came up behind her and interrupted her thoughts.

"What children?"

"Your customers will bring in their wee ones. You'll want to keep them content and occupied."

"I can serve hot cocoa."

"What about a fun tea experience?" He inclined his head. "Brew decaffeinated tea and give it an unusual name—like cinnamon toast tea served in a cup named Chip."

"A chipped cup?"

"From *Beauty and the Beast*," he prompted.

"Oh, right." She smiled. "Brilliant. Let's include that name on the chalkboard."

. . .

LATER THE SAME DAY, a $6000 invoice arrived for the double-deck gas convection oven. It was stamped OVERDUE.

Kathleen scanned the bill and gasped.

Sean peered over her shoulder. "Troubles?"

"How can the supplier expect payment if I'm not even open yet?" She set the invoice on the counter and began mixing dough for wheat bread. For her, baking was therapeutic and gave her something to do with her hands. "Financially, I'm stretched to the max."

"You can't apply for another loan?"

"I'm considered an upstart, and banks don't risk their money. I put up my parent's home in County Galway that was deeded to me upon their death as collateral. After $200,000 dollars, I'm tapped out."

He lifted a dark eyebrow, then perused the letter accompanying the invoice. "The company can shut you down if you can't remit."

"Naturally I pay my bills. Just not until the teahouse opens."

"I can help."

She placed the dough into the electric mixer and switched it on. "Sean, I refuse to accept your money. I know you're not a rich man."

The electricity blew out with a snap. The lights switched off, and the mixer stopped.

"Again?" she groaned. "Teddy said we may have an electrical issue if this keeps up, although the power company blames the problem on the new lines being dug in the area. I hope they're right, because I don't have an extra five thousand—"

"At present, it's an easy fix," Sean assured, finding the breaker box and switching the power back on. Once the mixer started running again, he showed up beside her.

"Kathleen, I have a business proposition for you," he said.

"I already had one."

"From your hotshot Miami boyfriend?"

She winced. She'd confided to Sean about Rob's job proposal. She wished she hadn't. A day hadn't gone by when Sean didn't bring up Rob, and his remarks were never flattering.

"I'm not selling my teahouse and setting back to Ireland with my tail between my legs," she declared, "so don't tell me to give up."

"We Irish have more pride than that."

There it was again. *We versus them.* The Irish versus the Americans, the bankers, even Teddy's crewmen if Sean disagreed with their work. He constantly implied the Irish were underdogs and appealed to her sense of patriotism.

She shut off the mixer, wrested the dough from the bowl, and began kneading. "What are you saying?"

"We share a passion for this type of place." He sidled closer. Instinctively, she moved back a step. "You and I worked under brass-hat Brady and watched him make difficult decisions."

"So?"

"So let's face the truth. You can't run a business. You're too emotionally involved." His tone challenged with a hint of mockery. "And there are numerous details, far too many for one person. You're in over your head, luv. Hey, you can't even make a decision about curtains without help."

Luv. She let the word go by.

She kept her head down while she rolled out the dough, then dusted her flour-stained hands along the edges of her apron. "As you obviously guessed, my specialty isn't interior design."

"This isn't about decorating. This is about realizing your strengths and admitting your weaknesses."

Rather than argue, she agreed, because she knew arguing

with him was useless. He was always willing to fight, and she didn't have the energy. Despite the never-ending work hours, her problems continued to mushroom. Somewhere along the way, she'd begun to feel powerless.

Maybe Sean was right. Her corporate sense wasn't strong. Sure, she'd been in positions of management, but that was different from owning a company where every choice meant financial loss and subsequent failure.

She sank onto a high-backed chair. "What are you suggesting?"

"As I said, I'm offering a firm proposition and subsequent solution."

Her eyebrows flicked upward, measuring him. "Which is?"

"I'll buy into your business." He watched her closely as he pulled up a chair. "Your financial worries will end, and you'll be free to bake and serve customers—the services you did best at The Ground Café."

"Your terms ..."

He slid his chair closer, then stretched out his legs. "A 60/40 split. In my favor."

"Absolutely not." Firmly, she shook her head. "I did all the groundwork."

"I'll continue your vision going forward, so don't go flashing those blustery eyes at me." With both hands on his knees, he leaned forward. "I'll take over all business aspects, financial and otherwise, and you can concentrate on a successful opening day."

"Sean, this is a difficult conversation." She rubbed the middle of her forehead and closed her eyes. "Give me time to consider."

"Rest assured I have your best interests at heart. In fact, I'll draw up the necessary papers." He lifted her chin. "It's best for everyone, aye?"

A heaviness invaded her body. Quieting, she gazed down at her rumpled apron, her washed-out jeans, and tried not to twist her hands. She was cornered, and her teahouse deserved no less than the best. She surveyed her supply of china cups and saucers stacked neatly on the shelves, the double-deck gas convection oven. What would happen if she lost her oven because of nonpayment? Her teahouse couldn't survive without the main oven and a large dough mixer, and she'd run out of funds.

"I'll think about it," she replied.

But what about Nancy, the new girl she'd hired, who seemed genuinely interested in learning the tea business?

Kathleen's mind whirled in a thousand different directions.

FOUR MORE DAYS WENT BY. Four more nights she spent staring at the ceiling in her shabby apartment, seeking the serenity of sleep before it vanished, forcing prolonged hours of insomnia and torturous deliberations.

And somewhere along the way, she stopped communicating with Rob altogether.

CHAPTER 11

On Wednesday of the following week, Rob strode over the tiny white blossoms lacing the front porch of Kathleen's teahouse. He knocked, then opened the wooden door. A tiny bell announced his arrival, though no one acknowledged him.

He'd texted his flight information to Kathleen the night before and she hadn't replied. In fact, he hadn't heard a word from her in several days. A quick query to Candee assured Kathleen was well, albeit "busy beyond words". Still, the silence had prompted him to return to Roses a couple days early.

Despite his focus on Miami and the mountain of paperwork yet to be signed, he congratulated himself. He'd successfully sold his business to a group of managers who'd worked in his bakeries for years. They'd pooled their funds, the bank loans were secured, and the closing was slated in a month.

"Sorry, fella. We're not open until St. Patrick's Day." A pencil-thin man sporting a dark beard and curly hair sat at a round table in the center of the main dining room. He was unmistakably Irish, his dialect quick, his sentences running together. He straightened from his sprawling position and refilled his glass of iced tea. "Come back Saturday for our grand opening."

"I'm aware of when March seventeenth is." Disregarding the man's hostile gaze, Rob strode further into the room.

"You Americans are smarter than people give you credit for."

"Who are you?" Rob demanded.

"Sean."

"Yeah, I figured."

"You?" came Sean's clipped inquiry.

"Rob."

"Aye. Without a doubt." Sean's derisive grin followed his flippant acknowledgement. He lifted his glass. "My only defense against the warm weather. In Ireland, March is a cold, rainy month. Here, the sun shines almost continuously and it's a bit warm for me."

"You'd melt in Miami then," Rob said. "How long have you been in Roses?"

"A few days."

Rob corralled his anger, focusing on the welcoming environment of the teahouse. The stunning renovation was a treasure trove. Orderly shelves displayed simple fruit jellies and preserves, and the counter was stocked with freshly ground coffee and an assortment of loose herbal teas in glass jars. The entire space was airy and bright. On the corner of each table, he noted a container.

Sean followed his gaze. "We added those for cell-phones. Kathleen believes in conversation with no interruptions."

Rob grimaced, recalling the number of times his chats with Kathleen had been cut off by his familiar cell-phone ping.

"Hungry?" Sean raised a silver tray laden with croissants.

"Nope." Rob avoided meeting the man's assessing stare. "Where is she?"

Sunshine eased through the floral curtains, lighting the cozy atmosphere, offset by candles shimmering along an antique sideboard. The cashmere comfort of a welcoming warmth enveloped him. In that instant, Rob saw the realization of Kathleen's remarkable achievement.

Well done, Kathleen.

"She's baking another Keiran O'Malley recipe in her apartment, because she prefers her small oven," Sean was saying. "Keiran has Irish relatives, you see."

"I'm aware."

"He's a decent bloke and has made me feel right at home. His pub is fierce and just the thing after a knackered day in a scorching kitchen."

"And I'm interested in Kathleen, not you." Rob crossed his arms. "I'll wait for her here and you can be on your way."

Since he'd entered, Rob had been struggling with an escalating annoyance, standing by while Sean lazily drank iced tea and tamped up croissant crumbs from his plate with his fingers. He felt like a panhandler waiting to be granted an audience with a queen.

"I'd suggest *you* should be the one on your way." Sean's sharp voice cut through Rob's thoughts. "You're acting like a Holy Joe coming to her rescue, but as you can see, we're ready for our opening and things have gone swimmingly. And we did it all without brainy old you."

"Excuse me?" In three strides, Rob closed the distance between them. "*We're* ready? *Our* opening? What's going on here?"

"I'll blame your questions on poor hearing because of your age and not poor listening. As you Americans speak frankly, I'll frame this so that you understand. Crack on and leave."

"Don't tell me what to do," Rob warned. "This isn't your place." He yanked out his cell-phone and typed Kathleen a text. *Where are you? I'm standing in your dining room.*

"On the contrary, it *is* my place." Sean examined his well-manicured fingernails. "Kathleen has agreed to make me her business partner. I'm here for the long haul."

For a moment, Rob couldn't trust himself to reply, his brain registering disbelief. His narrowed gaze examined Sean's blasé expression.

"I don't believe it. Kathleen is self-reliant."

Sean shrugged. "She's going in a different direction."

"Indeed?" Rob inquired. "Tell me more."

He'd been gone only a short while and Sean had triumphantly wormed his way back into her life. Slowly, something inside Rob began to crumble. While he was working out details and selling everything for her, she was handing over her business to this pompous Irishman.

He recalled his phone call with Kathleen when she'd sprung to Sean's defense.

"Do you remember Sean, my coworker at The Ground Café?" she'd asked.

"The guy who is supposedly interested in quitting his manager job in Ireland to lend you a hand in America?"

"I wouldn't put it that way, Rob. Sean isn't supposedly interested. He is interested and assured he won't accept a salary if he were to come here."

Rob scrubbed a hand over his face. He should've known Sean wouldn't waste a second quitting his job, flying over the Atlantic Ocean and coming to Kathleen's rescue. Nevertheless, she considered Sean a friend, so Rob was willing to endure the rest of the exchange for her sake.

"What are the terms of this offer?" Rob asked. "Because I can make her a better one."

"Can you? Mine is a 60/40 split."

"She'd agree to that?" Rob barked a laugh. "I'm surprised."

"We've always been brilliant together, and I'm her new fella. She's a fine thing, isn't she?"

Rob grappled with a stab of jealousy. "I can afford to give her the world," he said quietly.

"Your wealth doesn't impress me or Kathleen. How dare you flaunt your money around?" Sean enunciated each word in a vicious, thick brogue. "She's thrilled with our recent agreement."

"Oh, am I now, Sean?" Kathleen stormed into the room, her face emanating pure outrage. By the looks of the two steps she'd walked, she'd been in the doorway for some time. The green ribbon tying back her silky hair was askew, and her dark eyes sparked with fury.

Rob's heart thumped in double time, his gaze riveted on her. He trod closer, intending to take her in his embrace. She shrugged him off and marched to within a foot of Sean.

"How are ya, luv?" Sean grinned.

"Luv? Luv? I never decided on any so-called agreement."

"You were earwigging?" Sean shoved his glass aside and rose to his feet. "Eavesdropping on a private chat?"

She stamped her foot. "This is *my* teahouse, not yours."

Her outburst earned her Sean's hangdog expression. "Kathleen, I beg your forgiveness. Just teasing. Obviously, you're a bundle of nerves with St. Paddy's looming. If you'll only—"

"Get out and don't come back."

"What? And go where—" he sputtered.

"Back to Boston, or Ireland. You've ruined it for yourself by your underhandedness." She shook her head and whispered, "I should've realized. Why do I never learn?"

Without so much as picking up his glass or bidding a courteous goodbye, Sean twisted on his heels and blustered through the front door with lengthy, purposeful strides.

"A sound good riddance to him," Rob said as the door slammed. "Now you and I can talk."

Whirling, her glare blasted fury. "As if I'm starving for a chat with you when you're always so preoccupied. I don't need you, and I don't need Sean."

"We've been separated for a while, but now I'm retired. Let's sit down and have a friendly discussion over a cup of tea. Candee mentioned you received an overdue bill for the gas convection oven. I can help by writing out—"

Kathleen's eyes widened, and tears erupted. "How can you be so brilliant and yet think you can buy me? I know what I want, and I can achieve it on my own."

"But I can fix this." He paused. He loathed saying the same words his father had used on him, and it hadn't resolved anything.

Inside his jacket pocket, his cell-phone rang.

She stepped behind a high-backed chair, as if fortifying herself against him. Deliberately, she unclasped the skeleton key locket from her neck and placed it on the chair.

He felt as if his heart was breaking. He rubbed his fist against his chest. His eyes blurred with the effort.

His phone kept ringing.

"Aren't you going to answer?" she asked.

"Later." He came forward and closed his hand over her shoulder. "It's not important."

More tears leaked from her eyes and rolled down her cheeks. He brushed them away, and she flinched.

"Rob, return to Miami where you obviously belong."

They were so close he could see the mix of emotions crossing her face—trembling chin, lips pressed together, the slight freckles dotting her wet cheeks.

"You must know how much I love you," he said.

She drew an inward breath. "Everyone seems to love me

these days." Despite her quaking voice, she remained perfectly still.

"I realize you're joking. I know how you Irish love to—"

"This Irishwoman is deadly serious." Her voice rose. "And another thing, which I'm certain will come as a shocking surprise to you: this business is mine, and mine alone."

CHAPTER 12

$\mathcal{A}$t noon a day later, Kathleen sat in a high-backed chair in her teahouse and went through her text messages. Rob hadn't returned since their argument.

Instead, he'd called and left messages, saying he was staying at Candee and Teddy's home if she needed him.

Here's a final idea, he'd texted. *I've partnered with the Roses Chamber of Commerce for a ribbon-cutting ceremony on your official opening day. I know it's late but every bit of advertising helps.*

She hadn't responded.

I've done more market research and can set up a paid advertising media blitz which will coincide with St. Patrick's Day.

No. She'd set up all her online advertising ahead of time. She didn't need to lean on anyone except herself.

Why won't you let me help you? he'd asked again and again. *If you give us half a chance, you will remember how good we r together.*

That dart effectively pierced a nerve, and she'd closed her cell-phone and placed it in her purse.

A soft opening at the teahouse was arranged to begin at

four o'clock. This gave her and Nancy, the new employee, a chance to work out the crimps. Although the public was aware the teahouse was launching, Kathleen hadn't actively publicized it. Candee and Teddy sent their regards, as Joseph was participating in a horse show in Asheville and they couldn't attend. Keiran and Desiree were swamped at O'Malley's. And Sean had fled Roses.

Fortunately, another power outage hadn't occurred while customers dined later that evening, although the lock on the women's bathroom door broke.

Kathleen had also teamed up with Keiran and chalked his mushroom stroganoff as a main dinner entrée, quickly learning that serving the dish at five o'clock was too early and nine too late. Patrons preferred their dinner hour at seven, and she'd soon run out of mushroom stroganoff.

By nine p.m., the teahouse had emptied. After Nancy helped clean, she'd scanned a text message on her phone and departed without an explanation, forgetting her house keys in her haste. Because Nancy lived with her parents on the outskirts of Roses, Kathleen assumed she wouldn't need the keys until morning. Just in case, she put them aside near the herbal tea jars.

Kathleen dreaded the silence that enveloped the unoccupied rooms. It allowed her mind to dwell on all she'd lost. No longer could she hide behind work and busyness. She was forced to confront how much she missed Rob.

She slumped in the loveseat near the foyer and picked up her phone. She planned to make notes about the soft opening, tweaking her original vision. Despite her attempts, she couldn't focus, too intent on the honorable, caring man who had stolen her heart.

He'd been justifiably hurt and angry when he'd returned from Miami to find Sean lounging in her teahouse. And jealous, hiding his emotions by offering her money, hoping it would smooth the rift between them.

Her heart pinched. He'd worked for years to ensure a prosperous business, and desperately wanted her to succeed as well. He was the type of guy who helped people, soft-hearted and obliging. She knew he would never refuse her any favor. Rob was a man she could always count on.

He loved her. He'd told her so.

And what had she done when he'd proclaimed his love?

Why, she'd thrown it in his face.

"You must know how much I love you," he'd said.

"Everyone seems to love me these days," she'd responded coolly.

She read his numerous texts, pleading with her to give them a second chance.

She hadn't replied.

He had inquired about attending her soft opening.

I'd prefer you didn't. Please take my advice and stay in Miami.

And then he'd gone dark and hadn't contacted her since.

Dejectedly, she put her head in her hands and sobbed. Somehow, she'd done it again—succeeded in being involved in a heartbreaking romance with a man.

No. That wasn't true. Rob had given up his life in Miami, his thriving career, *everything* for her. And in the shared hours exploring a ghost town and dancing Irish jigs, amidst toppled tea cups and spilled vases filled with water and flowers, she'd fallen in love with him too.

Restless, she wiped her eyes, stood, and wandered through the vacant, lonely rooms, lighting night light candles and watering the potted green ferns.

Nothing was the same without him. The teahouse wasn't alive. He'd brought laughter, full of ideas, a ready smile on his face. And now he was gone.

She had driven him away, flatly refusing his help. She'd

seen the raw sadness in his blue eyes, the sagging around his mouth, when he'd said goodbye and walked out the door.

She leaned a shoulder on the windowpane and stared out at a cloudless night. Somewhere in the distance, a church bell pealed. When the time neared midnight, she sighted the star-shaped Big Dipper above the northern horizon.

Half-heartedly, she murmured, "Rob, how can you be so quiet after I told you to return to Miami? Did you forget me already?"

With a tattered sigh, she retreated to the back room and burrowed through the chest of drawers. She extracted the skeleton key locket and glided her fingers over the elaborate floral design. He'd confessed she held the key to his heart and requested she wear it always.

"Rainbows are brilliant in America too, Kathleen. And Roses is your new home."

And then the words that had dangled between them.

Here. With me.

She secured the locket, feeling better when it was near her heart, where it belonged.

With trembling hands, she texted him. If he accepted her apology and boarded a plane from Miami in the morning, he might arrive in Roses by midday. There was so much she needed to tell him. She'd been hurt by men countless times in her life and had been afraid to trust again. To love again.

But what was the world without love?

A FEW MINUTES after midnight brought a ping to Rob's cellphone. He'd been sitting by the guest bedroom's window in Candee's home, gazing idly outside at the familiar Big Dipper. The house was quiet, as the family was attending a horse show in Asheville.

"It better not be another manager texting me at this hour," he muttered, yanking the phone from his pocket.

Kathleen's caller ID appeared on the screen.

I miss you. Would you consider flying back from Miami?

And then: *1-800-IRELAND.*

He couldn't contain his excitement. He was already on his feet, his heart pounding with joy.

The drive to Kathleen's teahouse, which normally took under ten minutes, he covered in less than five. He didn't know what he'd say, wasn't sure how she'd respond. All that mattered was she had reached out to him and he was able to see her again.

He knocked once, hesitating only a second outside the teahouse's door, feeling the cool nip in the night air against his heated cheeks. Realizing the door was unlocked, he stepped inside. The tinkling bell announced his arrival.

She sat on a velvet loveseat in the foyer, her back to him, peering at a lengthy list. He recognized the business plan they'd drawn up together.

"Nancy?" Kathleen inquired without glancing up. "I put your keys aside for you. You'll see them by the tea jars on the counter."

He longed to rush to her, to pull her into his arms. She looked vulnerable, her red-gold hair shining in the delicate candlelight. Twice, he'd left her alone when he'd flown to Miami.

"Kathleen," he said.

She twisted and flew to her feet. "Rob?" All color drained from her complexion. "You're here? How?"

"I never left Roses."

"I thought you were in Miami."

"I couldn't leave." He strode to a cell-phone container and slipped his phone inside. "Our life together wasn't finished. It hadn't even started."

She moistened her lips, raced to him, and looped her arms around his neck.

He cradled her and guided her to the loveseat. She wore his locket over a starched white shirt and tailored black pants —the uniform she'd decided on for the teahouse. He traced his fingers along her high cheekbones. Her long dark lashes fluttered.

"I wish you'd been here, for the soft opening," she said.

"I wanted to. I'm here now. How did it go?"

"A few tweaks. Actually more than a few." She snuggled nearer his chest. "I learned people in Roses like to eat dinner at seven o'clock and be home early. The place cleared out by nine."

His lips brushed her forehead. "That's what a little bird told me."

She gazed up at him, this beauty he'd almost lost. "Who?" she asked.

"Nancy."

"My new employee?"

"Lovely woman, and absolutely exceptional. Sorry she'll no longer be working for you."

Rapidly, Kathleen blinked. "Excuse me?"

"Nancy will be working for me. Or rather, for us."

"You can't just walk in and steal my best employee."

"*Our* best employee."

"I'm not following." She frowned, her voice uncertain. "I finally ..."

He pressed a finger to her mouth. "I bought another place. A ghost town, actually."

"You bought ..." Incredulous, she stared at him. "You bought Hollan Farms? Now you'll be busier than ever."

"I didn't buy the town for me." He kissed her lips, softly, sweetly. "I bought the town for David to manage. I'm a silent investor."

She grinned, her face lighting with laughter. "The cow guy?"

"The one and only. And Nancy will help him." Rob twirled a lock of Kathleen's silky hair around his fingers. "Those two are young and ambitious. Hey, maybe it's the start of a budding romance. And you and I can oversee their progress once in a while."

"What will you do in the meantime?" she asked.

"I'm retired." He grinned. "But I'll be around, just in case you need my assistance."

"I do." She sat straighter, meeting his gaze with her own. "And I finally realized that accepting help isn't a sign of weakness, but of strength."

"You'll be far more able to reach your goals."

"Aye. So I've learned."

"Since you're so agreeable," he stood, then got down on one knee. "Will you marry an American man like me?"

"This is really happening," she murmured. "And my answer is, aye. Yes."

His smile reached his ears, and he went back to cuddling her on the loveseat. "After St. Patrick's Day, we'll look for a home in Roses," he said.

"I like the mild weather here. In Ireland, the days get dark quickly in the winter, and it's rainy and cold."

"In Miami, it's too hot most of the year."

Her deep brown eyes brimmed with tears. "Then Roses is perfect." She snuggled into his arms as his lips moved over hers.

"I love you more than anyone in the world," he whispered. "When you told me to leave, I vowed to wait however long it might take. I knew we had something extraordinary together."

"I've always wanted to visit Miami."

"I've always wanted to visit Ireland. I even have their toll-free number."

She laughed. "You don't really think that if you punch in 1-800-IRELAND, someone from Ireland will answer?"

With aching tenderness, he said, "I believe she will."

"I love you," she whispered.

"And I love you."

In the container by a table, his cell-phone rang.

She grinned up at him. "Ireland calling?"

"Toll-free."

"Aren't you going to answer it?"

"Nope. She's already answered all my dreams." He gazed around her comfortable teahouse, then at the exquisite woman in his arms.

A forever love.

THE END

RECIPE FOR AUNTIE PEGGY'S
IRISH BROWN BREAD

6 cups seedless raisins
2 cups rain water. Save after cooking the raisins

· · ·

COVER THE RAISINS WITH WATER. Cook until tender. Drain but SAVE two cups of the liquid after cooking.

DRY

7 CUPS SIFTED, all-purpose flour
  1 teaspoon allspice
  4 teaspoons cinnamon
  2 teaspoons nutmeg
  4 teaspoons baking soda

WET

1 CUP BUTTER, softened/room temperature
  3 cups sugar. Quantity is adjustable
  6 large eggs, room temperature.

IF YOU WISH, set aside the raisin water that is left and freeze it. Use the next time you cook the raisins. Then, reduce the sugar by a cup. If using fewer than six cups of raisins to start with, reduce the sugar.

ALL INGREDIENTS SHOULD BE at room temperature.
   Sift together all the dry ingredients in a large bowl and set aside.
   Blend the butter, sugar and eggs. (I like to use the KitchenAid mixer for this step.)

Add the 2 cups of raisin liquid to the wet ingredients and mix well.

Add the wet mixture to the dry mix and blend well.

Stir in the 6 cups of cooked raisins and blend well.

Pour into four greased loaf pans. Bake for 1 to 1.25 hours at 325 degrees.

The top will spring back when touched lightly or a toothpick/case tester works.

A NOTE FROM JOSIE

Dear Friend,

Thank you for reading *1-800-IRELAND*. I hope you enjoyed it. This the third book in my contemporary sweet romance series: *Flipping for You*.

This story continued in the charming town of Roses, North Carolina, and followed 1-800-CUPID, and 1-800-CHRISTMAS.

In 1-800-IRELAND, I gave Kathleen, from Oh Danny Boy, her own story. And, because Rob is a reader favorite from previous 1-800 books, I decided to give him his own book.

If you loved this sweet romance as much as I loved writing it, please help other people find *1-800-IRELAND* by posting your review, as well as for the bundle: Irish Hearts

1-800-IRELAND is available in ebook, paperback, Large Print paperback, Hardcover, and audiobook.

My Spotify Play List for 1-800-IRELAND is here.

Want more sweet Irish romances?

Oh Danny Boy: A reader favorite! This pot of gold could hold more than they bargained for...

Maeve: Set on the exotic island of Corsica, France.

He's all business. She loves to laugh. When business conflicts with pleasure, what could possibly go wrong?

Irish Hearts: 3 sweet Irish romances in 1 bundle!

ALSO BY JOSIE RIVIERA

Seeking Patience

Seeking Catherine (always Free!)

Seeking Fortune

Seeking Charity

Seeking Rachel

The Seeking Series

Oh Danny Boy

I Love You More

A Snowy White Christmas

A Portuguese Christmas

Holiday Hearts Book Bundle Volume One

Holiday Hearts Book Bundle Volume Two

Holiday Hearts Book Bundle Volume Three

Holiday Hearts Book Bundle Volume Four

Candleglow and Mistletoe

Maeve (Perfect Match)

A Love Song To Cherish

A Christmas To Cherish

A Valentine To Cherish

A Christmas Puppy To Cherish

A Homecoming To Cherish

A Summer To Cherish

Romance Stories To Cherish

Romance Stories To Cherish Volume Two

Cherished Hearts Six Book Volume

Aloha To Love

Sweet Peppermint Kisses

Valentine Hearts Boxed Set

1-800-CUPID

1-800-CHRISTMAS

1-800-IRELAND

1-800-SUMMER

1-800-NEW YEAR

The 1-800-Series Sweet Contemporary Romance Bundle

Irish Hearts Sweet Romance Bundle

Holly's Gift

A Chocolate-Box Christmas

A Chocolate-Box New Years

A Chocolate-Box Valentine

A Chocolate-Box Summer Breeze

A Chocolate-Box Christmas Wish

A Chocolate-Box Irish Wedding

Chocolate-Box Hearts

Chocolate-Box Hearts Volume Two

Chocolate-Box Double Hearts

Recipes From The Heart

Leading Hearts

New Year Hearts

SENIOR HEARTS

Summer Hearts

Christmas in the Air (1-800-Book)

A Very Christian Christmas

Most books are available in ebook, audiobook, paperback, Large Print paperback and Hardcover.

Many are FREE on Kindle Unlimited!